Ex Machina

Robert Finn

snowbooks

FX Machina

ISBN10: 1-905005-06-7
ISBN13: 978-1905005-06-2

Chapter 1

I've never actually been to prison, so this is a guess, but I bet when you get out you don't think *I know, I'll write my prison memoirs now, while it's all still lovely and fresh*. I should think the first thing you do is try to blot it all out (check your phonebook under BOOZE, HOOKERS, TATTOO REMOVAL, DISNEY WORLD®).

Like I say, I've never been to prison, but nevertheless these are my prison memoirs and I'm writing them now, before I forget, even though it's the last thing I want to do.

In case you're interested, what this has taught me is that a person really can change, but without doubt there's a price to pay. Starting over means you lose touch with who you were.

Your old memories begin to feel like someone else's, some person you don't know very well… which is a more than a little unsettling. It's like finding the aftermath of someone else's shopping spree on your credit card statement, someone else's low grades messing up your college transcript or someone else's hair clogging up your shower drain. (You'd probably got the message even before that last example.)

At any rate, the new-improved-you can still remember all of

the bad decisions the old-you made. Your memory is full of all those stupid things, but the motives no longer make sense to you. What was I thinking? Why did *that* seem like the smart thing to do? How could my thoughts have been so small?

Because the truth is that you find you can't squeeze back inside your old way of viewing the world anymore; the new you won't fit. You can't unlearn the lessons that caused you to grow and you can't wriggle back into your old, cramped mindset. That's what I meant about prison. I feel like I was trapped inside that claustrophobic maze of wrong choices and bad instincts for so long that it's a blissful relief to be free – despite what I went through. And I wish I could part company with that old me forever. But instead I'm clinging on to it, doing my best to record those thoughts before understanding evaporates, the way a confusing dream begins to evaporate once you wake up. I'm going to relive it all so that I can explain it to you.

So welcome to the old, even-more-annoying me. You'll have to put up with my day-to-day trivia for a little while before we get to the real meat-and-potatoes, because it's all bound up together.

So let's get on with it.

My name is Jo, which (regrettably) is short for Josephine, and the story I need to tell you starts in Cornwall. That's in the windy south-west tip of some rainy islands just off the north coast of Europe, in case you don't know. I've spent about nine of my twenty-six years in those islands, but I still think of myself as American. I prefer the big city, but at this point I'm a long way from what I prefer: I'm in the middle of nowhere.

How did I get here? Well, I think you could say that finding a post-doc slot was always going to be a challenge for me. But that's fine; I didn't really want a conventional position, the mainstream kind most people compete for. I'm not into that straight-ahead, plain-vanilla academia. Besides, all the fertile dirt is in the gaps between the disciplines. If you can find yourself a niche that's new and still a little precarious, you tend to find that the rules are looser and the people are weird enough that they don't notice your foibles. In between the disciplines there's not much status quo to disturb and no traditional way of doing things, so my (ahem) unconventional résumé is less of a liability. Under the right circumstances, it might even be a fun talking point. Whoop!

My problems started – at least this current set of problems – around the time I submitted my thesis. Instead of seeing it for what it was, my doctoral supervisor couldn't seem to get beyond the fact that...

None of which you need to know, so forget it. What with all the arguments and acrimony, though, I needed to find a new place to hang my hat – all the better if it was a long way from New York. Which is how I came to be back in the British Isles, my occasional second home.

Taking this post was a pretty straightforward decision, mainly because there were no other offers on the table – despite my mostly stratospheric grades, despite my publication credits, despite my fund of delightfully colourful tales involving legal wrangles with the governing board of a major East Coast college. Imagine. This was the only offer.

Now Cornwall is about a hundred miles further out from civilisation than many people think the UK extends. And while I suppose I don't actually *hate* the countryside, I do wish there was something there other than bugs and wet sheep. Somewhere to buy books would be nice. In fact, why not a variety of stores selling a rounded selection of modern consumer goods? Oh, and a choice of international cuisine too. And if the local residents could be exposed to the outside world occasionally, just enough to let them understand accents from non-agricultural parts of the English-speaking world, well that would be ideal.

None of those things being the case, I'd developed something of an enthusiasm-deficiency with regard to my new surroundings. The ill will over my thesis made me feel like I'd been wrongfully convicted of something, so Cornwall seemed like the unjust sentence that went with it. For the first few weeks of my banishment here I don't know that I did much except simmer and fume at the double-plus ungood way things had turned out. There was pretty much nothing about this new situation that I liked, on top of which there was nothing to take my mind off it.

The field station where I was based was run by Professor Shaw; the whole thing was his show. He was an old friend of my mother's (emphasis on old) and I suppose I should be grateful to him for offering me a post-doc spot at all. But honestly, I can't imagine there were too many other takers. And anyone who survived the cultural desolation out here would soon be scared away by the prospect of what joining this project would likely to do to their career. (How fortunate that mine was pre-wrecked!)

We were based in a few buildings that I think must have been used for some fish-related activity until recently. There was a large dormitory block adjacent. A ten-minute walk away was the village of Swaffet: ten houses, a post-office/general store, a church hall and two pubs. An hour away by bus – assuming they were running – was the nearest major town: half a handful of well-worn chain stores, no bookstore, no decent library, and a scruffy Pizza Hut bringing up the rear. Unless you had the use of a plane, your options for a fun night out were limited.

The outlook for our project was similarly non-stellar. If I'd had a career warning-light, it would have started blinking before I'd unpacked my bags. I'm not a history buff, but this place had 'fringe' written all over it. If these people were doing solid, mainstream work, you can bet it would all have been taking place back at the Professor's college in Cambridge, at the centre of the universe, not out here in the sticks. There's only one

4

reason you head out into the wilderness like this and it isn't to get away from the envious glances of colleagues or the feverish anticipation of the journals; it's so you can crawl away to die, academically speaking.

In fact it occurred to me that maybe Professor Shaw hadn't jumped; maybe he'd been pushed. Maybe this project and the field station were all about the college giving him enough rope to hang himself. Let him waste a bunch of taxpayer's money and they'd have a reason to show him the door. Otherwise they'd struggle to retire someone with his reputation and connections.

Insightful as that analysis might seem, the few times I tried to discuss our doomed mission with the other conscripts, I'd gotten a cold reception. They were obviously relishing their exile from the real world. And why not? No competition out here to show them up.

My part in the project started out with a disjointed list of responsibilities, some of which made sense to me, others not so much. I'd been told not to worry about publications yet or exactly what my final role would end up being; we'd deal with all that once I'd 'found my feet'. In the meantime, I was doing a little bit of everything – mainly rent-a-tech chores.

One of my first jobs was to set up a secure computer system. Not a problem for me, except that whoever had been working on it before I arrived had really messed it up. I'd hardly begun to get it unscrambled before I was getting flak about why it wasn't finished yet. And when I pushed everything else aside and made it my top priority, I got it in the neck for falling behind on my other assignments.

It wasn't the ideal way to recover from my doctoral fiasco. And to be honest, my spirits hadn't been that high when I arrived; a month on and they were falling fast.

Just for background, in case you care, I'd had a pretty tough time of it lately, and before that… well, more of the same really, with varying degrees of crappiness. So what would have been nice is if I had been cut a teensy little bit of slack. But was I? It turns out that I was not.

During the day, the nagging and the requests for 'updates' were really starting to make me stressed, which didn't help me work any faster, believe me. On top of which, what started out as polite enquiries about progress were getting bitchy and snide a lot quicker than I think was called for.

In fact, in record time I'd been made to feel totally unwelcome, out of step and unappreciated. Any chance I had of job satisfaction had vanished when the bitchiness started because I knew that when I *did* finally manage to get caught up, instead of 'Good job!' I'd be hearing an aggrieved chorus of 'About time!'.

The only part of the day I *almost* looked forward to was clocking off and trudging up the hill to The Red Hart (or The Retard as some of the team pointedly mispronounced it, in honour of its core clientele). There I could sit in ostracised silence and enjoy a couple of eye-watering glasses of *vin de sinus medicine*[1].

On my first couple of trips to The Retard I'd had some problems getting the alcohol dosage exactly right. Naturally, I wanted to suppress the newsreel that played in my brain, the one that looped endlessly through the day's little humiliations and setbacks. But on the other hand, when dealing with hooch of this calibre, caution was indicated. More than once I'd accidentally over-medicated my brain's vertical hold. I'd weaved back to the dorm to lie on my bed, not daring to close my eyes, for fear of triggering that queaseful head-in-a-tumble-drier feeling.

---

[1] Tourist tip: try not to ask for wine in a rural British pub. But if you do and the barmaid looks worried and says, "Ooh, I know we used to have some," then consider yourself forewarned.

A month in and I'd settled on an RDA somewhere between three-and-a-half and four glasses per night – a little more if I was off my meds (which topic I'll get to in good time). One lingering niggle was that however restrained I was in my drinking, the industrial run-off the vineyard used to melt the grapes always made for killer headaches the next morning.

After five weeks my reserves of perkiness had dried up, and now my problem-solving faculties were bypassing the question of how to get my assignments back on track and jumping right to exploring possible ways off the project.

And that's the way it was until – in amongst all that gloom and griping – I made a discovery. Out of the blue, I found something genuinely interesting.

In fact better than interesting: intriguing, fascinating, impossible.

It began to dawn on me that there was something going on at the field station besides the project I knew about.

The official line was that they were combing over some old documents, translating them and researching their backgrounds. This activity was being coordinated using some new project framework, which, when they were done, they were planning to publish. It included a certain amount of tricky IT and some clever process stuff – both of which I was going to play a big part in. But that was the extent of the project according to the outline I'd seen.

But I stumbled upon something else entirely.

My first clue involved the Procedures and Administration Committee. The committee would meet once a week, sometimes more, supposedly to discuss all the dull what-have-yous that kept the field station running: liaison with the distant main campus, project finances, maintenance, personnel, etc;

There were only six researchers at the field station, plus some support people, so you wouldn't have thought there was a mountain of work for an admin committee to do, but nevertheless they seemed pretty hard at it whenever I caught a glimpse.

Knowing what I know now, I've got to hand it to them: 'The Procedures and Administration Committee' is a great name. It's about the least tantalising title you could imagine – a fine example of reverse branding. The only hint of undisciplined ego was allowing it to have a cool-ish acronym[1].

The secure e-mail facility and the encrypted file-store I was asked to set up were for the committee (or the PAC as I later discovered they couldn't resist calling themselves). The Professor described their requirements and then took me aside to let me in on their 'little secret'.

Conspiratorially, he told me that the government were thinking of shaking up the way universities were structured and funded, and the Professor was on one of the working parties looking at alternative approaches. The implications, he said, were 'enormous'. This Procedures and Administration Committee had a secret mission. Hidden from the world, they were discussing ways of 'literally revolutionising post-graduate teaching in this country'. But, epoch-making though these changes might be, they were still only possibilities, only suggestions. If details of these embryonic proposals were to leak out it could 'set some hares running', maybe stir up opposition and controversy, even outrage, about initiatives that were still very much at the hypothetical stage. At this point, the committee's deliberations must remain *sub rosa*[2] – hence the need for a secure computer system. Better safe than sorry.

Wow. Imagine how excited I was to be let in on that scoop.

---

[1] Mind you, in the States, a PAC is something to do with politics. So not much shine on that particular apple.

[2] I've never known anyone like Professor Shaw for using a phrase like '*sub rosa*', when 'shush, it's a secret' would do.

The sense of awe and revelation I felt was comparable to the first time I realised that America used a political system that was both federated *and* bicameral. Amazing.

In other words: yawn.

But this was just another piece of hand-stitched, lovingly-crafted subterfuge. I'm sure the government does the same thing – and if they do, I'd like to think they call it 'drabbing': taking cool stuff they want to keep under wraps and making it sound so craptastically lame that you really can't be arsed[1] to pry into it. As in: "That's classified. I could tell you, but then I'd have to bore you." It was like finding out that by day Clark Kent was a mild-mannered reporter, but by night he… whittled ornaments.

So the big secret was nearly as boring as the cover story. Which might have been the end of it, except that I'm just a little bit nosey.

I created the e-mail accounts and the public/private encryption keys they wanted; I set up the secure file-store… and then I peeked.

It actually wasn't that easy to peek. My little buddy Daniel (more about him later) had obviously been asked to add a little security of his own on top of what I'd put in place. He'd set up some encryption that was independent of mine, the result being that neither of us could decipher a committee member's locked documents without colluding. Except that I soon found a way to log in as Daniel – from which point I could unravel his devious little tricks and get at the contents of their secret files.

Ironically, if the PAC hadn't decided to set up two separate layers of security I would never have bothered to delve into any of it. First off, by locking me out of their files they more

---

[1]   Excellent Brit expression: to not be arsed to do something. Unfortunately for Americans, you just can't say it right without an authentic British post-alveolar frictionless continuant.

or less challenged me to get access to them, wouldn't you say? And secondly, I was just a little bit suspicious that they were overdoing the cloak-and-dagger stuff – *enormous* implications for post-grad teaching notwithstanding, there was just too much security in place.

And once I knew that something was going on – something more than a government working party, that is – I noticed lots of other suspicious details.

My favourite bit of weirdness concerned a PAC-member called David Braun, who plainly had a thing going with the senior researcher there, Susan Milton. He was sort of good-looking in an ugly kind of way, and though he talked like a suit, he walked like a soldier. Everything about him said he was in control and he got what he wanted. Which is why I just couldn't quite take him seriously as a Catering Supervisor.

An explorer? Yes. Maybe a mountain-climber. Equally, I could imagine him in dress uniform getting a medal for something *hush-hush*. I could even see him as a Wall Street type, worth $200 million at 30, having started with nothing. But if he was a catering supervisor then my butt is a pumpkin.

Of course he didn't really have anything to do with catering and I found out later that the title was just part of the overall 'drabbing' – combined with Susan Milton's sense of humour.

David wasn't part of our research project; he just showed up for the PAC meetings. He'd obviously been somewhere hot recently, and not just for a few days. While the rest of them had that late-in-the-year British pallor from months (possibly years) without sun, David was burned a toasty brown – all except one wrist, which was much paler and looked a different sort of burned – not as in sunburned, as in acid-burned. It could have been creepy, but actually it just looked sort of rugged. Plus it wasn't like he had a claw or anything; his hand was fine, it was just the pigment that seemed to be messed up. It seemed like a clue.

As well as David, Susan and the Professor, there were two other members of the PAC: Daniel, my old buddy, and a non-entity called Theresa. She was mousy and unremarkable, and I never really discovered why she was involved with the team. Daniel, though, was a useful sort of a guy. Not *me* smart, but not a dunce by a long way. And for a history whiz, he was a remarkably fair techie. He was also a) in a band, b) reasonably buff and c) devoted to me.

But before you decide that he's a scrumptious muffin and I've got it made, I should tell you that he's two full inches shorter than me, has frizzy red hair, bad skin and has – to the best of my extensive knowledge – never had a proper girlfriend.

Which doesn't stop him making furtive little attempts to ask me out every few weeks. He doesn't have the guts to actually come out with it, of course, but he's always inviting me to things or complimenting me on something – like a shirt I've had for ages, or my hair, when it's exactly the same as it was the last time I saw him. Why he can't get it together sufficiently to say, "Jo, will you go out with me?" I don't know. I mean, I'd slap him down, but at least he'd have the satisfaction of being a man about it.

Sure, I know I treat him like crap, but deep down I really like having him around. For the most part. In small doses.

So anyway, once I'd got past Danny Boy's security measures, I took a quick look at what the PAC was saying to each other. I couldn't imagine any of it being very interesting, but I thought I'd see whether I was right about David and Susan having a *thang* going on.

I prised open one of Susan's archived e-mails dated a couple of weeks before I started on the project and hit the jackpot right away: Dear David, miss you, love you, blah-blah, snuggle-bunny, blah, murder, blah, hearts and kisses, yours Susan. So I was right. I patted myself on the back and thought no more of it.

Oh but wait. What was that about *murder*? I read that section carefully. Susan was responding to something David had said. He had concluded that a man named Teracus probably *had* been murdered by someone called Jan. David had been in mainland Greece apparently for the express purpose of investigating this guy Teracus's death.

The idea burst in my mind like a rammed SUV. My imagination lit up with the impact and all sorts of burning questions were thrown into the air. Who was David really? In what capacity was he investigating? Who could Teracus be (and what sort of name was that)? Who was this murderer, Jan? Why did Susan, a historian, need to know about any of this?

Then I got a foolish, sinking feeling. It dawned on me that the murder they were referring to could be some ancient event and Susan's interest was just part of her research. If I'd studied the liberal arts a little harder, would I have recognised the name Teracus as some historical figure, perhaps some Roman consul whose unexplained death was even now causing bunched underwear in common-room debates around the world? Was I following in the footsteps of the apocryphal New York citizen who, when asked what he knew of the murder of Julius Caesar, insisted that he hadn't seen a thing?

But that feeling of deflation and foolishness only lasted a moment. Reading on, it was clear that this wasn't some riddle from antiquity they were discussing. Susan's e-mail went on to say something about Teracus's hotel bill including a record of numbers he'd called. I cast my mind back to what little I knew of Ancient Rome. I was relatively sure that they didn't have phones in those days – or if they did, then I was quite sure that the technology to provide itemised billing by room hadn't been perfected until long after Rome fell to the Visigoths. My money was on this being a recent event.

So I knew that David and Susan were investigating a recent

murder. Next I wondered whether they were working alone or if other members of the PAC were involved. It seemed most likely that it would be a personal thing between the two of them. Maybe Teracus was some weirdly-named uncle of Susan's and David had seen so many Chuck Norris movies that he was happy to play the vigilante and volunteer to investigate. Maybe sleuthing was his early Christmas gift to her.

That in mind, I forced open a few of the Professor's e-mails, glossing over a couple of duds before I found one that answered my question – and raised about a million new ones. The bulk of the message concerned arrangements for the next PAC meeting; it also touched on the agenda, and there it was: a reference to Jan.

Towards the end of the message there was also an aside about Jan's name. The Professor, it seemed, had found a reference in Jan's notebook to his real or former name being 'Janu', which he believed meant 'life force'. "Ironic," the Professor concluded, "because it seemed to be the one thing he lacked, besides a moral compass, that is. Of course it also means 'knee' in Sanskrit, but I consider that an irrelevance. Even if we imagine it as some manly pseudonym, akin to a mafia *soprannome* or a wrestler's *nom de lutte*, it's a little out of kilter as a nickname. Fighters might revel in titles such as 'The Hammer' or 'The Fist', but I would think that attracting the nickname 'The Knee' is something you would be eager to live down."

I tried to find alternative ways of interpreting that note, wondering again if he could be talking about something remote, hypothetical, scholarly. But I just couldn't make it come out that way. It all seemed immediate and personal. The e-mail seemed to say that Jan was a) a murderer, b) known to at least one member of the PAC and c) apparently now dead. And let's not forget, Jan was on the PAC's meeting agenda. This wasn't about PAC members going off on a tangent about their outside interests; it was something they held meetings to discuss.

The tiny cogs in my brain were spinning like pin-wheels as I considered what I might do about all this. I was still thinking it over when an opportunity presented itself.

Now if you know anything about reading other people's mail you'll know it's not a spectator sport, so I'd tucked myself away somewhere private for my little session of electronic B&E. I was sitting in front of our server-farm's main console. The console, along with all the rack-mounted processors and the comms paraphernalia, was tucked into a storage room on the ground floor of the field station's main building. Apart from me, only the Professor had a key to the server-room door – and he had no earthly reason to use it, barring emergencies. The white noise of so many cooling fans tended to drown out conversation, and the expelled heat turned the room into a sauna, but the server-room was a good place to go if I didn't want to be disturbed or interrupted. (Nerds among you may like to chuckle appreciatively over the fact that I called the room the Fortress of Servitude.)

That said, as I sat there, turning over the content of those peculiar e-mails in my mind, I became aware of distant thumping. Someone was at the door.

I cleared the screen of any incriminating evidence (even though the monitor faced the racking) and then I unlocked the door and peeked outside. Daniel was standing there. He was wearing a t-shirt depicting a caffeine molecule and he grinned his shy grin as I put my head out to see what he wanted. I didn't smile; it only encourages him.

"Hi Jo," he said, "Sorry to interrupt you. I need to borrow a cable if I can."

"Yeah?" I replied, noncommittally.

"Have you got that mini-USB one? We need it for the meeting," he asked.

That's right. It was Wednesday afternoon and the PAC would

be getting together soon in the little conference room behind the Professor's office.

I was pretty sure they'd settled on that venue because it was so isolated. To reach it, you opened a fire door, went down three silly little steps and through a second door into the meeting room. The two doors were only five feet apart and they created a kind of airlock. You couldn't open the first one without someone in the room noticing, so that by the time you reached the second door everyone happened to be talking about the weather and most of the documents in the room were face down.

"What do you need it for?" I asked.

Daniel gave me one of his 'now don't be like that' looks – which always infuriate me – and said, "Well, I don't now that it really makes all that much difference *why*…"

He tailed off as he noticed the storm clouds gathering and my eyebrows getting closer together. There's something about his inoffensive, placid reasonableness that just makes me want to shake him.

Before I could pick a fight with him, he capitulated: "There are some photos we want to show. We need to hook the digital camera up to my laptop. It's not a big thing."

At that moment it really started to bug me that he was part of the PAC and I wasn't. Now that I knew it wasn't the ditchwater-dull snoozathon I'd imagined, it bothered me that they'd chosen Daniel and said nothing to me.

Irritated, I thought of asking him what a procedures and admin committee would need photos for, but now that I *knew* they were up to something I didn't want to seem too inquisitive. Plus, if I was honest, it was a dumb question. Even a *real* admin committee might find a reason to show pictures at its meetings. If I forced Daniel to tell me, he'd just lie and say it was holiday snaps.

I let the door bang shut and disappeared back inside leaving him standing there. A moment later I reappeared and held out the cable to him.

Then something occurred to me and without thinking I snatched the cable back as he reached for it.

"Oi," he complained, smiling, "No time for chase-the-cable. Work to do."

I suddenly realised that I wanted to listen in on this afternoon's meeting – and if I was going to eavesdrop then I would need a little time to prepare – not to mention get my nerve up.

To Daniel I said, "Sorry, I've just remembered this cable's iffy. If you can give me a couple of minutes I'll dig out the new one." I paused a moment and added, "You don't have to wait. I can leave it in the meeting room for you if you like." I gave him a big smile that I hoped looked authentic.

He looked almost suspicious for a moment – not about the cable, just about me volunteering to do him a favour. (It makes you wonder: if he's got such a low opinion of me, why does he want to go out with me?)

A moment later he smiled back, then glanced at his watch on its stupid, chunky wrist-protector strap and said, "Well I do want to find some grub. Can you drop it off before two? That's when the meeting starts." In other words, don't make me look bad. So he thinks I'm selfish *and* unreliable. That pretty much killed my fake smile.

Despite myself I snapped, "I *told* you I'd get it for you, OK?"

He made calming gestures with his hands and said, in his speaking-to-lunatics voice, "Alright, alright. That's great. Don't get your knickers in a twist."

So we left it at that and I ducked back into the server-room and locked the door behind me.

I already knew what I was going to do.

Chapter 2

At the far end of the server-room, the wall was covered with metal racking and shelving. The big spaces were filled with cardboard boxes stuffed to overflowing with all sorts of accreted techno-junk. I dragged one of the boxes off the shelf and began to rummage through it. Once I'd tipped most of the contents onto the floor I saw the old cell-phone I was looking for.

I turned it on. The battery was down to 50% and I wouldn't have time to recharge it, but a half charge would probably be enough.

Back at the server console I did a little searching and found the web-page of instructions I semi-remembered.

1) set the phone's ringer to mute.

2) short pins 2 and 6 on the phone's base.

I couldn't figure out an easy way to short the pins so I ended up kludging it by supergluing half a staple between them. Ugly but effective – and for a bonus point, I did it without permanently attaching the phone to my thumb.

The contacts on the phone's base were for connecting a

head-set and the pins I'd shorted were for the head-set's answer button. In effect, this hack was like having the phone's answer button pushed in the whole time. Now, whenever I dialled the phone's number, the phone would auto-answer without ringing. I checked that it worked by dialling it from my regular cell-phone, and with the call in progress I adjusted the volume for optimum eavesdropping performance.

With the rigged phone in my pocket, I grabbed a mini-roll of duct tape and the cable Daniel wanted, then I made my way towards the meeting room.

The Professor's office was empty, so I wandered in and over to the door that led down to the meeting room. With my nose against the little wire-threaded window I could see down the steps to the second door and, through its tiny window, a little of the meeting room beyond.

I wanted to know that the room was empty before I went in. If I met someone, I could hand over the cable as my reason for being there but I couldn't very well plant the phone. That would require a second trip, this time without the cable and so with no excuse for being there. If I had to make a second trip and I bumped into anyone it would be obvious that I was loitering with some sort of intent.

As I craned to see into the meeting room, I was surprised to find that I was pretty keyed up. It wasn't like I was going to be tortured if I got caught, but I was actually getting sweaty palms contemplating my plan. I'd been in that room half a dozen times without giving it a second thought, but this time it felt like I was heading deep into enemy territory.

I reminded myself that I was just having a little harmless fun with people I saw everyday; I wasn't spying on trigger-happy Nazis. In fact, I was only paying the PAC back. They'd started the trickery by lying about what they were up to; I was just asserting my right not to be taken in by it[1].

I felt a little better with that thought in my head. In fact, I was a little bit pissed off with them now that I thought about it. They hadn't seen fit to trust me with their secret; I was just there to keep the computers running and to believe any old crap they made up about what was going on. I mean, was the project they'd recruited me for even real? Or was that just a cover story too?

No longer caring whether the room was empty or not I let my little surge of righteous annoyance carry me through the door and down the stairs. With only a hint of hesitation, I pushed open the meeting room door… to see the Professor sitting there chatting to Susan Milton.

They looked up together and I felt a surge of blood rush to my cheeks. Dammit; despite my recent self-directed pep talk, I still felt guilty – so guilty I was sure my face glowed with it.

But they seemed not to notice, so maybe the blush I could feel was only on the inside. The Professor finished his sentence – something about timescales – and said to me, "Just the fellow, as it were. Where are we with those subscriptions? Any news?"

I experienced that unpleasant feeling you get when you realise you've forgotten to do something – or when you eat something and then it moves. I'd promised the Professor that I'd set up subscriptions to several online archives so that members of the team could use them in their work. He'd reminded me three times to get on with it, the most recent of which was yesterday. I'd promised him emphatically and without fail to get it done by midday today. It was about one o'clock now and I hadn't even started it.

I searched for an excuse and remembered the cable in my hand. "It's Daniel," I announced without thinking. Realising my words made no sense I added, "I mean I'm just doing this

---

[1] Damn, but I have wicked rationalising skills.

thing for Daniel… well, for the meeting really; he said you really needed *this*." I showed them the cable – and then realised they wouldn't know what it was for. I was making a mess of this little performance.

Still waving the cable I explained, "He wanted to show some digital pictures at your meeting. Finding this cable sort of delayed me, but the subscription thing is nearly done."

Somehow it seemed fitting to blame Daniel for my failings. Fitting because in Ductile Logic World – where I spent much of my time – Daniel had been chosen by the PAC instead of me and thus he was the reason I was having to lie about what I was up to. See? It *all* makes sense.

The Professor eyed me for a moment and I thought he was going to get angry that I was making excuses. He never really has done, but I can't help it; he's just someone I'm afraid of disappointing – or losing. When he went through a bad cancer scare the previous year, and lost all his hair, it frightened the life out of me. It still hasn't grown back and it's a constant reminder of what could have been.

For a moment, as I stood there, I wasn't sure whether I'd pushed my luck too far with him. Then he clapped his hands as though this was just the sort of thing he wanted to hear and asked, "And you have the list of subscriptions?"

Arrggh. I realised I didn't. I knew he'd given it to me but I couldn't recall what I'd done with it. It was partly his fault, I thought, for dealing in scraps of paper in an era of electric e-mail and horseless communication. I made a sort of uncertain sound.

He glanced at Susan and then chuckled, saying to me, "No matter. There's a copy in your pigeonhole."

He didn't sound annoyed at all and I felt relief spread through me – which in turn reminded me how spazzful I was being at the moment. I was really going to have to acquire some metaphorical *cojones* before I'd take home any awards for spying[1].

The Professor turned to Susan. "We can discuss the rest of this later. Let's have some lunch." She smiled in agreement and they both got up, gathering their paperwork to take with them.

"I'll just…" I said, holding up the cable again as though I needed to do something with it beyond placing it on the table.

"Good, good," the Professor said and the two of them walked past me and out the door.

Once I was sure they were gone, I fished out the reel of duct-tape and the phone and scrambled under the conference table to lay on my back beneath its centre. I ripped off a long strip of tape and attached the phone to the table's underside. I added a second strip to make sure it couldn't come loose – being careful not to cover the microphone.

I was just wriggling out from under the table when I heard the outer door bang. Jumping to my feet I jammed the tape back in my pocket, realising at the last minute that my dark sweater was now covered in a million flecks of nylon from the carpet.

David Braun came through the door just as I was trying to brush the worst of it off. I kind of froze as soon as he noticed me and just sort of stood there. He said 'hi' and set his pile of papers on the table. He was picking out a seat when he became aware – at about the same time as I did – that I was *still* just standing there.

He looked puzzled and opened his mouth to say something – most likely "Are you mental?" – but I just mumbled "Thanks" (I'm not sure for what) and headed for the door. I paused long enough to pick up the cable I'd left on the floor and to place it on the table, and then I bolted.

---

[1]   Hmmm. Do they have awards for spying? And if they do, do they announce the results or just lock the golden envelope away in a vault and let the winners figure out what's in it?

My heart was thudding as I crossed the Professor's office and headed for the server-room. There was no one around and I tried to calm myself down as I walked. I went over my pep talk again in my head, reminding myself that these were not ruthless drug lords I was dealing with, they were career historians who had no reason to suspect me of anything – historians who'd lied to me.

I was feeling less freaked out by the time I reached the server-room door. I paused there for a moment and got my brain working again.

I decided I should get the Professor's subscription thing done before he really did flip out about it and that would take my mind off all the deception-related spazzing-out I seemed to be doing. Then, in a little under an hour, I'd listen in on the meeting and find out what the project I'd joined was *really* about.

Of course, to take care of the subscriptions I'd first need the Professor's list telling me what I was supposed to be doing. I turned around and headed back down the corridor and towards the main entrance.

Just inside the main door was a recess with slots for each person's mail. In mine was a piece of paper, folded in half. On it, written in fountain pen, were the words 'I think you forgot this'.

I unfolded the piece of paper. Double arrgghh. It wasn't a *copy* of the list of subscriptions; it was the *original* list the Professor had given me. No wonder he'd asked if I had it. I'd obviously left it behind after our last chat. So he knew I wasn't 'nearly done' with it. It seemed even luckier now that he hadn't blown up at me.

I kind of wondered whether maybe I *was* in trouble over this, but the Professor hadn't seemed too upset so I put it out of my mind. I grabbed the list and scuttled back to the server room.

And wouldn't you know it, the job turned out to be a real pain in the hind-section. Each library service had a different system for arranging group access and none of them were very well thought out. Infuriatingly, two of them required 48 hours to process new subscriptions – though they'd take your money instantly. I was not going to win any new friends when the team realised it would be another two days before they could use these sites. Just when I needed to get something done quickly I was hitting extra delays. Which was pretty much typical of my luck.

I got as far as I could with it and then checked the time. I'd more than used up my hour. The PAC meeting would already have started by now. I quickly put the whole subscription thing aside and snatched up my cell phone, hoping I hadn't missed too much. I pressed redial, with my thumb hovering over the 'End Call' button because some part of my brain was telling me that any second now I was going to lose my nerve.

I had to take the handset away from my ear and check the display to see if the call had gone through because there was no sound of ringing. Sure enough, a call was in progress. I bumped the speaker volume up as far as it would go and found I could hear distant voices. The conversation sounded like it was taking place inside a mattress, but I could just about follow what was being said.

Susan was speaking: "…more important to stay undetected than to learn something new. We're not especially on the clock; we don't have to rush into anything. On the other hand, if the Army learns about us… Well, the point is that being in the dark for a little longer is preferable to bringing the roof down on our heads. We should be patient."

The Army? WTF?

Now David spoke, "Oh absolutely. We need to do two things, I'd say. First, make a really good plan for what to do if they find out about us. And second – and this is the important one – make absolutely sure they never find out about us."

Then I heard little Daniel clear his throat and speak. He was quieter and much more tentative than David. He sounded about twelve years old. "How do we compare... I mean to say, you and Doctor, erm, Susan, you've had experience with them, plus that was a while ago, so I should think you've progressed a little. I mean I'm sure you have, erm, progressed and I wondered whether there wouldn't be something you two might be able to do in the event of..."

Susan broke in politely. "Daniel, you're asking whether David and I could maybe handle these guys?"

Daniel found a little more confidence from somewhere and said clearly, "Well, respectfully, what I was wondering was how badly, um..."

"Right," Susan said, getting it, "how badly we'd lose. How badly they'd kick our asses."

I guessed that she glanced the Professor's way then, because I heard him mutter, "It's alright; I know about the existence of 'asses'; you needn't shelter me."

There was a pause, now that the question had been asked in a way that everyone (with the exception of me, of course) seemed able to understand.

A moment later, Susan said, "They'd kill us. They'd just plain kill us."

Again, I suspected she'd cast a look, this time at David, because he took up the explanation. He said, "Well, they'd probably have to work much harder at it than they'd like, but I don't think we'd stand much of a chance. We'd still be, um... Honey, what's the American for 'curtains'?"

Susan helped him out: "Toast. We would, in all probability, be toast."

I was struggling to make some sense of this. This didn't sound much like the *Army* Army. Daniel couldn't be asking if David and Susan could beat the *actual Army* in a fight, could he? Surely it hadn't slipped Daniel's mind about all the tanks and aircraft and men by their thousands with guns and how tricky it would be for one historian and a 'catering supervisor' to defeat the combined might of the military. So what Army could he be referring to? The Salvation Army? Even they weren't exactly a pushover – or so I'd heard.

With the phone still pressed to my ear, I turned in my chair and began typing at the console. As quick as I could, I created a little script that would fetch the documents in the PAC's secure store, one at a time, and run them through my decryption app. I was going to search their mail for answers while I listened to them talk.

The script was just a handful of lines long so I only missed a few seconds of conversation while I typed. As soon as a few plaintext documents were ready, I *grepped* them, looking for anything that contained the word 'Army'.

Straightaway I got hits. The first excerpt read: "The Army Who Witnessed Creation. Sometimes called The Witnesses. One of the groups known as the Awakened." So, not the Salvation Army; maybe not even the Jehovah's Witnesses. (Because clearly *that* would have made plenty of sense.) Plus, no mention of Jehovah. Obviously it was some other sect with a thing for the witnessing. I didn't have time to read any further because my attention was drawn back to the conversation I was supposed to be eavesdropping on.

Daniel was talking: "…I found some activity. I don't want to mislead anyone, but it looked like surveillance to me. But, you know, limited experience and all that."

Susan was obviously tuned into Daniel's wavelength as she said, "Which fits with one of the things I wanted to hear some discussion on today. Daniel thinks he found signs of electronic snooping; well, I'm pretty sure I saw signs of physical surveillance. I'm pretty much certain they're watching Jan's City Road place."

And, Dear Reader, just in case you wonder, this moment

here was when it got *really* weird. Daniel once again found a little more self-possession than I thought he was capable of and said, "Well, I've been thinking about the statistics of this. We're estimating around a hundred years between regenerations, but what's the duration of the regeneration window? If we just pull some figures out of our, um, out of the air we could say that any time after about the ninety-year mark you might put your name on the list for use of the Marker. Let's also take a flying guess and say you drop dead at around a hundred and twenty-five years after your last regeneration, but that maybe most adepts wouldn't go past one-ten if they still had the Marker available to them…"

Susan interjected, "We only have one document that suggests timescales and…"

What the *hell* were they talking about?

David said, "Honey," obviously wanting her to let Daniel finish, but Daniel didn't seem fazed. He ploughed ahead, "Right, but what I'm saying is this: if the spread of physical ages within the army is random – which it might not be for reasons we can come back to – but if it *were* then you'd have around one in ten of them looking to regenerate sometime soon, but little in the way of panicking. Ten years from now you'd have a fifth of them on the waiting list with a few of them getting pretty nervous."

Susan wasn't quite sure. She said, "Not *that* nervous. Using your figures, if they *choose* to regenerate at a physical age of about a hundred, but they can live to one-twenty-five, then they've got more like two decades before they need to panic. Could be a lot longer."

Daniel was still on a roll. "Definitely, but the point is when they *choose* to regenerate. It must be based on something. There must be a feeling that adepts start to lose their edge, start to slow down a bit at that age unless they regenerate. Even if the *actual* effects are negligible it doesn't matter because the perception is the important thing."

Susan wasn't following: "The perception?"

David was ahead of her and said, "I get it. If everyone agrees you should regenerate at one hundred if you don't want to start losing your marbles, then anyone who goes much past one hundred will be under scrutiny. There could be nothing wrong with them, but there'll still be muttering in the ranks every time they forget someone's name or knock over the salt."

Daniel took over again: "Exactly. Because if everyone agreed there was absolutely no problem waiting until one-ten to regenerate, then one-ten would be the norm instead. It's really more about the accepted norms of the group than about their physiology."

Susan had caught up: "You're talking about organisational stresses; that's where you're going with this."

I'm guessing from the couple of 'ahhs' I heard that Daniel must have nodded. He elaborated, "Any leaders who go beyond the consensus age for regeneration will be seen as less capable, possibly ripe for challenge. Any of the worker ants who go beyond that age will feel let down by their leaders. They won't feel the leaders are taking good care of them. Either way you look at it, it puts pressure on those at the top."

The Professor spoke, "An appealing institutional analysis, Daniel. Losing the Marker could trigger a coup long before its loss has any quantifiable physical effects. In turn, the *prospect* of a coup will influence decisions made at the top."

The Professor was silent for a moment and then went on, "Of course the relevance of that analysis depends upon their tendency to topple their leaders. If a coup is unthinkable in their world then the current leaders need not concern themselves. But given what we know of their warrior-tribal mentality, I would say that any perceived weakness in the leadership, either physiological or managerial, is likely to provoke challenges to their authority. I'm inclined to agree that those who lead the Army can't afford to twiddle their thumbs for long."

For the first time Theresa spoke, "But what constitutes a long time for people who live for hundreds of years? Maybe their idea of a knee-jerk response still takes a decade."

The Professor said, "I'd be interested to hear all of your views, but I find myself swayed by Daniel's point. I can't help feeling that the rank and file will expect concrete results after two or three years. Those in charge have nothing, so far as we're aware, to show for Year One in terms of progress in finding the Marker. If their stance has been passive until now – and of course we don't know that for *certain* – but if it has, then I think we will see them go on the offensive within eighteen months or so."

I was still listening avidly, but my mind had ceased to even process their discussion. I was taking the whole thing in with the intention of replaying it in my head for, say, about the next six months as I tried to figure out what planet we were on and why I didn't seem to recognize it any more. I'd also need to just explore the possibility that my colleagues were a psychotic cult of delusional lunatics.

These thoughts coincided with a lull in the conversation. No one spoke for a few seconds and then David said, "Someone's coming."

There was much shuffling of paper and the Professor said, "Perhaps this is a good time to take a tea break, if no one objects? I have one or two errands to attend to, I'm afraid; could we break for an hour?"

There were mutters of assent and I could hear the sounds of chairs being moved. Then I heard the door being opened and someone said, "Professor, I'm very sorry to interrupt, but there's a delivery that needs your attention."

That was plainly all I was going to hear for a while and my focus began to turn away from the muffled sounds of the meeting room and towards the memory of the words I'd overheard. I considered hanging up the phone.

Then, over the open connection, I heard a beeping noise which for a moment I couldn't place.

"Did someone forget to turn their phone off?" asked Susan a little accusingly. There was obviously a 'no phones' rule.

I heard "Nope" and "Not me" and Susan saying, "Well somebody's phone…" She was interrupted by the phone beeping again. At which point I realized whose it was. It was mine: my bug-phone. It was receiving a back-log of text messages. I mean, what kind of phone beeps while a call is in progress? Maybe that's why it had been at the bottom of a box.

I'd turned off the ringer, but I hadn't thought about texts. No one should be sending messages to that phone. No one for weeks now – except of course goddamned spammers. As though they hadn't caused enough irritation in the world they were going to blow my first attempt at espionage. Immediately, sweat began to prickle my forehead.

I waited for someone to look under the table, to remember my earlier visit, to check the phone's call log and to come and find me.

Chapter 3

But, what do you know, the finding of my phone wasn't the disaster that lurked just around the corner.

I heard Susan say, "I won't shame whoever it is, but make sure it doesn't happen again please. Phones off."

Then I heard her mutter, "It better not be you, Mister cell-phones-are-a-blight-on-society." I assume she was talking to David.

And that seemed to be that.

I wasn't necessarily in the clear yet – who knew how many spam texts were floating around in the system for that phone – but I figured there was a good chance they'd all just been delivered in a big clump. There was no reason for the phone network to drag it out. I might just have gotten away with it.

One thing was for sure, though; I wasn't going to try listening to the second half of the meeting. I was *preeeetty* sure that phone had a low-battery alert too. I'd avoid running the battery down with any more calls, then I'd retrieve the phone later.

I was kind of annoyed with myself because it was such a

silly slip and I should never have made it. But the annoyance couldn't really get a foothold; anxiety over nearly being caught and fascination with what I'd overheard were competing much harder for my attention.

Once the PAC seemed to lose interest in the subject of beeping phones, my fear of discovery halved – which allowed my upended sense of reality to grab the lion's share of my attention. What was this world the PAC thought they lived in? Was it some sort of game being played with straight faces? Were they just monumentally confused about… pretty much everything? Could any of what they were talking about be real?

I'd been doing some pacing while I thought about it all, but now I ended the phone call and sat back down at the console. I wanted more information.

I started opening the decrypted PAC documents and began reading. There was even more craziness contained in the first document I looked at than had been hinted about in the meeting. I read a note that discussed the powers of these 'adepts' and it seemed to be describing something akin to telekinesis.

If any of this was to be believed, the PAC had stumbled upon a whole world of strangeness, complete with super-villains, and the PAC-members themselves were trying to get their bearings while simultaneously working to thwart the forces of darkness.

I read on, mesmerised. It couldn't be real, but it was a mighty queer sort of hoax – and to what end? If it was all deception then it involved numerous conspirators and preposterous amounts of preparation – every member of the PAC had put on a show on the off-chance that someone was listening in. Unless this was all somehow for my benefit (and that way lay full-blown paranoid schizophrenia) it was clear that the PAC believed their own crazy version of reality. I didn't share their belief, but I was already sure that there must be *something* extraordinary going on here. They couldn't *all* be crazy, so they must either be right… or the hoax was being perpetrated on them. It was pretty fascinating, however you looked at it.

I paused to think for a moment and I happened to glance in the direction of my notes – the ones concerning the subscriptions I was supposed to be setting up – and I recalled my earlier fleeting thought about the Professor – the one where I was so relieved when he failed to freak out.

And it was at that exact moment that someone rapped sharply on the door. So much for the server-room being a good place to avoid interruptions.

What a tumble of paranoid thoughts that sound released. I wondered which possible source of trouble was waiting for me in the corridor.

I opened the door wide to see the Professor standing there. "Do you have a moment, Jo?" he asked. For a microsecond I wondered if I was becoming clairvoyant. I think of him and he appears. But this wasn't about seeing the future; it was about waking up to the inevitable.

The Professor stood there pursing and relaxing his lips in a strange way and it took me a second to read the meaning in his expression: he was furious.

A sense of dread settled on me. I'd never seen him this angry with anyone before. Did he somehow know I'd bugged the meeting?

I swallowed, not saying anything, and stepped back into the server room, holding the door so he could follow me. Whatever had pushed him over the edge, it was clear that he was about to really lose his temper with me.

I found I couldn't meet his eyes with mine. His voice was threateningly cold and horribly deliberate as he said, "I've just been informed that there are seventeen packing crates blocking the corridor in the dormitories. I'm told you arranged for them to be placed there." Seventeen crates? Crap. I was expecting one, maybe two boxes. God, this was going to look like I didn't give a damn how much disruption I caused. What peachy timing.

His gaze was hard and unblinking as he continued, "And the subscriptions… I didn't like to say anything in front of Susan, but we both know you haven't done a *thing* about them." I glanced up to see his eyes drilling into mine. "This really isn't good enough, Jo." The words weren't especially harsh, but his tone was heavy with a verdict of disappointment – so heavy I could feel it pressing down on me. He had made some sort of awful decision; I could tell.

Even before today, I had secretly known we would reach this moment. It had been coming for a while now. He hadn't even discovered the bugging; he'd just reached the limit of his tolerance – even without knowing the full truth. It was almost funny. Maybe, in fifty years time, I'd actually laugh about this.

But right now I was terrified. He couldn't be giving up on me, could he? That wasn't how this worked. He was the rock, the stern but dependable uncle-figure who might tut and grumble but who stood by me nonetheless. His patience wasn't supposed to be exhaustible, to run out. That was an important part of the lousy deal the Universe had forced on me. Professor Shaw was part-compensation for the loss of my mother and the fact my father had 'moved on, emotionally' as one therapist put it. That's why Professor Shaw's patience had to be limitless. If his distant, hesitating affection for me was all I got in place of two functioning parents then that affection had *better* be inexhaustible.

And what? I couldn't even have that now?

Whatever painful announcement lurked at the end of this conversation, it was fast approaching. He launched into it, still stiff with irritation: "I have come to accept your inability to think of others, so the chaos in the dormitories isn't unexpected. It is your attitude to work that *baffles* me. I know you're more than capable of completing the tasks you're set and you seem willing enough when they're discussed. And yet you seem determined to let down anyone you make a commitment to."

Was he going to throw me off the project? Was that what he was leading up to?

I knew my failure to speak up, to defend myself, would only make his anger worse, but I found I was trapped inside the realisation that I'd finally pushed to breaking point the one person I believed would always support me.

Then, thankfully, I heard myself begin to say something, to stand up for myself. Only what came out was this: "But you *said* I didn't really need to rush…" I couldn't finish the sentence; I sounded pathetic, whining, childish. I looked at the Professor out of the corner of my eye and now he *really* looked angry. *Here it comes.*

And I was right. His temper boiled over and he began to speak with unrestrained emotion now. His chin jutted and his eyes were wide and fierce as he said, "I have always tried to do what's best for you, Jo. I have been patient and I have made allowances. I know, too, that life has been difficult for you." He pointed a finger straight at me and declared, "But believe me, young lady, it has been *just* as hard on others from whom I never hear excuses, in whom I can safely place my trust and upon whom I can always rely. We have passed the point at which my tolerance seems to serve any useful purpose. It seems only to encourage you in your faults and to give others reason to suspect favouritism on my part." He drew up a breath and said, "Tell me, is there any reason why I shouldn't ask you to look for a position elsewhere? Any reason I shouldn't do that this minute?"

But I was way ahead of him. In my mind, I was already out of work and unemployable. The fact was, I had no family to turn to and no close friends. I had used my work to create some sort of framework for my life, to provide me with a direction, and that prop was about to be taken from me.

I had money, but what I didn't have was anything else to cling to – and that's a dangerous combination. Once I was kicked off this project, I wouldn't be offered another post, I knew that. *Then* what would I do? I knew I wasn't strong enough to start again, to find something new – or even to resist the temptation to let everything slide. I was terrified that the few strands of my life on which I still had a good grip were about to slip through my fingers.

Though I would have given anything not to, I began to cry – silently at first and then out loud. Fat tears rolled down my face. I knew how wretched and unsympathetic I must look, but that just made me feel worse, just confirmed the hopelessness I felt.

Brought up short by my tears, the Professor said, with hesitation, "Jo, I…" His voice was neutral now, the anger back on its leash.

Through my abject tears I saw something in him change and I thought for a moment he was going to put his arms around me. And I realised that I very much wanted him to do that. But whatever new emotion he was feeling, it wasn't pity. "Pull yourself together," was all he said and then he turned around and left.

* * *

I sat on my own and cried for a while.

When the tears eventually began to subside, I reflected on something a therapist once told me about personality problems. He said that whatever you have too much of – be it anger, sadness, paranoia or even confidence – all those excesses start with putting yourself too close to the centre of things, with believing that everything is about *you*.

So maybe the secret is not to take life too personally, not to get upset. Just let things wash over you.

But then what would be the point of living like that?

After the Professor left, I dropped into my chair and sat there, brim full of self-pity. My own feelings, my own predicament, filled the world and nothing else registered.

I might talk a pretty good game from time to time, but all the way back to the death of my mother I'd really just been papering over the cracks. I was beginning to think that by now I was *entirely* paper and cracks.

There was an irony as unavoidable as a migraine in the realisation that the arrival of my dead mother's belongings was what tipped Professor Shaw over the edge. It somehow seemed to close a vicious circle that had begun with her death.

My brain snagged on that thought and for maybe half an hour I dangled there, wretched and intermittently tearful.

Then, gradually, I became aware that my gaze had settled on my cell phone.

Pretty soon now, the meeting I'd been so keen to overhear would be back in session. Man, that all seemed like a long time ago.

The desire to know what was going on in that meeting seemed remote and sad for a moment, like reading a great review for a movie that was no longer showing. In another life, I would have loved the chance to follow it up, to discover what was going on, but there was no point now.

Of course, depression is like that: a familiar weight that settles on you so heavily that you can't move, you can't even *imagine* playing an active part in your own life. All you can think about is the weight and a feeling like falling.

Regardless, a single bright thought flitted to and fro in my gloomy mind, like a tiny, silvery fish darting through the silted hulk of a drowned ship. What if?

What if what? There wasn't much of my attention to spare for anything besides emotional wallowing, but mustering all the enthusiasm of a death-row inmate catching sight of the laundry instructions on his jumpsuit I gave this distraction a listless sliver of my concentration.

What if… I could prove myself?

It didn't cause much of a stir among my doom-laden thoughts. No more than a tag reading 'Wash strong colors separately' would distract you from thoughts of the gallows.

And anyway, who would I prove myself to? Why would it matter? Where would I even find the energy? And how would I feel when inevitably I failed?

Then again, this secret that the PAC was keeping was something big; what if I could help them with it? I was at my quirky best working in uncharted intellectual territory – in areas where the academic infrastructure wasn't built yet – and that was exactly the terrain confronting this project. Whereas most people couldn't work without a map, without some fixed points to steer by, I could. That was high on the list of reasons why I fitted in so badly wherever I went: I didn't like living inside someone else's framework; I'd kick at it, try to rearrange it, attempt to construct my own.

I suppose you could say I was kind of an intellectual off-roader. Plus, I didn't know a lot about any one thing; I just knew a little about almost everything and I could make connections. Boy, could I make connections. Which meant that maybe *I* was what this team needed – not some neat-and-tidy, colour-inside-the-lines team-player used to being told how to think, but someone like me.

Impossible as it seemed, I felt a little reflexive twitch of enthusiasm at this idea. Maybe it was just the last shudder before my motivation gave out for good, but this thought had somehow attracted my full attention.

As everyone knows, people with big brains don't behave any better than the rest of the population, they just rationalise better after the fact. Well, the idea that the PAC and me might be a match made in heaven was making more and more sense to me as a plan for the future – but it was making equally good sense as a desperately-needed rationalisation of my failure-strewn past.

I mean, what if trail-breaking, pioneering research wasn't just my forte, it was my oxygen? Well then naturally I'd have felt stifled where I was, stuck in the airless academic suburbs all my life. Maybe it was just my worthless luck to be born too late, into an era where most of the academic wilderness had already been paved over? Maybe I'd struggled all these years to fit in because I needed the kind of mental challenge that just didn't exist any more.

The signs were all there. I knew I was something of an academic cowboy but I'd always tried to suppress that side of me. But maybe what I needed all along wasn't a bit more discipline, maybe what I needed was a frontier to tame[1].

This new revelation took hold so thoroughly that for a second I couldn't think why my eyes itched and my nose needed blowing. Allergies? Oh wait, that's right, I'd been crying my eyes out a little while ago. Well that mood had well and truly left me now; the depression had been shoved back into the iron box it slept in. My tears had dried up, leaving only the rebound lightness you feel after a really good sob.

Now all I needed was a way into the PAC.

---

[1] OK, so cowboys didn't tame frontiers, they supervised cows, but we're talking 'in the popular imagination' here.

Chapter 4

As my mood lightened, I felt fired up and full of purpose (and *maybe* a little manic too). Somehow I would patch things up with the Professor. I wasn't sure exactly what my current, post-ragged-upon status was, but I didn't think I was off the project yet. I reckoned I was in the penalty box but still hanging by a thread (to use a well-known sports & embroidery metaphor).

I needed the Professor to forgive me and I needed to be drafted into the PAC – after which I could make myself indispensable (which at that moment I was convinced I could do).

(I didn't want to think about whether my new plan would actually work; I wanted to act before the moment passed, before this wonderful sense of purpose could desert me.)

I would definitely need to apologise to the Professor. I had to persuade him to grant me a stay of execution. Which he would do, right? Sure, I'd been pushing my luck with him for years, but this was the first time he'd really called me on it. So *technically* this was only 'swipe one' (as they ought to say in baseball when you *don't* strike the ball). Baseballing types get three lives, cats get a preposterous nine lives for sitting around licking their butts all day; *I* should get at least *one* chance to redeem myself[1].

Anyway, once I was out of the penalty box there were two things I would need to work on: intelligence and leverage. Intel, because I had to learn more about the strange world the PAC had uncovered if I was going to make myself useful to them. And leverage because I'd need a way to persuade the group – or at the very least the Professor – to let me join the inner circle.

Step one was my speciality: soak up everything there is to know on a new subject, organise it, then start filling in the gaps. Step two was just the opposite: my Achilles heel. I didn't have any leverage, any favours to call in and (face it) I wasn't likely to win through on charm alone. In fact the only person I could think of who still cared about keeping on my good side was Daniel.

Well, so be it; I'd start with good old Daniel.

And there was no time like the present. The Professor would need to cool off a bit before he'd want to hear anything I said – even if it *was* an apology – but I could still get busy. I'd go and find Daniel right now.

I checked the console's clock and thought about Daniel's routine. Then I let myself out of the server room and detoured to the ladies' toilets. During the day I don't wear make-up, at least not in the usual course of things, but Hysterical Blotchy Female wasn't the look I needed right now.

When I'd tidied my face up a little, I hot-footed it out the main entrance and round the side of the building towards the back-door to the kitchens. The PAC's hour-long break was nearly up but there was a fair chance that most of them, probably including the Professor, would still be loitering in the refectory, drinking tea. Clichéd though it sounds, it's what British academics do. But I knew Daniel liked to have a crafty cigarette with his

---

[1]   Though on reflection I might not justify myself using *exactly* those words.

cuppa, which meant he'd be out of doors somewhere, despite the intermittent rain.

Outside, the chronic drizzle was in temporary remission, but everything was still soaked. As I left the gravel drive, a certain reluctance around the lower pant-leg told me that the cuffs of my jeans were greedily drinking in the moisture from the grass. That was going to look glamorous.

I rounded the corner of the old stone kitchen buildings and, sure enough Daniel was there, talking to the scruffy cook in his stained white cook clothes, the both of them puffing on what the British still insist on calling fags. I wondered what these two had in common; were they discussing Charlemagne or casseroles? Or, knowing guys, perhaps they didn't bother with conversation. I'd heard that most male bonding is based on a primitive system of grunts.

The cook saw me approaching and said something to Daniel, then stubbed out his smoke and vanished inside. Daniel looked up as I got near. His hand dropped to his side and instinctively shielded his cigarette, like he'd caught sight of the principal – I think it was just a public-school[1] reflex. His expression, though, was relaxed and friendly. With his other hand, he raised a forefinger to tip the brim of his imaginary Stetson and said, "Howdy, Ma'am."

I collected myself and for the second time that year turned on a smile in his presence. I wasn't quite sure what I was going to say, but the best way to find out was to start speaking.

I said, "Can I have one?"

He looked surprised and said, "I thought you'd packed it in."

---

[1] You prolly know this already, but in the UK public means private. And private tends to mean special – as in 'he takes the *special* bus to school'. So public schools are the ones the public aren't allowed to.

"I still weaken when things get stressful," I said – so that he'd ask me to explain; though the truth was that I never smoked any more. It kicked up my asthma, so the fun had gone out of it. If I smoked at a party I'd spend half the night wheezing. Cigarettes = cool, but struggling to breathe = extra not-cool.

"So what's causing you stress?" he asked as he held out first the pack and then his lighter. I took a Marlboro Light – all anyone ever offered me – wondering if they even make other brands of cigarettes any more. Ever the furtive smoker, Daniel made the pack and the lighter appear from thin air and then disappear again once I'd lit up. I remembered that he could also roll his own with insouciant skill – something that I found simultaneously downmarket and a little bit charming.

I puffed without inhaling and said, "Well… too much boredom, mainly." I took a mouthful of smoke and added, "But I also screwed up." His expression became appropriately concerned.

I sighed, trying not to overdo it, and blew a little smoke into the moist air.

I said, "I'm really struggling to concentrate, what with the brain-dead stuff they've got me doing. It's so unbelievably monotonous that I can't help zoning out sometimes. But then I miss some silly detail and get in trouble. I need a challenge, you know? Something to keep me awake." Again I smiled at him and he smiled back, nodding. See how devious I can be?

He offered: "Yeah, but we're still setting up. There's bound to be some donkey-work to begin with. Once it's all up and running I'm sure you'll get something meaty to work on."

I turned to look at him. "Well, *you* seem to have plenty to occupy your brain," I said. "That procedures and admin thing is obviously a lot more interesting than it sounds." I looked away again, out over the expanse of wet grass, wondering what he'd make of that remark.

42

Out of the corner of my eye I could see him cast a nervous glance at me. I did my best to be nonchalant and kept my eyes fixed on the downcast sheep that dotted the drenched hills. A second or two later I could tell he'd looked away. My focus stayed on the sheep, giving him plenty of time to speak.

But he said nothing so I decided to make him sweat a little, make him think he'd given something away. I faced him and asked, "You've gone quiet; did I say something?"

"No, no," he assured me.

I pressed him, looking worried, "You sure?"

He said, "No, it's nothing."

Which meant I could say: "Daniel, people only ever say 'it's nothing' when it's something. Is there something about the committee I'm not supposed to know?"

Corny? What are you talking about? The word you're looking for is *masterful*. No way was Daniel an experienced enough liar to be *sure* he hadn't let something slip, now or in the past. I mean how else could I know that something was going on? By spying on him? Don't be ridiculous.

Daniel took a sharp drag on his cigarette and looked awkward. "Erm, Jo…" was all he said.

I threw him a rope, in my new role as master manipulator. "It's OK. You're not the first person to hint that the committee are up to something. I was just hoping that whatever it is, you might put in a good word for me; maybe I could be a part of it too." Simper, simper.

Now he really was uncomfortable – probably thinking through what he was going to say when the PAC hauled him over the coals for blabbing. He tried standing his ground: "What do you mean? I didn't say anything."

Again, courtesy of day-time soaps, that was an easy one to twist. I said, "You didn't *say* it, but you made it pretty obvious, don't you think?"

I was still searching for a way to make him open up. I gave him big eyes and said, "Pleeease. It's driving me crazy doing the mindless stuff. I really need, you know, a challenge before I go out of my mind."

Clang. Bad choice of words. It would probably be best if I left out the references to being a crazy person. But it was too late. His expression shifted from discomfort to concern. Couldn't he see I was being metaphorical? He said, "Listen, you're not back on those patches of yours, are you?"

That was the wrong direction for this to go in and it was an argument we'd already had more than once. I said, "That's got nothing to do with it. I'm talking about finding something interesting to work on."

He didn't take the hint. He softened his voice even more and said, "I just think you'd find everything easier without that stuff. You don't need it."

That preachy, hand-holding tone of his really gets on my nerves. I tried not to let it rile me but, trust me, it's instantly infuriating. I couldn't think what to say next... but that didn't seem to stop me blundering on: "I'm asking you to do me a favour. Is that such a big deal? Do you have to make it so hard?" Listening to my own words, I sounded anything but calm now. I wasn't even doing a very good job of keeping my voice down.

And apparently I'd encouraged Daniel on his little social-worker trip. He'd switched to his most calm, most caring voice – the one I especially hate. He said, "Of *course* I want to help. You know that. But if something's bothering you, we should talk about it. Then we can think about what to do."

Well, that wasn't even him talking; it was obviously some article he'd read about handling People with Problems. Is your friend on DRUGS? If you suspect that someone you know may be ON DRUGS, first reassure them that you're there for them. Crazy druggies need *a lot* of reassurance. Then patronise them to

44

within an inch of their lives while remembering to keep repeating their name – it builds trust. And remember, adopt the troubled but patient tones of a kindly uncle even if you happen to be a year younger than them.

It made me want to scream. Right on cue, he said, "Look, Jo, you know you can talk to me…"

I didn't let him finish. He obviously wasn't going to help me and I certainly didn't need him practicing any more of his Talking to Troubled Teens bullshit on me.

I held up a hand to cut him off. "Fine, fine," I said, "Thanks for the lecture; it was very helpful." I turned and walked briskly back towards the main entrance, leaving him struggling for words like a landed fish trying to breathe.

I was annoyed with myself for getting mad just as quickly as I always do. I couldn't seem to hit a compromise between fear of being found out and over-confident blundering.

Halfway back to the main entrance I realised I was still carrying a lit cigarette and dropped it into a puddle. It made an abbreviated fizzing noise that sounded a bit like the word 'snip' as it went out.

So much for Daniel.

It was a setback. I was bloodied, but unbowed though – not to mention hacked off, as they say in these parts.

I hadn't got anywhere with my first attempt to get some leverage on the PAC, but maybe I could focus on the intel for a while, until I'd regrouped.

I took some deep breaths of wet air, reminded myself I was on a mission, then I headed back to my lair. It was time to read the rest of the PAC's mail.

After all, when in doubt, research.

(Note: an even better maxim, learned some time later is: try not to let the research get you killed.)

Chapter 5

Once more I was back at the server room and now there was an envelope pushed under the door. It was the delivery note that came with the crates – the crates that were apparently blocking the corridor in the dorms.

This was hardly today's top story, but all the same I couldn't ignore it. If it didn't get sorted out pronto the Professor would never come down off the ceiling. And I needed him to get over his conniptions so that I could remain on the project. I also needed him to get over it so that he would consider asking me to join the PAC. And finally I needed him to get over it because I couldn't bear him being mad with me. It might be distant affection that I got from him, but I valued it all the same.

So the crates. And while I was thinking about that little chore and how I might quickly cross it off my to-do list, another chore came to mind. I needed to hassle the tenant of my house in London about rent and looking for lodgers and being less of a butt-pain. And I'd been putting that off because – surprise, surprise – I didn't want to do it.

Again, it didn't sound like a priority compared with

researching the alleged fight against superpowered evil, but things would really come unglued if I didn't tackle it soon.

Just before I'd left England to start my PhD in the States I used the majority of my father's Gewissengelt[1] to buy a house. I've been criss-crossing the Atlantic all my life, so I knew one day I'd be back. And buying property seemed like a smart investment in the long term. Plus in the short-term, it promised to bring in some rent and give me a base when I visited London. I mean, it sounds plausible, right? But, upon further inspection, it turned out that life wasn't that simple.

Like all good Americans, I'd believed my own propaganda. Confident in my plan, when I moved back to the UK I'd foolishly set things up so that rent from my tenants was the only thing topping up my bank account (unless you counted the drip, drip, drip of my miniscule project wages) and lately there'd been no rent. Which was a problem because bottles of Ouzo Extra Collapso don't pay for themselves. With no rent coming in, I'd drained my current account with impressive speed and kept on going. My overdraft had inflated alarmingly, bursting through its credit limits and triggering a volley of penalty charges like buttons popping off a fat man's shirt. While the adage 'ignore it and it'll go away' might work a treat on medical problems there seemed to be a dogged inevitability about debt that no amount of neglect could dispel.

Maybe I needed to spend a weekend in London to see if I could get things back on track. I could try to sort out all the rent-related nonsense and at the same time have a few days R&R away from Yokel-World and this project. It would give me a chance to think through the PAC revelations.

---

[1] My advice is to just ignore words you don't understand. I mean I'd probably explain them if they were important, right? Hmmm, now you've got me wondering.

For a moment that all seemed tempting, but to my surprise I realised I actually didn't want to leave right now. I'd got work to do here, what with the ingratiating and the snooping and the unravelling of forbidden mysteries, etc. So I decided to put off the London trip – though I'd need to slap a band-aid on the problem in the meantime.

I know, I know, this doesn't sound very relevant. But, boy, will you feel stupid if some of this stuff comes up on the test and you skipped ahead.

So anyway, something had to be done about the rent. *Or* I had to find another source of income. Admittedly, I could probably raise some cash if I didn't mind asking my father for help. But I *did* mind asking my father for help. I'd save that option until I'd run out of kidneys to sell.

Tucked away in my Fortress of Servitude, pondering my options, I was still feeling a little of that post-weep rebound-high; it was making me feel unusually dynamic, and I figured I should fix as many problems as possible before I slumped back into my trademark malaise. So I would head over to the dorms to call my lodger, Noola[1] The Pain-in-the-Ass, from my room and while I was there I could take a look at the distressing crate situation.

Before I set off, I took all the PAC mail and documents I'd decrypted and copied them to a flash drive. Now I'd be able to read them on my laptop in the privacy and squalor of my own room.

* * *

---

[1]   It even annoys me to write the word 'Noola'. I mean, why give your child a traditional Celtic name like 'Nualla' and then spell it phonetically? It just reeks of history absorbed from the backs of cereal boxes.

The drizzle had started up again (hooray!), but this time, as I tripped between the puddles, I managed to keep my jean cuffs from rehydrating. Sadly, now my hair was gulping moisture from the air and getting set to do its frizztastically adorable dandelion impersonation. Thankfully I made it to the dorm's outside door before my locks reached the point of no return. (In my case, water is to hair as heat is to popcorn.)

Up the stairs, through the fire door and sure enough: there were boxes running all the way down the dorm corridor. They weren't packing crates as I'd been picturing them, just reinforced cardboard boxes, and if they'd actually been blocking the passage when they were unloaded, they weren't now. Someone had spaced them out a little and it was no longer *impossible* to get past – providing you could walk with your knees pressed tightly together. I'd concede there still wasn't a lot of corridor left for foot traffic, though. Crap.

I really wasn't expecting so many boxes. What was in them all?

Last time I'd called up to check on my father (translation: to get some money) I'd spoken to Mrs Revilla, the housekeeper. She could hardly wait to tell me that Dad was getting rid of all Mom's things. Probably wife-number-two objected to all the mementoes of wife-number-one around the place. Or maybe it was current-girlfriend/potential-wife-three who was grumbling.

It occurred to me that as an added bonus maybe Dad had worked out that disposing of Mom's things would also erase any unpleasant reminders that he'd had a daughter by his first wife. Pretty soon, the only evidence that I'd once lived there would be a string of entries on his bank statements. Which is why I tried to make sure those little bookkeeping mementoes of me were as eye-wateringly memorable as possible.

Anyway, when Mrs Revilla had told me the plan, I did a little flipping out and a little ranting and I demanded that my mother's things be sent to me, rather than thrown in the trash. I wasn't going to allow her memory to be edited out of existence like that.

Let me stop there a second. Maybe I should be clear on something. Not that I think I should have to explain, but sometimes people act surprised when... What I mean is, Mom died a long time ago and sometimes people accuse me of acting like it was yesterday. I don't see that it matters, but yes I was very young and now I'm comfortably into my twenties, so perhaps a really well-adjusted person would view the whole thing as just some childhood setback or something. A hiccup best forgotten.

But that's just it, I *have* forgotten it. It's not something I've really talked about to anyone who isn't a registered therapist, but I have no real memories of my mother. I was five when she died and so, logically, I should recall all sorts of things about her. But everything I know is secondhand, learned from pictures and from talking to people who knew her. I'm sure if I was still seeing any of my former therapists they'd link that fact to my wig-out over the plan to ditch her things. My only connection to her is through the effects she left behind and I don't *care* that it's twenty years later; wanting a link to your mother is not a phase you grow out of.

Anyway, after the funeral, her clothes and a lot of her things were given away to charity. Someone had saved a few books for me, for when I was older, and the rest had been put into storage ever since. I imagined that by now we were down to maybe a photo album, some ornaments and a few bundles of letters. I was expecting a box or two like you'd get when you have a new stereo delivered; what I got was a *collection* of boxes like you'd get if you had a hockey team delivered. The thought that there was this unexpected mountain of her personal belongings still in existence, a whole consignment of clues to what she was like... well, it was a little daunting.

As I was unlocking my door I saw that the box nearest to

me had a plump envelope securely taped to its top. The word 'Inventory' was block-lettered on the envelope's front. I fished out my little Juice pocket-knife and snapped open a blade. I used it to slit the envelope free and open it up. Inside were a half-dozen sheets of laser-printed paper, stapled top-left, which exhaustively listed the contents of all the boxes. Box 6 immediately caught my eye as it mainly contained 'personal correspondence'. I could fit one box into the free floor space in my room without trapping myself in there permanently, and the lucky winner was going to be box number six.

Now, what was I going to do with the rest of it?

More or less straightaway I got an idea. There were two little windows in my room, high up on the wall opposite the door. I couldn't see anything from them – unless you count a piece of sky – without standing on the bed. And it wasn't worth the effort; if I did climb up to take a look, the view consisted of a muddy lane running down to a barn. A rusty red gate of tubular-steel was the only bright spot in the sodden green-brown scene – unless someone parked a car down there. The apron of stone-chips in front of the barn door seemed to serve the project team as an overflow car park.

I'd never really thought of it before, but that sort of implied that the barn was part of the same parcel of land as the dorm and the office buildings. If we could park there, maybe we had the use of the barn. Maybe I could stash the remainder of the boxes in there.

That sounded more like a question for Susan Milton than the Professor (or was that just my cowardice talking?). I'd have to talk to her about it once the PAC meeting ended.

OK. Now (deep breath) for Noola. I brought up the number on my cell-phone and hit send.

She answered promptly with a drawn-out "Yeah?" and already I was tempted to hang up. That accent.

I mean I'm hardly a xenophobe; I've spent nearly half my life outside the US. And I'm the first to admit that a lot of foreign accents sound delightful. I could listen to someone read bus schedules in French and find it charming. The story of Goldilocks told in Russian would stir my blood and leave me eager to join the epic struggle of bears versus tow-headed interlopers. But with some accents, a little goes a very long way. Noola's ultra-nasal vowel-wringing Australian was just plain wearying at the best of times. A compliment from her sounded like a complaint. So when she whined – which she did constantly – it was an adenoidal dirge that brought to mind stoned cats squabbling.

"Noola? It's Jo," I said.

"Jooooo. It's good you called; I wanted to taaaaalk to you."

"Really?" I said unenthusiastically, "what about?"

"Listen, this place is a dive. This neighbourhood I mean. Do you know what happened to me? I was mugged. Took my phone, my wallet. They even, can you belieeeeeve it, cut the ring my grandmother gave me for my eighteenth right off my goddamned finger. It was insane."

Gulp. "Are you OK?" I asked.

"Well, I'm still breathing, but believe me I'm not over the moon about it. Jerry and Katya moved out?" Wait, that wasn't a question, she was just doing that annoying thing where you twang up at the end of every sentence. "I've had to cancel my credit cards, buy a new phone and if I'm out late I have to get a taxi back. Someone should do something about this place."

For some reason, she was talking about all this as though it were my fault. I mean, I just wanted some rent; I wasn't planning to run for government on a law-and-order ticket. I said, "Erm, well, Noola. I'm sorry to hear all that and I'm glad you're OK… I mean not hurt. Listen, I was calling to ask about the rent situation you see I haven't…"

She didn't let me finish: "I can't belieeeve you're asking

me that." She sounded outraged and offended, as though I'd demanded to know how anyone could stand the sound of her voice. She launched into it: "I took this place because it was cheap. I didn't know that was because I was signing up to get robbed on my way home. You know, I could have been killed… or worse." I didn't ask what she meant by that.

I suggested as tactfully as I could: "Well, I understand that. But the place was cheap because you agreed to help me find lodgers. That was the deal."

"Yeah," she said as though I'd made her point for her, "and how many people do you suppose want to live in a house where they get attacked on their way home? Not that many, Jo. Not that many. Right now my rent money is going to pay for replacing what was stolen and on taxis so I can get home at night without having to worry about…" She gulped air and fought to finish her sentence, "… what might happen."

Her righteous anger had morphed into self-pity at the end there. She sounded like she was fighting back the sobs.

I didn't see how I could push it. I mean, *I'd* be pretty freaked if someone cut a ring off my finger. Wouldn't you have to wonder, just for a moment, whether they might take the finger too? Shudder.

"OK, OK," I said, "I'm sorry to bring it up. You're obviously pretty upset…"

She butted in with: "You're bloody right I'm upset," but she was more sad than angry.

I pressed on, "…so I won't bother you any more. Maybe we can talk in a week or so. OK?"

I was already sorry I'd called, but she wasn't finished with me yet: "To be reaaaally honest with you, Jo, I'm not even sure how I feel about living here any more. I'm going to have to see what I think about the whoooole idea."

She said it like forcing her to think was adding insult to injury.

Time for me to bail: "Well, OK. Listen I have to go, but I'm glad you're sort of alright. OK, bye then," I said.

She just sniffed and muttered something sorrowful. I hung up.

Well, that was a bust. Weirdly, I felt *almost* good about it though, because I hated doing things like that, hassling people for money. It had been a disaster, but then I knew in advance it would be and I did it anyway. Go me.

I hadn't solved the problem, but I could, in good conscience, put it out of my mind for a few days.

I spent the rest of the afternoon and the first part of the evening alternating between the contents of the PAC's filestore and the contents of Box 6. I struck a strange sort of equilibrium: first I'd take a tiny, measured dose of emotional turmoil by lifting something out of the box containing my mom's things. When the nostalgic swells threatened to turn into a dark wave of melancholy I'd plunge back into the crystalline surrealism of the PAC's world. Their actions were impossible and absorbing and had the power to pull me out of the unpleasant headspace inhabited by thoughts of my mother's last days.

From time to time I also glanced nervously at the door, expecting the heart-stopping knock that would mean my spying had been discovered, or that some other crappy thing had happened. But no knock came.

All in all, I didn't know how I felt about going through my mom's things; it was too big a feeling to get an overall impression of. But on that other matter, the PAC, I felt my feelings shifting, changing. There was the beginning of acceptance, of the idea that it wasn't a hoax or a mass-hallucination, but something else. I wasn't ready to believe it was all true yet, but I was increasingly sure that there was something solid at its core. And that, I can tell you, was a strange sensation.

I'd discovered an account, almost like a diary, of what had

happened to David, Susan and the Professor the previous year and how they had become involved with this guy Jan. It was interesting to speculate about why they'd written it. Did one or more of them worry that they might not be around to tell their replacements the tale?

I read it avidly and then read it again. The main points were these: someone called Dass was the head of a sort of superpowered mafia called the Army Who Witnessed Creation. Jan was an ex-member of this cult/crime family/coven who had now gone rogue. Jan stole something called the Marker from Dass. The Marker was supposedly some sort of passport to immortality for which Jan then needed the operating instructions. Jan killed the previous owner of those instructions, but the key documents, along with lots of others on the subject of supernatural powers, eluded him and ended up at the London School of Antiquities being studied by Susan Milton.

Meanwhile David Braun was hunting the Marker on behalf of Dass, initially unaware that he was working for a superhuman criminal mastermind and that the missing item was a magical artefact. When David learned there were documents describing the Marker, he teamed up with the expert studying them: Susan. The two of them ended up caught between Dass and Jan as old owner and new fought over the Marker. The Professor also became entangled as he tried to help his favourite student, Susan.

After Jan killed Dass and stole the Marker for the second time he came after David and Susan, who were by now on the run from him with the Marker's instructions tucked in their back pocket. Jan's vicious efforts to retrieve the instructions from the pair culminated in a showdown in which he nearly killed them both. What saved them was intervention by the Professor. He contacted the business front for Dass's organisation, and anonymously tipped off another member of Dass's cabal, a woman called Karst, as to Jan's whereabouts. Karst intervened, killing Jan and retrieving the precious documents. Jan, however, had refused to divulge the secret of the Marker's current hiding place to Karst. The PAC had every reason to believe that The Army Who Witnessed Creation, perhaps now headed by Karst, were still hunting for the Marker.

The summary of the summary. Karst and her superpowered colleagues were still out there. The PAC were laying low while learning all they could.

Phew. Not exactly an everyday tale of ordinary folk, is it?

It was around nine when I finished reading that account and I felt I'd earned a drink. I gave in to temptation, slipping out of the dormitories and climbing the hill to the pub. No one I knew was there and I drank my wine in silence while failing to focus on a couple of back issues of Nature I'd brought along. I sipped gut-rot and thought about what I'd read.

Having failed to find the Marker, how long before the Army came for David and Susan? They'd hopefully be aware that Jan was acting alone and that David and Susan were his victims not his accomplices – just as Karst must have been when she let them live. But once they'd exhausted other avenues of investigation, wouldn't the Army decide to 'interview' David and Susan anyway, just to find out what their exact role had been and how they'd ended up at Jan's mercy?

Fortunately for our plucky heroes, it seemed as though all the bad guys who had encountered the pair were now dead: Jan, Dass and his two assistants. Only Karst lived, and she would have little enough info to go on. She knew both of them had been injured and that they'd been forced by Jan to hand over a cache of documents, including the instructions for the Marker. It was difficult to see how she could learn their names from that.

Could Karst trace the history of the documents back to the School of Antiquities and find Susan that way? For a start, despite the fact that Jan was an ex-member of the Army Who, he didn't know how to operate the Marker without instructions. That suggested that the Army kept the trick to operating the Marker a secret, maybe to prevent exactly what had happened: an insider stealing it. But Jan had found a copy of the instructions elsewhere. It stood to reason that the Army had no idea that such a copy existed or they'd have done something about it.

Even once the documents had reached the School of Antiquities, only a few academics would have known about them. There were very few people who could describe those papers well enough for someone to establish that they were the same ones that Karst took away with her. On the other hand, Karst had those documents in her possession, each piece of paper neatly labelled in its own little plastic wallet. According to what Susan had written, they weren't a dead giveaway – they didn't have the college seal and a phone number printed on them or anything - but maybe Karst would find a clue in the wallets or the labels that led her to the School.

If Karst discovered that the documents had once been at the School of Antiquities, would that enable her to find Susan? Susan had only spent a few weeks there on a secondment. But on the other hand there weren't that many women associated with the project. Could Karst tie a memory of a bloody and battered young woman lying on the floor of darkened church to an academic secondment from Professor Shaw's Cambridge college? Or was there some way she could discover that the half-dead body lying among the pews was a man called David Braun? You wanted to say 'no' on both counts, but on the other hand was it something you'd want to hang your life on? David and Susan – and perhaps the Professor – must be living with the constant threat of discovery. I wondered if I really wanted any part of that.

Assuming I believed a word of it, of course.

Closing time rolled around soon enough. Not *totally* drunk, I tottered back down the hill – deciding on a whim to make a detour before returning to the dorms. I made my way to the main project building and slipped inside.

Moving through the darkened corridors, I sneaked into the Professor's office with the semi-inebriated intention of retrieving my phone from the meeting room. I mean, what could possibly go wrong with that bright idea?

Chapter 6

The Professor was firm, but not angry, as he spoke. He was almost his usual self, although he wasn't quite turning gleeful cartwheels yet. He said, "I hope you can see: I need to take some sort of action. I can't allow this to be a repeat of the previous times you have neglected your responsibilities."

I reckoned I was winning him over but I still had some work to do.

I was standing in his office, having pleaded my case. Today had been a good day and a string of successes had given me the confidence I needed to seek him out. And even now my luck was holding. So far, this conversation had managed *not* to veer off the rails and plunge into the tall grass.

Success number one today had come when I woke up and realised that I'd survived last night's impressively stupid decision to recover my spy-phone while under the influence of toxic grape-products. The main building had been deserted and dark, and there'd been no one to witness my heavy-footed tiptoeing, my missteps and self-shushing – followed by my weaving escape. You could say that I'd shot myself in the foot and missed. Hooray!

Then, this morning, finding myself with miraculously little in the way of hangover, I'd set to work scaling my chore-mountain and trying to clear the backlog of project work. I hadn't quite got caught up – I was *waaaayyy* too behind for that – but I'd taken a huge bite out of the problem. There was plenty to show for half a dozen hours of intense application.

And top of the notable achievements list was the fact that I'd called the relevant companies about our pending subscriptions and arranged a string of day-passes to tide us over while they futzed about with the paperwork. Then I'd apologised to the team for the delay. I'd very nearly done that in person, but, you know, that would have been a miracle. Instead, I *personally* emailed them to say I was sorry about how long it had all taken and to update them on the good news about the temporary fix.

That didn't just scratch an item off the Damoclean To-Do list; it actually made me feel good too. I almost got a kick out of being a good little worker-bee.

And there was more. I'd tracked down Susan Milton and wheedled the use of part of the barn so's I could store my crate collection. She'd agreed, on the condition that it was just for a few days, until I could arrange an alternative – but it seemed a good bet she'd let me extend it for longer than that. She was a little vague about what the team was currently using the barn for, so once she'd given me a key, I went to check.

She'd got part of the ground floor set up as a basic gym and there was a cleared area in the centre. I know she was an avid fencer and was maybe into martial arts, so I figured this was where she practiced. I was pretty sure that team money was paying the rent on the barn – and her training was hardly team business – so I figured I had just as much (or little) right to use the space as she did.

Anyway, once she'd agreed to share the barn with me, I phoned a man-with-van number I found in the yellow pages and persuaded a couple of local yokels to shift the crates into the barn for the princely sum of twenty quid. Not bad, and they were available that morning, so the whole thing was sorted by lunchtime. I'm *all about* takin' care of bidness [insert high-five here][1].

Towards the end of the afternoon, feeling pretty good about everything, I decided to tackle the most dauntingest chore of them all: generating a little détente with the Professor. And call me emotionally crippled, but I actually made some notes about what I was going to say before I sought him out – a refreshing change from my usual policy of stampeding around until I fall into a hole, as I'm sure you'll agree.

I figured that some apologising was required, but at the same time I needed to seem less of a neurotic mess than I'd been recently. The best way to persuade him not to give up on me, I decided, was first to persuade him that I could look after myself, that I wasn't going to be a burden to him however things turned out. I needed to appear capable, stable, productive – and appropriately concerned about repairing any damage done. Easy, right? So I went in and I told him that he didn't have to trust me, he could just let my future actions speak for themselves. I was putting myself on probation with him and if he didn't think I was doing right by him, then *I'd* remove myself from the team.

It was all pretty sneaky, when you think about it. I mean, no one enjoys the burden of propping up an emotional basket-case; but on the other hand, pushing them overboard generates a lot of guilt. I'd reframed the problem for him by appearing to have whipped myself into shape already. *Now*, if he threw me off the team, he wouldn't be jettisoning a neurotic wreck, he'd

---

[1] Hmmm. That makes me seem whiter than ever, doesn't it?

be creating one. In fact he'd be knocking someone down who was gamely trying to make a come-back. If he did that he'd be looking at a man-sized helping of guilt – so to seal the deal I offered to find my own replacement should he decide that I still wasn't up to scratch. I mean lightening his administrative burden on top of everything else, how could he refuse?

And refuse he didn't. But he didn't totally roll over either – though he seemed to be coming around. I guessed that his previous outburst had been a long time coming and that there'd been considerable momentum behind it. He wasn't about to rescind everything he'd said right away. That would be like admitting his big blow-up had been about nothing. On the other hand he was obviously looking for a reason to believe me. I couldn't tell yet which side of the fence he was going to come down on.

Worrying that I might be losing him, I mentioned the crates – hastily explaining that they were all taken care of and throwing myself on my sword a little more into the bargain. Then I told him what was in them.

I explained, "I knew they were coming, I just didn't know when they'd get here – or quite how much stuff there'd be." He was listening attentively so I went on, "But I suppose this has all been hanging over me ever since I called home. The PhD thing really knocked me back and then I found myself worrying about what was in the crates."

That all sounds very manipulative, but it was also true. I was levelling with him here.

"You were worried?" he asked, wanting to understand what I was telling him.

I explained, "Not worried exactly… but I knew I'd be finding out new things about Mom. I know that's what I've always wanted, but it's still a big deal. It's the unknown. I started thinking I might end up disappointed. Maybe she'd still be a mystery to me. Or worse still, I might find out something I didn't really want to know."

"I can see how you might find yourself thinking that way," he said guardedly.

Like I said, it was easy to say this stuff because it was pretty much true. But at the same time I didn't want it to edge over into some sort of charity appeal – you know, all 'pity me'; I knew what a turn-off that would be.

I said, "I know it's not an excuse. But I want you to believe I'm going to do all the things I've promised to do, and I figured if you knew what had been bothering me – and you knew that it was in the past now – you'd see that I meant it." This was scarily open and honest for me and I was glad I'd got it all out without becoming self-conscious.

He digested my words quietly and then asked, "When you say it's in the past… you've already made some headway looking through your mother's things, then?"

"Well, just the tip of the iceberg," I said, "but what I mean is, it was the *anticipation* that was stressing me out. Now that her things have arrived, you know… well, it's done; the die is cast, if you see what I mean. Whatever I find out, I find out. There's nothing I can do about it, so there's no point in freaking out."

I thought he might say something, show some sign of approval or agreement, but he was still looking thoughtful. Was he unconvinced? Or was he concerned about some other aspect of all this?

Delicately, as though wishing to inspect the contents of a can of worms without spilling any, he said, "This difficult business is still certain to upset you, I'm sure. Anything that brings you closer to your mother's memory is likely to rekindle your sense of loss, I would imagine. I would say to you, Jo, that there's no need to rush here. You can choose your own pace. This is not something that needs to be undertaken all at once."

When he said those words, he was obviously not thinking about my status on the project at the moment, he was thinking about *me*. I was relieved, both because it showed that he still cared about me and because it hinted that he was letting go of his previous anger. And yet he was obviously still hung up on something and I didn't quite see what it was.

I tried to sound self-assured and chock-full of resilience: "Right, but there's no sense in dragging things out. I can tackle this and then move on." I made a sound that was intended to be a brave little laugh, though it needed a bit more practice.

I continued, "Then I'll be able to focus properly on other things, like the project for instance." Was that too much? Too clumsy? It sounded a bit like toadying, but at the same time it was still mostly the truth.

Top of my wish list was still learning more about the PAC, but today's successes had also given me a tiny taste of how it might feel to be a good little chore-monkey, instead of a renegade – and it felt sort of… peaceful. I was wondering if it might *not* be the worst thing in the world to toil obediently in the salt mines for a while and to try a few tentative sips of that numbing brew known as (ugh) 'team spirit'. After all, I'd have my out-of-hours sleuthing to keep me from getting bored or feeling like a total sell-out.

The Professor, though, was still hinting at whatever it was he was hinting at. "Of course, of course. I'm just saying that you don't have to decide now. Keep on top of your work here and it's up to you how quickly you progress with your mother's… uh, with her things. If you find yourself a little overwhelmed, there's nothing to say you can't take a break for a while, now is there?"

Well, he certainly didn't seem to be angry with me any more. His tone was kind and full of concern. But I didn't quite see why he was labouring this particular point. I sort of wished he'd get past it and onto discussing my future. His words were a little confusing.

Then a possibility occurred to me. Perhaps he thought I'd discover something among my mother's things that would upset me. He was suggesting that I not jeopardise my attempt to get back on an even keel by rushing to learn more about her life. That suggested he knew something I didn't and he thought I wouldn't be able to handle whatever it was. That would fit with his words and his current demeanour.

I didn't quite know what to say... so I settled for blurting out the first thought that occurred to me: "Well, I know you and she went back a long way. Is there something I should know?"

He looked like he *really* didn't want to be asked that question. He prevaricated: "I'm just saying that you have been through a lot and you're obviously still coming to terms with..." He sort of trailed off, and made a gesture with his hands that I took to mean 'and so on'. Nice speech.

Suddenly we seemed to be past the part of the conversation where I pleaded for mercy and into some new phase where he hinted awkwardly and I became increasingly troubled.

"Professor," I said, "if there's something you want me to know, why don't you just tell me?"

He almost blushed – impossible though that sounds. What kind of secret could make him so awkward? In my experience there was a pretty short list of topics that could unsettle someone like that. He looked as ill at ease as if I'd asked him to explain to me where babies come from.

Of course that was a silly, stray thought but, just for a second, I wondered why it had popped into my head. He knew something about Mom; did it involve him too? And he was embarrassed about it. And now there was this thought in my head: sure I knew where *most* babies came from, but what about me? Did I know where I'd come from?

I'm not sure how old I'd been when I worked out that I was named after him. I've always been aware that 'Jo' is short for 'Josephine' and 'Professor' is short for 'Joseph', and I've sometimes wondered about it, in an absentminded sort of way. I figured that he'd been a really important person in Mom's life. But up until this instant I'd always assumed that his importance to her was entirely platonic. There was no way it could be anything else, was there? He must have been in his sixties when my mom was his grad student. At the very least he was in his late fifties and she'd only been twenty-something.

Though I knew they'd stayed in touch even after she met Dad and moved to the States.

"You're not telling me that…" I mumbled.

I knew Dad had been unfaithful, but it had never crossed my mind that Mom could have been. Plus, the Professor was a non-sexual being, surely everyone could see that – even my troubled and lonely mother.

Oh god, except that I'd always felt that she'd hooked up with Dad because he was strong and self-assured and someone she could respect. I figured she'd been looking for a little bit of a father figure and a little bit of a hero to worship. I'd felt that she didn't want someone to be close to, so much as someone impressive to look up to. And you couldn't deny that the Professor might fit that bill too.

I didn't know whether to be disgusted (which I definitely was anyway) or angry or upset or what. In fact I was sort of paralysed because in my mind I was conducting a high-speed review of the last twenty-six years, trying to examine every event I could recall, to see how it fit with this new possibility.

Everything was the same and yet I was seeing it all from a shocking new perspective. With each memory I could summon up, I asked the question 'how would this be different if Mom's old friend was really my father?' I mean, the more I thought about it, the more I realised that his presence in my life had always gone considerably beyond the call of duty if I was really just the daughter of a favourite student.

Without me thinking about it, my mouth sort of fired up of its own accord. "Are you trying to tell me that you and she were… that you were *involved*?"

He was a little taken aback. Maybe he was surprised that I'd figured it out without him having to say more. Unusually for him, he stumbled over his words as he said, "Not in the way… I mean to say, Helen and I had a bond, certainly, but if what I think you're saying or rather asking me…" He was really struggling with this now: "Your mother and I were, I suppose you could say thrown together by circumstances. I've never said anything to you because I really wasn't sure you were ready to hear…"

He had *that* right because I sure as hell wasn't ready to hear it *now*. His discomfort had obviously reached some sort of maximum. Short of outright fainting, there was no way he could look more awkward, seem more guilty. My mind was over-revving and I couldn't even tune in to what he was saying now, his attempts to back out of the situation he found himself in.

What was I going to find among my mother's things? Love letters from him? Did my dad realise he wasn't my dad? What had he thought when my mom wanted to name me 'Josephine'? Oh god, no wonder he always seemed to be competing for the title of World's Most Halfhearted Parent.

I cut the Professor off in his pained rambling and sniffed back the first unwanted but pathetically inevitable tear. "Listen Professor," oh god, I could hardly call him *that* any more, "I can't handle a long explanation right now."

I wanted to get out of there immediately because I could feel more tears on their way and I'd had enough of weeping in front of an audience for the time being.

"Maybe we can talk about this later," I said, hurriedly. My

voice was a starting to tremble as I spoke, but I kept going because I didn't want to give him a chance to start talking again. I didn't want him to start offering me details or telling me how he felt. I had plenty to consider before we got into any of the unbearable specifics.

"I appreciate…" I tried to keep my voice level as I sniffed back tears, "you keeping me on the project and I'll certainly bear in mind what you said about me staying on top of things, but if you don't mind, right now, I'm going back to my room."

I more or less ran out of the Professor's office and back to the dormitory block. And once I was in my room, I realised it wasn't far enough. I needed to get much further away from the Professor and this project.

So I called a taxi to meet me at The Retard, threw a bunch of my things into a big bag, and left the dorm building. The haste and busy-ness of my departure kept me from thinking. I made it onto the lane that headed up the hill without anyone spotting me or seeing where I was going, and frankly, that suited me fine.

Chapter 7

I know what you're thinking…

Well OK, I know what *I'm* thinking: I freaked out… again. And I didn't give the Professor any sort of chance to explain or clarify. But this wasn't about being fair to him or not; it was about not wanting to blow any more of my emotional fuses this week. He'd just finished advising me that I should take my nervous breakdowns slowly and in bite-sized chunks (always remembering to chew). And just because they're *my* breakdowns, that doesn't make them any more pleasant to be around, with all that wailing and distress. So I headed for the hills as soon as I realised that my emotional rollercoaster ride was picking up speed again. If it turned out I was going to make a scene, then I was going to do it in private like a grown-up for once.

In fact recent introspection had helped me come up with a theory. I was starting to think that emotions were like drugs – and not the good kind. If you can't 'just say no', then at least you should know when you've had enough.

I decided to handle this situation a little better than the last one – and to try to get myself back under control. And for that, I would need some privacy.

So I bailed, figuring that we could have our heart to heart and get into the sordid what-have-yous some other time. I'd take this crisis on the instalment plan, just like the-academic-formally-known-as-the-Professor had suggested.

Which reminded me of how, earlier in the week, I'd thought about going to London – and I'd decided against it. Well, I still thought London was the wrong destination, but I really wanted to go *somewhere* – somewhere away from it all.

Fortunately, all the isolation I could ever need was available, free for the asking, right on my doorstep. It was the very isolation I was always complaining about and it offered solitude in abundance. I decided to head to a place called Dartmoor, not far from the field-station.

Dartmoor is where the British armed forces practice surviving the elements. They dump their trainees into its expansive wilderness without proper equipment in order to teach them the value of… erm, paying attention in school so you can get a cushy desk job when you graduate – or something like that.

Anyway, I figured they prolly wouldn't choose that location to practice their survival skills if it was too full of picnic spots and friendly hikers. Comfiness is a hated enemy when you're trying to instil military-grade gumption. Yes indeed. Which made it the perfect place for me right now.

The idea of Dartmoor had popped into my head just as I got back to my room, so I'd dragged my giant holdall out from under the bed and started throwing anything that looked warm and/or waterproof into its dust-lined interior. Then I carefully added my laptop and a handheld GPS unit. Mind you, I had a GPS card for my PDA so I debated taking that for a minute. Oh and I'd need some books to read.

Then, remembering that a good storm-out required both spontaneity *and* speed of execution, I settled for grabbing whatever came to hand. And I only came back and unlocked the door once to snag a mini printer for the laptop. I reckoned that the best way to have an emotion-free weekend would be to concentrate exclusively on the Secrets of the PAC, and to put everything else out of my mind until further notice. To that end, I might want hardcopies of some of those secret documents so I'd have something to ponder as I prepared myself for the melancholy loneliness of the bleak, wind-scoured moors[1].

I'm probably making all this sound kind of flippant, but it wasn't at the time. I was feeling sort of jumbled up inside – not sure if I was really hurt or not, but not willing to think about it either.

As I shoved the printer into the giant holdall, some impulse made me pause a moment before zipping it up. A crazy idea had occurred to me. Quickly I fished out the key for the padlock that held closed the cupboard doors above my bed. In there was where I kept my jewellery box – mainly things of my mother's that I'd inherited. I didn't wear them very often, but I kept them with me.

Anyway, I fetched the box down and laid it in the bag, pushing it into the folds of a sweater. Then I resealed the bag. It was almost too heavy to carry now. Fortunately, I only had to lift it while I was getting it down the stairs; after that, the road up to the pub was just about level enough to let me drag it along on its diminutive little wheels.

Out on the lane, the din the bag made as it clattered over the bumps in the road, its tiny nylon casters whirring like turbines, sounded like someone feeding gravel into a hairdryer and I almost expected a crowd to congregate and follow me up the hill, curious to see what all the noise was about. But the lane was

---

[1] Such preparation quite possibly involving loitering in the nearest town, eating scones in warm tea-rooms.

deserted and I reached the pub without seeing another soul. Two minutes later the taxi arrived and I was off.

My first thought was to have the taxi take me to the nearest railway station. From there I'd get a train to one of the corners of Dartmoor. But once I was snug on the doughy back seat of the old Toyota, the tropical-pine smell of warm car-freshener in my nostrils, I wondered how much of a slog that trip would be. The driver confirmed that I'd need to change trains in Exeter. I could see a forty-mile rail trip turning into a whole evening of slow trains and waiting on damp platforms. Of course when I learned that the taxi driver could take a credit card payment for his fare, the problem melted away: it was going to be taxi all the way for me. It would bring the horrible day of reckoning with my bank a little closer, but at least this trip would be painless. And wasn't the point of this getaway to indulge in a little painlessness?

Once the driver had lobbed his entire stock of conversational-openers – and I'd listlessly batted them away – he turned his attention to the car stereo. He nudged up the volume to the point where it was just about audible in the back and nodded along to a selection of what the tranquilised-sounding announcer called 'classical mellow classics'.

I let the early evening hedge-rows and saturated meadows slip past the window and attempted to put questions of paternity far from my thoughts. Fortunately I had a once-in-a-lifetime distraction to occupy me. I'd reached the point in my reading of the PAC's secret files where things were starting to get not just interesting (I mean it was *all* interesting) but also revealing.

Susan Milton had concocted a sort of 'how to' manual on the special powers of the bad guys. I'd tried to read a little of it when I got back from the pub the previous night but for some reason the blurry words wouldn't stay in their proper order. Digging out my laptop now, I picked up where I'd left off and was pleased to find that focussing on the text was no longer a struggle.

One thing that struck me straight away was the implication that Susan was writing from personal experience. The bizarre abilities she was talking about were being described first hand. She'd even begun the colonisation of this new field of knowledge in time-honoured style: by coining some jargon.

A footnote suggested that 'magic', despite being the obvious description for the activity in question, wasn't really 'a helpful or appropriate term'. I'm not sure I agreed with that statement – I thought it summarised things very succinctly – but I could totally see why she'd shy away from that particular word. It was much like the way I'd prefer to be called a 'recovering survivor of emotional trauma' instead of a more conventional term like 'crazy person'.

Isn't it funny how much the words matter? I remember watching some old low-budget docutainment on TV, where a scientist was explaining that what primitive people thought of as witches might simply be young women with psychic powers. I mean, like calling it 'psychic' instead of magical counted as an explanation. No suggestion was offered for how psychic powers might work, but everyone seemed to feel better now that they'd switched to a modern, sciencey-sounding word.

The TV-show people obviously felt that the Powers of the Brain were somehow allowed to be mystical and unknowable, because of all the alpha waves and complicated structures and unwieldy Greek names, whereas magic had only nature to draw upon for its power – and nature was just a bunch of plants and rocks, right? A cool word like 'neuron' could make you think of all sorts of potent possibilities, whereas the word 'stick' probably wouldn't.

No doubt Susan Milton had covered this all in one of her arid academic-style papers: speculating about why brains are more appealing these days as sources of mystery than nature.

Oh and here's a thought: maybe the answer was that – as

people have been telling each other for decades – we only use 10% of our brains and who knows what we could achieve if we learned to tap into the rest? That's sarcasm, by the way. That 'statistic' makes me want to grind my teeth. I mean if I didn't know what 90% of something was for, I wouldn't shout about it, or get all superstitiously ignorant and label it 'Source of Mysterious Powers'. It was no better than writing Here Be Dragons on the bits of the map you hadn't visited yet.

Anyway, Susan's notes seemed to be turning the clock back on that neurons-versus-sticks question. Given a choice between explaining superpowers in terms of the outer world of nature or the inner world of neural physiology, she favoured nature. And I had to agree that it was a lot easier to hide an explanation of mystical abilities out there in the roomy expanse of the universe than it was to conceal it inside our rather cramped skulls.

In one passage, Susan had attempted to describe the knot you had to tie your mind in before you could command any of these powers; she had called that mental exercise 'Connecting' (with a capital 'C') – like there was a gap that had to be bridged before you could tap into some reservoir of magical power.

Just like with the Marker, expensive jewellery seemed to play a role. A gold band encircling each wrist and another around the forehead was apparently a pre-requisite for Connecting. Old hands at this sort of thing – those the PAC called 'adepts' – referred to it as 'tribute'.

I'd have been tempted to dismiss gold accessories as simply good showmanship, like an old-timey stage magician's silk top hat, but the PAC claimed that nothing would work without it.

I'd sat in on enough physics lectures to be totally intrigued at the role precious metals played in the PAC's weird world. The ability to work with purified metals underpinned the Industrial Revolution, and it seemed a strange coincidence that it should play such a big part in this occult branch of technology too.

The final piece of jargon Susan suggested was also intriguing. The list of magical powers was extensive but simple enough: Heat, Freeze, Shatter, Shield, Push, Presence and Heal (again, all with capitals). She called each of them 'Surfaces'. It was like each power had its own invisible membrane through which you could interact with the world. Reach out with your mind through, say, the Freezing Surface and you could lower the temperature of an object. Project your concentration through the Shatter Surface and an impact like a hammer blow would strike the point you were focussing on.

It seemed that Heal would work whether you concentrated on it or not, but it was most powerful if you focussed it. And Presence somehow warned you of the approach of other Connected adepts.

I just had to stop and wonder at this point: were they serious?

Even if they were, their words reminded me of the instructions that came with a blues harmonica I once owned. To bend a note, you simply had to "change the angle of airflow to put more pressure on the top of the reed" as you blew. Right. We were in explaining-colours-to-sightless-people territory here. This terminology might make sense to those who already had (or believed they had) experienced Connecting, but it left me confused.

Finally was something called Quell. It seemed that Connecting for the first time was hellish difficult, but the mind quickly adapted[1] and soon it took a conscious effort *not* to Connect if you had your 'tribute' in place. A mental exercise called the Quell state was how you held off Connecting.

Hmmm. The phrase 'intricate delusional structure' flitted

---

[1] Even then I wondered whether 'the mind adapted' really meant 'the mind was altered'.

through my mind. But it sure was interesting stuff.

So, what else did the documents say? One of the e-mails I'd read made it clear that the PAC still retained a secret electronic copy of the document cache that Army bad-ass Karst had confiscated. The PAC were still mining that cache for information – but keeping very quiet about it. And they'd found other occult documents to add to it since.

I wondered briefly how much research into magic was being concealed inside the legitimate work of the project. From what I could gather, stories of magic had been at the centre of Susan's previous work. But that was before she began to *believe* in any of it. Her run-in with various members of the Army coven – both current and renegade – had changed her outlook.

And with the Army Who still out there – and possibly looking to tie up any loose ends as they searched for the Marker – Susan had good reason to leave myths, legends and tales of the occult well alone. The documents that members of the project claimed to be working on now were all mundane histories of early Britain, and its neighbours, written after the withdrawal of the Roman legions. No magic here. No sir. Perish the thought.

The tricky thing for them was that once you start to look for it *all* old documents talk about magic. Every one of them. You read Homer and Virgil and there, in amongst the deeds of warriors and kings, are superhuman deities performing impossible feats. To pick another random example, the otherwise reliable Roman history of the conquest of Britain talks about Druids using magic to frighten the legionaries. It's the same for all ancient histories – especially the religious ones. The church may frown on any talk of magic today, but in the old days they made it their mission to *fight* magic, not to disprove its existence.

Susan and the gang had obviously worked out that some of the old documents floating around weren't superstitious bunk; they were the real deal. How they separated the bona fide stuff from the crackpot ramblings, I had no idea, but suddenly the way the PAC was wrapped inside our project made a lot more sense. If a document was reasonably magic-free they studied in their day jobs and talked about it at seminars. But if it seemed like it might contain nuggets of occult gold they sneaked it back to the bat cave and worked on it in secret.

That way they could analyse old documents and make use of every scrap. If an insight was practical, it went into the secret PAC files; if it was historical, it went into the public record for the project and helped to keep Susan and the rest of them off the Army's radar. It was all very clever.

That and the drabbing made me think that someone in the PAC knew a lot about operational security. That person was either ex-intelligence or they read a lot of spy novels. Knowing who attended the meetings, I was guessing the latter. A good geek can probably match the NSA[1] for ingenuity, and instead of costing billions of dollars, your only outlay in hiring a geek is a few buck's worth of ramen[2] and a handful of Amazon book tokens.

I found I was utterly absorbed as my mind romped through the details of the PAC's secret activities. When I next looked up from my reading, and occasional head-scratching, we were driving up the little high street of Meaves Edge on the borders of Dartmoor. This was where I planned to spend the weekend.

I had the driver drop me at the County Arms Hotel, the most impressive building in the town square, and twenty minutes later I was in a warm room, sprawled on an over-soft bed watching an undersized TV and thinking about dinner.

In spite of my hunger, I was suddenly tired and everything

---

[1]   The vast and secretive US National Security Agency, whose acronym is sometimes translated as No Such Agency.

[2]   The Brit translation would be 'Pot Noodles'.

– evil, the PAC, and certain personal questions of which we will not speak – all seemed better left for the morning.

I made a quick trip downstairs, where the hotel's bar brought me scampi and chips before I could doze off into my sauvignon. And it was well before ten o'clock when I tumbled into bed and gave myself up to the sucking quicksand of fatigue. And, while the fifteen or twenty times that doors slammed or that drunks yelled in the night might have pulled me close to consciousness, none of them could keep me from sleep. The next thing I was truly aware of was the morning light perforating the badly drawn curtains. My first thought was of today's big experiment[1] – the experiment for which I had brought along my jewellery box.

At ten o'clock I was in the hotel lobby waiting for a minicab to arrive. It would take me to one of the quieter roads on the edge of the moors and leave me there. By five minutes after ten, I was settled in the back seat watching the hotel disappear behind me.

As we left Meaves Edge, the Welsh-sounding driver was assuring me that once I was done with my hike, returning to civilisation would be 'a doddle'. He explained, "See, I'll tell Kenny, the gaffer like, where I dropped you. And when you call in, just say it was Davey dropped you off and he'll know what's what. Any of the drivers'll know this spot. And if Kenny's not on, which he won't be at that time, just tell the new guy, whatsisname. Remember to tell him Davey G. 'cos there's a Dave Williams on afternoons. Not that I've met the new gaffer yet, but I've heard he's alright and any of the lads will tell him who I am, they all know me. Not so much on the afternoons of course, because I don't work then, but there's bound to be someone around unless there's a match on, like today. Actually, come to think of it, Saturday isn't really your best bet. You wouldn't rather come out

---

[1] That is to say, *breakfast* and today's big experiment: they were my first thoughts.

here tomorrow, would you? Or Thursday?"

Annoying as it was to listen to someone who thought that reassuring me was somehow more important than actually being of assistance, I had a little bit of sympathy for him. Surprised? Well, it's not always about me, you know? Plus, he was doing something I do the whole time: telling people what they want to hear, filling the gaps in people's expectations with white lies and nonsense. It was like listening to myself as played by a confused Swansea-born cab driver. So in that sense, I suppose it *was* all about me. But as for what he was saying, I reckoned I'd take my chances: today I was feeling adventurous.

"How about this?" I suggested, "Drop me at a payphone and then when I call in, I'll give the address they print above the phone."

"Not too many phone boxes along this stretch, Miss," he warned, drawing in his breath. "One up at the point and the only other is outside the Wanderer's Ease and that's your lot."

Mustering some patience, I enquired, "Well, how about one of those two then?"

He considered it, and was prepared to concede: "I could drop you at the Wanderer's Ease, that way if the outside phone's not working you can go in the pub. Can't guarantee they'll be doing any food today, though. It's not really the season. Round here's deserted this time of year."

I didn't remind him that 'deserted' was what I'd asked for. I just told him I'd risk it.

He brightened: "Barry'll do you a toasty though, no problems. Just tell him Davey G. sent you. You might have to describe me, as Barry's a bit of dope with names and faces. Loves his football though so I don't suppose he'll be around today. Anyway, there's a path from the back of the pub leads up onto the moors. Council put in plenty of signs around there for walkers and so on, so you should be alright. Just don't let the beast get you."

He pivoted around for a moment to grin at me. "No, I'm only joking. There isn't any beast," he explained, very pleased with himself. Perhaps I was witnessing his first ever attempt at humour. What an honour.

When he let me out of the overheated taxi I stood for a moment in the cold October air, savouring the drop in temperature. I was bundled up like Bibendum[1] and that cab had been stifling. Now the snapping breeze snatched away all that excess heat, leaving a delicious, refreshing chill.

The sharp wind was delightful for all of twenty seconds… then I felt the first shiver start as a droplet of rain on a horizontal trajectory caught me in the eye. But pluck and gumption were in good supply today and I strode towards the hills before hypothermia could get so much as a toehold. It so happened that I had the, ahem, robust physique of a walker; it was time to find out if I had the constitution to go with it.

* * *

Tired, bedraggled and frozen solid to the touch in a few places, I sat in the Wanderer's Ease an impressive four hours later. Impressive because I wasn't dead – although the moment didn't seem far off. In the meantime, blessed Jameson's Whisky was melting the ice crystals in my bloodstream and stuffing my pounding head with soothing cotton-wool.

I'd trudged for half an hour, trying to keep my bearings and looking for a sheltered spot where I could see but not be seen. Probably I needn't have bothered. I saw no living creature, except a crow, while I was out there. I began to imagine that the crow was circling after a while, maybe waiting for me to collapse, before he feasted on my carcass. But perhaps he was

---

[1]   The Michelin Man. Jeez, get an education.

just curious to see what I was up to. I was after all, attempting to perform magic.

I'd sat and stood, paced and pondered, chanted and concentrated for two hours until I began to worry that my body temperature had dropped into single figures. A print-out of instructions from the PAC's secret library was in one numb hand, a pattern for me to concentrate on was gripped in the other. A doubled-over gold chain was doing a fine job of drawing the remaining heat out of my brain and dissipating it on the bitter wind. Likewise, an unfamiliar weight of gold chain dragged at each wrist. All very bling I'm sure, but it made me feel like an idiot. No, better yet, it made me feel like Mister T's dumpy white niece, and as the great man might have said himself, I was a 'fool'… and maybe an 'ugly mudsucker' too.

I'd got nowhere; nothing had happened. Not a tingle, not a twinge, not (as they say in these parts) a sausage.

The fact that there'd been no audience watching me didn't help much. I felt as foolish as if a crowd had gathered and tickets had been sold. Magic? Me, who had sat in more science classes than Albert Einstein had had hot dinners. Me, who could (after half a dozen vodka and Red Bulls) tell you the technical flaws in virtually every episode of The Next Generation, DS9 and Enterprise – and even come up with a few suggestions about how each one could have been corrected. Me, who knew more physics than any biologist, more biology than any computer scientist and more computer science than anyone who didn't have a y-chromosome and a listing on the Nasdaq. I'd somehow talked myself into believing that magic was worth an afternoon of frostbite and peri-terminal exposure tying my head in knots. What was next? Pyramid worship? Crystals? (shudder) *Astrology*?

Well, I'd learned my lesson. First, I was going to dose up on excellent, restorative Gaelic spirits. Then I was going to get a taxi back to the County Arms Hotel and soak in very hot water up to my nostrils until coldness was but a fading dream and damp clothing a distant memory. Then, tomorrow, I was going to read through every document I'd brought with me and figure out what was *really* going on with the PAC.

Chapter 8

By three in the afternoon on Sunday, the day after my unsuccessful hike'n'hex, I was starting to feel human again. I'd like to claim that when I woke up that morning, all my physical woes could be traced to the psychic after-effects of a near miss with the supernatural. Or just to an afternoon spent in the ice box of moorland a few miles from my hotel room. But in the interests of total accuracy I have to admit that the bar immediately *beneath* my hotel room was at least as much to blame.

I'd been feeling pleasantly fuddled and moderately thawed by the time the taxi took me away from the Wanderer's Ease. Back at the hotel, I found that the whisky had parched my throat and after a long soak in the tub I was getting a dehydration headache – and I was ravenous. Fortunately, downstairs, the hotel bar was once more ready to meet the challenge. A damn fine roast beef sandwich, a basket of chips and a family-sized helping of mulled wine served in something that looked a little like a beaker arrived in minutes. I settled in to munch and slurp and apply juice to as much of my face as possible. And when I was done, a minion emerged from behind the bar and, through the wonder of modern ingenuity, lit an instant fire in the grate. It was gas-powered, fake-logged bliss.

I had them refill my beaker on several occasions (although my recollection is not entirely clear regarding the exact number). And I vaguely recall trying out a toddy the barman recommended from his time in the navy[1]. Beyond that point, I have one or two snapshot memories of talking to (or at) strangers in the bar, a single impression of pressing my overheated forehead to the cool window back in my room and a final vague sense of searching for the bathroom at around 3 a.m. As usual, no dreams came. And so endethed that particular day.

Someone hammered on my door at about ten the next morning, calling out something unintelligible in the baffling glossolalia favoured by maids the world over. I managed to send them away and went to stand under the shower for a while, waiting for order to return to my magimixed wits.

I felt a lot better once I'd had some breakfast… and it had stayed down. I wasn't yet up to the challenge of reading or even thinking, but I could look at the people walking past the hotel's front window without feeling sea-sick.

After breakfast, I went for a slow totter around the village, bought a bulky Sunday newspaper (which later went into the bin still sealed in its taut polythene), and contemplated the merits of smoking a cigarette… but abandoned the idea as I usually do. Ibuprofen, vitamin C tablets and a cold yoghurt drink seemed like a better idea.

The middle of the day passed in slow motion, including the taxi ride home. I was back in my dorm room at the project field station by two o'clock.

I'd had the cab drop me off a little way from the buildings and I'd managed to make my way inside without encountering

---

[1] I think that should have been a warning, right there.

anyone. I wasn't tired enough to sleep, but I wasn't alert enough to do much except brood a little. I laid on my bed, a soft pillow under my head, and let my mind wander.

I tried not to think about my last talk with the Professor, but that was one of those don't-think-about-pink-elephants deals where the harder you try the less you succeed. Our last disastrous encounter action-replayed in my head a couple of times and I discovered that somehow my feelings had shifted. Right after it happened I was full of emotion, feeling like I might burst with it. The Professor's words had seemed laden with significance and hidden meaning. But now that impression had evaporated and I couldn't muster a sense of panic as I recalled his awkward protestations and oblique hints.

In theory, he could be my (gulp) father – nothing impossible about that – but I found I didn't believe it. Shocking and uncomfortable as the thought had initially been, the truth was that it would be too *convenient*. A wrenching revelation like that would be a great excuse for me to obsess, act out and generally behave badly.

If my suspicions had turned out to be true, it would simply be the latest and largest in a line of crisis-of-the-week bombshells that I continually manufactured as a way to keep me firmly at the centre of my own little melodrama.

The tired reality was that I had a listless father who had been drawing away since before I was born. And that offered no fuel for my emotional burn-outs, no ongoing justifications for my graceless behaviour. A tectonic upheaval in the structure of my family, my background, would be just what my inner drama queen needed to keep the turmoil rolling, but it didn't have the weary weight of truth.

And I knew that once I overcame my horror, the Professor would have made a much better father than the one I'd been assigned at birth. Deep down this was more of a wish than a fear.

Nevertheless, the Professor had been trying to keep *something* from me with his butter-fingered dissimulating, something he was horribly ill at ease over – and I'd pretty much convinced myself that what he was hiding wasn't a shiny new parent for me.

When the conversation had got uncomfortable for him, his nervousness seemed to take precedence over his not-inconsiderable need to scold me. It seemed like he'd rather turn a deaf ear to my failings than risk revealing some agonising truth in my presence, so I was pretty sure I wasn't going to like it, whatever it was. 'What could be so bad?' I thought, unpleasantly aware that it was a phrase that would work well as famous last words.

* * *

Round about six-thirty the ebb and flow of queasiness seemed to recede for good and I was left washed-up on the far shore of Hangover Straits feeling weak but alive. Now that I was out from under the weight of all that alcohol, my curiosity was coming back to life. And it was beginning to pluck metaphorically at my sleeve.

The first time I'd pried into the PAC's secrets, my picture of the world had cracked right down the middle; either magic was real and everything else I've thought in the last twenty-six years needed reassessing, or it wasn't and the riddle of the PAC was an unexplained hole in the otherwise tidy fabric of the world. I was still in need of some answers.

I pulled on my boots with the sudden idea of taking a stroll down to the barn where my mother's things were now stored. But I wasn't after clues about my mother. Rather, I'd realised something about Susan Milton. She had an office in the project building and a 'set' (which was college-speak for a small suite) in the dorm building and yet she chose to keep some of her things in the barn. Intriguing, no? I was a good way through my reading of the PAC's electronic documents and I was as confused as ever; I wondered if it was time to have a glance at the *non*-electronic goodies they kept squirreled away at the bottom of the lane.

I stepped out through the front door of the dorm block. Somewhere, behind the smoky looking clouds, the sun was touching the horizon. The damp air nuzzled unpleasantly at my exposed neck and tickled my nostrils as I slipped and tripped my way along the mist-sheened cobbles of the lower lane.

Reaching the gate I glanced up at the barn's top windows: they were dark, which was good. In the most ungainly way imaginable, I hauled myself over the top bar of the gate and crunched – as quietly as I could – across the gravel drive towards the barn's side door. The main doors were wide enough to admit a tractor – or for that matter a brass band riding on llamas – but they were shackled closed. The side entrance was secured by an ancient mortice lock, to which I'd been given a long, iron-black key.

I undid the lock and paused, thinking I'd heard something – a gasp, perhaps. I held still, waiting for it to repeat itself, and wondered if it was some common rustic occurrence – anxious badgers perhaps – or something man-made from inside the barn.

A sharp sound, like a slap, came from the interior of the barn. Opening the door a fraction of an inch, I could see that a dim light glowed from the far side of the dark space, but my view was blocked by all the junk stacked near the entrance. Clearly there was someone in there.

I considered my position for a moment. I had a reason to be here: my mother's things. So if I encountered anyone, I was in the clear – providing they didn't catch me doing any pantomime-style skulking. So if anyone approached, I'd just clump about to make it clear I was here for entirely-non-clandestine above-board-style activities. But until I was discovered, I'd do my best to imitate a tiny church mouse.

Carefully, I pulled the door wider until I could fit my head through the gap, and took a proper look around. The sky behind me was fading into murky twilight and it was nearly as gloomy outside the barn as in, so there'd be no sudden burst of sunlight to announce my arrival.

There seemed to be no one at my end of the barn. But from behind the dark shapes of cupboards and racking I could see a faint, flickering light emanating from the far corner and hear indistinct sounds as if a struggle were taking place.

Seeing no one near me, I slipped in through the gap and allowed the door to swing softly shut behind me. Under its own weight, it would stay closed but wouldn't latch – which suited me fine.

I took several silent steps into the shadows and towards the light. And I heard what sounded like a man's voice say something I couldn't catch and then a woman laughed – almost a giggle. It began to dawn on me what I was sneaking up on. Ahead, some unidentified couple were enjoying a little private snuggle-time.

Which should have seemed like none of my business, but I found I was just as curious as if I'd walked in on a secret meeting of the PAC. Assuming one or both of them were on the project team, who were they? We each had our own rooms, and there were no anti-fraternising rules that I was aware of, so why would anyone sneak out here? I couldn't resist a puzzle.

I glanced up at the top window and noticed that it was covered, though I couldn't see with what. No lights would show to anyone outside; someone wanted to visit this place without broadcasting their presence.

I edged forwards, careful not to step on a rake or snap a twig – the two main hazards in any stealthy endeavour. With careful positioning, I found I could peer through the tangle of junk hanging from the beams and on into the open area beyond – and I could do so with very little chance of being seen.

Thirty feet away, a single bulb illuminated a tangle of sweaty limbs and shining steel.

David Braun and Susan Milton were in some sort of intimate clinch – albeit a fully clothed and heavily armed one. With a gasp they separated and I could see a little more of what they were up to. Both of them were smiling as they circled one another, and both of them were carrying swords. Clearly they were duelling, though their expressions suggested that they had no intention of actually hurting each other.

David was exploring Susan's defences. Watching the easy discipline with which she blocked his probing attacks and the unhurried precision of her ripostes caused a memory to surface. I remembered someone telling me that Susan was a fencer – and it looked like she was extremely skilful – not that David was exactly clumsy. He was fast, powerful and accurate, but his expression showed concentration, whereas Susan's was simply playful. She was the master here.

Suddenly Susan put up her sword with a move so quick that I could hear the whip of steel scoring the air that accompanied it.

"Let's use the blunts," she said, "I want to show you something." Bending to one side, she slid her sword into its vinyl case and picked up two others, which appeared to be made of wood. One of them she flipped towards David.

For a moment, I couldn't believe what happened next. The wooden sword snagged in mid-air, just outside David's reach. He set aside his rapier and a moment later the wooden sword was released from its frozen trajectory to drop into his empty hand.

"You're getting pretty nimble with those Shields," Susan said, appreciatively. "You don't have to stick your tongue out anymore."

"You're not too old to put across my knee, you know," David said, rotating his shoulder and settling the wooden sword in his hand.

A moment later, Susan attacked.

Impressive though their earlier engagement had been, I realised now that they had been holding back. Now I could hardly see tips of their practice swords, they moved so swiftly. Susan's smile had given way to a blank look of intensity while David was concentrating so hard his face was like a machine.

This time Susan was on the offensive and she hardly waited for David to parry each cut before switching to a new angle and driving in again.

"See," she said, through tight lips, "how I'm coming in high and to your right over and over. Gradually your elbow is coming out and you're opening up your left side."

As she said it, she struck low to David's right. Instinctively he dropped his arm to counter and she rotated her blade through a full three-hundred degrees, rolling her wrist, to bring the sword crashing in towards the left of David's head. Letting the power dissipate at the last minute, she angled down to tap him firmly on the shoulder.

"Nice," he said. "But I could Shield that side pretty easily, couldn't I?"

"Try it," she suggested.

David hesitated for a moment, like he was doing mental arithmetic, and then raised his blade. Once again, Susan began a rapid metronome beat of attacks, the majority of which were high and to David's right. Now that she'd pointed it out, I was fascinated to see his elbow moving away from his side as he struggled to block the onslaught.

And, just as before, once David was open enough on his left, she struck low and to the right. Just as before he dropped to block it and with ferocious speed Susan rolled her wrist to bring her weapon around and down again on David's exposed left side, aiming for his head.

With a woody thump, the weapon impacted – but instead of striking David's face, it slammed to a halt eighteen inches from his cheekbone, stopped short by the suddenly solid air. I was almost too stunned to follow when Susan reacted. The moment her blade struck the non-existent barrier, she recovered and lunged, cutting down towards David's feet.

Taken by surprise, he skipped to his right, anxious to get his shins out of the path of her sword even as Susan completed the move, slicing only emptiness. Then, as though she'd done it a hundred times before, Susan pushed her blade straight out ahead of her and into David's side.

"Ow," he yelped, though it didn't look as though she'd done him any real harm.

"The way you want to think of it," she explained, "is that as soon as I hit your Shield, I'm going to alter my attack so that the Shield is in your way and not mine. With your Shield covering that side, you can't parry on your left, which is fine. But for mobility you keep your Shield well clear of the floor, so I attacked under it. You had to jump back. You still didn't have room to parry on your left, but now you're not protected by your Shield either. And voila."

David patted his side thoughtfully and shifted the preposterous terry-cloth headband he was wearing (I noticed Susan had one as well) so as to mop the sweat from his forehead. "You make it sound like Shielding your vulnerable bits could be a bad idea."

Susan nodded. "I reckon it's smarter to place Shields a little to one side of the vulnerable spots. You can duck behind them quickly enough, but they don't limit you. And of course, if they stop an attack, you should move them immediately, because now your opponent knows where they are. It's probably best to have at least three different ways of arranging your Shields and to secretly switch between them to keep your opponent guessing."

"Sneaky," David said. "But let me have one more go at that attack. I want to try something else."

Susan gave David a moment to prepare himself and then began her attack again, just as he'd asked her to. Again, she pressured him so that his parries left him increasingly exposed on his left. Again, when he was suitably open, she cut low and then rotated to attack his left at head height. And again her weapon slammed into an invisible barrier, prompting her to lunge and cut towards his ankles. This time, however David hopped with his back foot, allowing the blade to whip beneath him, and then came down on his front foot… and kept dropping.

Susan had withdrawn and was beginning her strike along the centre-line, even as David allowed the leg supporting his weight to collapse. It looked like he was about to fall on his butt in order to get under her attack. But then, as Susan's blade came forwards, it became clear that David's little hop had allowed him to twist his body. It was like he was performing the world's lowest roundhouse kick: step, hop, kick – but performed while dropping into a crouch. It was how a Cossack might kick, one leg folded under him, the other arcing out to the side. At full stretch, his head was too low and too far back to be in range of her thrust, while his sweeping, outstretched leg was still able to snare her feet and whip them out from under her.

She tumbled lightly onto the crash mats behind her. Before she could get her feet under her, David was on top of her, pinning her hands to the mat. He lowered himself so that she could hardly move at all.

I wasn't sure if this was still part of the fight.

"Yes?" she said, enquiringly, looking up at him.

"This is as far as I'd thought it through," he said, letting go of her wrists and bending his head down towards hers.

"I warn you, I smell bad," she muttered as he bent to kiss her.

A moment later, he broke the kiss, saying, "No you don't. You smell pretty." For the first time, I felt a flush of embarrassment about spying on them.

Plus I'd probably seen enough. I took a couple of silent steps backwards towards the door. If they'd finished with the swordplay they might be leaving soon – or they might decide to move on to the, ahem, close-quarters stuff. Either way, I reckoned it was time to retreat.

But this was obviously just a quick snog-break, because Susan laughed, saying, "Get off me, you big animal," and gave David a playful thump on the arm. He collapsed, as though she'd wounded him, allowing her to roll to her feet. A moment later he was standing too.

"Tired?" he asked.

She glanced at her watch – an incongruously dressy-looking thing – and said, "Ten more minutes?"

"Sure," he said. "What do you want to do? Tank training?"

Susan curled a lip in disgust but said, "Probly better. I'll be 'it' first, shall I?"

David nodded and retrieved his wooden sword. Susan went to stand at one edge of the open space. "I'll see if I can get to the towel over there," she said, indicating a splotch of white in the gloom, about thirty feet from where she stood. Her weapons lay abandoned on the crash mat.

"Ready?" David asked and when she nodded, he stepped forwards and began to swing his wooden sword quickly from side to side, striking alternately at Susan's unguarded sides. She, in turn, simply stood her ground, hands by her sides, with a look of deep concentration on her face, and let each hefty blow slam into the wall of air surrounding her.

Without letting up, David hammered away at her, striking high and low. And, while every blow landed hard, none of them came closer than a foot or so to Susan's body.

Stepping around Susan in order to attack from a fresh angle, David had to pause for a moment as he shifted his feet. In that second, Susan moved forwards, taking a step towards the towel.

In the next few minutes, Susan took advantage of four more hesitations, each time shuffling a step closer to her goal. When she finally said 'Stop' and checked her watch, she was still only halfway to the towel.

Now it was David's turn to be the piñata[1]. He managed perhaps three feet more than Susan before he raised his hand, but when Susan checked her watch it turned out he'd had a minute longer than she had.

While David caught his breath, Susan began zipping weapons into bags.

"Jog?" he asked.

"Went this morning," she said, sounding self-satisfied.

"I might skip for a bit then," he said, not sounding enthusiastic.

I was backing towards the door in earnest now, since they were obviously packing up.

"Sure," she said airily, gathering up her things. "It'll be nice to have the shower to myself for a change."

David looked up sharply. "Good point," he said. "Skipping can wait."

I was slipping out the door now and I could hear their voices getting closer. Trying not to make a sound, I latched the door and eased the giant key into the lock. I'd barely had a chance to re-lock the door and remove my key when I saw the doorknob twist.

A moment later, a muffled voice said, "Honey, have you got the key?"

I raced towards the back of the barn as silently as I could and ducked around the corner. Then I stopped, my heart thumping

---

[1] A sort of mexican cocktail made from papier mache coconuts.

from my five-second sprint.

I could hear the door open, then close, followed by gravel crunching away into the distance as the pair moved off up the hill.

I waited for several minutes before peeking around the corner. The sun was long gone and it was pretty much pitch-black now. From what I could tell I was alone.

I figured I'd stay put for a few minutes longer anyway, just to be on the safe side.

Lowering myself to the ground, I leant my back against the side of the barn and stared up at the sky. A single gap in the clouds revealed a handful of stars directly above me.

I thought about what I'd seen in the barn and once again I felt my sense of the world shifting.

Chapter 9

So now I knew.

It should have made things simpler, but the simplicity didn't seem to have kicked in yet.

Was I sure of what I'd seen? Yes. Could it have been anything other than magic? Well, yes, I suppose it could, but I couldn't imagine what. If it wasn't magic then it was some other thing that you might just as well call magic.

OK. But then why hadn't it worked when I'd tried it? And why hadn't Susan and David needed gold like the PAC documents said?

The answer to the first question could be simply that I'm a klutz and a raging incompetent. The answer to the second one didn't take much deduction: there was gold in the ridiculous his-and-hers terry sweatbands they'd both been wearing: one at the forehead, two on the wrists. (Well, to be accurate Susan was wearing a fancy gold watch on her left wrist instead of a sweatband, but same deal.) It was an easy way to keep the gold hidden and comfortably in place – I just hoped it was worth the risk if the fashion police found out about it.

So, what did this all mean? Was everything in the PAC documents gospel?

I thought I should probably reserve a little bit of judgement, just in case. But there was no getting away from the heart of it. Magic. It was real and I'd seen it. (Or I was in my huggy-jacket in a padded room somewhere, hallucinating all this through a haze of Thorazine.)

Long after David and Susan had left the barn, I was still sitting on the damp ground ordering my thoughts… and then doing it all over again. The clouds cleared for a while and I stared upwards, unseeing, at the gallery of stars. The sense of vertigo from watching the heavens wheel above me matched how I felt. Then the cover closed in and a mist of rain began to fall, pattering against the trees. It was time to move.

I stood up, aware that more than two hours had passed and now my legs were achingly stiff from the cold and my butt was numb from sitting. The banged-up cartilage of my right knee was throbbing too; it never missed an opportunity to remind me of a long-ago moment of stupidity. And my jeans were soaked through. But at least while I'd been out here I'd managed to make some sort of peace with the events I'd witnessed in the barn.

I sneezed explosively into the quiet darkness, which served to break whatever rapture had held me in place. Twice now in one weekend I'd found myself half-frozen. I clumped along on my cramping, tingling legs, eager to get inside and into the warm.

Back in my room I put the convection heater on and angled it towards the bed. I snapped on the reading light and then, slipping out of my grass-slicked boots and clammy jeans, I turned out the main light and wriggled under the covers still wearing my thick sweater. With outstretched fingers I was able to pull my laptop towards me without getting up again.

Shivering, I hunkered down, waiting for the room to warm and began once again to read the PAC's secrets.

It was after two in the morning when I found I was dozing more than I was reading. Mostly I was going over things I'd read before, but this time I was thinking about what they implied, instead of wasting time wondering whether they could be true. What I'd seen in the barn had left me with no other option: I now believed the PAC's enemies were real.

But imagining danger when you're swaddled in duvet and warm as a biscuit is tricky. Instead of fear, I felt excitement and anticipation. Where I should have seen a nightmare ready to come to life, I saw an adventure.

I turned off the heater, the laptop and the reading light and laid down to sleep. For a moment, dreams rose up and I felt a Christmas-morning sense of promise and wonder, as though I were entering a new and brilliant world. But then the promise fell away and I dropped into my usual dreamless slumber.

* * *

The tiny gods of Random Play that live inside my music player chose Volcano Girls, by Veruca Salt, as my wake-up tune. Listening to the irresistible first verse it was a struggle to stay lazy and immobile, but somehow I managed it. As a concession to getting with the program, though, I opened my eyes and saw that it was light in my room.

Better get moving, I thought and then a colossal sneeze rattled my skull. *Sick*, I thought. *I'm sick*. In the night, creeping particles of *blah* had colonised my sinuses, my joints and the lining of my throat. Crap.

I rolled unsteadily out of bed, thankful that my room was warm, and grabbed sweatpants and a hockey shirt out of the pile on the back of my chair. Today would have been an ideal day to declare a 'sickie', but illness would just have to wait. I had Things To Do. Maybe I could get whoever was going in to town today to bring me back some cold remedies to help me soldier on.

I got myself ready and made it down to the refectory before the cook finished serving. I was happy with cereal, toast and tea, so he left me to it, scowling his usual scowl in my direction.

Theresa was talking softly with Blondy on the other side of the room, both of them holding mugs of coffee. Of course Blondy wasn't really her name, but I could never remember what it really was. Vanessa? Stephanie? Felicity? Who knew? I never knew what to say to them so I endeavoured to ignore them, hoping they would reciprocate.

They were still there when I finished eating so I slipped out unnoticed… except I was stopped in my tracks when the cook yelled 'Oi' in my direction and pointed to my dishes.

I was sure that the girls were laughing at me as I carried my breakfast things over to the counter, my chin reflexively tucked into my chest doing the Tall Girl Slouch, and added my crockery to the pile. Then I escaped without making eye contact. Just another day in Loserville.

A fresh sneezing fit overcame me as I neared the server room and I was scrabbling desperately and unsuccessfully to remove a Kleenex from my pocket when Daniel found me.

"Unclean, unclean," he intoned, as I finally clawed a tissue free and dabbed at my dripping nose. "You under the weather, then?" he asked.

I shrugged and made a face. "I'm alright," I said, unconvincingly.

"I'll tell you what you need," he chirped, not waiting for a response. "To do me a favour."

"Really?" I said, sceptically.

"I want to convince the landlord of The Retard to let Wounded Panther play a gig there," he said. "I need moral support. I'm going up there this evening."

"I dunno," I said, wondering what excuse I could give. And then I added, "I thought you were called Hammerhead."

I was trying not to sound interested.

"People weren't getting the irony," he explained. "Anyway, you're up there most... um, you know, a lot of nights. So it's not out of your way." He wheedled, "Go *on*."

I felt another sneeze coming on. "I'll see how I feel," I said, which seemed to satisfy him.

"Cool. Gotta dash," he said and skipped away. I rooted the key to the server room out of my pocket, accidentally dropped my Kleenex and felt an unpleasant wave of headrush as I bent over to retrieve it. Germtastic.

First things first: machine check. Everything looked good. Then I fired up my e-mail reader and was pleased to see that all our subscriptions were now set-up. I sent a group message to the research team letting them know the happy news.

OK. What next? Mindful of the unhappy role handwritten notes had recently played in my life, I let myself out of the Fortress of Servitude and went to check my mail slot. Bingo. Though not the good kind where you won things. There was a note from the Professor which glossed rapidly over our last exchange – he acknowledged that it was a difficult time for me – and then detailed a passel of scutwork that needed the Jo touch.

Automatically, my frustration levels began to surge. But then a thought struck me. This could be a test, to see if I'd meant what I'd said. The Professor might be looking for proof that my line about turning over a new leaf had some substance behind it. If I knuckled down and got this done without any wailing and eye-rolling I could maybe earn some useful Brownie points. *After a difficult start, Jo has learned to apply herself. She would make an ideal addition to any occult-crime-fighting organisation.*

With a quick tug of the forelock I got down to it. Despite frequent trips to the bathroom to steal more tissues – which

I used to polish my nostrils a shiny red – I toiled away until lunchtime, at which point I quickly grabbed a sandwich and retreated once more to be with the machines. I even managed to avoid any human contact on my trip to the canteen.

After I'd eaten, I checked my e-mail again to find a note from Sebastian, Susan's doctoral student, asking for help with his laptop. I'd pretty much finished the Professor's trial-by-boredom assignment, so I headed upstairs to find Seb.

It turned out that everybody in the team had some techie problem or other that they needed help with. I felt a little put out to have this sprung on me, but the good news was that by the end of the afternoon I'd resolved every last niggle. In fact, if I hadn't drawn out the last couple of fixes I might have finished even sooner. But when we'd gone down for tea mid-afternoon, the Professor had come over and whispered discreetly that he'd like to see me in his office once I was done for the day. Hence the foot-dragging. I reckoned I was currently in the clear on the work front – in fact I was doing a bang-up job – so I wasn't expecting complaints there, but undoubtedly what he really wanted to talk to me about was our previous heart-to-heart – and I wasn't looking forward to picking up where we left off with that.

Nevertheless, five-thirty rolled around and I realised I couldn't put it off any longer. Like a condemned man being led to the bellows[1], I shuffled downstairs and tapped on the Professor's door.

"Come in," he called and I entered to find him fussing over the contents of one of his bookcases.

"Jo. Sit down. I've just made a pot of tea; would you like some?" he asked, all smiles. I nodded. It would postpone the inevitable for at least thirty seconds.

He had a tray of tea-things on his desk and he poured us

---

[1]   Or whatever it is they're led to.

both a cup, even remembering to add sugar to mine. I sat in the visitor's chair in front of his desk, leaning forward to take the cup and saucer when he offered them.

He settled himself behind his desk and after a moment he said, "I'm sorry about how things went last time. I don't know quite what impression I gave but I'm sure it wasn't the right one." Perhaps he'd rehearsed this speech because his voice was calm and confident, very different from Friday's awkwardness.

He took a sip of his tea – what you might call a little English courage – and pressed on. "The last thing we discussed… Well I want to be clear: your mother and I were never involved romantically. I think I may have inadvertently left you with the idea that we were." He looked up to gauge my reaction. To the best of my knowledge, I gave no evidence of one. I was holding myself in, waiting to see where this went.

He continued, "Helen and I were certainly friends, though. Good friends, but no more than that. She came to me for help and…" here he faltered slightly, "…and support. And I did whatever I could."

He went on, "Your mother had many obstacles to contend with and I happened to be near for some of her most trying times. I hope I was some comfort to her; I certainly tried to be a steady friend."

I said nothing and after a while he added, "So I hope that clears things up."

He sipped his tea in silence and I sat with mine on my lap, untouched.

I wasn't sure what I thought. Was I happy or sad? Surprised or relieved?

And then, out of nowhere, a swell of anger was suddenly upon me. He still hadn't told me the truth and he was hoping he wouldn't have to. I said, "There's something you're not telling me."

I could almost see him considering his options: deny it, play dumb, feign a heart attack. He took too long making up his mind. Whatever he said now, it would sound like a line, a tactic.

I gave him a little encouragement. "There's something in my mother's things you're worried about me finding. But I *will* find it, so you might as well tell me."

"I…" was all he could say. He set down his tea and we both waited for a moment.

Long seconds passed before he was ready. I held very, very still – almost like I wasn't there. I wasn't sure that I was any more eager than he was to hear what was coming.

He asked, "I imagine you know that your mother was often unhappy. Depressed, in fact."

Yes, I knew that. I nodded.

"Sometimes it would get very bad," he said, "*very* bad and she'd stop coming in to the department." He gave a sad smile. "She told me that some days she couldn't even get out of bed."

I knew she'd had problems. Maybe I hadn't appreciated how serious they were.

He gave another sad smile and continued, "I was used to her absences and I knew the reason for them. I always made light of them because I knew it would be difficult enough for her to return to work without worrying that a court martial awaited her. I made sure she always knew she was welcome."

Someone thumped along the corridor outside and he paused until they'd gone past. When he spoke again, his voice was no longer steady: "One day she didn't come in and I got a call from the hospital. She had tried to kill herself."

I felt the pit of my stomach drop and I thought I might be sick. He'd enunciated the words so carefully. There was no mistaking them.

He went on, expressionless now, sounding like a recording: "I sat with her until she woke up. By chance, she had been found almost immediately and the hospital had pumped her stomach. They found sedatives and rather a lot of gin."

I noticed a tear on his cheek as he caught my eye and explained, "Your mother detested gin. She told me later that she'd chosen it deliberately. A comforting taste wouldn't have been right, she said. And if she survived she'd have a colourful excuse never to touch it again." Again, the sad smile.

Numbly I asked, "So she expected to survive?"

He shook his head. "I don't see how. It was a winter morning, still dark. It just so happened that there was an accident in her building, one of the undergraduates cooking food in her room, lots of smoke. The fire brigade were called and the building was evacuated. No one could find Helen. A girlfriend said her bicycle was in its usual spot and someone else noticed that there was a light in her window. A fireman forced her door open. An ambulance was called. She couldn't have known any of that would happen."

I knew my mother suffered with mental problems; I'd always known it. I figured I'd inherited my hang-ups from her. I'd heard lots of muttering about her problems from my dad's domestic staff, and from relatives, when I was younger. I even knew that some of them believed her death was no accident. But that was just cruel gossip. They had their facts wrong. That's what I'd always believed.

That's what I'd always *known*. But the Professor's words told a different story.

He turned away for a few moments and blew his nose. When he turned back he was more composed. And he had more to say: "When your mother moved to America, she stayed in touch. I never allowed a letter of hers to go unanswered for more than a day or two, especially when she moved into the new house after you were born. I know she found it difficult to make new friends and with your father so busy… well, I think our correspondence helped a little. She told me that she saved my letters; they reassured her that sometimes life could be normal. She claimed she meant that as a compliment. Unless they were lost in all the upheaval I would imagine those letters are somewhere inside one of those wretched boxes.

"Towards the end…" he struggled.

And then tried again. "Before she died, we discussed her depression, the black moods that wouldn't leave her. How her medication wasn't helping. I didn't want you to read those letters not knowing what to expect, to have it come as a complete surprise." He leaned forwards. "But the truth is that I hoped I could persuade you not to read them at all." He was getting choked up again as he said, "You have had a lot of sadness of your own, Jo, a lot to deal with, and for the *life* of me I can't see how you could benefit from sharing in your mother's misery. Goodness knows it was more than *she* could bear. I didn't want you to read those letters because I didn't want you reliving your mother's pain. She wouldn't have wanted that either."

I realised I was crying, but I didn't say anything. I just sat there. I was afraid I would spill my tea with my trembling so I set it down on the desk and then let my hands cover my eyes. I was sobbing quietly now.

That last day, Mom went for a drive, something she normally didn't do. She didn't like driving but she travelled right over to the other side of town; we never found any reason for it. It was an industrial park; just factories and warehouses. Then she stopped the car and got out, leaving the engine running. A truck hit her as she stepped out into the street. It had never made much sense. But now I knew why it had happened. It had happened because the first time she'd tried it, back in England, she'd been rescued.

I felt a hand on my shoulder and I realised that the Professor was standing by me. His face was so sad as he looked down at me. "Dear girl," he said, patting my shoulder. "Dear girl."

I reached up and he took my hands in his, and held them while I cried. "I'm so sorry," was all he said, repeating it softly.

Chapter 10

You're probably used to me being upset by now. Boo-hoo, twenty-four seven. Then the jokes, the flippancy before the next big drama. You're probably pretty tired of it. I know I am. Well, take comfort: we're nearly past that point now. I'll just say that this last slump was a big one. I mean even a stable, reasonably-together person would be hit hard by something like that, right?

I'm sure I don't need to explain why the discovery of my mother's suicide knocked my legs out from under me. You're human, you have empathy, you get it. But there were sides to the whole thing that deepened the hurt. Like for instance what it meant for my future. She was past caring, but what sort of legacy had she left me? How much of her self-destruct mechanism had I inherited? Was its timer counting down towards zero in *my* head now?

I knew enough to understand that traumas run in families. And since I don't suppose anyone *chooses* to lose their grip on the world I have to imagine it happens to you whether you want it to or not.

And besides the question of what she might have passed on to me, there was the question of what had been lost with her death. I didn't have any close family. My dad had long since decided to re-cast himself in the role of distant uncle. My mother had always been the one I had yearned to be closer to, to know more about. The fact that I couldn't remember her, even though she had died just before I was sent away to start school, had left me desperate to learn more. First she'd left and then I'd had to – Dad said it had already been agreed before she died – and it opened up such a chasm between us that I desperately wanted to fill it with something.

It had made me search for evidence of her in my personality, my mannerisms. I wanted to bring her closer, to soak up whatever I could about her past, her character, and to absorb it into me so that I would have some link to her, the one person I really thought of as family. Now, with this sundering, this axe-blow, I was suddenly horrified by the idea of being linked to her, of finding echoes of her within me. It was the last thing I wanted. Her influence suddenly seemed like the touch of a disease that I had to wash off.

And above all I felt betrayed by her. She'd left me alone in the world with only her example to guide me. And what an example it had turned out to be. My father hadn't known what to do with a daughter and it turned out neither had my mother. So whose idea was I? I mean, what was the point of me?

I'd been sent off to boarding school as soon as I was old enough, but I'd always wanted to believe that if my mother had lived she'd have kept me near her. And I had to let that hope go now. Neither of them knew what to do with me.

Ridiculous though it sounds, it made me think about Frankenstein – not the movies, but the book. In the original, the creature is having such a lousy time of it, he seeks out his maker to find out why he was created. He only becomes a monster when he learns that there is no good reason for his existence. He was a whim, an intellectual experiment – and ultimately a mistake. It makes you think; if the one who gives you life doesn't want you, has no purpose for you, doesn't care for you, then why should anyone else[1]?

Ironically – if irony is the right word for it – discovering that my mother had been seriously mentally unbalanced was threatening to push me over the edge too. Maybe this was what the Professor had been worried about when he learned that his old letters were in my possession: that I couldn't handle the shock of the truth.

I don't remember how I eventually came to leave the Professor's study. I remember being glad that he was there trying to comfort me – glad and pathetically grateful that someone still loved me – but I was still inconsolable. I think perhaps he brought me outside to get some fresh air after everyone else had left the office for the day.

Anyway, once outside, an instinctive desire to be alone came upon me. When that black weight presses down on you, some reflex makes you want to get away from other people. Other people interfere, they hold off the worst of it and that's not what you need. You have to be by yourself, and let it rage through you, unrestrained, so that you can find out how bad it is, whether there's hope, whether there's any point in fighting.

But I knew the Professor wouldn't let me go unless he believed I was coping. I had to persuade him that I wouldn't do anything stupid so that I could get away from him. I found that if I concentrated on the fact that I would be alone soon then I could stop the tears for a little while. Knowing that in a few minutes' time I could let it all out helped me get myself under control

---

[1] And it makes you wonder whether Mary Shelley's parents were freaks like mine.

for a while. I dried my eyes, lifted my head up and squared my shoulders.

We were standing near the back door of the main building, outside the dark windows of the empty refectory. The sun had set some time ago. "I'll be alright," I lied, "I think I just need to walk it off."

He took some convincing, but by now I was breathing normally and meeting his eye. I even tried to smile. I think it came out more as a grimace but nevertheless he relaxed a little.

"I understand," he said, "Just don't stay out here and make yourself ill. I think you might be coming down with something." He gave my shoulder a last squeeze and let me go. Hands jammed into my pockets, I walked up the path towards the dorm building and the lane beyond.

I didn't know where I was going but it didn't really matter.

In the end, my feet carried me past the entrance to the dorms and on up the hill. I didn't think about it; I just kept going. If I was going to really lose my grip on sanity, this would be my chance, the moment when the full force of it would hit me and I'd snap. I waited for the storm inside me to reach its peak.

And as I walked up the lane, passing between dark fields, there was so little light that I was barely able to make out the hedgerows on either side of me. My feet knew this path – I walked it most nights – I was headed towards the pub. And though the last thing I needed was company, the lane didn't end at the pub; it wound on. I could turn off onto a quiet track, if I wanted – walk for miles and not see a soul, or be passed by a car.

The lights of the pub came into view and I could hear muted conversation and the music of the stereo. I hugged the opposite side of the road, keeping as far from the light and sound as possible. The cheeriness of the place was repellent to me.

And yet, I found I wasn't crying any more. The churning emotions had made me sick to my stomach but they hadn't overwhelmed me yet. I felt alone but not quite lost. Maybe it still hadn't hit me fully. Or maybe it had and I would survive.

"Jo," someone called out. Despite myself I turned. It was Daniel. He stood beneath the pub sign, his back against the pole. He had a scarf wrapped multiple times around his neck and his hands too were plunged deep in the pockets of his denim jacket. He looked frozen. Had he been waiting for me out here? I'd forgotten all about him.

I didn't say anything but I stopped walking. He ran over to me.

When he saw my face, the red eyes, all the signs, he knew I'd been doing some serious crying. I wanted to be irritated with him for breaking in on my solitude like this… but I found I wasn't. He looked at me with so much concern, and yet he wasn't crowding me. I could see that he wanted to help me, to comfort me, but he also wanted to give me space, to let me choose.

Into the quiet, I blurted, "Daniel, I found out something about my mother." I said it before I even thought about it, before I even knew I was going to speak. Hearing the words out loud stirred things up inside me again, and I knew I couldn't say anything else for a minute or I'd break down. Even my breath was catching in my throat.

Carefully, respectfully, he put one arm around my shoulder and led me towards the pub, explaining, "There's a table right at the back of the garden behind the wall. Everyone's inside. No one will know you're here." Somehow he knew that I wanted to be invisible.

Steering clear of the main building, he led me around to the back of the pub, through the darkened garden, with its empty tables, and into the deep shadows beyond. An ancient wall screened off the furthest corner from those inside and one battered table lay behind it. The upper storey windows in the main building let out just enough stray light for us to find our way.

Daniel sat me down and headed back towards the pub. He said nothing before he went, just lifted a strand of hair out of my eyes and departed. Two minutes later he was back. He put a drink of something down in front of me and then fiddled with the gas heater, one of those tall metal mushrooms that radiate heat from the glowing mesh beneath their hoods.

"They said I could put the heater on if I promised not to pester them anymore about playing a gig here," he said, smiling. The heater soon began to glow, its mesh rippling with heat. I found I could see my glass now.

I picked it up and sipped. Southern Comfort, no ice. I hadn't thought I liked it, but it tasted strong and sweet and it spread warmth through my chest when I swallowed. The heater, too, was starting to work and the feel of my cold skin thawing made me feel a little better.

For a moment I felt like laughing with relief. I felt crappy, but the drink, the warmth, Daniel's patient silence all helped. I was hurting but I wasn't dying. On an impulse I grabbed his hand and squeezed it. He nodded, as though he understood, but said nothing.

We sat there without speaking for a little longer and I continued to warm, both inside and out. I finished my drink and asked Daniel if he'd get us some more. I held out some money. He carried away the empties and was soon back with a couple of fresh drinks in each hand and some packs of crisps clamped between his teeth. He opened his mouth, dropping the packets on the table, and passed me another Southern Comfort.

Very softly, he said, "So. I think you must have had a horrible day." His voice was a whisper.

I pressed my lips tightly together and nodded, tearing up a little. I sniffed the tears back, aware of just how ladylike that must look. I suddenly wanted to tell him, to explain everything, but I worried that I wouldn't be able to get the words out without triggering a meltdown.

In the end, when I started to speak I couldn't help crying, but it was a different kind than before. It felt healthier, like I was releasing something that had been trapped. The words came through in spite of the tears.

Daniel listened quietly. At one point, I faltered as I was telling him what the Professor had told me; he reached up and brushed my face, gently resting his fingers against the hot skin of my cheek for a moment before pulling back. Other than that, he just let me speak. And best of all, he didn't try to make this about *us* or to rush me and I realised for the first time how much he cared about me.

When I'd run down, exhausted all the words in me, and come to the end of the tears, he asked me, "What can I do? Is there anything you want?"

I considered it for a moment, then sniffed and smiled, saying, "Get drunk with me."

He looked a little unsure, just for a second, and then he nodded and said, "You're the boss." After that he looked around him as though he'd lost something. A moment later his gaze settled on the lights of the main building as though he'd only just noticed it. "Blimey," he said, "a pub. That's handy. I'll be back in a jiffy."

"Moron," I said, politely, as he gathered up the empties, and the scattered crisp packets, and walked back up the garden. He was gone for a few minutes, but I didn't mind the wait. I was warm, the alcohol had lit a crackling log fire inside me and I felt peaceful… in a slightly fuzzy way. I nearly giggled with the feeling of it. The world hadn't ended. I was talking with a friend who adored me and the pain, for the time being, had slid away.

When Daniel eventually returned he was carrying a tray. On it were more drinks and a couple of toasted sandwiches. As soon as I saw them I realised I was ravenous. I could have kissed him.

113

He held up a hand as if to halt me. "Now don't worry about this, but Tammy might join us," he said. "She works here and you might think you won't like her but you will. The sandwiches are on her."

For a moment I felt a bit put out that some stranger was going to intrude on our little haven of calm. I wondered if I was annoyed. But then I realised I really didn't mind. I trusted Daniel. At that moment I found I trusted him completely.

We'd had *several* more drinks and we were getting a little bit giddy by the time Tammy finally appeared. I was feeling happy enough to start teasing Daniel about his band. He was laughing and calling me unflattering names.

Tammy appeared out of the darkness and came over to the table, setting her drink down. In the dim light, I could see that she was beautiful – dark-haired, dark-eyed, with perfect skin. I realised I'd seen her in the bar plenty of times but I hadn't thought she was staff. She was wearing a giant, formless biking jacket that hid her shape and I remembered the regulars in the bar sneaking hungry glances at her whenever she moved. I prepared to hate her.

"Hi Jo," she said, like we were old friends, "I'm making some more food; are you interested?"

"Well I…" I said, a little uncertain. The sandwich had been delicious but it wasn't really enough.

"It's only chips; is that alright?" she asked "I'll make something else if we're still hungry."

"Great," I said, finding myself smiling. She went back inside for a minute and returned with a basket of chips in each hand. She had a chip clenched between her front teeth and was trying to blow on it. She looked ridiculous and she obviously didn't care. So perhaps I wouldn't hate her. Right now, I didn't think I hated anyone.

I soon discovered that Tammy was the new singer in the ever-changing line-up of Daniel's band. She told me the story of the disastrous gig they'd played that Saturday, making it all seem like her own fault. Loosened up from laughing at her exaggerations, I found I was happy to talk, so I told her a related story about a disastrous gig that the *previous* incarnation of the band had played back in London – and I made it all seem like *Daniel's* fault. Daniel wriggled good-naturedly with embarrassment.

At one point, I felt a stab of jealousy as Tammy suddenly snuggled up to Daniel, squeezing her slim hips close to his on the bench. But a moment later she pushed hard and slid him onto the ground. He lay there looking hurt but also laughing.

"What was that for?" he asked, looking up at her.

"It was Jo's idea," she explained, "She says you never get a round in."

Daniel attempted to say something in his defence but she sternly hissed him into silence with a zipping motion across her mouth. "Go," she commanded and then turned back to me, smiling. "So do you know any secrets about Daniel? Tell me something *really* bad that he's done. No, something *embarrassing*. Ooh, better still, something *evil*."

Reluctantly Daniel trailed back up the garden leaving us to gang up on him. He seemed to be gone a while, but it was getting difficult to tell because by this time I was starting to feel pretty drunk. Tammy was easy to talk to and I was feeling chatty. I realised that Daniel had been right to include her; it opened things up, stopped me from obsessing. At least that's what I *hoped* Daniel had been thinking.

Made brave by drink, I suddenly asked her, "Do you have a *thing* for Daniel?"

She looked surprised and a bit uncomfortable. "Well," she said, drawing the word out, "he's great and everything, but he's a bit old for me."

"What do you mean?" I asked, my mind not at its quickest.

"You're…?"

"Nineteen," she said, sounding embarrassed. For some reason, that news made me very sad. What was the point of being twenty-six if you could be funny and confident and likable at nineteen. I felt old and crushed and useless. For a moment I forgot to speak.

"Besides," Tammy said, "he won't shut up about you. It's a bit of a turn-off." She laughed and I joined in. It's not easy staying grumpy with that much booze inside you.

Daniel came back then, with more drinks. "Did you know it's nearly closing time?" he asked me, "Can you believe it?"

I shook my head. "I thought it was about nine o'clock."

"Me too," he said. Then he turned to Tammy. "Dom might join us in a bit, once he's locked up. He says he wants to talk to you about where all the Southern Comfort went."

"Well he's a big old soft sod, then" she said, her accent sounding local for the first time that evening.

By the time Dom joined us, I was feeling I'd probably had enough to drink. I might even have passed that point a while back. It was getting very difficult to think and the minutes were starting to skip past in sudden jumps. Everything was getting hard to follow.

Dom, it turned out, was a kind-looking man the size of a mountain gorilla with a big gut and lots of white hair. He came out carrying a pint of ale, perched on the end of the table, and told us stories for a while. At one point he stood and picked Tammy up, twirling her around to illustrate some point or other. She yelled to be put down but could do nothing about it. She was only about half my size, but even so… I was amazed at how easily he did it and I wondered, like a child, what it must be like to be so strong, for things to be so effortless. Moments later she was back on solid ground with no harm done.

Time skipped ahead again and I realised that I'd tuned out

116

for a while. Daniel was whispering to me, "I think we should go home." I'd rested my head on his shoulder for a minute and I think I must have fallen asleep.

Dom helped me to my wobbly feet and I gave him a big hug, which was wholly out of character for me, until you factor in my level of consumption that evening. I hugged Tammy too – she seemed to be mainly jacket – and she hugged me back, saying, "I hope you feel better. It was really nice talking to you." She sounded like she meant it.

And then Daniel held out his hands to lead me away and I hugged him too. "I'm going with you," he said, laughing.

"Still get a hug," I insisted, tripping on my words.

Everyone laughed and I focused for a moment on Tammy; she was staring at Daniel and the look on her face was hard to read – but not impossible. *She does like Daniel*, I thought, decoding the softness in her eyes. And then I looked at Daniel and saw that he was staring in my direction. *And Daniel likes me*, I thought, feeling smug.

We said some goodbyes and then Daniel and I went weaving down the lane. I'd had a great evening and I kept telling him so. "Good. I'm glad," he said each time.

At one point I'm pretty sure I kissed him and he said 'Thank you', very formally, and then we carried on walking.

I was fairly unsteady on my feet by the time we reached the dorm building and Daniel had to help me get up the stairs. He rummaged about in my jacket pocket for the key to my room, which tickled me like mad. "Hold still," he whispered as I wriggled and giggled.

"*You* hold still," I told him.

Eventually he found the key and helped me in. I flopped back on the bed and just lay there. When I realised I couldn't hear him anymore I sat up. He was gone and the door was open.

He returned a minute later with an empty waste bin and a pint

117

mug of water. "Ooh, is it a magic trick," I asked, excited. "Do you need a roll of newspaper? I've got one somewhere."

He put the bin by the side of my bed and handed me the glass. I realised I was thirsty for something other than alcohol and glugged a quarter of it straight down.

"Will you be alright?" he asked. "Do you feel sick?"

"I'm fine," I said. "I had a lovely evening."

"Excellent. Well, goodnight then," he said. He turned on my reading light and put out the main one. He was backing towards the door.

"Was I a big embarrassment?" I asked.

He lent forwards and gave me a tiny peck on the nose. "You were lovely," he assured me. And then he left, pulling the door quietly closed behind him.

I flopped back on the bed again and thought about taking off my clothes. It seemed like a lot of effort. My eyes fluttered closed... and then snapped open again as my stomach lurched. I sat up quickly and the nausea subsided. *Better not lie down for a while*, I thought.

I swept some clothes onto the floor so that I could sit in my one armchair. Doubled over and grunting from the exertion I finally managed to unlace my boots and get them off my feet. That was much better.

I drank a little more water and thought about putting some music on. Provided I didn't close my eyes, I felt fine. Three sheets to the wind, but fine. I knew in the morning, I'd probably be all upset again, I could sense it lurking just over the horizon, but at that moment I could think about my mother and not feel bad. Maybe my thoughts were too jumbled to feel anything, but I was safe from the pain for now.

That feeling of safety led to an idea. I located my keys and used them to open the bottom drawer of my desk. Inside was a little plastic case containing anti-depressants. They were patches, like the ones to help you give up smoking, and they would feed a steady dose of medication to my bloodstream. I thought it was pretty likely that I'd be needing some extra help in the coming weeks. It was just a shame they took a while to kick in. But maybe there was still some in my system from the last time.

Need some skin to apply it to. I pulled off my coat and my thick sweater, then wriggled out of the thermal camisole I had underneath. There was already a patch on my right shoulder and it was due to come off. This one was something else; something called oxymethylphenidate. A doctor had prescribed it for me once when I had difficulty studying. The idea had been to take it for the few weeks of exam season, but it turned out it helped with more than just the studying. I ordered it over the Internet now whenever my supplies ran low.

I peeled off the old patch and applied two new ones: an anti-depressant and one full of OMP. Then I shivered and pulled a hockey shirt on. The alcohol had suppressed most of my cold symptoms this evening, but now my nose was beginning to run. I pulled the last of the tissues out of the box, nearly falling on my ass in the process, and wondered blearily what to do with myself until it was safe to lay down to sleep.

My eyes wandered round the dimly lit room before coming to rest on my unpacked weekend bag. *Yes,* I thought, *that would do nicely.*

Chapter 11

Something was different.

I opened my eyes and looked around my room. It was in disarray: clothes, boxes and bags everywhere. But that wasn't it. My room is often like that. I'd obviously made it worse before I settled down to sleep was all.

So what was different?

Like the bursting of one of those giant fireworks they have at expensive displays (black sky suddenly blossoming into rich colour) I remembered the dream. I never dream, but last night, when I finally settled down to sleep, I had – and it was still with me, vivid and powerful, almost more real than the room in front of me.

But that wasn't it either. I sat up in bed. I suddenly wondered what the hell I was wearing? The top half of me had clothes on but like I'd been playing dress-up.

I swung my feet out of bed and stood on an empty patch of floor still trying to put my finger on what was different. Then I got it. It was me. I felt fantastic. No cold, no hangover; my head felt like a winter morning in the mountains, everything crisp and clear.

I remembered the trip to the pub last night and before it my talk with the Professor. I touched that memory carefully, like it was a bone that might be broken, but there was no sudden splinter of pain. Last night's catharsis seemed to have worked a miracle.

After the pub I'd come back to my room. I remembered sitting in the armchair, careful not to let my eyes close in case the nausea enveloped me. What had happened next? I sat back down on the edge of the bed and tried to run the videotape of my memory past that point, but it kept skipping ahead to the dream, the amazing colour of it and the endless sound of the ice.

Before the dream, I'd apparently scrambled the contents of my room and tried on some clothes; I'd been more than a little drunk. Maybe if I'd been sober enough to form memories I wouldn't have been fooling around like that. Perhaps there was nothing worth remembering. Except the dream; that would be difficult to forget.

I remembered that I'd been inside the dream for a while before I realised it. First of all everything was white – or at least colourless – like low cloud on a dull day. There was nothing to see and I had no sense of being anywhere. The light was weak, filtered, so attenuated that there were no shapes, no colours, just the impression of distance. There was sound, though – a whole geography of sound.

Imagine floating on your back in calm water, your eyes half-focused on the featureless grey cloudbanks above. Then imagine that you could hear every ripple and swell of moving water all around you. Ten thousand individual sounds spread out like flowers in a meadow, like trees in a forest, on every side of you.

For a while, that's where I thought I was: floating. Then, in a synesthetic moment the sounds became flickering points of light against blackness and I was a speck at the centre of a twinkling, rippling aurora as wide as a thunderstorm. And then the sounds were sounds again and I realised that they didn't ripple, they creaked. And I didn't float, I was simply suspended.

The landscape around me, indistinct as it was, began to make more sense to me – not clouds but ice. Miles of ice. It had drained the light of its power, its definition, its ability to render shapes. I was at sea but it was a sea that had frozen, back before anyone could remember, before there were even people *to* remember. And I realised that the light which I'd thought was colourless was the most amazing pale blue – the colour of a billion tons of frozen ocean. Every photon of light in that vast plane was the same colour, which was why it hadn't registered as colour at all.

I listened to the creaking and cracking, like a heavy sailing ship flying before a strong wind. The ice creaked like rigging and cracked like the snapping of sails and shifted over itself in a million tight spaces with a sound like the roaring wind. It was like the ice itself was dreaming of the ship, yearning for it, and the sense of its motion was exhilarating.

My whole awareness of the world was through these sounds, but gradually I became aware that I could also see something. As one part of my mind rushed endlessly forwards, drawn along by the dream-ship as it raced ahead of the surging waves, another part of me puzzled over a shape that was forming before me.

In a minute I had it. A figure, distorted and compressed, caught like an insect in that weird, blue *azul* amber.

I stared at the slumped figure for a good long while before I realised that it must be me.

But there was more to the scene. Another shape was there, but this one was empty, insubstantial. It was the husk of a person and it lay there in front of the me-figure, almost at its feet. And there was one more element, one more presence that I struggled to resolve.

Finally I understood: it was the source of light. Right by that first figure, that twisted representation of me, was a pool of radiance. Something that glowed, but not like a lamp – more like an open window on a sunny day. It didn't create light, it merely admitted it to the scene, allowed it to flow out in all directions.

What was I to make of this? A human shell, long dead, and standing over it two shapes: one a dark figure, distorted, the other a perfect light, unblemished. Were they all aspects of me? Had the light been present all along or had it just now come into existence? I couldn't tell, but perhaps the being of light, devoid as it was of detail or features, was simply the possibility of something now awakened within me. The dark shape was a grotesque distortion of my image, hardly recognisable. How long had it lain trapped in the ice, collapsing, decaying? And the empty shell: if I peered closer would I recognise it? Would I see the vanished face of my mother, echoed in the dust of its ruined form?

Since my own mind was the source of these images it seemed I had only to open myself up fully to understand their meaning. Some part of me already knew the truth and I willed everything else into silence so that its message could be heard.

With a growing sense of certainty, I realised that the two versions of me, the twisted-dark and the glowing-light, would be with me for some time to come – they were both aspects of my nature. I couldn't expel the flaws of a lifetime in an instant, but I could begin the process right now. I could work to erase that dark, twisted version of myself and allow the other, brilliant me to come more fully to life.

But the vacant shell nearby – which I took to be my mother's lingering, haunting presence – I realised I could be rid of that influence right now. There was only one role left for her in my life; she could help me by serving as a warning. She would be a beacon to keep me off the rocks. By renouncing her in everything I did, maybe I could avoid her fate.

All this came back to me as I sat on the bed. The immediacy of it was intense, like the grip of a nightmare, but I wasn't frightened; I was filled with calm resolve. Immersing myself in the vibrant recollection of that dream seemed to have unlocked my memory. I now recalled the final events of the previous night and I shuddered at my stupidity.

There were still gaps and omissions but I could remember the heart of it. After a few minutes of sitting in the armchair, I had risen unsteadily and tipped out my weekend bag, trying to find the rain-crumpled pages I had studied on the moors. From a zippered pouch I had removed the gold jewellery that proved so useless two days before when I stood in the grassy lee of that windswept ridge. And once again I forced myself to focus on the rhymes and rhythms of a nonsense mantra, the interlocking geometry of a labyrinthine design, and I strove for that moment of clarity and control that had escaped me on the freezing heath.

Then, full of weary confusion, stifled pain, alcohol and the mingling drugs of my pharmaceutical support system, I achieved what had escaped me when I'd had a clear head and a hundred acres of solitude. The feeling that Susan Milton described as 'Connection' came over me.

Did I feel or just imagine the crackle as my throat and lungs were swept clear of cold-viruses, each one spitting out of existence like water droplets on a griddle? Was I imagining the twist of realigning cartilage as my right knee-joint slid free from its decade-old injury and lost its ache? I *knew* I wasn't imagining the sudden expansion of my senses. It was like watching the world through a bank of cameras and when I turned my head, they all panned at different speeds. It should have been disorienting, but it was just the opposite; the cascade of images complemented each other. My awareness of my surroundings was so much more rich than before, and each new sensation seemed to find some previously unused part of my brain ready to process it.

And I knew that if I'd wanted to, I could have ripped the door to my room off its hinges simply by thinking it, then roasted the wood to cinders just by wishing it so.

At that moment I realised that alcohol was what you chose to get drunk on if you couldn't get your hands on power.

I was sitting on my bed remembering all this and I didn't know what to think. Even once I felt that I'd recovered all the previous night's events I realised that there was still something missing. I could remember Connecting and the initial impressions of what that felt like, but what had happened next? *That* memory was gone.

Glancing down I could see that my wrists were still wrapped in gold. I checked my bed and, sure enough, between my pillow and the wall was wedged the heavy gold necklace I'd wrapped around my head. It seems that I'd actually gone to sleep wearing what the documents called 'tribute'. I just couldn't imagine what I'd been thinking, keeping all that on in bed. Had I simply passed out before I remembered to take it off?

The final surprise came when I stripped off my remaining clothes ready to take a shower. I was wearing even more jewellery – a necklace in fact – and I didn't recognise it. I fumbled at the back of my neck looking for the catch, while trying to see the necklace in the mirror. It didn't look familiar but I'd turned out so many boxes last night, including a bunch of my mother's newly arrived possessions – perhaps I'd discovered it amongst them. Try as I might, I couldn't retrieve the last of the missing memories.

I gave up trying to remove the necklace and instead studied it in the mirror for a moment. I could see that it was beautifully made and as I inspected its reflection a distant memory began to surface. I recalled my mother's interest in handmade jewellery.

I vaguely remembered someone telling me that she'd created a number of pieces herself. Gazing at the wonderful design of it I had a growing sense that I'd seen it before. Somehow, last night, pretty much smashed out my mind, I'd managed to find this beautiful thing among her other possessions.

Lovely though it was, I wasn't about to celebrate her memory by wearing it. I was feeling so calm today that I found I was able to think about her with no more emotion than if I were pondering a shopping list. My dream-revelation seemed as right now as when it first struck me: her example should serve as a warning. I no longer felt any need to be close to her; her presence in my world was reduced to the role of a haz-mat sticker applied to a section of my life, something I could glance at to remind me of danger.

That said, maybe that was exactly why I *should* wear her necklace. I never go in for low necklines so no one would even be aware of it. Only *I* would know it was there and only *I* would understand what it symbolised.

The idea appealed to me so much that I resolved not to remove the necklace until the transformation I'd glimpsed in my dream was complete and the danger had passed. The necklace would come off when I no longer needed reminding of the terrible consequences of weakness.

And this new sense of determination felt good. It was a strange feeling to be so positive about the future and I wondered for a moment whether Susan and David experienced this whenever they Connected. They had certainly seemed happy enough when I spied on them. Maybe Healing worked on the mind as well as the body – though I hadn't seen any mention of it in the PAC's documents. Perhaps I was just feeling a buzz like the one you get from your first couple of cigarettes, a buzz that disappears when the novelty becomes a habit.

Hmm. Thoughts of smoking took me back to the night before

and the feeling I'd had in my lungs and throat as my cold left me. And I remembered my knee injury, the excuse I'd been using since high school to get out of exercising, and how last night I'd felt it heal. Had it really, though? An unfamiliar thought occurred to me – a way to test my health that no one who knew me would ever expect me to try.

Like a lot of people I owned a pair of running shoes that had never been party to anything faster than an amble. Now I dug them out from under my bed, nearly choking on the dust, and then searched around for some clothes to run in. Half of modern fashion is sportswear, so even *I* had something suitable. Finding the right bra was more of a challenge; if this was to be more than an isolated occurrence I'd need to do some shopping.

When I stepped outside a few minutes later I was surprised at how early it still was. The sun was up, but only just, and no one from the project was around. It was pretty cold out, even with a fleece over my t-shirt, but my newly repaired lungs were able to cope. Maybe my asthma was history too.

Watching my breath steam in front of me, I trotted slowly up the hill.

I didn't set any records, but for someone with my lifestyle it wasn't a bad start. I ran for about two miles, starting really slow and speeding up a little, once I was warmed through. The damp air tasted great, and the shallow Autumn light glittering off the frosted meadows was remarkably beautiful. Best of all, my knee was giving me no trouble at all.

When I got back, I lingered outside for a couple of minutes, doing my best to remember the stretching exercises I'd seen runners perform. My muscles felt warm and full of blood; my breathing was deep and easy, and I suspected I was having my first proper hit of endorphins. Why wouldn't anyone in their right mind want to start their day like this?

Except that tomorrow, I might make it a little bit earlier. That way I could see the sunrise and it would give me a little more time before starting work. My room desperately needed a spring-clean and I doubted I was going to finish it this evening.

For a moment I was almost giddy with the rush of well-being. I was going to have to be careful that my head didn't fly off. This feeling was a little disorienting. I calmed myself down and concentrated on my stretches.

I *would* get up early tomorrow, though. Nothing had changed in my desire to learn more about the PAC and to find a way onto the team and it wouldn't happen if I was lying in bed sleeping. There was work to be done and I wasn't going to waste another minute.

I headed back inside to change and get ready. When I was finished showering and dressing I walked over to the main building to look for some breakfast. The cook was just setting everything up and no one else, as yet, had arrived.

"Morning," I said, adding, "I'm Jo," in response to his rather blank look. I realised I'd never really spoken to the cook before.

I said, "Can I ask you something?"

He nodded, without enthusiasm, and I said, "Listen, I want to try being a little bit healthier. I want to stay off the fried food for a while. What do you think I should be eating for breakfast?"

He scratched his chin and looked a bit surprised. Maybe he didn't get asked for his advice very often. But I figured he'd probably had to sit through a bunch of catering college lectures on this stuff and it was probably easier to get him to fix me something if it was his suggestion in the first place.

"Well, we've got the muesli," he said, "Some of the girls go for that. Did you want to do a bit of, what do you call it, de-tox then?"

"I don't know," I said, "I don't know much about those things."

"Well, for a de-tox I think you'd want to eat a lot of fruit,

128

specially for breakfast," he explained, warming to his role as teacher. "Maybe drink some green tea. I've definitely got some somewhere because Doctor Milton likes it. And lots of water, which I always put out anyway." He pointed over to the big metal jug on the end of the counter which I'd never seen anyone touch.

I'd always found him kind of surly and aggressive, but it seemed like he could be pretty helpful if you asked nicely. I gave him an encouraging look because it seemed like he might have more to say. He thought for a moment and said, "I could get in a bit of fruit if you like, kiwis, citrus, a bit of colour. I've got an order to place this afternoon."

"You'd do that?" I asked appreciatively.

"Oh yeah, that wouldn't be a problem. Probably won't be in before Thursday though. Maybe try the muesli in the meantime. There's skimmed milk to go with it in the jug at the back," he indicated the table with the cereals on it.

"That's really kind of you," I said and then looked awkward. "I'm sorry but I can't remember your name."

"I'm Ray," he said, jutting his chin like it was a source of pride. "And you're Jo, then" he said, and for the first time since I'd joined the project I saw him smile.

Interesting.

"Thanks Ray," I said and headed over to get myself some muesli – though I wasn't feeling much enthusiasm at the prospect. I'd had it in the past and found it boring, but really it wasn't too bad, it just took a bit of eating. I was still chewing away when Daniel came in. His hair was all angles and he hadn't shaved yet. He didn't look all that well.

He seemed surprised to see me and came straight over to join me. "Hey. I was going to come and look for you once I'd had some tea – check you hadn't slipped into a coma. We guzzled a *boatload* of booze last night."

The cook wandered over and put a white mug of tea down in front of Daniel and said, "Wasn't sure you could fetch it yourself. You on the pop last night?"

Daniel just laughed and put his head down in his hands, pushing his fingers through his hair. "Yeah. It all went horribly wrong. Cheers for the tea, Ray."

The cook wandered away to finish laying out breakfast. Daniel took a couple of sips of hot tea, sighed with relief and said, "You look fresh as a daisy. I thought you might be feeling the effects a bit this morning."

I couldn't very well tell him the secret of my rapid recovery, so I made something up. "To be honest," I said, "most of what I drank came back up before it had a chance to do much damage."

He swallowed, queasily, and I added, "Sorry to be gross."

He cleared his throat and carefully avoided my eye. "The main thing," he said, "is that you seem like you're not letting it get to you." He wasn't talking about the booze, of course. "Probably a night out wasn't a bad idea. And, you know, if I have to, I'm prepared to risk my liver and do it all over again. If it would help." Then, sounding exhausted, he added, "But not tonight."

I caught his eye – to make sure he knew I meant it – and said seriously, "You've helped a lot already, thanks."

He was maybe a little surprised by my easy directness – it wasn't something I often achieved – but I could tell he was glad to hear the sentiment. He met my gaze for a moment and then he looked thoughtful, confused even. He said, "You know, you look *incredible* this morning. And your cold is gone. You should write to the Southern Comfort people. Offer to sell them your story."

"I do feel pretty good," I admitted. I wasn't planning to tell him about the magic, but I couldn't see the harm in sharing part of what I'd experienced – maybe enough to stop him becoming suspicious. "I had the most amazing dream last night and it really made me think. Made me realise some things."

"Yeah?" he said, meaning *go on*.

I hadn't actually intended to go into details, but he seemed so interested. "Well, you know dreams are always weird, right?" I said. "But I saw myself stuck in the middle of all this ice and I was just looking awful, falling to bits in front of my own eyes, if you see what I mean." And suddenly I didn't want to tell him the rest of the dream. I don't know why; it just suddenly seemed too personal – plus it sounded pretty dumb.

He saw my reluctance and said, "I won't make fun. I promise."

It would seem weird to just clam up, so I compromised a little and said, "It just made me think. I could stay stuck in the same rut for the rest of my life or I could change my approach, try something new. Be like this ball of light instead of staying trapped inside the sad, old me until I fall apart completely." I realised I'd been waving my hands a lot and I put them down now. "OK, I didn't explain that very well, but do you know what I mean?"

He shrugged agreeably and said, "Well, I understand the idea, definitely. I suppose the imagery is whatever makes sense to you. If I had that dream it would probably be about being on stage or something. Anyway, it obviously got your attention." He looked nervous for a second and said, "I was worried that maybe you'd, um, opted for a little bit of *chemical* assistance this morning."

Curiously, this suggestion didn't annoy me. Daniel knew about my patches and had never approved, so this wasn't anything new. I found the only question his words raised in my mind was about what sort of impression I wanted to leave him with. Was it better if he thought I was propping myself up with medication or if he thought I was fine without it? I figured it was easier not to have him fussing over me. "No drugs," I said, holding up my hands. "We had a really good evening last night and when you consider what I'd been through yesterday, that's a miracle. My weird dream just made me realise that if I could do it once, then I could probably do it everyday. It's about time for a change, is all. And you were a big part of helping me see that."

I was laying it on a bit thick, but why not? He was a good guy and if I wanted to keep counting on him I should probably give him some recognition occasionally. Plus, if I were being cynical, I could say that his ego would now keep him from doubting me because he couldn't take the credit for my improvement while simultaneously being suspicious of it. So whatever.

He gave me an appraising look. "You're not going to become a Buddhist or anything are you? This is just about remembering to look on the bright side a bit more, right?"

I nodded reassuringly, and he seemed satisfied. He looked over to the counter where the cook had finished laying things out. "OK," he said, "Well I need bacon or I think I'm going to croak."

"Right. See you at lunch. If you live," I said, and headed for the door. I gave Ray a wave on my way out and he nodded back. Not even nine o'clock and I'd made a friend.

And the day just kept getting better. I felt good, I was feeling really strong for once and people seemed to respond to that right away. Of course there was a part of me that didn't trust this transformation. God knows I've turned over a new leaf or two in my time – quite recently in fact – but this was a little bit different. This wasn't the usual ten-minute makeover. I had, after all, undergone a major physical tune-up last night, so there was every reason to think that it might have fixed up my mental machinery too.

I mean it had always seemed weird to me that anti-depressants could work, because it was absurd to think that the root cause of depression was a lack of *pills*. But on the other hand, what those drugs did was boost your serotonin levels in a few key areas. If 'Connecting' could cure the common cold and straighten mangled cartilage, it could probably blow the cobwebs out of your brain too.

When I started the day, this new leaf was just a good idea; by the end of the day it had become a reality. I'd managed one full day without screwing up, giving in, curling up, lashing out or blaming anyone for anything, myself included. I mean, hallelujah. And if I could manage one day then maybe I *could* manage another, particularly now I'd had a taste of how good it could feel.

With this frighteningly stable version of myself working on the problem, could it be long before I'd won over the PAC and earned a seat at their table? More than ever that was what I wanted and I'd never felt more capable of getting what I wanted in my life. I fairly hummed with purpose and drive. Even at the end of the evening, it almost took an act of will to stop bustling, to lie down and sleep – despite the fact that I'd had the busiest day I could remember. My final thought as I began to drift off was the realisation that I actually wasn't afraid – of the future, of other people, of what I might say or do. I had stopped being afraid.

I slept that night in total peace, and although I dreamed – endless visions of colour and movement – in the morning the details had all slipped away. I woke rested and ready to begin again.

Chapter 12

So it's true that *ideally* I wouldn't still be spying on anyone. But I couldn't really afford to wait outside until the PAC invited me in. I needed to know what was going on right now. I couldn't afford to be excluded.

Now, for anyone who doesn't know, there's a place in London called Tottenham Court Road. Nerds call it TCR and it is one of their holy places. You can pretty much buy any gadget you want there – including off-the-shelf surveillance equipment. You'd think you'd need some sort of licence or official permission to buy hidden cameras, bugs and sound-recorders that look like pens, but you don't. You don't even need to make a trip: a web browser and a credit-card is all it takes.

In fact, my needs were positively pedestrian compared with what else was on offer. I just wanted an audio bug with a short-range transmitter in it and then I needed something to pick up the signal. Right away I found a bug that was made to look like a mains adaptor – one of those dealy-bobs you use when you've got two plugs and only one wall outlet. It was voice-activated and drew its power from the mains current – and it was available for next-day shipping. I mean they were making it difficult for anyone with a healthy level of curiosity *not* to bug people, if you ask me.

So a week had gone by since I'd first Connected and I hadn't wasted a moment of that time. I was still feeling terrific, but my mood had settled down a little. I wasn't having those moments where I had to fight the urge to grin like a fool any more. I'd just fairly *torn* through every task assigned to me (while remembering not to make it look *too* easy); I'd built or repaired bridges with several members of the team and I'd continued to study the PAC's documents in detail.

A couple of times, when I headed out for my dawn jog, I'd taken my bag of gold knick-knacks with me so's I could do a little practice with the magic. I needed to get a minimum of a few hundred yards from the project buildings and the barn on the off-chance that one of the other members of the team was doing the same thing. The Presence Surface was like sonar for other adepts; when I Connected I'd become visible to them – and if I were detected the PAC would think the enemy was upon them and there would be a lot of running around and yelling and other stuff I didn't want.

But I had no problems with that or anything else. In fact just the opposite. Call it luck or call it natural talent, but I just took to the use of magic like I was born to it. From my reading I knew it had taken days before Susan had even basic control of a Shield. And it took her weeks of diligent effort before she could manipulate any of the other Surfaces worth a damn. Not so for me. I found I almost didn't have to try; my first instinct was unfailingly the right one. And in what amounted to my spare time, I had mastered what others had taken months, even years, to learn. I didn't kid myself that I was on a par with the Witnesses, many of whom had centuries of experience behind them, but I was certainly on the fast track.

My control was good enough that I was able to turn my two-twists-of-necklace headband into something a little more professional. I wound a filament of steel wire through the loose links so that the necklace would hold a shape, then I got it settled properly on my head, adjusting and twisting it until it was both comfortable and planted firmly in place. Then, for the next step, I'd borrowed a gold necklace from a non-PAC researcher called Nicola. I needed it so I could Connect in order to work on my own headband. I used the Heat Surface to raise the temperature of the gold links until they began to fuse together. It took half an hour, and persistence was definitely required, but the result was pretty impressive. I pulled out the steel wire when I was done and admired the result: a custom-made gold headband that wouldn't fall off.

So my accelerated progress with magic was certainly good news. Things were moving a little more slowly with my ingratiation into the PAC – but that was a people thing and they always take time. A week is an eye-blink when it comes to changing people's attitudes and I had a lot of fences to mend (along with building those bridges I mentioned). And while we're extending metaphors, as part of my overall self-promotion I'd also been planting a few seeds – a comment here, some gentle pressure there – which I hoped would bear fruit soon enough.

For instance, I knew Daniel was impressed with how well I'd got my act together, but I could tell he was worried it was temporary. With a few carefully chosen remarks I helped him conclude that what his pal Jo really needed was a purpose – ideally one she could share with those around her. Without it she might grow disillusioned, isolated and turn inwards again, but with it she might continue to improve and be gradually drawn out of her shell. In other words, I made sure he'd want the PAC to offer me membership because it was the right thing for *me*.

The Professor, on the other hand, was from an earlier era.

He understood about purpose, but his generation were largely motivated by duty. I suspected that when he was growing up, young people weren't encouraged to keep their options for the future open or obsess about whether they were happy; they were told it was better to keep busy and get on with something useful. I made it clear to the Professor that shouldering some responsibility was really helping me to steady myself. It was an impression I tried to create with my behaviour rather than my words, whenever possible.

Like Daniel, he was sure to wonder how permanent my new diligence was too. I figured he'd feel most comfortable if he could keep an eye on me to see how I was bearing up, so I made sure we often found ourselves with a few minutes to chat, just the two of us. Sure, I'd go a little quiet from time to time, just to show I wasn't manic or a machine, but in all my dealings with him my watchword was 'steadiness'.

Susan Milton was a tougher nut to crack, partly because I knew very little about what made her tick. I knew she was a hard worker and very bright. And I knew she had a soft side, as evidenced by her closeness with David Braun. Beyond that, she was still largely opaque to me.

My best guess was that her main concern would probably be with my flaky personality. I had an idea that being a team-player didn't come naturally to her. I suspected that her instinct was usually to tackle everything on her own. If she found teams naturally uncomfortable then she'd want to keep things simple by making sure that no volatile personalities were added to the mix. She'd want to avoid any situation which might require too much complex diplomacy.

She also struck me as a 'good girl', someone who'd never really rebelled; she was therefore less forgiving of others who had. This was guesswork but the course it suggested wasn't a high-risk one. I decided that my priority with Susan would be to seem calm, reasonable, even a little unimaginative – in short, less of a highly-strung liability than my background suggested. Her priority would be the good of the team, rather than my welfare, so I did my best to seem like an asset.

So that was how I behaved; I was also making some changes to how I looked. That Saturday I got the bus into town and did a little shopping. It was basic psychology really: one way to change the impression that I was flaky was to get rid of as many of the outward signs of flakiness as possible – anything a person might conceivably associate with a troubled personality. So gradually I started to take better care of myself. Nothing over-the-top, because drastic change is also a sign of problems, but I made sure my nails were neat and unbitten, my hair was tidy and presentable and I put a little more effort into keeping my chin high and making eye contact. I gave up slouching and I stopped being so jumpy around people. From time to time, in a restrained way, I even smiled pleasantly, to show that I wouldn't bite.

On my shopping trip I picked up a few clothes in lighter colours than I usually went for. Again, nothing jarringly out of character, but I had a habit of wearing old jeans and patterned sweaters in muddy tones and the overall impression it gave was that I wanted to be inconspicuous, that I wanted people to not look at me.

Now I wanted my appearance to say 'look or don't – I'm comfortable either way'. I wasn't trying to grab attention but I wasn't actively deflecting it either. So I found some lighter-weight sweaters in solid colours, no patterns, and a couple of pairs of jeans in shades other than denim-blue. My plan was to still revert to the bulky, dowdy, blah outfits occasionally but to balance them by doing something more imaginative with my hair or maybe (gasp) applying a suspicion of eye-liner and popping a pair of colourful studs[1] in my ears. (In fact I hardly needed cosmetics; my skin tone and circulation were so much improved that make-up would have been overdoing the transformation.)

My room, too, I kept neat and tidy. Not Marines-Corps neat, but orderly – like I cared about the space I spent time in. Two decades of on-and-off therapy and psychiatry might not have helped me *achieve* a healthy mental balance but it was just the thing for helping me *fake* it.

* * *

Towards the end of my second week as a member of the occult fraternity, I found out that the PAC were planning to have a meeting. I thought it would be a good opportunity for them to start the process of including me in the group, so I laid some groundwork to that end.

I came up with a few technical tricks to help with the project work. I thought it my impress the PAC members and help them to see how useful someone like me could be to them.

Also, on my own initiative, I tracked down an ancient book that was coming up for auction in Edinburgh the following week. I had chosen it carefully because it was an occult title that I was sure would pique the curiosity of the researchers. Then I approached Susan and asked if she thought it might be of interest. She was very keen to know more and I apologised for not having any more details, explaining that I'd discovered it while looking for other items on the project's behalf, but that I wasn't sure *this* was quite their thing. (I didn't want to let on that I knew about

---

[1]   OK. Studs rapidly gave way to clips. One problem with occult regenerative powers is that they interfere with a gal's piercings. Would anyone spot that I no longer had pierced ears? Unlikely. But I made a mental note to check the ear-lobes of anyone new I met.

their interest in the occult.)

She assured me that it was just what they were looking for, so the next day I sought out Susan again and told her what else I'd been able to discover. Not only had I researched the title that was up for sale – and written her a little gloss – I'd also researched the seller, discovered what else he might have in his private collection and made suggestions on how he might be persuaded to sell some of it. The point I wanted to make was that I could trace things and people, and pull together background information on them, in a way the PAC could surely use. I was careful not to give any hint that I was making that particular point, or that I suspected more was going on with them than met the eye.

But I knew the PAC were still delving into the loss of the Marker and were trying to track it down without alerting the Army's spies. They were going to need skills like mine.

I'd given the whole thing a lot of thought and with growing certainty I'd decided that the Marker was the key. If I could help them find it, my credibility problems would be a thing of the past. Now I was looking for a way to get started on that.

The final piece of groundwork I laid for the meeting was the most important – and it involved Daniel. The evening before the PAC meeting, I invited him out to the pub. The plan was to enlist his help and get him to sponsor me for membership of the inner circle. But I had to do it without letting on that I knew what they were up to. Effectively, I had to apply for the job while appearing not to know it existed.

Unexpectedly, the first hurdle came when we arrived at the bar and he offered me a drink. The phrase 'no thanks' was on my lips almost before I realised it was a little out of character. For this stage in my rehabilitation, I should be coy and say *Well, I shouldn't,* or I should make it clear that two was my limit, something like that. I shouldn't turn down the offer without a little internal struggle, or a slight suggestion of regret. I'd turned over a new leaf, not become a Puritan.

Truth be told, I don't suppose Daniel would have noticed either way; it was just a reminder to me to watch what I said. It had also taken me a little by surprise that I actually *didn't* feel like a glass of wine. It reminded me of those tests they give you when you go to the opticians. You know the ones, where they flip a little monocle of glass backwards and forwards in front of one eye and then ask, "Better with or without? Now look again. Better with or without?" In the past, my view of the world had always been 'better with' a little alcohol. But now that I wasn't feeling any pain and I had good reasons to want a totally clear head, alcohol seemed like a distraction. I was becoming 'better without'. Fine and all, but it had crept up on me.

"Listen, before I forget," Daniel said when we'd got our drinks, "Tammy's having a party on Saturday and she wondered if you wanted to come. A few people from the project will be there, Seb, Felicity... moi."

Even the new me felt a hint of jealousy when I thought of Daniel and Tammy and the implied chumminess of him doing her inviting for her.

I snuffed out that feeling immediately. Jealousy I could do without; it was corrosive and pointless – especially now that I had enough guts to go after what I wanted. The new me was (I was pretty sure) quite capable of grabbing Daniel by the lapels and saying, 'Forget Tammy, concentrate on me' if that seemed like the thing to do. So why seethe inside when you can just seize what you want? The only question was: what *did* I want?

Cold though it might sound, I didn't need Daniel as anything more than a friend. I'll admit, until recently I've occasionally thought about us becoming more than that – if only I had the guts to do something about it. It was something I'd daydream about from time to time. But that was then; I had other considerations

141

now; I had work to do.

On the other hand I needed Daniel's help and keeping his friendship probably meant keeping his interest. Which meant not letting distractions – like pretty part-time barmaids – absorb too much of his attention. I needed to perform a little adjustment of his attitude here.

"Oh that's such a shame," I said, "I'm probably going to be in London this weekend. I need to take care of some things at the house." It wasn't just an excuse; I was really considering it.

"But you *might* be around?" he asked.

"Well, it's *possible*," I said. Then I looked downcast, put my hand on his arm, and said shyly, "Anyway, you'll have more fun if I'm not there. You know I'm not big on parties. It'll give you a chance to spend some time with Tammy."

He looked a little awkward and had to hunt for his words. After a moment he said, "But I'd much rather you were there. I wouldn't have asked you otherwise."

I made a little bit of eye contact and teased him: "I thought the invitation was from Tammy?" He said nothing and I added, "Well don't have too much fun without me, will you?"

I figured that was enough – a bit of flirting, a bit of guilt-tripping – I doubted anything too irrevocable would be happening this Saturday even if I wasn't around to keep an eye on him. On to other matters.

"Listen," I said, "I wanted to ask you about something."

"Sure," he said, agreeably, sipping his pint.

"So… it's about the project," I said. "I mean, you can see I'm making an effort to do my bit and make up for the, um, horrors of the past. Right?"

He gave a firm nod, which seemed to mean 'absolutely'.

I went on, "I'm not asking for a favour; I don't want to put you in an awkward position. I'm just hoping that if you think I'm doing a good job on the project and that I'm ready to take on a bit more, that you could let the team know. I totally understand that I've got some way to go before I'm considered anyone's first choice, but I'm really trying to do my best not to let anyone down. I just want to make sure someone notices."

"I can tell you," Daniel said, "everyone's noticed."

"Really?" I said, "Well, that makes me feel better. The thing is, though, because I've screwed up in the past, everyone's pretty careful not to give me anything too important to do. And I don't see how I'm going to prove to anyone that I can be reliable until someone trusts me with a challenge."

"Well, I'm sure no one wants to overload you, particularly when you've been through the wars lately," he said.

"No, no, I get that. I do. I'm just saying that when you get to the point where you *personally* think I could handle something more challenging – *if* you get to that point – will you make sure the others know it? That's all I'm asking."

He shook his head, as if to say it wasn't even a question I needed to ask. "Of *course* I will," he said. "In fact I was planning to say something at the meeting tomorrow."

Which was just what I wanted to hear. I thought about driving the point home, but I'd got what I wanted; I should quit while I was ahead.

So with that out of the way and dealt with, we chatted for a little bit longer, mainly about Daniel's work. I was attentive for as long as I could manage, but my attention started to wander after a while. As soon as a decent interval had passed I made the excuse that I was tired and headed back to field station.

In truth, I was trimming back on my sleep at the moment because I had so much to do. It was so easy to do that I was a little appalled with the amount of time I must have wasted in the past, snoozing when I could have been doing something useful. But, since I'd wasted most of the hours I'd spent awake too, I didn't the see the benefit in dwelling on it.

Before I returned to my room, I dropped into the main building. Almost everyone had gone home – which suited me, because I needed to plant my bug. But first, I ducked into the server room and rummaged around in my box'o'bits for a cable. The receiver for the bug was a black metal box about the size of a pack of cards out of which protruded eighteen inches of aerial. I taped it behind a tower server in the corner of the computer room, letting the aerial run up the wall. Then I plugged the audio output of the receiver into the sound card of the computer. Finally, I logged onto that server and downloaded a copy of Wavepad from the net so that I could record, clean up and edit whatever I overheard. Once it was ready I let myself out, locking the door behind me, and went to plant the bug.

I tapped on the Professor's door and got no answer, so I went in. The room was in partial darkness, only a desk lamp was still on and the man himself wasn't around. Quickly I slipped through the far door, down the steps and entered the pitch-black meeting room. I had to feel around for a moment to locate the light switch before I could see anything.

Placement of the bug was going to be tricky. There were two wall sockets, neither of them in great positions if acoustics were your main concern. I selected the far one because it was out of sight unless you were tucked right in that corner. There was a recessed slider on the back of the adaptor/bug and I used a fingernail to drag it to its 'on' position. Once it was plugged in, the bug would be live.

It was an awkward stretch, the table was in the way, and I had to contort a little to reach it. As I stood up again, Susan Milton was coming through the door. "Oh it's you, Jo," she said, obviously expecting the Professor.

What a difference a couple of weeks had made. There was no crescendo of panic inside me, no rabbit-in-the-headlights expression on my face. I was as cool as a bushel of Icelandic cucumbers.

Big smile, to show I was happy to see her (not guilty or surprised – happy). I said, "Oh hi. I'm glad there's someone else around; this place is a bit creepy at night."

She nodded, but didn't depart. She was obviously going to want an explanation for my presence. *Keep it simple*, I thought. "I borrowed the mains adaptor from in here," I said. "Figured I'd better put it back in case Daniel needed to plug his laptop in for another slide show."

"Right," was all she said, not giving much away.

"Anyway, all done," I said cheerfully and breezed past, adding, "G'night."

I headed back to the Fortress of Servitude and hit stop on the recorder's toolbar. I could see from the squiggles on the waveform display that something had been captured. I converted the file to MP3, named it 'Neil Sedaka Live pt1'[1] and plugged my severely-hacked-and-modified iPod into the server in the corner. Then I copied the recording to the player and took a listen. Not bad at all. I could hear myself a lot more clearly than I could hear Susan (and boy, did I sound weird) but everything was intelligible.

With this set-up I could leave the recorder running and transfer it to my iPod later to see what I'd captured. I could even log in remotely, re-direct the audio stream over the network, and eavesdrop live from my dorm room if I wanted.

If I'd done my preparation properly then during tomorrow's

---

[1]   You remember when you learned Venn diagrams in school? Well, in one circle put all the people who are tech-savvy enough to poke around the directories of someone else's iPod. In the other circle put all the people who like Easy Listening music from the Seventies. The overlap of the two circles is called the 'intersection' of the sets. Notice how it's empty.

meeting, the PAC would consider admitting me to their hallowed circle – and I'd be listening in.

Chapter 13

It was a couple of hours before dawn on the day of the PAC meeting and I found I'd had enough sleep already. I boiled my little mini kettle and made some of that weird tea that Ray, the cook, had recommended. It was sort of addictive in a bitter kind of way. But from what I could gather, of all the things in the world with addictive properties, green tea is about the healthiest of them.

I wrapped my quilt around my shoulders, folded my legs underneath me and settled into my armchair to read the final instalment of the PAC documents. Actually it was the final instalment of documents actually *written* by members of the PAC – their collection also included a lot of PDF[1]s of more ancient documents – most of them in languages I didn't speak).

These last few were speculative essays discussing the

---

[1]   Just ignore any jargon words I use that you don't understand. If it matters that you know exactly what I'm talking about then I'll explain it. That said, if you don't know what a PDF is I hope you've got a good reason, like you're Amish or you were born in 1850.

origins of magic. I have to admit that when I first found out what the PAC were into, the thought that most intrigued me was: if magic *did* work, then *how* did it work? Since then, the question had been rather edged out by other considerations and I found that my interest had waned. But I remembered turning the possibilities over in my mind and wondering who else had tackled this question, and whether they'd come up with any possible answers.

And now, for the sake of completeness, I was reading the PAC's thoughts on the subject. I *had* wondered whether the preponderance of history majors in the team would result in a lack of scientific curiosity about the underlying mechanisms of magic. Not so. David Braun, it seemed, had studied engineering, and unsurprisingly that mindset led him to wonder about the rules and origins of magic. Little Daniel too had taken all manner of science-side courses in his time, including some philosophy of science classes. His main interest seemed to be the implications of magic for a universe that ran on science – or vice versa. In other words, either magic was a sort of science or science was a sort of magic – or the universe operated according to two separate sets of rules. That last possibility threatened to blow my mind – and I was pretty sure it was a nonsense scenario. It seemed to me that whatever the rules were that governed our reality, they must be consistent with both magic and technology, because both of those things existed. Medieval peasants might have thought magic was supernatural – beyond nature – but I didn't. Discovering magic had to be the same kind of thing as finding a novel sub-atomic particle, only more so: it was all part of the same puzzle.

So I felt sure that magic must also be good physics at some level. What I couldn't quite get my head around was the question of whether magic could function using just the physics we currently knew about – the four forces, the ever-growing menagerie of particles, the hotly-debated complement of dimensions – or would we find that to explain magic we'd have to discover a whole new field of physics?

Naturally, I couldn't answer that question, but it made me think of Arthur C. Clarke's often-quoted third law of prediction: "Any sufficiently advanced technology is indistinguishable from magic."[1] Turn it around and what it says is that anything that looks like magic must really just be technology that's very advanced. Deep.

Actually I fudged the syllogism there, didn't I? Clarke's law really only says that something that looks like magic *could* just be advanced technology – in other words, it could be science that someone has harnessed to serve a purpose. Logically, the other possibility is that magic is science that doesn't need harnessing; it's just built into the world. Again, deep. Did magic work because human brains had somehow evolved to be remote controls for the hidden forces of nature?

I decided to stop thinking about this stuff and just read. Because my purpose in going over these essays wasn't to unravel the secrets of the universe; I was more interested in any clues they might contain about the PAC, the Army or the all-important Marker.

By the time the sun's first rays were lightening the gloom outside my window I had satisfied myself that there was very little of immediate use to me in any of those papers. So I shucked off the quilt and changed into my running gear.

Two weeks of running, a bit of healthy eating and a complete

---

[1] Do you care what the other two are? Do I? Here they are anyway:

i. When a distinguished but elderly scientist states that something is possible, he is almost certainly right. When he states that something is impossible, he is very probably wrong.

ii. The only way of discovering the limits of the possible is to venture a little way past them into the impossible.

magical overhaul of my physiology had done wonders... although I was still a slightly pudgy twenty-something with chunky thighs and no upper-body strength. But I was in no rush. After a year of this I was sure I'd be in great shape. And who knew how buff I'd be after a couple of hundred years. (Yup, increasingly, everything led back to finding the Marker.)

* * *

Meeting time rolled around soon enough. I hit record on my monitoring software and checked that I was picking up good audio. At this stage of the meeting the noise came mainly from the motion of chairs, papers and mugs of hot caffeine, but I also detected the odd 'hi' and 'excuse me' so I knew the bug was going to do its job.

As the meeting began I listened in for a while, but the first order of business was a yawn. The Procedures and Admin Committee might be a front for a group of occult White Hats, but from time to time they still used it as a forum to discuss actual procedures and admin. I double-checked that my recording set-up was capturing everything and then I set off to put this time to better use.

I wonder if the PAC realised that the one weak point, from an operational-security point of view, about gathering themselves together in a (supposedly) private room, was that it left them exposed elsewhere. Any evil mastermind will tell you that you need henchmen: full-time big, dumb, totally obedient minions who stand around and guard your stuff and keep an eye on the prisoners.

The PAC, on the other hand, were all officers. They didn't have a flunky class who could patrol the perimeter in ill-fitting black jumpsuits while the higher-ups strategised. They probably thought it would be impolite to treat someone like a second-class citizen and exclude them from meetings by having them do the gruntwork. Man, evil gets all the breaks.

So, blessed as I was these days with bucketloads of icy sang-froid, I dropped into Susan Milton's office and poked around among her things for a while. In my hot little mitt I clutched an anti-virus install disk – my excuse for sitting at her desk in front of her computer should anyone come in. And it was a bust. Of course I didn't really need to be in the room to work on (or spy on) her computer – I could do that from afar – this visit was about physical items of interest: PAC-related paperwork, maps with Xs on them, glowing amulets, etc; None of which I found.

I retreated. Then I screwed my courage to the next highest sticking point and ventured into the Professor's office. For a moment I considered having a proper nose around. But in the corridor outside I could hear other people in the team passing the door. Plus, you never knew when someone in the PAC meeting might nip out for a comfort break. The chances of detection were a little too high. Undoubtedly I could bluff my way out of any awkward encounters but it didn't seem worth the risk. I'd be better off coming back at night.

So I withdrew, opting to bide my time. Maybe I hadn't learned anything from my physical snooping, but in the meantime my bug would have recorded around three-quarters of an hour of the PAC's cloak-and-dagger conspiring. (At least I hoped it was cloak-and-dagger; I didn't have much use for a recording of the fierce debate over personal use of the photocopier.)

About then a growl from my stomach interrupted me, so I made a detour via the refectory, on my way back to the server room. I grabbed a plastic carton of what I hoped was a tuna salad, plus a bottle of water, and waited for Ray to finish what he was doing so he could take my money.

Then a strange thing happened.

Blondy, who I think I decided was really called Felicity, was in there reading a dry-looking book and sipping from a steaming plastic cup of what appeared to be hot water. Did thin girls really drink hot water? No wonder they were so grumpy.

Anyway, I paid and started to walk out. Felicity looked up as I passed her, caught my eye and beamed me a smile. And what a smile it was. I vaguely remembered hearing that she was into girls – or was that Theresa? – anyway, the look she gave me definitely registered, even on my low-powered, straight-person's gaydar. Not that I cared what she did to amuse herself, but what unnerved me was the smokingly coy look I'd given her in response. Oh. My. God. I hurried out of there.

I'd as soon not talk about this, but the fact is that what with my bouts of depression, the anti-depressants to tackle the depression, a head full of neuroses and the black hole where my self-esteem should be, I pretty much had the libido of a bonsai tree. If a nice-looking guy smiled at me, I'd freeze. Or so I always imagined. I couldn't remember it happening in reality. Anyway, Felicity had checked me out and I'd fired back a smouldering look of barely disguised interest. WTF.

Was it possible that as my libido thawed after years in suspended animation I'd discover that I was gay? What was I, living in a soap opera?

I realised that for the first time since the dream, and my big decision not to follow in my mother's footsteps, I was freaking out. For a moment I was in danger of dropping my salad[1]. I took a deep breath and shut down this cacophony of thoughts. A momentary echo of the ice dream flashed into my mind and I focussed on the untroubled cool of that scene. Calm. I was calm again.

I'd think about this some other time, but I couldn't help considering what would surely be the *ultimate* talk-show

---

[1]   That sounds like a euphemism for something but it isn't

question: did magic make you gay? Or maybe just into girls, whatever biological equipment you happened to be fitted with. Was that why adepts were 99% men? Was that why the church got such a kick out of burning witches – they were really burning ungodly lesbians? There was obviously more going on here than I'd prepared myself for and it made me wonder if I was the only one who'd experienced this, ahem, side-effect.

I mean I'd been there in that barn, and if Susan Milton had come over all SSO[1], she was hiding it magnificently well. Which meant there was a pretty good chance that this had nothing to do with magic-use. Gulp.

Anyway, I put all that out of my mind. Since I wasn't actually having any sex, what did it matter what kind I wasn't having? The Catholic church and I would have to agree to differ on that point.

Thankfully, I'd put my little panic behind me by the time I sat down behind the main console in the server room. My spring-cleaned psyche seemed to find its way back to equilibrium so much quicker than in the old days. And when I put something out of my mind, it actually worked. My focus was now on the record of the PAC meeting. I had fifty minutes of audio to listen to and I began hopping through it in one-minute increments, searching for the end of the admin chatter and the beginning of the secret-squirrel stuff.

I had to jump forwards nearly half an hour before I heard Susan say, "OK. I think we can move onto the next section. Daniel, there was something you wanted to say before we get on to Theresa's update?"

That sounded good. Chances are it would be about me. I hadn't been certain that Daniel would be direct in his methods, but I was pretty confident that he'd find *some* way to champion

---

[1]   Same-sex oriented.

my cause. He wasn't exactly a bulldog, so I thought he might opt to have one or more quiet one-to-ones with other members of the team, but here he was having requested a slot on the meeting's agenda.

He cleared his throat and said, "Thanks. If it's alright with everyone, I want to say something about Jo Hallett. And I want to make a suggestion, even though I reckon there'll be some fairly strong reactions."

He went on, "You all know that Jo and I are friends, which maybe means I'm prejudiced. But it also means I know her pretty well. If you've worked with her then you know that she's one of the most intelligent people around. You also know that she lost her mother when she was younger and she's not had a very stable upbringing. That doesn't sound great, I know, but I don't think it should put us off either. What I've got in mind is that we should think about bringing her into this group.

"I reckon if it was just a question of her abilities, there'd be no problem. She's just unbelievably clever and she has a ton of knowledge on all sorts of useful subjects. And a lot of what she knows is in areas where this group isn't especially strong. Not only that, but they're areas we *ought* to be strong in." He paused a moment. "The downside is that in the past Jo's been… well… unreliable, difficult and touchy. To be honest, she can be a real pain to work with, but lately she's put in a huge effort to improve. Personally I think right now she's as sorted out and together as she's ever been. I'd say she's at least as together as I am," he laughed, but no one else joined him.

He went on, "I know some of you might need a bit of persuading, but I think Jo would help a lot more than she'd hinder. And if we don't choose *her* then we need to look for someone else with the same skills… and I'd rather take someone I know and that the Professor knows – even though she has problems. With a stranger we'd have no idea what we were getting."

There was a lengthy pause, and I guessed that eyes had turned towards the Professor because he started to speak. "It's *true*..." he said hesitantly, "Jo has put in an absolutely heroic effort of late. And bear in mind that she's not tackling the most rewarding of assignments currently. I've withheld from her some of the more fulfilling tasks, largely to see how she fared when she had only her own work ethic to sustain her. And I have to say that she has distinguished herself. But I also have to say, her improvement comes hot on the heels of some very conspicuous low points."

Daniel, bless him, jumped in: "But Professor, you know she always struggles around the anniversary of her mother's death."

I hadn't realised that Daniel knew the date my mother had died. And if I was worse around that time then *I* hadn't spotted it. Nice job Daniel. That, and the unexpectedly strong case he was making on my behalf had really surprised me – you know, in a good way.

Daniel went on, "Now that that's passed, she's really settled down." He cleared his throat. "I understand she recently found out a few things she hadn't known about her mother and they knocked the wind out of her for a bit, but I think overall she's better for it. I think it's helped her get over some of her bad experiences. I mean, you all must have seen how hard she's trying now."

There were a few seconds of quiet and then Susan spoke.

"Daniel," she said, and just from the way she said his name I knew this wasn't going to be good news. "I know she's your friend and I don't mean to insult her, but to be frank, Jo's a disaster area when it comes to responsibilities. It might not be her *fault*, but that doesn't change the fact. And from what I can tell, she's always been a disaster area. I'd have serious misgivings about taking her on even in her *current* capacity, now that I've had a chance to be around her. I'm certainly not about to trust my life to her – and that's what membership of this group means. We all trust each other with our lives and I think you all know that's not an exaggeration. Jo might have some skills the team needs, but she'd also be its biggest liability – right from day one. I'm sorry to be harsh, Daniel, but she spends most of her free time so drunk she wouldn't know what she was saying or to whom. And the things this group knows aren't just about trust; they're also about how well you can carry a burden. We can't place the weight of the world on the shoulders of a girl whose idea of an impossible challenge is starting work on time."

Well that was that. I couldn't see anyone supporting Daniel's suggestion now that Susan had taken a wrecking ball to the idea. The Professor had clearly had his reservations even before she spoke. And I didn't expect Daniel to be able to mount a defence against someone as forceful and sure of herself as Ms. Milton.

But once again Daniel surprised me. "Hold on, though," he said. "I'm not disputing what you're saying, although I don't think Jo's problems are as bad as you make out. But maybe there's a way to compromise. I agree with you that being in this group is about trust, and handling the responsibility, as well as having the right skills. But that's also true of anyone else we bring in instead of Jo. They'll need to somehow prove themselves because to start with we won't be sure of them. We won't know how they'll cope or whether they're going to let us down. So if we want to get someone with Jo's skills we're going to have to put that person through a probation period before we make a final decision on them. Well, why not give the same chance to Jo?

He pressed on before anyone could cut in: "On the down-side, we know she's been flakey in the past, but on the up-side, in a sense she's already one of us. The Professor, if you'll excuse me pointing this out, has done more for Jo than her own father ever has. If she's loyal to anyone, it's to the Professor – and to me. With an outsider we'd have to figure out their loyalties and we'd have to hope they didn't blab about us to whoever they share their secrets with. Well, in Jo's case, I'm pretty sure the two people she's closest to in the world are already in the group. I think if a total stranger can have a trial period, a probation, then Jo deserves one too."

Damn. Nice recovery. Daniel was on tip-top form today. I'd been hoping things would go a lot more smoothly than they had, but Daniel appeared to have hauled my figurative ass out of the fire.

I listened to the debate for a few minutes more. David Braun spoke up and said that he didn't know me, but he trusted Daniel's judgement and that a probation sounded pretty reasonable to him – if they could figure out how to test me without trusting me with the whole enchilada (or kit and caboodle as he put it).

Then Theresa chimed in and said, "I'm sorry Daniel; I know you like her and you think she's a good egg underneath it all, and I know you're close to her Professor, but for my money Jo Hallett is poison. She might not mean to be but she can't help it. I agree she's a genius, but as a human being she's a nightmare. She'll be trouble from the word go."

Several people tried to respond to that, including a slightly shrill-sounding Daniel, but the Professor won out. "Dear boy," he said, and I understood that he meant Daniel, "don't concern yourself; you'll have a chance to speak. But let me see if I can save you the trouble."

In his best may-it-please-the-court voice the Professor said, "Theresa, can I ask, is it your opinion that Jo would let us down at the earliest opportunity, or thereabouts?"

Sounding awkward, Theresa said, "I'm not being mean about her. If anything I feel sorry for her, but that doesn't mean I want to trust her with my life."

The Professer persisted, "But you don't think she'd be able to acquit herself satisfactorily for any extended period of time?"

"No," Theresa said.

I could now see where the Professor was going with this. He went on, "So if we *did* allow her a trial period to prove herself, provided that it was of reasonable duration, you'd be confident that she'd make a hash of it?"

"I suppose," Theresa agreed.

"So, although you'd be averse to her joining the group, you wouldn't actually be averse to allowing her a trial period," he asked, his voice calm and intelligent, like a trial lawyer lining up a key witness.

If Theresa disagreed, I couldn't hear any evidence of it. The Professor was almost at his summing up now. "And do you feel the same, Susan?"

She replied, "I can't say that I'm delighted at the idea, but I can't think of a good reason to deny her a shot – provided we're careful about what information we share. However, I wouldn't want her to join the group *automatically* even if she somehow survives the probation period without screwing up."

"Fair enough, I should say," the Professor agreed. "Does *anyone* object to the idea of a probationary period?"

After a pause, which I took to contain both silent agreement and unvoiced resignation, he said, "Very well. And how long should it run for?"

There was some horse-trading and some unhappiness on both sides of the matter, but the discussion remained remarkably grown-up. And from Daniel's continued silence I concluded that the Professor had guessed his thoughts correctly – and probably handled the matter with a little more deftness than Daniel could have brought to bear.

When everyone had been heard from, the probation period had been talked down from six months to two. Whether that decrease was a triumph for the Professor's and Daniel's confidence in me, or Susan's and Theresa's certainty that I'd screw up quickly, I couldn't say.

Unfortunately, two months was still a hell of a long time to twiddle my thumbs for. I could do it if I had to – behaving myself wasn't much of a challenge any more – but that time could be put to much better use. Jumping through training hoops for the PAC was certainly not the most productive thing I could be doing.

I decided I'd take no action of my own until I heard the exact terms of the probation and discovered what kinds of tasks they were going to test me with, but in the meantime I'd cover my bases by coming up with a plan of my own – a plan for recovering the Marker without their help or their permission.

If I was able to secure the Marker and the group still excluded me, they'd be sabotaging their own plans. And possession of the Marker would make my probation period irrelevant.

In fact, if I had the Marker, I had to wonder whether the PAC didn't become a little bit irrelevant too.

Chapter 14

It was two days after the PAC meeting and I was finally due to have a proper meeting with the Professor late that afternoon. The previous day he'd come over to talk to me as I sat in the refectory during the afternoon tea break. I was in nerd-heaven reading a book on wifi security written by three wily Russian dudes. Not exactly Anna Karenina, I'll grant you, but likely to do me more good in the short-term.

When the Professor said he wanted to see me, he hinted that he had something important to talk over besides the usual chit-chat about current and future chores. Three guesses what that was about. We set a time and then he went on to say something about the team's plans for the Christmas holidays. As I sat looking up at him, my mind wandered away from what he was saying and a random detail that had been tickling at my subconscious for some time finally clicked into place. I realised I should have worked it out at least two weeks ago.

See, I was thinking about the health problems the Professor had had. I'd known for a number of years that he had some sort of illness, but when I met up with him about eighteen months ago,

I remember being shocked at his deterioration. I had dropped in to see him at his home in Cambridge – this was before the field station project had even been mooted – and when he came to the door he looked like a ghost. His skin was nearly translucent and his cheek bones bulged like hip joints beneath his thin flesh. In a weird way, he looked more alive than he had for a while and there was a superficial improvement in his appearance: the lines were less visible and his complexion was unblemished, glowing almost. But it was an unnatural sort of vigour. The disease was thriving, not him. The changes resembled good health about as well as a bruise resembles a tan.

He was reluctant to talk about it, but I suppose there wasn't much to say. I could tell it was bad – but I didn't feel I could push him to say more than he wanted to. So we talked about me.

Gradually, though, his mood lightened and I began to suspect that I'd dropped in at a particularly low moment, because over the course of half an hour, the sense of weary resignation had completely left him and he became as perky as ever. By the time I left, I wondered if things could really be as bad as I'd initially thought.

He'd been busy for the next couple of months – and I knew part of that time was spent receiving treatment for his condition. And then he decided to get away for a while, to recuperate down in Cornwall. (I knew now that he'd gone down there during the business with Jan and the Marker.) When I was next in the UK, he happened to be on a flying visit to Cambridge, tying up loose ends, having decided to relocate to Cornwall permanently, and we met up for lunch.

He was transformed – a new man – and almost giddy with his new lease of life. He announced that despite ominously long odds, his treatment had been a great success and he was free of cancer for the first time in years.

That was the only time he put a name to his condition, but I'd guessed anyway. Looking back on it now I can imagine what lay behind his miracle recovery. He had obviously discovered the same wellspring of health that I had.

Try as I might, I couldn't picture the Professor using any of the other magical abilities besides Healing. But my imagination conjured an image of him sitting in the back parlour of his Cambridge cottage. Having bolted the door, I could see him settling into an armchair, his eyes closed and gold twinkling at his temples. In my imagination, his head was still covered in fine, slightly unruly white hair. The man who stood in front of me now, though, had not a single hair on his head.

He'd told me that his treatment had caused his hair to fall out and that his doctor wasn't surprised when it declined to grow back. And that was the detail which now resolved itself in my mind. His hair *hadn't* fallen out, I realised. He had shaved it off and continued to do so – his eyebrows too, though I hadn't noticed before. Why? Well, I was pretty sure I knew the answer to that: because his hair wasn't grey any longer.

In fact, I reckoned he was probably rationing his use of Healing in order to keep his appearance broadly consistent with a man of his supposed years. (I realised I never *had* known his exact age). He looked a vigorous seventy, just as he had when I'd been growing up.

Thinking about it, moving to Cornwall had made sense for Susan Milton, and to a lesser extent David Braun. The assassin Karst had seen Susan's face and perhaps David's when she had arrived to dispatch her ex-colleague Jan. But the Professor too had a reason to get away. He looked like a man barely out of his sixties when I was reasonably sure he was actually well into his eighties – and that disparity would only get more noticeable. Coming to magic so late in life, he'd never possess that vastly extended youthfulness of the lifelong adept, but I suspected the Professor would still look a year or two off retirement age on his hundredth birthday – assuming no calamities befell him before then.

How weird must this last year have been for the Professor? From what I could gather, magic use hadn't changed David or Susan very much – at least physically. Even if they'd been twenty years older the change would have simply been a matter of degree; but a dying man in his eighties who suddenly found the years rolling back towards his youth would have a great deal more to adjust to.

A few weeks back, at the height of my floundering and flailing, I'd been shocked when the Professor had lost his temper with me over my various failings. Sure, he'd had ample reason, but it was out of character for him, not just in our relationship, but for his behaviour in general. But then he was a man coming back to life. It was no surprise that his temper flared more suddenly and burned hotter than it had for years and that it sometimes got the better of him. Everything would seem more real, more immediate. I wondered if he chafed at having to act older than he felt.

I caught myself envying him, but for the life of me I couldn't think why. I had every advantage, every opportunity that he had – and more besides – so it was a strange thing to think.

I tuned back in again, just in time to catch the gist of what he was saying. They were closing the field station for ten days over the Christmas period, so wherever I was going to be then, it wasn't here. Perhaps I should surprise my father on whichever resort island – and with whichever woman – he was spending the holidays? Hmmm, I think not.

After tea break was over, I got back to work. These days I was spending more time in among the researchers and less time in the server room. Partly that was because I was taking an interest in what they were up to, partly that since I wasn't dodging work I didn't need to hide away so much – and partly it turns out that not being afraid of people had suddenly made total solitude less appealing. Besides, a person could log into any computer from any other computer, so being cooped up with the servers was more of an excuse than a necessity for most tasks.

When I was done for the day, I headed back to my room. Shipshape as it now was, there was still some residual clutter that needed lobbing overboard. I'd finally managed to get all my correspondence and financial paperwork sorted out. I couldn't pretend that my finances themselves were in very good shape, but at least I had a picture of what was going on. High on my list of non-magic-related chores was to schedule in a butt-kicking trip to London to put my deadbeat lodger, Noola, firmly in her place. Most of my net worth was tied up in that house and it needed to start generating an income for me. Immediately.

Here too, I reckoned that not being afraid of people was going to make a difference. Noola wouldn't really stand a chance. And if she gave me a hard time I could always break every bone in her body with the force of my mind. You know, not that I would of course. But there was nothing quite like knowing you could snuff a person out like a gnat to put you at your ease with them.

Anyway, on the clutter-removal front, I finished separating out all the odds and ends I wanted to get rid of into a big cardboard box. Then I began the hassle of dragging it out to the dumpsters behind the dorm block. Fortunately for me, I encountered Daniel as I was half way down the stairs and he offered to help.

The box wasn't that heavy, but it was bigger than you could get your arms around, so two pairs of hands made the task a lot more manageable.

"Any news on your plans for the weekend?" he asked, walking carefully, one step at a time, backwards down the stairs.

"I think I really need to spend a weekend in London," I said. And since the truth wasn't a problem here, I added, "I haven't had any rent for a few months now and I'm pretty much broke. I need to get something sorted out."

He looked disappointed, but he nodded. "So what's in the box?" he asked.

"Oh, just junk. The landfill needs this stuff a lot more than I do," I said.

"Right," he nodded. "This is one of the boxes that your…" I knew the next word he was going to say was 'Mother's' but he made a last second substitution. "…delivery came in."

"Like I say, the landfill needs it more."

"Sure, sure," he said, anxious not to ruffle my feathers even though I could see he was working up to attempt just that. "You're not going to throw all your mother's things away though, are you?" He was trying to sound reasonable, conversational, lighthearted.

Wow, it was so nice not being crazy any more. Instead of flying into a hissy fit, I shrugged (as best I could while carrying something heavy) and said, "Some of this is my junk, not hers. But, you know, I don't need this stuff and she won't be coming back for it." Hmmm, that came out a little darker than I'd intended. Maybe I wasn't *totally* cured. On the other hand, I wouldn't have *attempted* this conversation three weeks ago; we'd have been knee deep in wailing and used Kleenexes by now.

"I guess not," he said, sounding like there was still some doubt about it. "But, you know, we could just as easily take this down to the barn and stick it with the rest of the boxes. If you suddenly remember you dropped your passport in here, you won't have to mount an archaeological dig to get it back. Plenty of time to throw things away later."

"Thanks, Daniel, but this isn't really a spur of the moment thing. I'm not doing this because I'm all worked up; I'm just clearing some space in my room," I said.

"Not emotionally distraught. Got it," he confirmed.

"You could even see this as healthy," I said, as we reversed through the fire door and out into the late autumn chill. The sun had set and a dim light the colour of hot coals was all that remained. Whether Daniel was convinced or not, he let it go, silently carrying his end of the box all the way round to the little dumpster corral.

We manhandled the box into the maw of the nearest giant bin and then walked back towards the dorm-room entrance. "I'm actually heading back to the project building," Daniel said as we turned the corner. "I'll see you later."

Going off to brood, by the looks of things, I thought. Still, not really my problem.

I scooted back inside, happy to get out of the cold. Originally my plan for this evening was going to involve putting in a little preparation for tomorrow's meeting with the Professor. He was going to ask me to do something related to the PAC, but something sufficiently tangential that it didn't let too many cats out of their bags regarding the PAC's true mission. I'd intended to get a head start on whatever it was tonight, before being asked, but I found that my espionage skills hadn't been quite up to the job of discovering my assignment ahead of time.

When I'd reviewed the recording of the PAC meeting, I was expecting to hear them decide what my first, probationary penance should be. What I'd heard instead was an agreement between Susan and the Professor to discuss it after the meeting… in the Professor's office. Which was a pain because I hadn't bugged his office. I hadn't even purchased a second bug just in case I needed it. Very poor.

Anyway, since I couldn't prepare for tomorrow, I had an evening free. I spent it writing an anonymizer: a chunk of software that an Internet sleuth (like myself) could hide behind. When I was online, searching for clues to the Marker's whereabouts, I didn't want the Army tracing my location – assuming they were out there.

I was going to set up the anonymizer on some free webspace I had my eye on, hosted out of Taiwan. From what I could gather it was run by asylum-seeking Chinese anarchists, who I was pretty sure wouldn't be sharing their records with anyone. So that's where my Internet trail would dead-end.

But just in case someone got through that, I had another trick in mind. Lots of people connect to the Internet over wireless links these days and most apartment buildings are full of these wi-fi signals. What you might not know is that there are people who cruise around mapping all these signals and logging their findings online. Thanks to them, I'd found two Internet connections in the same building – an apartment block in Capetown, as it happened – and neither of them had changed any of the security settings from their defaults. I was going to hijack one wireless base station and use it to connect to the other. Anyone who traced my activities back to South Africa would find a wireless point in someone's apartment and assume I was somewhere nearby, using my laptop to log in.

By midnight it was all ready. All I needed now was a target. But that was a job for another time. I called it a night, cleared my mind and was asleep in minutes.

Faded azure sea-ice filled my dreams and some time in the night the unending icescape gave way to flickering images and whispers of conversation that when I awoke I couldn't recall properly. But neither could I get them out of my head for some hours.

Chapter 15

The Professor was talking. "I'm sure you have many questions and I'll answer them all... eventually. For now there are some explanations that I would rather postpone." He gave me a moment to digest that and went on, "If that's not acceptable to you, or you're uncomfortable with a request of this nature then you should say so. I'll drop the matter and we'll say no more about it."

Necessarily, I was playing the fool, not letting on what I knew. Mind you, I only had the half the picture, so it was only partly play-acting. I asked, "Isn't this a matter for the police? I don't want to get in their way."

He explained, "They are no longer actively pursuing the matter. You have to understand that while the stolen documents were of enormous interest to us, they were not especially valuable in monetary terms. Quite simply, the police have better things to do than hunt for our missing paperwork. Their main interest in this case was resolved when the criminal behind the robbery met his end. The evidence relating to the crime led to him and so the enquiry died with him. They have no leads on finding his associates and I suspect they place criminals killing their own quite low down on their list of crimes which must be stamped out."

"Yes, but why would a gang of criminals steal documents that only academics put any value on?" I was almost enjoying asking questions that I knew the Professor couldn't give truthful answers to.

"Ahem, well, um…" he said, clearly collecting his thoughts. "They might have stolen the collection in error. Those documents were housed in the same building as various objects of quite considerable value. And they couldn't be expected to hand the collection back once they realised their mistake."

"No," I agreed, "they'd most likely just destroy them all. Wouldn't they? Do we have a reason to think they didn't?"

Again he took a moment to construct a reply. "Quite. But we aren't searching based on the probability that they *did* destroy the collection; we're searching on the *possibility* that they didn't." He went on, "And anyone interested enough to steal items of historical interest might show some reluctance in destroying them. Flawed though the theft might have been, an expert was certainly involved, and it's difficult to imagine an expert who doesn't have some attachment to his subject matter."

Not a bad piece of yarn-spinning, really, for someone thinking on their feet. The Professor was a halfway reasonable liar when he wanted to be, though his delivery could use some polish.

"OK, Professor. It certainly sounds like a challenge; I'll find out what I can," I said.

He held up his hand and looked positively grave as he said, "The most important point I must impress upon you is the need to avoid attracting unwanted attention. I know you are exceedingly knowledgeable in these matters, so I'll leave it to your judgement. But before you begin I would like you to estimate the risks of inadvertently alerting any remaining members of the gang to our presence. If you don't think you can do this *in silenzio*, I would ask you not to undertake it at all. A determination from you that it is unsafe to proceed would be even more useful to the team than the successful recovery of the collection. I say that because ensuring the safety of everyone concerned is our highest priority here."

He went on, "We must assume that the criminals have computer experts of their own who may very well be lying in wait, so to speak. I previously asked Daniel to explore our options in this matter and his conclusion was that we should leave well alone. He believed that someone *out there...*" he waved his hands vaguely, presumably to indicate the Internet, "was keeping electronic watch. He felt it would be exceedingly difficult to uncover any useful information without coming under scrutiny. He said that it was best abandoned completely... unless we could enlist *you* to handle the matter. He has an opinion of your skills that borders on the reverential, and I'm prepared to take his word for it."

I nodded slowly, to show that I appreciated the gravity of what I was getting into. "I understand, Professor. I'll be extremely careful. I have a couple of ideas for concealing myself that, to the best of my knowledge, have never been penetrated by anyone."

The Professor obviously wanted to spread it on thick. He added, "The initial loss of the collection and the events surrounding it were notable for the sheer number of violent attacks, and even deaths, that occurred. These are tenacious and ruthless people whose attention we must not attract. I would rather not spend my twilight years hiding in the Falkland Islands disguised as a sheep farmer. Discretion, caution, stealth – please let these be your watchwords."

"Hey, it'll be me on that island too, if I screw things up," I said. "Just me and the sheep. And some annoying old farmer constantly muttering 'I told you so'."

"Well, it sounds like we have a meeting of minds, then," the Professor said, with the flicker of a smile.

"Yup. I would like a little time to work on this, though. The better I prepare, the more invisible I can make myself. I'd like two weeks to get ready, if that's OK. There are programs I need to write," I said, adding, "I'll still be able to get some of my regular project work done, but this thing will need a reasonable chunk of time if I'm going to do it properly."

He pursed his lips thoughtfully. "A fortnight sounds acceptable. Are there any other resources you will need? Any assistance?"

Thank you for asking. "Well, there are some bits and pieces back in London that would make the job easier. Plus they have computer stores there..." I spread my hands to indicate the lack of such things here in Cow Country.

He was considering it. I went on, "It makes the job easier, plus it's one more level of security. It's harder to trace anyone in a big city and it gets the focus away from the project. If anonymity is our big thing, we don't really want to attempt this using the only high-speed Internet connection for miles around."

"And you'll give me updates on how it's going?" he asked. He was clearly leaning towards saying 'yes'.

"Why don't I phone you at six pm each day? Just to check in," I suggested. "You can keep me up to date with all the gossip."

"Well, it *would* give us a chance to discuss the latest celebrity indiscretions," he said thoughtfully. He'd obviously made up his mind and had moved on to the sarcastic part of the conversation.

"Ex*actly*," I enthused. "If it's alright with you, I'll head to London on Saturday morning and use the weekend to take care of some personal things. I'll get to work on Monday and call you that evening."

He nodded agreeably. Which, I reckoned, concluded our

discussion. I said 'Adios' and left him to it. My next stop was my dorm room to get my coat. It was still a few minutes before sunset and I wanted to get out and go for a walk. I had some thinking to do… among other things.

I wandered up the lane, flexing my fingers to keep them warm and stamping my feet. I was thinking about the assignment I'd been set and how it tied into the overall situation with the Marker. The Professor and Susan had made an interesting choice for my first probationary task. They had asked me to track down the collection of documents that Jan had stolen from Susan's old workplace –which had subsequently been swiped by Karst, once she'd dealt with Jan. The documents were presumably in the possession of whoever had taken over from Alessandro Dass as local big cheese of the Army – quite possibly Karst herself, if Susan's recollection of her tailoring was any indication of her status.

But this wasn't really about the collection. After all, I knew that the PAC had an electronic copy of the entire collection. No, this was about spying on Dass's organisation: the Army Who Witnessed Creation. The Professor needed a way to make an investigation like that seem psuedo-legitimate, so he'd invented an academic angle to all this. He'd admitted that the Procedures and Admin Committee were up to something – Daniel must have told him that I suspected as much – but he hadn't admitted what it was yet. Instead, he'd asked me to do something very unorthodox which nevertheless maintained the fiction that this all related, however indirectly, to an academic project.

In his version of what had happened to the collection, the Professor had allowed the lines to blur between Dass's organisation and their rogue alumni, Jan. In his version, a gang had stolen the collection, and in an internal squabble a couple of gang members had been killed, including the mastermind behind the robbery. This implied that someone else was in charge now. He was letting me think that I was investigating the people behind the robbery, when the truth was that the thief, Jan, and those who killed him were working against each other.

And naturally there'd been no mention of magic or the Marker in his version of events.

From reading the PAC's secrets, I knew what had really happened – that Jan had stolen the Marker from Dass and then taken the instructions for its use from the museum Susan was working in; he'd also killed Dass in the process. Then Dass's agent, Karst, had killed Jan and taken the collection away with her. The Marker remained wherever Jan had hidden it. Or so we assumed.

It was possible that the Army had already discovered its hiding place and retrieved it. We wouldn't necessarily know if they had. But we knew they'd looked pretty hard for it in the months after Jan's death. Daniel thought they were still looking.

Of course, maybe they were just being tidy-minded, but it seemed more likely that they were still hunting for it in earnest. The PAC believed the Army were also lying in wait, in case someone else made a grab for the Marker. If some third party found it, the Army could swoop in and take it from them. If they failed, the Army could still swoop in – to interrogate them and find out what they knew. And I *really* didn't want to be someone the Army tried to prise information out of.

I wondered, did the Army think some accomplice of Jan's might try to retrieve the Marker? We were fairly sure that Jan had acted alone.

Or maybe the Army were specifically looking for the man and woman Karst had glimpsed that night in the church. She'd seen two injured people who weren't Connected, who weren't wearing gold, and she'd ignored them. They were just civilians who'd got in Jan's way. But if she hadn't given them much thought at the time, you can bet that her attitude had changed once the Army's other lines of enquiry had dried up. By now I was fairly sure that Karst wished she'd asked to see some IDs before leaving that night.

But the Professor mentioned none of that. He was hiding one search inside another and so would I. Hunting for the collection was his way of having me spy on the Army – but I'd use the investigation as cover to look for the Marker itself – though I wouldn't neglect the Professor's assignment completely. If I got anywhere *near* the Marker, I'd certainly want to know what its previous owners were up to and whether they were right behind me. So I'd spy on the Army *and* look for the Marker – and, fortunately, I could use the same technology for both.

Relocating to London was an added bonus. I wouldn't have to hide what I was up to from those around me, plus I could sort out the lodger situation while I was at it. And there was one more advantage: I wasn't planning to limit myself to Internet sleuthing when it came to finding the Marker. If I unearthed any clues as to its whereabouts, I was going to follow them up. In person.

If the Professor thought it was dangerous trying to track Dass's people online, he'd be horrified at the thought of me risking their wrath face to face. Three weeks ago, I couldn't tell a lie about a late subscription without panicking; now I was planning to get between a society of ancient killers and their most precious possession. I supposed it was as good a way as any to find out how much progress I'd really made since then.

Chapter 16

London. They say when a man is tired of London, he's also tired of quotations about London.

I got the "fast" train back to Paddington station, caught the languorously torpid Bakerloo line down to Waterloo and changed onto the Northern Line. My house was near Stockwell tube station in an area I'd selected as being up-and-coming. Unfortunately that was four years ago and it still had just as far to up-and-come. Stockwell needed to pull its finger out.

There was a big cheery sign just outside the exit of the tube station informing travellers that they were now in a high-crime area where muggings were routine. Which was nice. If I remembered correctly, this was also the place where the Met had first implemented its shoot-to-kill policy concerning Brazilian electricians[1]. Clearly I wasn't about to sell up and make a profit any time soon.

My route took me away from the main road and into the

_____

[1] If you're reading this in, like, the year 2255, ask your talking computron to find the relevant Old Earth news story.

warren of side streets and cul-de-sacs beyond. The quickest way to cover the last few hundred yards to the house was to cut through an alleyway linking two streets. It ran behind a disused warehouse and it was dingy, and frequently smelled appalling – but sticking to the sun-lit streets added five minutes to the walk. I was dragging my huge roller suitcase and I didn't want to haul it one foot further than I had to.

The bag's wheels sounded especially loud as they rumbled and crackled over the grit of the path as I turned into the secluded alleyway. I was struck by how isolated you could feel in the middle of the city if you found the right (or maybe the wrong) spot.

Halfway down its length, where you couldn't see what was up ahead because the path detoured around the metal fence-stakes of an electricity sub-station, I heard something: a human sound I couldn't identify. I looked around and saw no one.

To the left, ahead of me, a set of iron stairs ran up to the warehouse's boarded-over rear firedoor. Beneath the open treads of the heavy steps, the gloom was all but impenetrable... until I suddenly realised that a man was hiding in the shadows there. Despite my newfound steeliness, my heart gave a little thump of alarm. (I suppose it's possible that even the steeliest of folk benefit from a little shot of adrenaline from time to time.)

I kept walking, my gaze flicking between the path ahead and the half-seen figure in the shadows. As I drew level I got a better look at him in the feeble, slatted light penetrating the ironwork of the stairs. He was sitting on the ground, legs out in front, his back propped against brickwork that was furry with mould and grime. He had on greasy black jeans and a filthy, punk-style angora sweater hitched up at the waist exposing a triangle of pallid abdomen. He looked like the day-old corpse of a homeless Ramones fan. He had slipped one ghostly pale arm completely out of the sweater and stretched it out by his side – a syringe hung by its needle from the flesh.

For a moment, I wondered if he was even alive – whether a good Samaritan should maybe call an ambulance for him. But then a feeling of disgust welled up in me and I was neither afraid of him nor concerned for his wellbeing. I'd seen human refuse like him all my life and they never changed. They were parasites and that was how they deserved to be treated. If he was still there the next time I came this way I might put him out of his misery myself.

I kept moving, and just before he was lost to sight I saw him move and a sound like a hiss came from his lips. I realised his eyes were open and he was staring at me. The look was unwavering, predatory, malevolent. I had to admit that if I was going to encounter him like this, with my 'tribute' buried in my bag, it was probably a good thing that he was incapacitated: laid out by the heroin, and unable to pursue me.

A moment later I laughed quietly at my own cowardice. I didn't need magic to handle a hundred and ten pounds of busted veins and opium-addiction.

She hadn't been specific, but my shrewd deductive mind reckoned it was a fair bet that *this* was where Noola had been robbed. She'd been coming home from a night out, probably late in the evening. And in my experience, junkie-predators like this one tended to keep vampire hours, so pub closing time fell squarely within their working day.

They also tended to find themselves at least one partner in crime, it being difficult to mug healthy members of the public when your body has to extract most of its usable calories from poppy juice.

In summary, this would be a good spot to avoid once the sun went down.

I was glad of the fresh air and the light when I emerged into daylight on the other side of the alleyway.

Moments later I reached the house and let myself in. All was quiet and the living room was empty (though I noted three ashtrays that were full – not bad going if only one person was living here). I dragged my case up three flights of stairs and unlocked the door that led to the top floor, which was my private part of the house. Nothing seemed to have been disturbed, though the place was a little musty. I pushed up one of the elderly sash windows, letting in the distant traffic sounds of South London, and a hint of a breeze. Then I changed into old clothes and got busy.

By five in the afternoon, when I heard the front door open and close, I had done the unthinkable: I'd cleaned, vacuumed and tidied. The place hadn't been in a *really* horrible condition, but neither was it very well looked after. In fact, if I hadn't lived most of my life with the domestic instincts of a dung beetle, I'd have probably been more disgusted with Noola's housekeeping than I was. What was weird was that even in the old days I'd never liked living in squalor, but for some reason it hadn't seemed like my job to do anything about it.

I was downstairs in the kitchen when I heard Noola's shopping bags rustling in the hallway. I was interested to know how she'd play this confrontation; I suspected she'd go on the offensive with her usual mixture of bullying combined with playing the aggrieved victim. It was not only a potent combination for getting one's own way, but it tended to frighten the life out of me with its sudden emotional tangents.

What was different on this occasion was that I could hear Noola's heavy tread approaching and I didn't feel anxious. I wasn't dreading her complaints, her demands and her sheer volume as I usually did. When I thought of her now, I no longer felt like a child about to be told off by an angry and unpredictable grown-up. If anything, she was the child now. I even found myself smiling and looking forward to her opening salvo, fascinated to see what preposterous complaint she'd use to put me on the defensive.

"Oh my *god*, Jo," she screeched, "You frightened the *crap* out of me. I thought someone had broken in. You know what a bundle of nerves I am since the robbery. Why didn't you call to *warn* me you'd be here?"

I noted that her hair was now my least favourite style in the world: bleached-blonde dreadlocks. The skin around her nose-ring looked angry and red. Much like the rest of her.

The smile on my face grew broader as I turned to face her. I was smiling because I was immune to her. I could feel myself wanting to apologise, to explain – or at least to answer her question – but I held myself in check.

She was irrationally angry and blaming it on me: every instinct I had told me to placate her. Deep down, I'd always suspected that people got angry with me not just for the reasons they gave, but because I irritated them with my poor social skills and my thoughtlessness. They were *right* to be angry with me and I knew it. I deserved it.

Except now, that all seemed like nonsense. I kept the impulse to give in to her under firm control. It was amusing, really, to see how she set about pulling my strings – and to feel myself wanting to respond. But this conversation wasn't going to be directed by her.

She had put down her bags in the doorway, blocking any exit I might wish to make, and now she was glowering at me, one hand on her hip, the other tapping the air in front of her in time with her words, like it was the eject button for my self-esteem.

My turn to speak. "*I'm* wondering whether to throw you out," I said, conversationally, "Or maybe I should give you another chance."

She drew herself up. "Well, of all the *gall*," she replied, sounding especially incensed. "I could have been *killed*. If I knew what was good for me I would have walked out and never come back. But I stayed, I took care of this place and I tried not to let what happened rule my life. I thought it might be too much to expect some concern, to expect that you'd ask me if I was feeling any better, to maybe say '*thanks*, Noola, for not leaving me in the lurch'. Because you see, where I'm from, Jo, people don't burst in and threaten someone who's been through what I have. I really expected better from you."

Her anger had crescendoed and then given way to outraged pain. The old me, which I could still sense lurking somewhere in the back of my brain, begged to be allowed to make excuses, to whine. It was a small voice, though, and it no longer had any power to make me do anything.

"Let me explain something," I said, in a calm, almost regretful tone which Noola initially misinterpreted as defeat. "You don't pay rent, you don't find anyone else to pay rent and you don't do a good job looking after this place. That's all I'm interested in. I couldn't care less if you were chopped into kebab meat the next time you stepped out of that door. It's not my problem. You're my lodger, not my girlfriend; you understand that, don't you?"

I could almost see the grinding of mental cogs as she failed to process my amiably offensive tone, my coldness, my ridiculous question. She just simply had no response. It was all I could do not to laugh out loud.

But I was feeling generous – and a little curious – so I didn't hassle her. I gave her a few seconds to recover her wits. I wanted to see what she'd come back with.

Her eyelids flickered for a moment with impotent anger and at last she spluttered, "I could *sue* you. I could take you to court and make your life a misery. Anyone who would take advantage of a person like this, when they were at their most vulnerable, deserves what comes to them. If you're not careful I'll end up *owning* this place with the damages I could get. You'd better *really* be sure you want to mess with me." Her defiance seemed to have once again energised her and obliterated her earlier hesitation.

Now let me stop there for a moment. I'm going to tell you what happened next in just a minute – but first let me tell you a scenario that didn't happen. It didn't happen, but it appeared in my head, fully-formed – including details of how Noola would react. This is what I imagined:

I imagined holding up my hand to cut her off.

"When you were 'attacked', Noola," I saw myself asking, "was it in the alleyway over there?" I would point in the direction of the cut-through I'd used.

"What's that got to do with anything," she would demand.

"Was it in the alleyway?" I'd snap loudly, taking a sudden step towards her.

She'd flinch with alarm, as though she was worried I was going to lunge at her, but she wouldn't reply.

"Let's assume it was," I'd say more calmly. "What do you suppose would happen if I took this key," I'd hold up my front door key, "and gave it to one of the junkies back there? Just handed it over."

She'd look shocked now, and uncertain. "What are you *saying*?" she'd demand, as though I'd switched to a foreign language.

"What if I told them to just let themselves in?" I'd ask, savouring the words.

Then a thought would occur to me: "What time do you usually go to sleep?" I'd ask – and then wave the question aside. "It doesn't matter. I'd just tell them to make sure it was really late, two or three in the morning maybe." I'd be genuinely interested as I asked, "What do you think your *lawyer* could do about that? Do you think he could come round and make sure that you were alright, that nothing *unpleasant* happened to you?"

She'd be staring at me now as though I was poisonous, her eyes bugging with fear. "What are you *saying*?" she'd ask, repeating the question – only her voice would get quieter with each repetition. She'd be gone by the morning, I knew that.

But I didn't say any of those things. I simply possessed the sudden and clear knowledge of how it would play out if I did. Whole and complete. And to tell you the truth I was a little shocked at myself. I mean, creepy much? I've invented little revenge fantasies before, but this was so efficient, so ruthless, so professional. It wasn't a fantasy of terrifying Noola; it was a *technique*. Not that the words I *actually* said were all that warm and fuzzy. In fact they made me sound like an evil, scheming bitch, but they had a little less of the decompensating serial killer about them.

What *really* happened was this:

"Well, the thing is, Noola," I explained, "I've been going through my paperwork and there's a problem. I forgot to renew your tenancy agreement when it expired and you forgot to remind me. You add that to the fact that you decided not to pay rent a while back and on paper at least, it doesn't even look like you live here any more."

"Of course I live here," she insisted, testily, "all of my *things* are here."

"Are they?" I said pleasantly, giving her a moment to think about that question. "See I decided that you should be in the small room, so I boxed your things up and locked them in there."

Before she could explode at me, I pressed on: "So you can get lawyers involved if you want, but it puts me in an awkward spot. I mean I could *cover* for you: tell the authorities that you really live here, that I believe you *intended* to pay your rent. Tell them that even though your tenancy agreement appears to be entirely verbal I consider it binding. In other words I could *help* you to sue me..."

Again I gave her a moment to think her situation through. "Or I could gather up your stuff and take it to the dump," I concluded brightly. Then I set about applying some salt to the wound: "Then I could ask the police what I should do about an ex-tenant who's made a copy of her door key and lets herself in when I go out." I played out the hypothetical phone call I'd make, for her benefit: "Yeah, I think she's in the UK on some sort of *visa*. What? Yes, she's used threatening language to me, but I don't *think* she's stolen anything. Maybe I should check?"

Enough play acting. By the look on her face I suspected that if I looked hard enough I might just find that she'd liberated one or two little trinkets from around the place. But more importantly, she was realising that I could certainly tell some convincing *lies* on the subject. I summarised the situation for her: "If it's that, or lose this house, well frankly I'd rather it was *you* on the street instead of me."

She was thankfully speechless – and rather deflated looking. I stepped over her shopping bags and headed for the stairs. "I've got some work to do," I said over my shoulder. "Have a cup of tea and think about it. Either you're gone in the next twenty-four hours or we get back to normal. You pay your rent – including what you owe – and you start looking for some housemates."

From halfway up the stairs I added, "If you write me a cheque this evening, I'll even let you sleep in a real bed tonight."

I reckoned even if she decided to go, I'd probably get at least *some* back rent from her, out of fear. She knew I could make a lot of trouble for her and she probably knew now that I'd really do it. She'd either go quietly or she'd stay and behave. I didn't think she'd try to fight me. But I did have one nasty surprise in mind in case she wanted to cause trouble. I'd swiped an out-of-date credit card of hers when I moved her stuff, lifting it from her dresser using a Kleenex, being careful not to smudge any fingerprints.

If she provoked me, I'd change the locks and then snap off her credit card in the front door, making it look like she'd tried to jimmy it. I particularly liked the fact it would make her look incompetent as well as criminal. Which of course she was.

It was all a matter of resolve, of how far I'd go. I could scratch my own face and tell the police she attacked me. I could break some crockery and claim she went berserk. I could daub some paint around and call her a vandal. Sure, she was a cunning and ruthless manipulator, but her range was limited: it was all verbal sparring and amateur theatricals. I could take it to the next level where she'd be hopelessly out of her depth and she knew it.

In the grand scheme of things she was such a minor annoyance that she really wasn't worth the effort, but that's how you keep things minor: you make sure that you're prepared to go further than they are and that they know it.

Once I was back upstairs, in my attic room, I got to work setting up a couple of workstations that I'd need later in the week. I tended to keep all the valuable computer stuff locked away, so it all needed hauling out now and cabling up. It kept me busy for quite a while and I only thought of Noola again when it started to get dark. I went downstairs to see what she'd decided.

She was still there – sitting on the sofa, a mug of cold tea in her hand. She looked sad.

Time to throw her a bone. I'd rather she stayed and got the place organised instead of me having to go out and look for a new tenant. I'd shown her what I was made of, I'd given her good reason to be afraid of me; now it was time to have her forgive me.

"Noola?" I asked gently, "What does your mother do?"

She glanced up at me, a little nervously, and gave me a forlorn look. "She's a school teacher," she said, without a hint of defiance.

I sat down on the other end of the sofa, keeping to myself "A little while ago, I found out that my mother killed herself," I said. Noola looked surprised, though it was difficult to guess exactly what she was thinking. She looked at me properly now, giving me her full attention.

I went on, "My dad remarried. He never wanted kids in the first place. I've moved around too much to have a lot of friends. It's just me. Me and this house."

Noola put her mug on the table and studied me, but there was a hint of softness about her look.

"My mother never fought for things," I said. "She made excuses and went with the flow and eventually it dragged her down. She wasn't able to handle anything. Not even being alive."

I turned to face Noola now. "I'm sorry about before," I said, sounding humble yet sincere. "I was very hard on you."

My hands were clasped together and I squeezed my fingers tightly now, to show how much emotion I was holding in.

"But I'm not going to end up like my mother. I can't let that happen. It might make me a bitch…" I said. And I let out the breath I'd been holding and gave a weak smile. Noola smiled a little too. "…but that's better than giving up."

"Listen…" she said. She sounded respectful now, even concerned.

But I pressed on, "You see, I don't trust anyone right now. I wish I *could*, but I can't." I gave her a brave smile. "I want us to get along. I *like* having you here. But I have to look out for myself because no one else is going to."

Then I made eye contact and said, "You *will* stay, won't you?" I sounded anxious.

Earlier, I'd knocked the stuffing out of her. Now I'd humbled myself. Her pride would no longer be telling her to leave. If she stayed, she could tell herself that she was being gracious:

accepting my apology, taking pity on me. And I'd made it her choice. All in all, it would be a lot easier for her to stick around… and we all want an easy life.

Sure, in a week or two, her confidence would return and she'd try to reassert herself, but all it would take would be a sharp look, an edge in my voice and she'd remember our little showdown this afternoon.

"I had no idea," Noola said, referring to my mother. "I don't know what you must think of me going on about my problems all this time, after what you've been through. Of course I can stay."

I'd never seen Noola like this but I'd been sure she must have other scripts she could follow, other roles she could play besides just the pushy whiner.

I'd shut down the whiner and, lo and behold, here was a whole other side to her opening up. Probably this was how she was with kids or people she was looking after: this was her in the role of 'protector'.

And often that's all there is to controlling people. They have a handful of roles they're comfortable playing – or at least familiar with – and if you want to bump them out of one then you have to make it easy for them to drop into a different one. You can't deny them all the roles they're familiar with or they become unpredictable. They get hysterical or they close themselves off completely.

I was fortunate that Noola possessed a compassionate side; I hadn't been sure. Now I knew that she had a protective role she was comfortable in, I could feed that: I could ask for her help, lean on her for her support.

On a hunch, I gave her a hug and made sure it was a little bit pathetic on my side. She didn't reject me. "It'll be alright," she said. "We can look out for each other. After all, I'm eleven thousand miles from home," she laughed. "We're in the same boat really."

Excellent.

Well, that was more than enough female bonding. As soon as I could do so without appearing to hurry, I got to my feet. Looking sheepish but reassured I made to head back upstairs.

Oops, I thought. I'd probably better head off a confrontation over her room.

"Listen," I said, "I want to get your old room redecorated, really make it nice – do something special. Will you be OK in the spare room for a bit?" I handed over the key.

She nodded. Good. And who knows, I might even make good on that promise to redecorate. Either way, it would buy me some time.

"I, um," I said awkwardly, "I have some work to do," by way of excusing myself.

"Right," she said, "Maybe later we could go out for a curry or something. What do you say?"

It would probably be a good idea, just to cement this new version of our relationship, but I didn't really have the time. I had to be careful about rejecting her, though.

"I have to sort through some of my mother's things," I said, sounding a little choked. "Maybe another time."

That should do it.

Then I put Noola out of my mind and climbed back up to the top of the house thinking about my next task: to learn what I could about the life and times of a man called Jan.

Chapter 17

It was Monday morning: day one of my investigation. I'd spent Saturday night and Sunday morning finishing off the cracker's toolkit I'd need if I wanted to explore other people's systems with anonymity. The only problem was that I didn't have a target.

For me, the idea of tracking someone online was a strange hybrid of the familiar and the unknown. I knew about IP addresses and cookies, digest access authentication and traceroute, http and email headers – all that gobbledy-gook. On the other hand, I knew nothing about land registry records, credit checking, voter rolls, tax records, Companies House and community charge payments. If you broke down the act of tracing a missing person into individual tasks, half of them I'd fly through and the other half would mystify me.

I had many of the skills I'd need but no idea where to apply them. It was like searching for your car keys with a microscope. I really needed pointing in the right direction.

But, in the absence of a guide, I decided to let my starting point be the information I already possessed. Thanks to the PAC,

I had three former addresses for Jan and the aliases that he'd owned or rented them under. In addition I knew the name under which he'd bought and insured a car. And I had scans of a US passport in a fifth name that Susan had found among his things.

The residences were what drew my attention. It wasn't just that Jan might have left clues behind; they were also mailing addresses: destinations for revealing correspondence of all sorts to pile up in – especially now that he wasn't around to tidy it away. Ideally I'd poke around and find an invoice for a safety-deposit box, but I'd settle for something less obvious.

But would his old properties still be empty? Wouldn't his death have triggered some process of resale and liquidation? I didn't really know happened when a person died[1]. But with all those aliases in play, and no corpse to examine, it seemed unlikely that news of his death had reached all the relevant officials. If the bills were still being paid then one or more of those addresses might be just as he'd left them.

Unless, that is, the Army had got involved. They would be used to slipping in and out of identities just as Jan was. It would be easy for them to provide a wife or son or daughter ready to inherit from each of his aliases. It would give them fuss-free access to everything. Which meant those addresses were either treasure troves of information or traps – maybe both.

I wondered how far I dared go to find out.

I wanted to look around Jan's house and maybe read some of his posthumous mail, but I wanted to do it without being captured, tortured or killed. I'd have to take things one cautious step at a time.

To start with I'd limit myself strictly to surveillance – just looking for signs of the Army's presence. Actually getting inside

---

[1] One of mankind's oldest questions. But I'm thinking more in terms of bureaucracy than theology here.

would be stage two and it would only go ahead if I saw nothing – absolutely nothing – to indicate there was a trap waiting for me.

I quickly settled on the Notting Hill address as my first target. It was undoubtedly the coolest of the three properties. All other things being equal, if you owned a really nice place you'd want to spend the biggest chunk of your time there. Or so I reckoned.

It would be an easy trip too – under an hour door-to-door. And I was only planning to look around the neighbourhood, so there wasn't much need for preparation. That morning I made the decision to go there and by early afternoon I was on my way.

I wore regular street clothes; the only bit of spycraft I indulged in was a detail I'd picked up from Susan's diary: I took a carrier bag of Tesco groceries with me. Weird I know, but it's pretty much built into the human psyche that you can't be suspicious of a woman lugging a bag full of toilet rolls, pots of yoghurt and oven cleaner. Plus it was a handy place to hide my tribute, along with a pair of dusty Victorian opera glasses – which was the closest I could come to binoculars at short notice.

On my way there, I ran through a few scenarios. There was a limit to how much I could learn by peeking at the house from the end of the road – and even doing that was a risk. On the other hand, if I got up close there was a better chance of being seen – seen and followed – followed and investigated – and from there it all might unravel.

So I settled on a third option – what you might call an occult fly-by. I'd find myself somewhere to hide that was close (but not *too* close) to Jan's house, I'd Connect, and I'd check the Presence Surface for other adepts active in the vicinity. If I detected nothing I wouldn't really be any the wiser, but if there *were* contacts, that would tell me all I needed to know. I'd break the Connection, hide my tribute and bug out, never to return.

Or that was the plan. It seemed easy enough, although when

I got near to the house I hit my first snag. This was an expensive neighbourhood: the houses were huge, the gardens were wide and the walls were high. It wasn't the sort of street that had bus shelters, alleyways and corner shops for people to skulk in. Each residence had that subtly fortified look that nervous millionaires tend to prefer: the kind where the architect's priorities seem to have been space and light, closely followed by good fields of fire and defendable access points, just in case the revolution came a little sooner than expected.

In the end I found a pedestrian path that led through to a pocket-sized park one street over. The path ran between a couple of houses and it was close enough to Jan's old residence to just be within range of the Presence Surface while still being out of direct line of sight.

Before I tucked myself away there, I took a good look at the house in question – but there was nothing especially revealing to see. It was a corner property, it looked well-maintained, the curtains were open and there were no obvious signs of life. To learn more, I'd need to make use of more than just the usual five senses.

About twenty feet down the path, I found a handy tree to stand behind. Then I waited until I was sure there was no one approaching from either direction and I put on my tribute.

Instantly I felt a jolt of adrenaline. My attention was fixed on the Presence Surface as it unfurled around me and spread out to touch the world. And immediately, pushing up through the Surface, were a string of contacts the colour of desert sunlight – bushy blossoms of light, each one a Connected adept. I counted seven before my scrabbling hand managed to snatch the headband from around my temples. Jan's old house was crawling with enemies.

I was momentarily shaken and did nothing. But a second later a thought pushed its way into my head: *Run*.

I felt foolish. I was out of sight of the house. I'd arouse more suspicion if I broke into a sprint than if I simply put my weary head down and carried on walking, groceries in hand.

Run, the voice in my head insisted. And despite myself I got moving, setting off down the path, moving as quickly as I could without breaking stride.

Run, the voice thundered and just then I became aware of the nearby squawk of a walkie-talkie; it was coming from just over the wall I was standing behind and it was moving. Just up ahead, was the gate for that garden. I would need to pass it in order to get away. I ran.

At the same time, I snatched the headband out of the shopping bag, stuffed it into my jacket and let the bag fall to the ground as I sprinted along the path and towards the gate.

As I reached it, the gate rattled violently but didn't open. Whoever was on the other side shook it frantically and I heard a voice, so close that the speaker might have been by my side, yelling for the key.

I pounded down the path hoping to reach the far end before the gate opened. I was running flat out now, thankful beyond words for the morning jogs I'd been taking, and all I heard behind me was rattling and swearing.

At the far end, I dashed around the corner, sprinting for the patch of greenery beyond. As I left the path behind me I heard a shattering crash and the sound of splitting wood. I guessed that whoever was back there had got impatient. Who knows how many months they'd been staking that place out and at the critical moment, someone had mislaid the key. My good fortune was almost certainly someone else's extended beating.

Fifteen seconds later I was through the little park, out the other side and onto a main road. There were cars, shops, lots of people and plenty of places to conceal myself.

I slowed to a walk and ducked swiftly into a charity shop

– figuring that it was the last place any sane person would expect me to hide. Any self-respecting enemy of the Army would have had a black Range Rover with tinted windows idling at the kerb ready to roar off with a squeal of smoking tyres. Instead I peered out from behind a rack of second-hand wedding dresses and tried to keep an eye on the street.

A slim man with the build of a dancer and the dress sense of an Italian film star flew out onto the street and stopped dead, turning one of the fastest sprints I'd ever seen into a nonchalant saunter in the blink of an eye.

He looked first one way and then the other along the street, his eyes apparently taking in every detail. I was sure it was impossible for him to see me through the shop window, behind my barricade of voile and taffeta, but nevertheless I pulled back even farther and watched him through a gap in the shelves of children's books.

A moment later my view was blocked as a bus pulled up at the stop in front of the charity store and two old ladies got out. I seized the moment and moved quickly out of the shop, jumping onto the bus just as the last passenger boarded.

I flashed my travelcard and rushed past the driver to stand halfway up the bus's stairs, where I would be hidden from view from almost every angle. The bus doors closed and the vehicle moved away from the stop.

Again, I took it for granted that no adversary the Army had ever faced would flee on public transport, and once the bus was a few hundred yards down the road and round a corner I set about coaxing my heart-rate back down into double figures, reasonably sure that I hadn't been seen and wasn't being pursued.

It happened more quickly than I'd expected – my breathing returned to normal and a sense of calm purpose pushed aside my anxiety. I was back in control.

I'd learned a couple of lessons here. Firstly, I'd reminded

myself not to underestimate the Army: they were real, they were active and they were following the same trail that I was. And secondly, I'd learned that in future I really should listen when that inner voice tells me to run.

Chapter 18

Tuesday, day two of sleuthing and today I thought I'd try a new approach. I'd maintain at least a minimum quarter of a mile distance between me and anyone trying to kill me. Today would be all about coffee and the Internet.

So what did I know now that I hadn't known yesterday? Well, I knew that the Marker wasn't in any of Jan's houses. How come? Well because the Army had been there and they would have crawled over every brick, plank and tile of each address. If they hadn't found it in a year, then it wasn't there.

The obvious, no-brainer conclusion was that Jan hid the Marker somewhere other than his known residences – and he didn't leave behind any obvious record of it, because either the Army or the PAC (who had a notebook of Jan's) would have noticed.

He had put it somewhere we hadn't looked – and yet it would also need to be somewhere that Jan could have quickly retrieved it from if he'd needed to. He would have wanted to be ready to make a run for it at any moment and I wondered what sort of hiding places were convenient, discreet and always accessible

– and whether any of them would leave a data trail.

The classic I'd already mentioned, the safety deposit box, would imply bank records, a key, account details. In these days of cross-selling and direct marketing, wouldn't any commercial deposit service be writing to him every five minutes? Naturally, he could redirect correspondence to another residence or a post office box but they too would generate paperwork. At the very least a locked box needed a key. If the Army had found any mysterious keys, they'd had a year to figure out what they opened. So a commercial hiding place, like a lock-box, wasn't the likeliest answer in my view.

What about public property? A loose stone under a monument, a crypt, a hole in the ground in the woods somewhere? That could work, I suppose, but this needed to be somewhere Jan could reach easily, so it was probably in Central London. He just didn't have time to head off to the countryside. And how much public property was there in the middle of London that wasn't scrutinised, frequented, patrolled or covered by security camera? Jan would want 24 hour access, but he wouldn't want to be observed or risk anyone else discovering his hidey-hole. What was public, but secluded and open night and day? A church? A station? A park? A hotel? There were dozens or even hundreds of each of those.

Again I seemed to have reached a dead-end, but my plan was to keep at this until I came up with something I could act upon, so I tried coming at this from a different direction.

What if Jan couldn't reach the Marker for some reason and didn't want anyone else to find it? After all, if he got captured he couldn't very well spring into action at *that* point and conceal it. What he'd need was a system like a dead man's switch, something he had to keep resetting while he was around. Then, if he was somehow removed from the picture, the mechanism would be triggered and automatically hide the Marker.

Something like that might allow him to hide the Marker in his home, right where he'd want it, while still allowing him to keep it out of reach of his enemies if anything went wrong.

Now, *that* was a promising line of enquiry.

So what might fit the bill? Refuse collection was the first thing to spring to mind. But unless he actually kept the Marker in the dustbin by his back door, the scheme wouldn't work. Plus, would you really want to trust the miracle of the ages to foxes, unreliable collection schedules and one's ability to separate platinum filigree from eggshells and bacon rind once a week?

I wondered what else might work in a similar way.

I tried to think laterally. What about buying something on hire purchase? If you failed to keep up the payments – because you were dead or captured – then it would be repossessed. Hmmm, except that repossession would probably take months and require getting a warrant to break into the house. I discarded the repossession idea.

But the idea of payments led onto another avenue of thought. If Jan *had* constructed a dead man's switch, he'd need to use some sort of scheduled collection. Something like that would probably cost him money and that might leave a trace. If the collection itself was something innocuous, something that no one would suspect because it made sense for reasons that had nothing to do with the Marker, then the relevant payments might be overlooked by the Army.

I pictured Jan hiding the Marker among his shirts and then removing it before the laundry service collected it each week. No, that wasn't it either.

It was a farfetched scheme, but that was what I liked about it. All the easy options would have been explored; I could take that as read. I mean, stash the Marker under the mattress? The Army would have checked. On top of the wardrobe? The Army would have checked. I needed to look somewhere they wouldn't have thought to look and this idea fit the bill. If it got me nowhere, I could always go back to the more conventional possibilities.

So what was my next step? Well, ideally I wanted to get into Jan's bank records to see if he'd been paying for any sort of collection service, but that was easier said than done. Why couldn't he have done the decent thing and left a laptop lying around with the details of an online banking service still in its web cache?

I wondered if a man like Jan would even use something like Internet banking. Wouldn't a person who relied on magic be kind of a luddite? But then I remembered seeing a news cutting in the PAC's private store which mentioned that Dass's killer had used a radio transmitter to track his victim's car. So Jan obviously had a little experience when it came to technology.

And thinking about online banking triggered another memory. Susan had scanned Jan's notebook into a file and then made some annotations. One of them concerned a couple of numbers and a word that Jan had written on the back page of the book. They were:

```
10183461
1555635971
Punarbhava
```

Susan's annotation read "Password? It's the Sankrit word for 're-birth'. But what do the numbers mean? "

You probably think I should have checked that notation out as my first priority, right? But, really, what do two numbers and a word mean? They could be anything. I mean even if you knew they pertained to something on the Internet, there's still a lifetime of possibilities to check – and we *didn't* know it was an Internet thing. They could be details of Jan's tailor for all we could tell or maybe the location of a hidden stash of weapons in Patagonia: a map reference and a phone number in some far off land, plus somebody's surname.

Except they weren't.

I'd tried logging in to nine other UK banks or building societies before I found one that required two numbers of the right length and a password – and of course I did this all from behind my anonymizer[1] via my wireless cut-out in Capetown. I keyed in the digits, provided part of the password…

…and I was in.

Sweet.

First of all, I noticed that Jan had just over nineteen thousand pounds in his current account and a hundred and six thousand in his savings account. The second thing I noticed was a line in the top right-hand corner of the window that read 'Last log in:' and then gave a date and time from last year.

Well, it couldn't be helped. The next time someone logged into this account, that last login info would be displaying *today's* date and it would be obvious that I'd been here. That's to say, I hoped it wouldn't actually be obvious that me, Jo Hallett, had been here, but it would be obvious that *someone* had logged in.

Hmmm. The last log-in date was around the time of Jan's death. Did that mean no one else knew about this account? It was definitely possible. I checked the preference screen and saw that he'd ticked the boxes instructing the bank to make any correspondence electronic rather than paper-based.

Then I clicked on another link and found a facility to view old statements going back two years. When I pulled up the first page of a statement, there was an option to download a copy in a choice of formats. Handy. I chose Microsoft Excel format… and then realised that I was using an anonymizer; it would ruin my concealment if those files came directly to my home machine. I wasn't going to be able to download files unless I rewrote my

---

[1] And for all you techno-pedants out there, I first spent a considerable amount of time rewriting it to handle HTTPS. Happy now?

damn software for a third time. So I settled for viewing them in a web-browser and taking screen prints of each statement. I consoled myself that it was probably a lot more secure this way. I wasn't sure if the Army themselves had the techno-chops to trace me once they became aware of this account, but if they'd successfully impersonated Jan's next of kin, they could always get the police to work on the case for them.

Even if they involved the police, I was pretty sure that no one in a nylon shirt and clip-on tie was going to unravel *my* security.

When I'd copied all the current account statements, I did the same for his online savings account and his Visa card. And then I copied a lot of very boring 'messages' offering him mortgages and insurance, just in case one of them pertained to something other than selling more financial services. With the brutal latency introduced by the various cut-outs, all this took forever.

Finally, there were only two more items to copy: a list of standing orders and direct debits, and an e-mail address that was listed under the account-holder's contact details. Interestingly, the name on the bank account was Mr N Harrington and the e-mail address was `Niall.Harrington@onlineuk. com`. It wasn't an alias that I'd seen anywhere else, which meant I might be in possession of some information that the Army didn't have yet.

When I was finally done, I had just under ninety pages of print-outs. I wiped the logs of the wireless access points I'd used in Capetown and told the anonymizer to destroy itself and then run a program that would lunch its way through the hosting server's records. I wouldn't be using either of those systems again. If I needed to do any more online sleuthing I'd load the anonymizer onto a new server somewhere, and see if I could locate a fresh wireless link elsewhere in the world – perhaps in Johannesburg this time, just in case anyone bought the idea that a South African was behind this.

Tomorrow I'd start the job of going through the screen-prints line by line looking for something that matched my dead-man's switch theory: a gardening company that cleared bags of leaves, a charity that collected bric-a-brac… or failing that, a payment to 'Acme Safety Deposit Boxes Inc'.

Chapter 19

Monday had been brush-with-death day[1]. Tuesday had been taken up preparing for, logging onto and copying Jan's bank records. And Wednesday was mainly eaten up going through each entry, trying to figure out what it might pertain to and making some sort of guesstimate on whether it was a red herring or a golden goose.

Fortunately, I could put a lot of those payments to one side for now because I was only looking at recurring entries. If some service was making regular collections then I'd imagine they'd want regular payments, so I made a separate list of all repeating monthly outgoings. Quite a few were utilities or services that obviously didn't involve any sort of collection. I worked through the rest and by the end of the day, I'd crossed *all* the entries off my list and had nothing to show for it.

Then I tried adjusting my definition of 'recurring'. After all, Jan only came by the Marker shortly before his death. To arouse the least possible suspicion, he'd have weaved his concealment

---

[1]   Part of Flossing-with-Danger Week

mechanism in with a service he'd been using for a long time. But maybe he hadn't thought that far ahead. I started looking for regular payments which only started up six months or more before he died.

There was only one new entry and it was an insurance company. So far as I know, the only thing they collect is money, so that one was out as well.

Even when I just looked in the last three months before his death, I found only a single additional payee: The Clipping Service. I knew what a clipping service was; they collected press cuttings on whatever topics you set them. Was this a firm that collected news stories on Jan's behalf or was it just a cutesy name for a gardening firm? The latter would suit me better, although the former would still be intriguing.

I did a little digging, no pun intended, and learned that The Clipping Service was in fact a hairdressers[1]. A lesser woman might be getting frustrated by now. My patience, fortunately, was limitless these days.

It had also occurred to me that my dead man's switch theory could be correct without there actually being a regular payment or collection. Like, maybe he made a telephone call each week that said, 'nothing to collect this week'.

Then again, the more I thought about that idea the more it seemed to suck.

Maybe he'd had an accomplice after all. An accomplice would just notice that Jan was dead, grab the Marker and scarper (as they say in these parts). Sure, a commercial service, like a gardening firm who cleared away garden refuse, was a very clever way of making it seem as though the Marker had just vanished, but on the other hand, there was such a thing as over-thinking things.

---

[1]   What's the link between hairdressing and puns? Do they all have to have names like Curl Up And Dye, or From Hair To Eternity?

An accomplice could just flat-out sprint for South America as soon as he'd snatched the Marker. Maybe there was accomplice and he'd simply managed not to leave a trail, and that's why the Marker was still unaccounted for.

Plus the dead man's switch idea didn't make sense with just any old service. A gardening firm wouldn't file the leaves and grass they collected; it would probably burn them. And even if they mulched them instead, you wouldn't really want a piece of priceless platinum to be lost among tons of rotting grass.

I couldn't tell if I was making progress in puzzling out Jan's scheme or gradually demonstrating to myself all the reasons it couldn't work.

At the end of each day, the Professor was there to receive my call and we would have a pleasant little chat. I tried to exude the kind of older-and-wiser, weary strength that you expect from felons who were going straight or Country singers who'd kicked their forty-year bourbon habit. I didn't have much to tell him about progress on the search, but then I reckoned I had at least a week before he could realistically expect any revelations.

After I put the phone down following our Wednesday call, I thought back on the conversation. Then I thought about the fact that the Professor had offered to call me tomorrow instead of the other way round... which led me on to thinking about Jan *getting* a phone call each week rather than making one. Why this train of thought was worth mentioning, I couldn't say. But there was something there; I just didn't know what yet.

I also found a few minutes on Wednesday to dash out and deposit the rent cheque I'd received from Noola. She appeared to be planning to stay and to pay her way. With minimal 'handling' from me she was behaving herself and even tidying up around the place. Assuming the cheque actually cleared, I could consider the Noola situation dealt with, for now.

On Thursday, having checked all the repeat outgoings from

Jan's account, I started looking at all the one-off expenditures. Dead end followed dead end, and by the end of the day I had nothing worthwhile to show for my efforts.

Friday dawned and before settling down to work I went out for a run. I wasn't sure the net effect was actually beneficial when you factored in the carbon monoxide, the volatile organics and the unpleasant nitrogen compounds in the London air, but exercise was good for my brain chemistry. Endorphins and a healthy blood-sugar level made it easier not to be depressed. Plus, I just found I liked starting my day that way.

While I was out jogging, the answer to that earlier puzzle came to me. I could call the Professor or the Professor could call me. Jan could pay a collection service or a collection service could pay him.

Suddenly I wanted another look at those statements. I wanted to check whether there were any regular *incoming* payments in Jan's bank records. I picked up the pace a little and then took a chance. I cut back through Mugger's Alley in order to save a little time. I figured it was waaay too early for junkies to be up and about. At this hour of the day they were probably still fast asleep dreaming of bugs under their skin.

I needn't have worried; the alley was deserted and I was home a minute later. Eager though I was, I waited until I'd taken a shower before re-examining Jan's bank statements. Wrapped in a thick terry robe, with a pink towel twined around my head like fondant topping, I sat down with the print-outs and a highlighter pen.

I couldn't find a recurring amount, but I *could* find a recurring name: Achtung Antiques. The payments had only been running for two and a half months, and the amounts varied greatly, but they were weekly, which immediately caught my eye. Granted, there were a couple of weeks with no payments at all, but there was still enough of a pattern to make it seem worth investigating.

I put another shovel full of coal on the Internet connection and went in search of Achtung Antiques.

There wasn't that much to find. Google Local showed a store by that name less than a mile from Jan's Notting Hill address. They didn't appear to have a web-site.

The good news was that I had something promising to investigate; the bad news was that I would have to do so in person. This needed to go better than my outing on Monday had.

I'd need a cover story to use when I visited the shop and started asking questions – and it had to work whether I was talking to a real shopkeeper or an Army stooge on the look-out for suspicious visitors.

I needed to ask the payments that had been made to Jan's... I mean Niall Harrington's account. I could pretend to be a relative, or a cop, or someone from the lawyer's office handling his will. I could even tell the truth, sort of, and say Mr. Harrrington was a bad, bad man and I wanted to retrieve some property he'd taken, which the police had given up on finding. But that sounded idiotic and the other suggestions I'd come up with were all straight out of TV Clichéland.

In the end, I figured that it was about 90% certain that all those payments from the antique store would turn out to be exactly what they appeared to be: Jan selling off some antiques. Which meant I could use the least suspicious line you could use in a store: "Hi, I'm interested in buying something."

Unfortunately for me, I didn't know exactly what Jan had been selling so I couldn't go in and ask for it specifically. But if I said I'd been to his house, then I could just ask if they'd handled the sale of *any* of his things – and that I liked everything of his that I'd seen. And if it turned out that those payments *weren't* for antiques, it still didn't look totally suspicious. Who had a big house in Notting Hill without at least a few antiques? It would just suggest that someone else had handled the sale.

Next I really needed a reason to have visited Jan's house that would hold up under the scrutiny of a genuine shopkeeper (easy enough) and also a spy for the Army (much trickier).

I decided to keep it vague. I'd be a neighbour who had been to Mr Harrington's house on a couple of occasions, for reasons left unspecified, and who was interested in buying anything he'd parted with. I figured it would sound ghoulish if I said I knew he was dead, so I'd claim that when I asked after him, I was told he'd sold up and moved away.

So now I needed to look the part. What do women my age wear if they're rich and privileged? I did a little research courtesy of Hello magazine and some other, less deferential publications. It was scary what you could find out. It was easy enough to pull up a list of the brand names favoured by Prince William's current girlfriend, complete with pictures of when she'd worn each item and marks out of ten for how she looked. Sadly, most of those clothes would make me look like a moose in fancy dress, but then she *was* nearly ten years younger than me. Fortunately there were other, shall we say sturdier members of the British nobility, who still wanted to look their everyday best when they weren't on a horse or at a ball.

I suspected that women who ran antique shops in expensive parts of London had a keen nose for class, income and pedigree, so just to be on the safe side I made an appointment to get my hair styled and my eyebrows plucked. Despite many years of living in England, on and off, my American accent hadn't diminished much – which probably worked in my favour. The relationship between class, accent and wealth was much less obvious on the other side of the pond. Plus, my daddy didn't spend all that money on private tutors just so that I could sound like the downstairs maid.

Maybe all this preparation sounds like overkill; I'd probably only be in that shop for ten minutes. But the Army don't kid around. If I was going to cross the Afghan border at night carrying false papers you'd expect me to get my story straight and not to muddle my chadri with my kameez. This might not be a war zone, but it was still enemy territory. Dass had nearly killed David Braun at his smart home in Belgravia just because he was a loose end. If it could happen to him in Belgravia, it could happen to me in Notting Hill.

In the end, it was Saturday morning before I was finally at the door of a very exclusive looking store round the corner from Portobello Road. The windows had far too little stock compared with the few antique stores I was familiar with. I suspected the less in the window, the more it cost.

I'd spied the place out quickly the day before, but hadn't approached. The name Achtung Antiques had been bothering me and I wanted to check it was selling actual old antiques and not Modernist salad tongs in red and yellow plastic. My outfit said 'old money' not new bohemian. I needn't have worried, though.

As I pushed open the door, I could see my reflection in the glass. I looked virtually unrecognisable. A month ago, I would rather have been dipped in barbeque sauce and fed to the dingoes than wear a Chanel rainbow-tweed suit and a silk blouse. My hair alone would have had me reaching for the hemlock. Man, but you needed some chutzpah to dress like this and not feel self-conscious. No wonder nobility inherit their titles; unless you're raised to this sort of thing from birth you don't stand a chance.

But that was hardly a helpful way to think. I was smarter and far deadlier than the women who customarily dressed like this. One day soon I might even have in my possession the means to live forever. Didn't I have reason enough to act aloof?

A little bell tinkled as I entered the store. I let my gaze wander, ignoring the welcoming smile and head-tilt of the proprietoress. She fluttered over a couple of minutes later and said, "Celine Dubois. *Do* let me know if there's anything I can help with."

"Hmmm, I don't see it here," I said.

"What were you looking for, Madame? Perhaps I can help you find it," she asked brightly. Her accent was hard to place. It seemed like it wanted to be French but was keeping its options open.

"A friend of mine, I think you bought a number of pieces from him; I was hoping that you still had some of them," I said. Antique-lovers call old chairs and things 'pieces', right?

"Oh really," she said, sounding delighted that I was telling her things, "and what is your friend's name?"

"Niall Harrington. He was a neighbour of mine and I always admired his taste. I remember once he recommended I drop in here and look around. I was hoping if I did that I might find some of his charming pieces," I said.

She looked sad. "Ah, Mr Harrington had so many lovely things. I was very sad when our business was concluded," she sighed. I noticed that she dropped the 'h' in 'had' but not 'Harrington'. It really made you wonder which part of France the Dubois family called home.

"Yes," I said, "when I enquired after him, I was told he'd moved away. It was a surprise."

"Oh no," she corrected me, "he'd been planning to go for a couple of months. He was unable to take his collection with him and so he'd decided to let it go." I assumed by 'let it go' she meant sell it. From her phrasing you'd think he had simply allowed it to evaporate into the air instead of doing something pedestrian, like swapping it for cash.

So he had told her he was leaving, but she didn't appear to know that he was dead now.

"*Do* you still have any of his things?" I enquired. I think I'd worn out the word 'piece' in the first few seconds of my visit.

She glanced at the table I was leaning against and said, "Well, of course you'll remember this lovely 18th century card table. Although I think this particular item has at last found itself a new home."

I was definitely getting the impression that when operating in this price range, one didn't actually refer to money changing hands. Instead all parties had to pretend that antiques simply moved on of their own accord from time to time – a little like wild birds visiting your garden; you could try to coax them, and they might linger with you for a while, but you could never be sure when they'd flit away again.

"Really?" I said, attempting to admire the table, "This was his too?"

Then I decided to take a chance. I needed to find something bulky enough that it might hide a secret compartment. This card table was positively anorexic. I was looking for something with a little more meat on its bones. I said, "He had a desk I rather liked. I only caught a glimpse of it, but I wondered if that had made its way to you."

"The Davenport or the Secretaire?" she asked.

Having no idea what those words meant, I went with the one that sounded weightier. "The Davenport."

"Ohhh," she said, sounding as though I'd given her bad news. "No longer with us."

Well, we could play this game all day. I needed to get to the heart of the matter. If Jan had hidden the Marker, it would presumably be in the last consignment of furniture they collected from him.

"Niall said that you had rather an unusual arrangement. You would send someone to pick up a few items from him each week. Did I get that right?" I said. If I was wrong, she might give me a strange look, but probably wouldn't rush out into the street yelling for the police. Even if she was an Army spy, it didn't really give grounds to be suspicious. From the Army's point of view, just saying I knew Mr Harrington was the interesting part.

She looked embarrassed for a moment and then said, "Well, he asked me not to talk about it." I gave her a friendly smile and plenty of silence – which she could choose to fill if she wished.

After a few seconds, she appeared to take some sort of decision and said, "But since you're telling not asking, I can't see the harm. And anyway," she said, glancing pointedly towards the back of the shop, "since when is it unprofessional to have an actual conversation with a customer?"

I nodded and smiled some more, full of encouragement. "Exactly," I said.

She added quietly, "My name's really Cheryl, by the way. Doesn't mean I don't know antiques, does it?" Her French accent obviously knew when it was beaten. It had withdrawn and her underlying London vowels had burst through.

With a look I attempted to convey my shock that anyone would think otherwise. "Well obviously," I agreed. "And Niall *has* left the country. I can't see him minding now," I pointed out, hoping I sounded conspiratorial and chummy.

"We still have most of his *final* few pieces, but I have to say I always wondered why the rigmarole," she said. "You don't happen to know, do you? Why the business with the weekly collections?"

So there *were* weekly collections. I was feeling heartily gruntled that I'd been right. I said, "I imagine he held on to his favourite things until the last moment. He didn't want to part with them until he was just about to leave. In fact, maybe he was already gone when you collected them."

She nodded, as though I was very wise. "He said they'd been in his family a long while. I suppose one forms attachments. He didn't seem like a sentimental man, but it just shows you can miss the signs."

"I'm fascinated," I said, hoping I wasn't laying it on too thick. "How did it work? He left a few items out for you each week, then?"

"That would have been a *trifle* unusual. This was *much* more peculiar," she said. "He had that giant workshop space all cleared out and filled with some fabulous things, mainly Victorian, a lot of furnishings. Each piece had a card on it and each week he'd redo all the cards."

I nodded, wanting her to go on.

"Well, the only things the cards had on them was a date and a price. And the prices were always bargains. You were supposed to compare today's date with the date on the card. If it was still in the future you'd leave the piece; if the date had passed, you'd take it. That was the arrangement," she explained.

It was very clever, I thought. For whatever reason, he had some antiques to sell off, but instead of disposing of them in one go, he'd parcelled them out to last several months. And then each week that he *didn't* include the Marker was another week when he got to check that the collection system was working properly. At the most superficial level, there was nothing suspicious to find. A man about to go on the run had gradually sold off his furniture. Only the collection scheme was peculiar and you'd have to suspect it existed to go looking for it.

She concluded, "And one day we turned up to find all the dates were in the previous week. So we took away everything. I had to have the men make a second trip. When he first created our arrangement, he said when that happened, when we'd taken everything, then that was it, our business was at an end and he'd prefer me not to discuss it with anyone."

She nodded her head gravely, as if to say: *yes, it was all very strange*. And then she seemed to realise that she hadn't exactly kept her word to him. She looked doubtful for a minute.

"I won't tell a soul," I reassured her. "And I'm sure he wouldn't have mentioned the arrangement to me at all if he hadn't wanted me to know about it."

212

That seemed to satisfy her and she began to lead me round the showroom, pointing out the three other items – two chairs and a sideboard – that had belonged to Mr. Harrington. She told me there were three more pieces in their store room at the back: an armchair, a bureau and a credenza (whatever that was).

"So how many of the pieces in that last collection are still here? What have I missed out on?" I asked.

"Well, we've already parted with a lovely Queen Anne escritoire and a Regency pedestal desk," she admitted.

Hmmm. The desk and the escritoire (which I had in mind was a thing with drawers and a flap for writing letters on) were both losses. You could hide a thing like the Marker in either one.

Clearly, I was going to have to come back here when no one else was around and check over all the items from Jan's last consignment. And if I didn't find anything, I'd have to track down the two items she'd already sold. But at least it looked like I'd only be breaking in to the premises of ordinary mortals. Now that I'd had my theory about weekly collections confirmed, I was sure that Jan had concealed the Marker this way. Which meant that the Army didn't know about this place, otherwise they'd surely have recovered it by now.

"I know it's an imposition," I said, "But could you show me the items from your store room? Once I've seen everything I can go home and think about what I might have room for."

"Of course," she said and led me through a doorway and into the large dusty area beyond. It was a great expanse of cloth-draped shapes. I made a mental note of the layout and where Jan's pieces sat in the overall scheme.

When I'd spent a suitable amount of time appreciating what I hoped were the salient features of each, Cheryl escorted me back to the sales floor.

"I'm afraid I forgot to ask your name," she said, as we neared the front door.

"Anne Wexham," I said. 'Wexham', because it was one of the surnames Jan had used elsewhere. I figured if anyone asked questions later about my visit, that surname would send them on a wild goose chase: they'd think they were looking for an accomplice of Jan's. And I chose 'Anne' because I figured if it was good enough for a princess it would work for me.

Just before I left, something occurred to me. I said, "Do you mind if I ask you something? Where did the company name come from?"

Cheryl looked around before answering and even then she kept her voice low. "Well, they're terrible snobs here. The owner maintains it was a condition of one of the firm's investors, a wealthy German gentleman. But the truth is that when they moved to Notting Hill, they changed the name to sound more up-market and European. It used to be Acton Antiques."

She chuckled and I joined in. I knew my London suburbs just well enough to see why she was laughing.

As I let myself out, I made sure to take careful note of the alarm sensors on the front door, the transducer in the corner for the ultrasonics and the closed-circuit TV cameras.

I had some breaking and entering to plan.

Chapter 20

I hadn't seen any mention of it in the PAC's notes, but a person who was Connected could see pretty well in the dark. I didn't need the sun to be up for me to get a good look at the back of the Antique store.

Of course, it wasn't exactly 'seeing'. It was more like an extended sense of touch. I could feel things close by, though anything more than forty or fifty feet away was just a mushy blur. Distant buildings were bulky and indistinct, like trying to read a Braille headline with your shoulder. The cinder block by my cheek, on the other hand, was pocked and coral-edged: almost crystalline in its sharpness.

It had seemed obvious to me: if you could Shatter something on the other side of a wall, it stood to reason you needed a way to see it was there, didn't you? But the PAC still seemed to be in the metaphorical dark on that point. Which, irony fans, was probably because they didn't spend enough time in the literal dark. I'd guess they did pretty much all of their training in well-lit rooms. And even if you did dim the lights, you tended not to really notice these extra sense impressions if your eyes were open and you were straining to see. You had to really concentrate on the Surfaces – and to start with, it helped if you kept your eyes closed.

It was easiest if you used the Push Surface, the one for applying pressure to the objects around you. It really was like a sense of touch, because if you focused too hard on the texture of something, you could find that object sliding away from you. It reminded me of an electron microscope I'd once seen demonstrated, where the target was a dried housefly. As the operator zoomed in, to show the delicate hairs around one of its compound eyes, the hairs drooped. The act of viewing them applied enough power to cook them.

Seeing with the Shatter Surface was similar to using Push, but there was more of a sense of tunnel vision. The Freeze and Heat Surfaces had their uses too. You could tell the difference between a mannequin and a live human even in zero light, just by sensing their temperature. Of course learning to use each Surface in this way could take years – and decades more to really master.

I was in my element, though, unperturbed by the lack of light. It was like that venerable adage about night being a dear friend to the old and a cloak to the young – which, take my word for it, sounds better in Latin because of the amiculus/amiculum friend/cloak wordplay.

Which was… nothing to do with anything. What was I going to say? Oh yes. When I'd left the antique store the previous morning, I'd lingered in the street talking into a silent mobile phone, while using it to snap pictures of the front of the building.

Later that day I'd returned on a scouting mission. It was just before sunset when I found myself spying on the goods entrance at the back of the store. By then my perfect hair had been jammed into a woolly hat and I'd undergone a sort of reverse makeover

216

– part of which involved issuing a last minute reprieve to an old fisherman's jumper and a pair of scruffy jeans that otherwise would have gone into the garbage. I'd dowdied myself up and removed every trace of make-up. You'd have had to really have a thing for staring at frumpy women to recognise me as the fancy-pants shopper from earlier that day.

So, cunningly disguised as myself from a month ago, I'd found my way to the road that ran behind the antique store. You could reach the back of the shop from there by turning off the street, which was mainly residential[1], passing through a pair of high chain-link gates and walking fifty feet down an asphalt driveway.

The first section of the driveway was shared with another business, which made it sort of communal ground. I'd reckoned I could loiter there for a little while without attracting attention. Remember, it didn't look like the Army, with all their wary paranoid deadliness, was involved here. So I just had to make sure I didn't look too much like a furniture thief and I should be fine.

From where I'd stood, I'd been able to see there was a large yard leading to the store's rear loading bay, and a ramp to one side, for wheeling things up to the level of the store room entrance. The entrance itself consisted of a reinforced door adjacent to an enormous heavy-duty metal roller-shutter, which was wide enough and high enough that you could carry a grand piano through it… on its end, if you felt the need.

The setting sun still provided enough light to get a good look at the rear of the premises, but from that distance there wasn't much to see. So once I'd committed a few details to memory I

---

[1] Britain has only the haziest grasp of zoning. A country that can put a nuclear power station next door to a nature reserve can't get worked up about commercial premises adjacent to family homes.

headed off to pick up a few pre-heist essentials and then I went home.

Now I was back for the third time, in the early hours of the next morning, standing thirty foot away from the rear loading bay, crouched behind an old storage bin full of de-icing grit. I'd hopped over the chained-up security gate easily enough and I was tucked behind the last piece of cover before reaching the back of the building. Before I got any closer I was checking that I hadn't missed any security cameras on my earlier visit.

It was just after 3am on an overcast night and the neighbourhood on all sides of me was asleep. There was very little sound and nothing to suggest trouble ahead.

I peered into the dark corners of the building's recesses as best I could using my eyes, and then I pulled my hood down and used the Surfaces to explore in more detail. Still no sign of a camera.

A CCTV camera with a good lens can register an image when it's so dark that owls are stepping on each other's feet, but you still need *some* light for them to work. For that reason, security cameras that are intended for night-use are normally sensitive to infra-red and have a special light-source built in, or maybe slung underneath. Of course, being infra-red, you can't actually see the beam the light-source puts out with your eyes, but it would show up fine if I used the Heat Surface to look around. And I wasn't detecting any such IR illumination.

On the other hand, cameras with Passive IR sensors might only switch themselves on when a warm body came near. With that in mind, I removed a chemical hand-warmer from my pocket and activated it. When it was toasty warm, I hurled it towards the building. A little nudge using Push and it struck the rear door right by the lock. The packet dropped onto the concrete and lay there, clearly visible to me through the Heat Surface, blazing away in the infra-red. Hand-warmers run a little cooler than human flesh so I gave it a little encouragement with Heat, just to make sure it would trigger any sensors. Still no sign of any IR light-sources, so I reckoned it was safe to approach.

From what I could tell from my previous two trips, all the doors and windows had magnetic switches to register when they were opened. Any windows that weren't made to open had conductive-film strip-sensors fitted, which could tell if the glass was broken. From outside, I could sever the connection to any of the sensors using magic, but that would only trigger the alarm. I needed another way in.

When I reached the rear of the building, I climbed up the drainpipe near the bottom of the ramp and swung myself onto a flat section of roof. While skilful use of Push made it easier to haul myself around, I still had to remind myself that my muscles weren't very strong. Even when they only had to carry half my weight, my fingers sometimes struggled to maintain their grip.

I could only marvel at the person I'd been. I'd known for most of the last twenty-six years that my body, being female, had only a fraction of the testosterone of a man's, so I was always going to find it difficult to maintain muscle mass. But had I compensated by doing plenty of strength training? I'm surprised you even have to ask.

Now that I was up high, I could see over the security fence into the next property. It looked like a good direction to head in if things went, as the English would have it, pear-shaped. Fortunately, with the lack of a moon, I wouldn't be all that easy to see up here. The black clothing would help too – and not just because it made my thighs look slimmer.

I didn't have to worry about being seen from the street at the front of the shop because the building itself hid me. The front of the building had a high, pitched roof, with the ridge running parallel to the road. The lower rear section, where I stood now, was flat, punctuated by a couple of vents and a new looking heat exchanger for the building's climate control. I shuffled over and examined one of the vents to see if I could remove the metal louvres of the cowling. The dimensions where the vent passed through the roof were a little small for a grown-up to get through. Even if I could remove the whole cowling unit, it would be a tight squeeze.

(Probably) no harm in trying though. It would be a lot of metal to burn through, and trying to Shatter it free would make a noise like a grenade going off. I ran my hands over the metal and used the Surfaces to probe the joints inside, trying to find a weak point. I could sense two bolts which held the main part of the assembly fixed to the frame it sat in. With a little science and a heaped helping of concentration, I reckoned I could break the bolts without waking the neighbours.

First I Heated the bolts, dividing my concentration equally between them to make sure they were both properly roasted. After a couple of minutes, I could feel the temperature really start to climb. Through the Heat Surface I could sense the metal glowing yellow, then orange – ripples of hot colour pulsing against the washed-out ambience of the background. I kept Heating, all the way up to a cherry red. That was hotter than many adepts could manage, but I needed the high temperature to make the steel brittle. One final burst of Heat and then, with all the speed I could muster, I Froze them, pushing hard, dragging them down from red-heat, to room temperature, and quickly on down below zero. Moments later I could sense flakes of frost piling up on the bolts' glassy threads.

Then, gathering my focus, I Shattered the bolts at their mid-points, first one, then the other. They fractured loudly in the dead air. But it wasn't a troubling sound like glass shattering or a dog's bark starting up. It sounded like deep ice cracking and for a moment I saw the pale-blue light from my dream.

No time for that now, though. With a bit of jostling and

twisting, I pulled the vent-cowling free of the roof. From immediately below I heard the thump and tinkle of a sheared bolt dropping onto some priceless heirloom and then bouncing away into the gloom. Between their AC and the damp climate, these vents probably didn't get much use and this one was filthy. I set it down on the roof next to me and peered into the hole.

The floor was about twenty-five feet below me: a long way to jump for someone with the muscle tone of a boiled Muppet – even with occult assistance to cushion the fall. I'd need to hang, *then* drop – while attempting to miss the chest of drawers immediately beneath.

I lowered my legs through the hole and, as gracefully as possible, wiggled my hips through the gap. Careful not to snag my backpack, I slid down until I was hanging by my hands. The metal edge of the vent's frame dug sharply into my palms, cutting through the fabric of my gloves, but I held on long enough to rock my centre of gravity a little to one side. Then I let go and was falling through empty space. (Without meaning to, I found myself imagining the sound a person might make if they dropped twenty feet to land on a glass display case.)

Again, I needed to use a little Push to avoid impacting coccyx-first, but my trajectory allowed me to reach a strip of empty floor and avoid the many looming, cloth-shrouded mounds of slumbering Victoriana. Then I hit the ground and an electric crackle of pain shot through my ankle.

My eyes watered, involuntarily, and I sat down with a bump.

Pulling off my gloves, I sat there for a moment massaging the fire in my tendons with my bleeding hands. I still had many of my old, self-pitying instincts from all those years as a willing victim of life's unfairness and it took me a couple of seconds to suppress the swirl of pain and tearfulness I felt. I touched the necklace at my throat to remind me to be strong and that did the trick. The door slammed shut on all that neurotic nonsense and I was once again all business.

I took a few minutes to focus on my hands and my ankle, working the Healing surface over the damage. My palms had only superficial cuts; I would have ignored them completely except that I didn't want to leave pools of my blood at the scene of a crime. My ankle required a little more work – and, plus, it wasn't optional: I needed to be able to put my weight on both feet, maybe even run if it came to that.

Ten minutes later my ankle felt fine. It wasn't back to full mobility but it was pretty close.

Next, I directed my concentration to the lip of the frame far above me. I worked my way around the sharp edge, scorching the metal with Heat, until I was sure I'd barbequed any blood I'd left up there: a precaution in case the London bobbies watched CSI.

Then I pulled on my gloves and stood up to look around, picturing the layout from when Cheryl brought me back here. The dust-covers draped over so many boxy shapes made the room look like a miniature town after a massive snowfall, all banked sides and softened outlines – particularly so, as the Surfaces couldn't discern normal colours, rendering the scene as pale as a ghost's breath on a winter morning.

I found the bureau first and pulled the cloth from it. It looked very promising as a hiding place, with drawers all up the base and a hinged front that opened flat to reveal more recesses. Of course, I was looking for a *hidden* drawer or a secret compartment, but still, there was enough wood here, and enough structure, to offer plenty of opportunities for concealment. Carefully, I slipped my focus in through the joints of the frame, along the smooth timbers of the carcass, behind the backs of the drawers and under the surface of the inner compartments. It was tricky, delicate work, and I found nothing except wood, glue, handmade screws and some tufts of cotton rag entombed since the bureau was made.

On to the next item, which was an armchair. It was even trickier than probing the inside of the bureau. The metal springs in the stuffing and the taut threads of the webbing confused my senses. I was tempted to tear the thing apart, but in the end I ran through the internal space of the chair using Freeze and after that I found I could distinguish the chilled metal from the warmer organics. Now I could focus on the multitude of metallic loops and twists and it became obvious that they were all springs and pins, not platinum filigree.

The credenza was a bust too, and because of its size it took a lot of checking. I'd already eaten up an hour since I jumped over the gate, which made it 4:00am now – and I still had the three items out on the sales floor to check. I'd wanted to be out of there by 4:30, because I knew there were people who actually get up at five on a Sunday. Granted they were mostly golfers and fishermen, but just because they were crazy didn't mean the police would necessarily ignore a call from them.

On the other hand, I hadn't wanted to get here any earlier. London is such a boozy, good-time gal of a city that half the population is still busying throwing up their kebabs at 3am – and the police are out in force keeping an eye on them. It's a real challenge finding a good time for bad deeds.

So I'd checked out the furniture in the stock room and found nothing. Now I approached the door that led out to the sales floor. I stopped in front of it to look for alarm sensors.

There was a magnetic switch fastened to the frame that would set off the alarm if the door was opened without taking some sort of preventive action first. Fortunately for me it was on my side of the frame. Evidently burglars were supposed to force their way in at the front of the shop and work backwards from there. Silly me for breaking in all wrong.

In the pocket of my jacket I had a double-syringe of rapid-setting epoxy. I took it out now, uncapped it and applied huge globs of resin around both halves of the sensor. Then I warmed it a little to speed the reaction along. Time was ticking and I could sense some part of me growing restless over how long this was taking, but it wasn't a good idea to rush these things. By now I'd had some practice at ignoring the little voice in my head that wanted me to panic or lose my cool or give up.

I probed the room behind the door as I waited for the glue to set.

I gave it ten minutes, keeping the glue at about body temperature to aid the curing. Once it was hard to the touch, I went back to the storage area and over to the workbench on the side wall. When I'd been shown around by Cheryl, I'd noticed a tool chest there and now I started pulling open drawers looking for suitable tools. I found a razor-sharp wood-chisel and a large screwdriver with a taped handle. I brought them back with me to the door and began using them to gently pry the magnetic sensor out of the wood. Naturally I had to help the process along with a little magic, warming the wood fibres and pushing the screws out from the back.

Gradually, the sensor was coming loose but it was taking an age.

I checked my watch and decided to take a risk in order to save some time. I packed the sensor in a tight Shield and applied a little Shatter to the frame of the door, directing it along the grain in the areas around the sensor. The hundred-year-old wood split neatly and the sensor came free, complete with a patch of gloss-painted woodwork, forever joined to the two halves of the sensor in one resinous lump. I was sure that no one outside the building would have heard a thing.

I collapsed the Shield and let the sensor assembly dangle from its wires. Then I reached in and pushed the tumblers of the lock mechanism aside, unlocking the door. But I didn't turn the handle yet.

First I directed Freeze at the two PIR sensors in the corner of the room beyond, until I could sense ice building up on the front of the detectors. Then I frosted up the lenses of the security cameras. Only then did I open the door and step out onto the shop floor.

I felt very exposed, being able to see out through the tops of the shop windows, over the furniture on display, and into the deserted street beyond. There were lights on in the display windows, but painted backdrops screened off most of the store from anyone looking in. I could see spits of rain hitting the glass of the window which was a good sign: bad weather made it even less likely that someone from the Neighbourhood Watch would be taking a stroll at this hour. But if someone did pass by, all they'd see beyond the top edge of the window display was blackness. It was dark as a starless night in the back half of the sales floor, except for the lone constellation of twinkling LEDs that belonged to the phone, the cash register and the thermostat.

Moving swiftly now, I made my way to the card table. It took only moments to check and then I was on to the first of the chairs. I was beginning to get a sinking feeling as I finished it and started probing the second chair. Now there was only the sideboard to check. It took me nearly ten minutes to be sure, but when I was done, I'd satisfied myself that the Marker wasn't in the store.

Damn it.

Which meant it was in one of the pieces they'd already sold.

Now I would have to find the store's records of its sales.

While the storage area at the back was a single storey construction with twenty-foot ceilings, the front of the building, which was clearly much older, had an upstairs – in fact, the outside windows in my photographs suggested an attic space above the first floor[1].

How many doors with how many sensors would I have to get past? How many cameras? I didn't know, but it wasn't like I could pack up and go home. I paused a moment just to think through my options.

OK, I suppose I *could* go home and come back another night, but the owners would know they'd been burgled, and like most people once the horse has bolted, they'd probably fit newer, stronger stable doors. Alternatively, I could say to myself, *hang the sneaking around*, and just rampage through the place, gambling that I could find what I wanted and get out before anyone reacted to a triggered alarm. The third option was just to carry on, let the clock keep ticking, and trust either that I wouldn't be discovered, or if I was, that one or two standard-issue policemen wouldn't pose much of a problem for me.

Actually, even half a dozen *armed* police weren't going to slow me down much; it was just a question of much of a ruckus I was prepared to raise if I found myself cornered. All in all, it seemed best to keep going, keep quiet and trust in the universal instinct to laziness that keeps most nosey people in bed on Sunday mornings.

The decision made, I was maybe five minutes into this plan, when I decided to change tack. Why? Well, I was still working on the door that led to the next floor when an urgent peep-peep-peep noise started up; it was coming from the direction of the store room.

I dashed out to investigate and found the main panel for the climate-control system lit up like a radioactive Christmas tree on the fourth of July. Above the sound of the alarm, I could also

---

[1] That's the British use of 'first floor'. Confusingly, if I were back in the US, I'd *already be* on the first floor. Which would have saved me some time. Huh?

hear the sound of rainwater pattering onto the dust-covers from the hole in the ceiling. Crap. The weather was getting in and it had set off the temperature/humidity sensors.

I ran back to the sales floor, placed one hand on the door to the stairs and blew the lock out through the other side of the frame. Then I threw the door open and ran upstairs, feeling ahead of me with my mind, looking for the heavy, resonating bulk of a filing cabinet. Doubtless, everything was electronic these days, but I was sure they'd still store their signed delivery notes for a while.

I had to shatter another lock before I found the right office and then I had to calm my heartbeat so that I could concentrate on the tumblers on the first of three filing cabinets. Not even *I* could read ink on paper without using my eyes, so I turned on the overhead light and quickly ascertained that all the paperwork in front of me pertained to wages and employee records. I was just Pushing open the lock on the second cabinet when I heard the heavy metal shutter of the loading bay downstairs being opened. I glanced out of the nearest window, which overlooked the street in front of the shop, but saw nobody down there yet.

Now something cold shifted inside of me and I really began to move quickly. Checking the second filing cabinet, I could see the files I was looking for. I clawed my backpack off, grabbed a wedge of delivery notes six inches thick and thrust them into the pack. Then I grasped an equally thick sandwich of goods receipts and shoved them in next to the delivery notes. I zipped up the pack, strapped it back on and ran from the room.

I turned, and with something icy squeezing my heart, I ignited the remaining contents of first one and then the other filing cabinet. Then I burst through the door of the room opposite, figuring it must lead to the back windows of the building.

Into the room – and in the corner I spied a safe. Perfect. I lashed out at it through the violence of the Shatter Surface, cratering the door with a single heavy blow.

Good enough.

Turning back, I blew out the rear windows as the fire began to roar and to light up the hallway behind me. This was just like the old days: no time to hesitate. I leapt out onto the flat roof and sprinted to the back edge of the building. Without pausing to see who was below, I jumped, Pushing into a high arc over the security fence and dropping down into next door's parking area. It was a thirty foot fall from the highest point, but for this manoeuvre I had plenty of room to land. I rolled as I hit the concrete and this time my ankle held.

I tore through the next fence as quietly as I could, aware of the gathering orange glow immediately behind me, and then scrambled up, over the roof of the next building and down onto a footpath beyond. From there I could thread my way through back streets, moving rapidly on quiet feet, until I was half a mile from the shop. I took a deep breath then and found the cold weight in my chest loosening its hold.

I smartened myself up, tucked the hood, gloves and gold into my backpack and stepped out onto the main road to look for a cab. I got lucky and I was just settling into the black leather of the back seat when the first of the fire engines blew past.

Chapter 21

This was a strange feeling. All the elements for panic were present, but I was calm. It was like watching someone stick a scalpel into an anaesthetised arm – my arm. I should feel something: react, scream and shout, but I didn't. My calmness was unbreakable.

But somewhere, beneath the calm, I *was* reacting. Like a madman in a cramped cage, in some deep dungeon, one part of me was silently, impotently freaking out about the previous night's events. Torching the store, the destruction, and the memory of a frigid feeling like flying as I crashed through doors, tearing up anything in my way. In a carefully sealed off part of my mind I was half hysterical because for twenty years, whenever I'd lost control of a situation, I had always turned inwards and imploded. I was always the first and only casualty of my meltdowns. But last night had been different, uncontained, explosive. I'd radiated an angry, surging wildness that felt unpleasantly familiar. My brain had pulsed with destructive impulses, they'd multiplied like bacteria, until they burst out of me, assaulting my surroundings like a shockwave. I knew I would have cut down people with the same savage efficiency that I used to demolish inanimate obstacles in my path.

But the dominant part of me maintained an arctic composure, gliding across an emotionless surface beneath which my tiny, weaker self was trapped. After all, there was no problem. I wasn't seen last night, I didn't fail. No harm was done to my plans. I came away with everything the situation had offered me. The Marker wasn't there, so the next best thing was information about its whereabouts, which I now possessed. There was nothing to berate myself over. The mess was someone else's to clear up and nothing linked me to it.

The only uncertainty was over the police follow-up. There was no sign that I'd tried to steal any antiques, so the investigation was unlikely to view this as a conventional burglary. I didn't especially want the owners of the store to notice the gaps in their paperwork, put two and two together, and warn their clients that someone might be coming to rob them. So I'd had to improvise a false motive for the break-in. On the spur of the moment, the best I could do was to hint at an employee theft gone wrong. The botched safe-cracking would point the police towards a different kind of robbery and the torched employee records would hint that a former member of staff was involved; why else set light to the files unless it was to cover your tracks?

I thought there was a fair chance that the false clues would send the police down the wrong path. And if it didn't work, if the police somehow concluded that the break-in was about stealing client invoices, and the recent customers of the store were warned to be on their guard, well so be it.

It had been noisy – showy even – the way I'd handled things, but there was nothing to be ashamed of. And yet this other noise in my head wouldn't stop its bleating. It was extremely distracting. So I clamped down my emotions – squeezing as hard as I could – until that twittering voice was throttled into silence.

230

The effort set off a headache that came from nowhere and seemed to bury its sharp sting just behind my right eye. For a horrible moment, I thought my struggle for composure was going to rupture a blood vessel. But then the headache passed and my control returned. I was feeling fine again – and there would be no more whining and flailing. I just would not stand for it.

I'd taken a shower when I got in and then laid out on my bed for a while, hands behind my head. I couldn't sleep, but then I never had slept much. It was enough that I was able to breathe, to feel my chest rising and falling, to be free.

I wondered how swiftly I would need to act now, to follow-up on last night's captured intelligence. It seemed more important to be thorough than to be quick. The only other task with a conceivable claim on my time was the job of investigating the Army on the Professor's behalf, and really, that didn't seem all that important any more. I told myself, my whining other self, that I would take care of it sooner or later, but privately I was rapidly realising something: I was finished with the PAC. All I cared about now was the Marker.

* * *

Around 7 am, I put on some coffee and found bread and fruit to eat. Noola, if she was in, was still sleeping; her door was closed. I took the coffee back up with me to the top room, pushed the bolt across and spread out the papers from last night's raid.

First, I turned to the receipts. They listed each purchase the shop had made, and somewhere in the pile would be one detailing the last collection from Mr. Niall Harrington. When I found it, I compared the items it listed with my stack of invoices. When I found a match, I could see from the invoice the name and addresses of the customer who bought the item.

Cheryl/Celine had said that only two items from the last

Harrington collection had been sold and I hoped she was right. Two was a manageable number when you were planning break-ins.

My money was on the desk being the Marker's hiding place. I had it in mind that a 'Regency pedestal desk' would be about half a ton of intricately worked, endangered hardwood – a perfect blank from which to whittle out a secret compartment. To an anxious adept with something to conceal, it would feel like a safe hiding place.

By 10 am, I'd double-checked the paperwork and confirmed Cheryl's version of things: only two items. I had the contact details for the owners of both the desk and the escritoire, neither of which were in London. So I'd soon be making a couple of road trips. Well, *one*, if I got lucky first time. I decided to get the train out to where the owner of the desk lived that afternoon. Depending on what I found, I might even stay over and attempt my raid on the place that very evening.

The house was near Penshurst, a village in Kent, that according to the sheaves of entries Google retrieved for me was plenty picturesque and mucho historico (I'm paraphrasing). It certainly looked that way from the pictures. I pulled up some maps and saw that I had quite a trek from the station to the house in question – not a problem when I was reconnoitring the place in daylight, but not ideal for a fast getaway after I broke in. Train travel for something like this was a joke. I was really going to have to find myself some adequate personal transport.

I brooded on that for a while, eventually deciding that it was important enough to be worth delaying my retrieval of the desk. I'd still take the train down that afternoon and 'case the joint', as they (used to) say; I'd maybe hike a little through the nearby countryside too, to get a feel for the surroundings, but I wouldn't break into the house until I could come up with something better than a brisk jog as my getaway strategy.

And I already had an idea for how to solve the transport problem, so I did a little research – memorising what I read and picturing the instructions in my mind. A bite of lunch and then it was time to make my way to London Bridge to catch a train to the Kent countryside.

* * *

The trip to the manicured wilds of Kent was uneventful but a success. I returned with photos and sketches of the house where the pedestal desk now resided; I knew what the occupants looked like and I could make some sort of estimate of how best to raid the place.

The owners seemed to be a couple in their sixties, plus a cat; none of them seemed likely to pose much of a problem.

I came back to London in the early evening and headed home for a little nap. I was finally feeling tired enough to need a couple of hours of sleep. In the end I slept until 10pm, which was fine; I only had one more task to perform that day and there was no point in starting it too early.

Before going out, I found some dark clothing, a black wool cap and a heavy leather jacket, and then I left the house heading for the West End. I'd printed out a list of central London multi-storey car parks and now I made my chilly way, on foot, from one to the next. I finally found what I was looking for just round the corner from Leicester Square: half a dozen motorcycles parked on the deserted roof of the car park. And most importantly, there were two of the same high-end make and model: Yamaha YZF-R1's, both in dark blue, both a few years old.

I loitered in the shadows for a couple of minutes, waiting to see if anyone else was around, and simultaneously checking out the closed-circuit cameras. Under my cap I was wearing tribute and now I Connected in order to burn out the sensors in both of the nearby security cameras.

As well as the two R1s I was interested in, there was another bike at the end of the line-up, a ratty old BMW tourer, which had a new-looking helmet padlocked to its seat. I cracked the lock, pulled off my woolly hat, and put the helmet on my head – being careful not to dislodge my headband.

Then I went over to the R1s and got to work removing their number plates and swapping them over. The one on the left looked a little more dinged up, so I decided that would be the one I'd leave behind.

Next I cracked the two shackle-locks securing the bike I planned to take. I hopped on, placing my hand over the slot for the ignition key and concentrated.

It was a fiddly lock, but after thirty seconds or so, I had lined up the tumblers and twisted the cylinder. The bike's instrument panel lit up.

Now for the moment of truth. Sitting astride the R1 I started the engine.

It was a very different thing *reading* about riding a bike to actually doing it. But then again, the only two bikers I knew were a little lower down the intellectual pecking order than the average drummer. If they could do it, so could I.

Kick-stand up, clutch in, put it into gear, little gas, let out the clutch. Not bad. I actually got the thing rolling. No stall and no rubber-scorching wheelie. I ran the bike forty feet across the roof, moving slowly, heading for the edge of the down ramp – and then I brought it to a halt. Turning my head I closed my eyes and reached out, finding the back of the R1 I'd left behind. I Heated the rear licence plate until it was just a lump of charred and smoking plastic. Then I did the same for the front plate.

When the police identified the bikes I was about to wreck, I wanted to make sure they relied on chassis numbers for the R1. When they figured out that one of the bikes was missing and started looking for it, they'd be searching for the plate numbers I'd just incinerated.

And if anyone ran a check on the plate number I was using, they'd find a description that matched this bike, and probably think no more of it. One day soon, those records might list the bike as 'destroyed', but that was better than recording it as 'stolen': the police don't go looking for destroyed vehicles.

Next, I sought out the gas tanks of each bike in the row, lining them up in my mind and *squeezing* Heat into them. I tried to cook them all up together, but it was tricky doing it evenly. At any rate, when one finally ignited, the others blew immediately.

The explosion was a little more than I'd been expecting; it blended into a single, colossal crash which actually sent a couple of pieces of debris hurtling my way. Something hard pinged off my visor, and a piece of metal thumped into my upper arm, causing me some pain even through the leather. I reckoned next time I'd put a Shield in place first.

Filthy black smoke poured out of the fire and flowed along the concrete ceiling, occasionally revealing heat-rippled glimpses of the roasting and broken machines inside the flames. It looked like a scrapheap in hell.

I turned away from the fire and gave the bike a little throttle, letting out the clutch and pulling slowly away from the scene of my second count of pyromania that weekend. I managed not to tip the heavy bike over in the corners as I spiralled carefully down the car park's ramps. I had to Shatter one more camera that might otherwise have captured a clear image of the bike, then I forced up the exit barrier and gave the throttle a little blip as I pulled out onto the dark street.

Belatedly, I remembered to turn on the bike's lights, but even with them on, at slow speeds I found it much easier to ride with my head down, my eyes closed, *feeling* the road, concentrating on my balance and the revving of the engine.

I kept my speed down, heading away from the West End, and drove around the quieter back roads near the edge of the City for most of an hour, getting the hang of the bike. Then I turned south, crossed the Thames and threaded my way back to Stockwell. A couple of times I opened up the throttle, just to see what it was like, whether I could handle it – and it felt fantastic. I managed not to fluff any gear changes or have the thing topple on me as I sat at the lights – though on one occasion I only managed that with a little occult shove at the last minute.

I reckoned I'd give myself a couple of days more practice before I officially declared this bike my getaway vehicle. I'd also rig something with the ignition switch. I couldn't afford to spend best part of a minute concentrating on fiddly tumblers every time I wanted to start the thing. I figured I'd disconnect the multi-position key-switch Yamaha had fitted and instead route the wires to a regular switch and a push button. Flip the switch, push the button and anyone could start the bike in seconds. Just to make sure that anyone didn't, though, I'd wrap the new controls in polythene, smother them in Epoxy and glue them under the tank cover. The bike would be adepts-only then. Only someone Connected would be able to reach under the seat, *through* the glue, and flip the controls. Regular humans would find it a distinct challenge to steal.

I left the bike a couple of streets away and walked the last two hundred yards home. I wasn't tired – in fact I was a little bit psyched from riding around town – but I was happy to lie on the bed, letting my thoughts drift. Instead of sleeping, I spent a couple of hours in a Healing trance, letting it do the job of sleep – and a little more besides. It was an old trick and a good way to always be at your best. Then, around four-thirty, I went for a walk. And as my feet wandered the empty, dayless streets, my mind wandered among the many branching paths of the plans I was making.

236

Chapter 22

Jeez. I saw why they made those bikes so fast; with that engine noise you're not going to be able to *sneak* away. Fortunately, if I kept the revs down to little more than an idle I could almost convince myself that I was being stealthy as I drove through the back roads of the Kent countryside. If asked whether they remembered anything, I didn't want half the county to say, "Well I did look out of my window when I heard a sound like a fighter jet taking off, and I saw this girl going by on a blue motorbike."

A week had passed since the weekend of the antiques fire and the car park fire. I'd swiped the bike in the early hours of Monday morning, initially thinking that I might take it down to Kent the next day. But I'd gone for a long walk after my hog-heist, and I'd done a lot of thinking. I'd worked through each step of my plan to recover the Marker, and I'd visualised as many contingencies and branch-points as I could. Different scenarios might come to the fore depending on how the previous step turned out (i.e. what went wrong) and I wanted to pre-think all of it.

I reckoned my chances of finding myself surrounded by a contingent of Army assassins rose dramatically the closer I got to the Marker. If they were on to me, I'd need to have my escape route planned before I made that last dash to grab the Marker.

On Monday I checked in with the Professor, even though I really wasn't planning to go back – but I figured there was no sense rushing to burn any bridges yet. If I failed to find the Marker, the PAC might still be useful to me.

The Professor was eager to hear if I'd learned anything new, so I threw him a bone. I told him that I'd discovered Dass was part of some secret society called The Army Who Witnessed Creation. It wasn't news to him, of course, but it proved I was making real progress on the sleuthing.

Then, a few days later, I shared a couple of titbits on the non-magical history of the sect that I happened to recall – nothing terribly useful, some famous names from the past, a few details on the evolution of their territory. It was old news really, but it captured the Professor's imagination. He was very impressed and wanted to know where I'd found that information. For a moment I couldn't recall, so I made up a lie about managing to hack into Interfinanzio's computer system and finding some of Dass's personal files.

He sounded me out on that, clearly wondering if I'd stumbled upon any references to magic, but he didn't want to come right out and ask. So I played dumb: as far as I was concerned, this was still Harriet the Spy, and not the X-Files.

Checking in every day was starting to become a pain, so I also told him that I was coming down with something and I probably wouldn't phone for a little while, until my poor throat was feeling better and I was ready to get back to work. And we left it at that.

So it was the middle of my second week in London before I was ready to head down to Kent. I'd taken the bike out a half a dozen times, and driven round for an hour or so. While I wasn't ready for [insert the famous bike race of your choice] yet, I was feeling pretty comfortable getting around on the thing. The one hiccup had come when I ran low on gas and pulled into a petrol station. I'd stopped at the pump before I remembered that filler caps have locks on them – and without tribute, I wasn't going to be able to be able to open this one without a hammer or a cutting torch. So I headed home, grabbed my tribute, sprang the lock, and made it to the nearest petrol station without running out of gas completely. I left the filler cap unlocked after that and hang the risk of petrol theft.

* * *

On Wednesday evening, I made my final preparations and then drove down to Penshurst. I got there about 7pm – comfortably after dark – and parked the bike outside a nearby pub where it wouldn't attract attention. Then I walked the couple of hundred yards to the house. It was red-brick with a tile roof, but it was old – I'd guess at least two hundred years. The windows were mullioned or bastioned or whatever the word was. They were made from coaster-sized diamond-shapes of glass set in a lead lattice. They'd be child's play to get through.

I found a way to get off the road and circle round to the back of the property. The land behind the back garden was open and beyond their fence there were lots of trees for cover, and after that farmland. I've never been much for climbing trees, but it seemed the sensible thing to do here. So I hauled myself up and found a good perch from which to observe the back of the house.

Downstairs, the curtains were drawn – though I could see the lights were on – but upstairs the curtains were open and I had a view right through into the master bedroom. Several times I caught glimpses of the lady of the house as she passed the window. She was getting ready to go out. She had on a floor-length gown in grey satin and she was fixing her hair and trying on jewellery. After twenty minutes or so she went away for a minute and came back carrying a mug of something that steamed. She went somewhere with the mug in her hands and a minute later the upstairs lights went out. Soon after that I glimpsed her downstairs, checking that the kitchen door was locked.

They were definitely going somewhere, which was perfect.

In the still night air, I heard a car door slam and the distant echoing ring of a doorbell. I was fairly sure I could hear an engine idling too. Intrigued, I sprang down from the tree and trotted back round until I reached the road. I didn't emerge out onto the lane but loitered in the bushes – from where I could see a taxi on the sweep of gravel in front of the house. A moment later, the couple came out, the man in a tuxedo and the woman with a fur wrap over her grey gown. The man dallied for a moment, just inside the door, kind of hunched into the wall with one hand up by his nose. It took a second for me to figure out what he was doing: he was pushing numbers on a keypad to set the alarm. Then he closed the door behind him, they both got into the taxi and it pulled away.

So the house was going to be empty. And an alarm wasn't any trouble. This was looking like child's play – assuming children burgled houses – which I'm sure they do these days; the little tykes.

I went back to my tree at the rear of the property and waited, giving the owners twenty minutes to come back for their tickets or to remember that they'd left the bath running, but they didn't return.

From my perch I could tell that the road at the front of the house was fairly quiet – maybe one car per minute – but you'd still have to be ODing on testosterone to break in the front way. The back garden, on the other hand was very private. The house had only one near neighbour, whose curtains were all closed. If I went in that way, there was no one to see me.

I shuffled along my branch, leaned out and then jumped. With a little Push I was able to clear the back fence and roll lightly onto the grass of the lawn. Very nice. It was a strange feeling: one bit of me calmly controlling my tuck and roll, the other part of my brain jabbering that I'd never had a gym class in my life that didn't end badly. Fortunately the capable side of my personality seemed to have settled into the driving seat on a permanent basis.

I loped up the lawn and stood to one side of the back door, in the deep shadows there. There was a window just next to me, which appeared to be for an old-fashioned pantry. There was a ventilated mesh thing that I associated with the larders of old houses.

Reaching out with my mind, I probed around the edge of the pantry window. I could feel a smooth plastic lump on the other side of the frame: undoubtedly a sensor. Concentrating on the fine detail I could tell it was in two parts, just like the sensors on the doors back at the antique store. It was just a simple magnetic switch – separate the halves to trigger the alarm.

Now, as you'll undoubtedly recall, lead melts at 327°C. A little hot for a sauna, but still an achievable temperature to aim for when you're planning to do a little occult metalwork. Working my way all around the lattice of the window, I applied Heat to the lead beading until it began to wilt, and the lattice of the window started to come apart. With a gentle application of Push I made sure that it slumped out towards me, rather than inwards.

I slipped out of my leather jacket, held it like the net firemen hold for jumpers, and caught the drooping nougat of soft lead and chunks of window glass as it sagged free from its frame. I should say I caught *most* of it; a couple of diamonds of glass dropped a foot or so onto the flagstones. They clattered a little, but didn't break.

It didn't sound like much: no louder than someone dropping

a metal fork onto a hard kitchen floor. Even so, I set the glass down, put my jacket back on and stayed where I was, ready to move, waiting for any sign that I'd been discovered.

I gave it three or four minutes, which felt like thirty, and when nothing happened, I climbed in through the empty window frame – being careful not to kick the magnetic sensor with my boot. In the darkness, I could sense the jars and bottles on the shelves around me and I managed to move past them without knocking anything over. I had to use Push to release the catch on the pantry door before I could open it and step out into the shadow-filled kitchen. The house was silent around me.

I left the lights turned out and stood in the centre of the kitchen, reaching out beyond the walls to investigate the nearby rooms. Beyond the kitchen I could sense the cavity of a hallway just inside the front door. From there, doors led off to other ground floor rooms and a staircase doubled back on itself to connect with the upstairs landing.

The largest pocket of empty space I could discern lay the other side of the staircase. Leaving the kitchen, I quietly crossed the hall and opened the door into a large sitting room. The space felt cool and dusty, compared with the kitchen – unlived in – and various pieces of old furniture were arranged around the room, including a baby grand piano by the window.

No pedestal desk though. Neither was it in the other main room on this floor: a warmer space that contained a TV and a gas fire – both recently turned off but still leaking heat into the room.

So I made my way slowly upstairs trying to minimise the creak and chirp of the old timbers as I shifted my weight on the treads. The time-warped wood amplified every movement and my footsteps seemed like they might bring the staircase to life, causing it to start up like a steam organ at a fairground. Sure, I wasn't making a fraction of the noise needed for the neighbours to hear, but I couldn't help feeling that a professional would move a little more stealthily.

As it turned out, there was a better reason than just professionalism for keeping the noise down. As I reached the upstairs landing, the tread of the top step croaked like a frog as my weight lifted. A moment later, a bleary voice called out, "Mum?"

I froze, ready to run or fight. The door ahead of me opened and a woman in her early thirties shuffled out, her hair a snarl of bed-pressed curls. She was wearing thick, fleecy pyjamas and holding a Kleenex to her stuffy, red nose.

"Did you guys…" she asked and then saw me, a stranger, clad in heavy black clothes, my head hooded, standing at the top of her stairs, illuminated by the light spilling out of her room. She started as she caught sight of me, and then a moment later jumped back with a yelp and tried to slam the door to her room.

Chances were that she had a phone in there. I leapt forwards, getting my shoulder to the door before she could close it. For a second we struggled and then I added some Push from my side and she was rammed backwards, stumbling over her own feet. She back-pedalled, colliding with a dainty-looking table and went down.

I took one step into the room and had to duck as something heavy and made of marble smacked into the wall beside my head, its weighty corner punching through the wallpaper and kicking out chips of plaster. She'd heaved one of the ornaments from the toppled table at me. I took another step and looked around for a phone; maybe she had a mobile. A moment later she grabbed the other ornament, a tall, thin African statue of a face. It was made of some dense-looking black wood and she leapt at me swinging it like a club.

I reacted without thinking, punching her out of the air with a pulse of Shatter. I saw her head slam sideways off the door of the wardrobe hard enough to splinter the wood and then she went down like a marionette with its strings cut.

For a moment I stood panting, unsure of myself. I'd nearly hit her a lot harder, except I'd messed up the attack. Even as I was lashing out through the Shatter surface, pouring force into the blow, I was simultaneously pulling back, draining the power of the assault. A part of me had tried to stop the blow even as I had summoned the energy to attack her.

But despite my inner conflict, she'd been thrown pretty hard into that door.

I just stood there, wandering what to do next.

A moment later I heard an unpleasant sound. Blood was bubbling as the woman breathed. She was alive, but her head was arched back, her arm under her. It was painful to look at her in that contorted position.

I took a step forwards, determined to help her, before my self-control kicked in. We were here for one reason alone: the Marker.

As a concession to my clamouring conscience, I decided that when I was done here I would take the phone off the hook and dial the emergency services – just before I left – but not until I'd found that desk and got what I came for.

The desk wasn't in the woman's bedroom – which I imagined her parents used as a guest room when she wasn't visiting – and I doubted it was in the back bedroom I'd spied on earlier from the tree. (I remembered the hot drink the mother had been carrying now and realised who it had been intended for.)

I extended my senses and tried the next room along. I could feel, even before I pushed the door open, that it was a study.

The desk I was looking for sat under the window. I crossed the room to place my hands on the leather inlay of its top surface. I spread my fingers and set about infiltrating my senses into the structure of the wood, feeling out the mechanism of the drawers, testing the spliced joints of the frame.

There was something here. Something.

I could sense a space inside the desk, barely an inch under the tooled leather top. I explored around the edges of the cavity, trying to see how the parts of the desk fitted together. A few moments later, I found the hidden lock. The maker of the desk had added a strip of wood that ran in a groove along the underside of the desktop. If a person opened the top drawer, stuck their hand in about ten inches and felt upwards with their fingers, they would find a depression just deep enough to get some purchase on. Placing two fingers in the depression and pulling forwards would slide the strip in its groove and unlock a hidden catch.

Except that someone had severed the strip. Pulling on it did nothing now. There was no way to undo the lock anymore... unless you could reach inside the desk with your mind and manipulate the locking mechanism through an inch of solid mahogany. Like my bike, this hiding place was adepts-only now.

Probing carefully, I found the break and moved my focus past it until I reached the internal lever it used to be attached to. Then, I applied Push to activate the mechanism. An unseen catch beneath the front of the desktop released, allowing it to angle up like the hood of a car, pivoting on secret hinges.

I lifted the lid, sending a lamp, some stationery and various knick-knacks sliding onto the floor. Inside, under the lid, was a shallow tray, lined with velvet. In the tray were papers. I lifted them out, looking for something beneath them, looking for the Marker. Surely this was the hiding place: somewhere that only Jan could reach.

But there was nothing except papers.

I crouched over the opened desk and probed the velvet lining: was there another layer? Did the tray itself lift out to reveal something beneath? I focussed so hard that I could feel each indentation in the cloth. With a surge of adrenaline I found a depression in the nap that matched the shape of the Marker. It had been here once, pressed into the velvet. But now it was gone.

I felt rage mounting inside me. Not the meek, whining, emotional part of me. Now, for the first time, the ruthless, calculating part of my brain was feeling rage and it *refused* to be thwarted like this.

I sat down on the floor next to where the lamp lay and turned it on. Despite its fall it still worked, and by its light I examined the papers, hoping that they would give me the information I needed. For a while I couldn't make them out, but as I hurriedly scanned them, hope rekindled itself and the rage drained away. There were details here of another place that Jan owned and a sketch of something. It was another hiding place – a *final* hiding place; I felt sure of it.

I took a moment to shut the desktop, clicking the catch closed. Then I put on a show for the police: ripping open a couple of drawers until I found a wallet containing banknotes in several currencies and a number of savings books. I grabbed them, bundled them together with the papers from the secret compartment, and zipped them into my backpack.

Back out on the landing, I headed for the stairs… but found I was desperate to look in on the injured woman. I couldn't help myself; I wanted to see if she was still breathing. I was imagining a spreading pool of blood, her ragged breathing catching and slowing until it ceased.

I shook my head, pushing those thoughts out of my mind, and headed downstairs. On the hall table I passed a telephone and I stopped in front of it. With my gloved hand, I laid the receiver to one side, punched the digits for the emergency operator and made to move towards the back door. For a second I couldn't force myself to leave; I was frozen in place, and then I heard the voice of the operator repeating her question: "Which service do you require? Hello?"

"I need an ambulance," I yelled towards the receiver and that seemed to free me to move my feet again. I ran into the kitchen and turned towards the pantry intending to leave the way I'd come in.

But another rebellious thought stopped me. I'd give the injured woman one more chance at getting some help. I remembered her father configuring the alarm before he left, which meant it was on.

Instead of heading for the pantry window, I ducked down behind the kitchen countertop, focussed on the back door, and blew the lock inwards. Still attached to a chunk of door, it bounced past me across the tile floor and slammed into something out in the hall. The backdoor was flung inwards and now, from the front of the house, I could hear an alarm bell starting to ring. I ran out through the open door and down the garden.

When I reached the rear of the property I jumped, Pushing myself up and over the fence, tucking into a ball as I crashed through some tree branches, and landing on all fours among the leaf litter. I stood and dusted myself down, then I trotted through the woods, and across the corner of a ploughed field, until I could see the roof of the pub. I hopped a fence, finding myself on a footpath that led along the side of the pub's car park.

I Froze out the single light that illuminated the path and stood in the darkness, feeling with my extended senses across the expanse of asphalt beyond, hunting for the bike.

I found it, and spread out my focus looking for observers. At that moment, the car park seemed to be empty of people. Narrowing my concentration once more, I felt my way along the bike's frame until I located the epoxied controls and I started the engine.

Once it was running, I sprinted to the end of the lane, stepped over into the pub garden and walked briskly back to my idling bike. I pulled on my helmet, jumped on and shoved the bike forward on its kickstand, dropping it into gear and moving quickly out onto the road. I flicked on the lights but kept the revs low and the throttle barely open until I'd covered a half mile and I dared to make a little noise.

Throughout all of this – right from the moment I'd slammed that woman's skull into a wardrobe door – I'd been in shock. The ruthless, practical part of me was in sole charge, while whichever remnant of my old self it was that possessed a conscience looked on in stunned horror. Only twice in the following ten minutes had my humanity surfaced: once to make that phone call, the other time to trigger the alarm.

I roared back up the A21, staying under the speed limit, and tried to keep my mind from fracturing into two separate halves – with whatever consequent loss of sanity that might entail.

The impact of skull hitting wood played over and over, and I knew that something had changed.

Chapter 23

Do you ever have dreams where you watch yourself from the outside? I've heard that sometimes people who've come close to death say they saw themselves from above, as though their spirits had left their bodies and were looking down on them.

I felt like that now, except my spirit was trapped inside me – no longer wholly connected to my body but still imprisoned within it. I could monitor myself, see what I was doing, but I wasn't in control.

The sense of paralysis and dread that crept over me as I realised what was happening brought to mind something disturbing I'd once read in a medical journal, about the recipient of a limb transplant who was gradually driven to the edge of madness by the feeling that his pale new flesh, though a part of him now, still wasn't his own. He had finally insisted that the hospital cut off his new hand so that he could get some peace. With a feeling that grew like an itch beneath my skin, I thought I knew how he'd felt.

When I'd first used magic, when I had the ice dream, I had thought that magic was freeing me, fixing me. I thought it had cured me of whatever it was that had always held me back, that had screwed things up for me. I'd welcomed this improved, stronger me – unfamiliar though it was. That new strength was disorienting but wonderful and everything had suddenly seemed so easy, so effortless. But now I'd come to realise it was effortless because it wasn't me doing it. I found everything easy because all I was doing was watching, while someone (some thing?) pulled the levers, took the strain and made my decisions for me.

What ever was happening to me, I was no longer in charge of my life.

The feeling that things were badly wrong in some new and horrible way had been growing inside me for days. I had watched myself with an increasing sense of isolation, even disapproval. I found myself acting even before I'd considered what I wanted to do. And if I did reach some sort of decision ahead of time it seemed to have no effect: I'd see myself follow some totally different course of action.

So why didn't I fight? Why didn't I even realise what was happening? Well for a time I thought I knew what it was: it was simply the old, neurotic me reacting with spite and resentment to my new, capable attitude to life. The old me *liked* being miserable, was comfortable in its familiar pit of despair, so *of course* that part of me felt unsettled, hijacked even.

Long ago sessions with half-forgotten therapists had even warned me this would happen. The old and bad would feel familiar, the new and good would feel strange. I had to embrace the new. But I'd never managed it, partly because the bad voices were the ones that seemed most like *me*. So initially, when I'd noticed this growing sense of split personality, that's what I thought was causing it.

And even then I'd felt like something bad was happening, but somehow I hadn't been able to dwell on my concerns; my mind refused to lock on to the problem. As soon as I started to focus on the *wrongness* I was feeling, everything slowed, it became difficult to concentrate, and my mind wandered. But if I abandoned that train of thought I felt better, more purposeful. My head only stayed clear if I concentrated on the task in hand: the search for the Marker. Nothing else mattered.

I now realised that some internal censor in my head had been pulling the plug on more than just my sense of wrongness. There were questions that I should have been asking, riddles that had fascinated me just a few weeks before, that I couldn't seem to find time for now. Like, where did magic come from? How did it work? Given who I was, I should have been obsessed, *relentless* in fact, when it came to those questions. But I'd hardly given them a thought – hardly *been able* to give them a thought.

I'd caught myself thinking over past events and remembering things that had never happened; I recalled facts that I'd never learned, like the information about the Army that had just popped into my head when I was talking to the Professor.

I mean, *I* didn't know Latin; I certainly didn't have a pet Latin maxim about the dark, even though I'd chuckled to myself about it. *I* hadn't watched opium devour old friends, yet I felt the residue of that anger as I walked through the junkie's alleyway. *I* shouldn't have known how to manipulate the Surfaces like a master of two centuries' standing but it came to me like I was born to it. None of this was me.

Then this evening something had shifted; something had torn. I had been too horrified by my own actions to carry on as before. And with my conscious awareness of the rift, came a change, a divergence. Now that I knew – absolutely *knew* – that some other agency was at work here, I found my true thoughts starting to separate themselves from their impostors. Someone was still steering the motorbike, watching the road, mulling over the contents of the documents from the desk, but it *distinctly* wasn't me. *I* was mentally huddled in a corner gibbering to myself and panicking.

It now seemed obvious to me that magic was something more than the PAC had realised; it was more than just a way to affect the world. It *did* something to you. It implanted itself in you.

But it didn't just alter what it touched; it added to it. So where did those extra memories come from? Someone's agenda had overridden my own – where did it originate? Was there an actual personality at work here? Could there be some sort of intelligence behind magic, a being at the heart of it all who could influence adepts, who could subvert them while letting them think they were in control?

Yet I didn't think Susan or David had experienced this, or the Professor. Had Jan? Had Dass? Why hadn't I heard of this phenomenon? If other adepts had felt what I was feeling, sooner or later they'd for-damn-sure notice – or those around them would. Not only had I read dozens of the PAC's documents on the nature, tradition and application of magic without seeing a mention of such a thing, I had also glimpsed the layers of knowledge and memory that had coalesced in my mind from elsewhere – knowledge that allowed me to manipulate magic like a master – and it didn't include the memory of being influenced, of having to guard against being controlled.

And yet there was something…

I 'remembered' (though it couldn't be *my* memory I was drawing on) a facet of the training embarked upon by new adepts (in the days when there *had* been new adepts – that was another fact that appeared from nowhere). I recalled an exercise to ward off distracting influences and fey moods which might otherwise settle upon the novice. The more I thought about it, the more it seemed to hint at an outside agency invading the vulnerable minds of those new to magic. But it was a fleeting, tenuous thing they were guarding against – like an unwanted daydream or a gloomy mood that was difficult to shake – all in all about as much of a problem as an annoying song stuck in your head. Was that some mild strain of the full-blown affliction I was suffering from? Was I the only one to get the virulent form of this malady? What was so special about me?

But wait. Hadn't there been something else? I vaguely remembered pressing 'delete' in exasperation, shortly after I began to read one of the PAC's scanned, ancient manuscripts. Which document? Why had I deleted it? I struggled to recall the moment, and that effort detached a scrap of sequestered memory and allowed it to float up to the surface. The outside influence in my head had forced me to erase a document in which someone began to recount a dream they'd had and I wondered what I would have found if I'd read on. A clue perhaps, an echo of my own predicament?

It was tantalising, but whatever else that document contained, I was sure it wasn't the sole surviving mention of a legion of possessed adepts, their minds all slaved to some controlling entity. There was no getting around it: if others had had their heads invaded by something with the same implacable strength as the force that was controlling me, then the PAC's collection of manuscripts should be full of warnings.

As far as I could see, these were the only possibilities: 1) Those possessed aroused no suspicions in others and were unable to tell anyone that they were possessed – which didn't fit, because lots of people had noticed a profound change in *me*. 2) Every adept was possessed so there was no one left unaffected to raise the alarm – but I didn't believe that David, Susan, the Professor and the Army Who were under the same influence as me – for a start wouldn't we all be one big happy family? 3) I was pretty much the only victim of this force.

I couldn't think of any other options. Either I was the only one, or few enough others had been affected that the PAC documents held no mention of them. I'd somehow fallen victim to a side-effect of magic use that everyone else was immune to.

It figures, I suppose.

And there was another, perhaps more disturbing way of looking at this[1]. I mean, if it was just me, how did I know that magic was to blame? How did I know this wasn't a problem more psychiatric than occult, if you see what I mean? Instead of fixing me, could repeated exposure to the Healing surface have scrambled some important circuit in my brain? Had magic taken a mind weak from two decades of neurosis and created a fracture – a full-on psychotic break? Maybe this whole crisis was bubbling up out of a crack in my subconscious. Perhaps I was inventing these foreign memories and concocting a mission for myself the way a paranoid schizophrenic invents voices and weaves them into some urgent, but ultimately deranged objective.

At least I hadn't killed anyone. Yet.

This was not a happy line of thought.

If it was my own mind that was disintegrating then how could I hope to battle that? I would be fighting against my self. But then the alternative – some sort of demonic possession – didn't appeal much either. All you could say in its favour was that at least if my oppressor was real (whatever I meant by that) then maybe they could be beaten.

Then something obvious and duh-worthy struck me. If this was all part of some psychosis then that meant I was inventing everything, that I was conjuring up my false memories and my impossible knowledge out of thin air. So how come I was doing such a good job of it? A schizophrenic might imagine himself to be Jesus Christ, but that didn't mean he could walk on water. Thinking you were Napoleon didn't make you a military genius. If I'd *fantasised* all these insights into the use of magic, how

---

[1] Or, given that we were talking about possession here, maybe it *wasn't* more disturbing.

come they all worked? I might still be crazy, but that didn't mean I was imagining things.

Someone else was in my head.

* * *

So, like I say, I was in shock. After I left the house in Penshurst and the injured woman, I had withdrawn inside myself; I had let the other me run everything while I tried to come to terms with what I'd seen and felt. I've given you the gist of it, but getting to the point where I knew this other personality was real, that someone – or something – external was influencing me had taken several hours of fevered introspection – with revelation alternating with disbelief – in which time my body drove itself home, courtesy of its eerie new master. When I started paying attention again, I found myself looking at the papers I'd (we'd?) removed from that antique desk. They were spread out on my bed and I was stretched out next to them examining them minutely. My tribute lay on the bedside table next to me.

There were official-looking bills, handwritten notes, confusing scribbles. Since my eyes were looking in that direction, I decided to give them my attention for a little while. Whatever else happened, I needed to understand the mission I found myself on.

I joined my puppet master in looking over Jan's secret papers. From what I could make out, Jan had another address, a place we hadn't known about. But there was something strange about it. Among the papers was an invoice for all sorts of charges relating to this new property and many of them made no sense to me. I couldn't figure out what most of the abbreviations meant. In fact the address itself was strange. It clearly wasn't a conventional house, but I couldn't work out whether it was a flat in an apartment block, a room in some commercial building, or just a plot of sub-divided land. The address was in East London, in somewhere called New Charlton, along from Greenwich, south of the river.

Yes, I would go there tomorrow to spy out the location.

But that wasn't me talking. *I* hadn't just decided to go there. It was so easy to mistake the thoughts of this other presence for my own.

I was going to have to examine every notion, every impulse that passed through my mind, in order to decide where it had come from. How else could I begin to trust – and perhaps to reclaim – my own mind?

But I realised I had an advantage. Ever since my new owner had arrived, he had been doing the same thing – separating my thoughts from his and pushing his to the front. (Wait, did I say 'he'? I realised that I thought of this other personality as male; somehow I knew that.)

OK, well *he* had been using something a lot like 'cognitive therapy' on me. From my own experience I knew it worked by teaching someone to recognise their negative, destructive thoughts and to shut them down – or at least interrupt them. That's what he'd been doing to me, except he'd been derailing any thought process of mine that didn't fit his plans. My brain already had several weeks' practice at this internal censoring process. Now all I had to do was flip things around and apply that same process to cutting off *his* thoughts instead of mine.

And this interloper hadn't had it all his own way. He hadn't met with total success. The real me, the old me, had got past him on a number of occasions. It was the old me who stopped him killing that woman tonight. (A wave of guilt rose up as I thought of her. I'd attacked her with such violence that it horrified me.)

But then it wasn't *me* who'd done it; at least I knew that now. *I* was the one sabotaging the attack, metaphorically grabbing his arm. Even so, I felt horrible. I should have fought harder, realised sooner what was going on. For a while I couldn't stop thinking about that woman, wondering if she was alive, whether she was still lying there, drifting closer and closer to death.

But then I caught myself. I'd done what I could and obsessing wasn't going to help. I would think about this guilt later; right now I needed to focus on things that would help – like figuring out how I was going to extricate myself from this mess.

A moment later it dawned on me that I'd just successfully tested my new weapon: I'd cut off an unproductive train of thought about the injured woman. In the old days, I'd have disappeared into my own head for hours when faced with that much guilt, but this time I'd seen that line of thinking for what it was: a distracting mental loop that would prevent me from fixing the situation. I had recognised a bad impulse and shut it down – and *he* was next. I had no idea whether I could beat him, but I could sure as hell fight him.

There was even a chance that I could *force* him out if I just concentrated hard enough. Maybe I could stand up to him and take back control by exerting my will powerfully enough and refusing to let him manipulate me. After all, it was my body; I'd grown up in it; it was used to taking orders from me. Surely I had what followers of golf, or was it hockey, called 'the home court advantage'… if I could only use it.

I stood up, right that moment, scattering papers onto the floor. I could sense him trying to stop me but I forced my body to obey me. I willed myself to step over to the table and then I grabbed my mobile phone, calling up Daniel's number. I didn't even need to think about it; he was the one person I could trust to believe me and to help. I pushed the button to dial.

It began to ring.

And ring. Then it went through to his answerphone.

Damn it.

"Daniel Maclay has left the building… for the time being.

Please leave him a message." Then there was a beep.

What the hell should I say? I just started talking: "Daniel, there's something I need to tell you. Actually it's something the whole PAC needs to hear. It's about me, about how I've been behaving. I... it hasn't really been me, not the *real* me. I need to see you all as soon as possible. Call me when you get this. It's important, Daniel." I hung up.

It was a ramble, I knew, but I hadn't wanted to spell out the details any more explicitly, because then I'd have come off as crazy. You just couldn't blurt out something like this in ten words or less. You really, at the least, needed to set the scene.

Throughout the call I had feel the presence fighting me, but I had got my way. I put down the phone and sat back down on the bed. It had been an immense effort – taking back full control for thirty seconds had exhausted me as though I'd just run a marathon – but I'd done it. The strain hung heavily on me now, though underneath I was feeling elated. This seemed like the first taste of victory.

And then the fatigue got worse, ratcheting up and up in sudden jumps as though someone was pulling out the fuses, one-by-one, that fed power to my body. Suddenly I was struggling to even keep my eyes open.

I let myself flop back on the bed, worried that I'd fall if I didn't lie down. I was still in control, able to direct my limbs, decide what I wanted my body to do, but it was a body drained of energy.

I felt darkness starting to close in, as though I was being lowered into the ground. I was still looking out at the world, but it was from the bottom of a hole that kept getting deeper, and which took me down with it.

Was I dying?

Now the world was a diminishing circle far above me and I knew that soon it would disappear completely.

Just before I passed out, something came to me. The clash with my invader was twisting and buckling the seams of our shared consciousness and the vats of memory were beginning to spill over. I realised this: that my mother had never made jewellery. The necklace I was wearing was nothing to do with her. Why had I thought otherwise?

It was from him.

That seemed important somehow, but now my eyes were closed and my arms and legs weighed so many tons that I couldn't think how I could move them. The bed underneath me pressed into my back and it felt wonderfully, sinfully soft. And then the light was gone and blackness was everywhere, and all around me I could hear the ice cracking and shifting as it had done for uncounted centuries. In the faraway dark I began to make out the threads of pale-blue sunlight, filtered through miles of frozen seawater. And then, once more, I was gliding across the ice sheet, imagining I was on the deck of a ship racing ahead of the wind. There was nothing to think about except the driving arctic gale hammering and snapping at the sails, and the naked exhilaration of speed.

It was just as I'd experienced before, just as that long-ago writer had detailed in his journal... the journal I'd glimpsed momentarily on my laptop screen, just before a sudden, forceful impulse had brought my fingertip down on the delete button. The document had disappeared, just as the world was doing now.

Chapter 24 – Told by Susan Milton

The barn was quiet; I was on my own. David would still be in the air – moving further away from me with every second. He wouldn't be landing for seven more hours. For the first time in what seemed a long while I had no training partner.

I wondered how he was doing. He wasn't crazy about planes although he refused to admit it. And I worried that when he got to Hong Kong he'd get himself into trouble somehow. It was like a gift with him. But, bless him, he was also tenaciously good at getting himself out of trouble too. Maybe it was all the practice he got.

I wish I could have gone instead – not least because there was a reasonable chance that he'd buy the wrong manuscript and pay over the odds for it – but everyone else had been unanimous: I should keep a low profile. As they pointed out, Karst barely got a look at him back in that church.

Add to that the fake information I'd given the hospital when they tried to treat his injuries and it was clear: there was far less chance of the Army Who tracking him down compared with me. If only I'd done a better job of covering my own tracks then I could be sitting next to him now, annoying him and biting his earlobe when he tried to sleep.

But I hadn't *entirely* forgotten how to train solo. I limbered up and worked through a few fencing drills with the sabre. It made just the right ripping noise as it cut the air and I could feel my balance, centred and responsive, shifting properly through the steps.

A year of Healing trances had done good things for my range of motion. It had been fine before, excellent even, but now it was back to that double-jointed springiness I vaguely remembered from competitions in my freshman year of high-school.

David had been teaching me some Kendo katas, so I worked on one of those next. But I fudged the changes and messed up the footwork, so I abandoned that idea. He'd have to show me it again.

Without my training buddy, I couldn't practice combat properly, but I decided it might be a good chance to work on something less athletic. There were some concentration and control exercises I wanted to spend more time on. Dexterity through the Push surface had been a big thing with me for a while now – really, ever since I'd first Connected.

And in my pocket I always kept one of those little plastic mazes with the ball-bearing inside to help me work on my fine control. David bought me a new one whenever he travelled – or I should say whenever he passed a really cheap-looking novelty store – and I had some horribly garish treasures in my collection. I realised after a while that he was buying the ugly ones on purpose. That tricky sense of humour of his playing up again, no doubt.

Anyway, I had a new exercise of extreme, fiendish difficulty to work on; though it sounded easy enough. I dropped a tennis ball and then bounced it, just using Push. The closer to the floor one kept the ball, the more accurate one's timing had to be: lots of small, quick, regular taps. And even if you made things easier and bounced it high, to give yourself more reaction time, that just made directional control trickier. The concentration required was intense. It just wore you down the longer you worked at it.

Today seemed like a day to really test myself. I thought maybe I'd been letting myself off too easy lately. I'd make this a real fiery test of stamina. And it was less of a problem to really push myself if David wasn't around; I'd been on at him not to over-train so I was always careful to follow my own advice in front of him. Today, though, I felt like going for it.

The worst thing with this exercise was that I tended to bunch my shoulder muscles and give myself a stiff neck and a headache. I'd tighten up my shoulders even though this was supposed to be a purely mental exercise. I'd *really* be missing David when I had no tame masseur to rub my neck later.

Anyway, I threw the ball out into the middle of our sparring circle and gave it a slap with Push. It spun off at some crazy angle and I had to start again. Pretty soon, though, I found a good rhythm.

After a while I really got into it, trying variations, walking the ball around the circle, bouncing it from side to side. It would get away from me and I'd have to start over, but I kept the drill going. I was totally absorbed and I quickly lost track of the passing time. I finally had to stop because the sweat was running into my eyes and I couldn't reach my towel without taking my eyes off the ball.

I mentally called break time and stopped to catch my breath. This was hard work. I rooted out my water bottle from my bag and sat on the edge of the old couch. I swallowed half the water without pausing; I reckoned I'd sweated away easily that much already.

The tiredness I was feeling wasn't just from the exercise; I was fairly sleep-deprived too. I hadn't slept all that well the night before and it seemed to be catching up with me now. I was used to David being around and I'd kept waking, thinking that he'd got up and wondering what was wrong, if there was a problem. And each time I had to remind myself he was in London, because he needed to be at the airport in the morning.

Sitting there, I was tempted to call it a day, but I found I was just a little annoyed with myself. The plan had been to make this a marathon session and I knew I had a little more in me. I found David's jump-rope and tried some skipping. I really went at it, getting my heart pounding and my blood flowing.

When my legs started to cramp and I couldn't stop the trembling in my calves I switched to the punch-bag, pounding the cracked leather until my shoulders and lats were screaming.

A moment of dizziness brought me back to reality and I decided to stop and sit down for a minute. I've got a lot of stamina but I was coming to the end of it now. This work-out had become kind of brutal.

It was exactly what I told David not to do. I liked to think that I'd helped him get a little better at spotting the difference between discipline and masochism, and since I'd stopped him over-training, he was actually in better shape than when I'd met him. So I really should have known better than to torture myself like that.

I found a spare bottle of water and perched on the arm of the couch to drain it. I was actually feeling sick from the training; I couldn't remember the last time that had happened. Sitting there, panting, I realised that the lack of sleep, and the strain of pushing myself so hard, were really starting to gang up on me.

I let myself slide off the arm and down onto the couch itself. It felt so comfortable that it was actually a little bit tempting just to take a nap here. But I'm used to that temptation. I'd never get any training done if I gave into it. I made to get up…

But I didn't; I stopped. There was some stray thought

wriggling in my mind and it seemed important. But it had flitted away for now. I wanted to capture it before I got up and maybe drove it away for good.

Nope, it was gone. Even so, I decided to give myself a couple more minutes rest. My heart was still thumping and I wasn't feeling great. And this ratty old couch felt like a feather bed at the moment. I leant back, stretching and then relaxing, and allowed my eyes to close just for a little while, as I tried to find that important thought again.

My mind wandered and for a few minutes I think I must have drifted off entirely. For a while, probably less than five minutes, I was dead to the world – and I had the most extraordinary dream – a dream that for a while I couldn't quite recall. Only my reaction stayed with me, the sense of something strange and vivid, but the detail itself had passed behind a cloud and I couldn't make it out.

I wondered why the experience seemed so sharp, so unusual… but then I *was* sitting upright with my neck stretched back over a dusty sofa – it wasn't exactly conducive to normal sleep patterns. I was a little surprised that I didn't dream of being folded in half backwards.

I woke from my doze with a start, and rescued my neck from its painful stretch. For just a second I didn't know where I was. *Man*, I must really have been out of it.

I got another little jolt of surprise when I noticed I was still wearing tribute. Whenever I wore it I thought of myself as being ready to fight, it was like strapping on my mental armour or something. And I didn't like the idea that I'd fallen asleep like that; it sort of mocked the whole idea of being in steely-eyed combat mode.

I must be getting old, I thought to myself. Dozing off during the day wasn't something I ever did. But growing up I remembered how my grandfather could fall asleep in a chair practically in mid-sentence. But he had been ancient when Adam was a lad, as David would say. I rarely found sleep that easy.

As I mulled over the residue of my dream, I found that my thoughts had drifted to the subject of Jo Hallett. I still didn't know how I felt about her as a person, even though she'd won over the Professor and maybe David. Daniel Maclay, of course, could see no wrong in her. But for my part, I didn't totally trust her recent transformation; it seemed too good to be true.

If she'd changed for the better and put her troubled past behind her then I'd have liked to know the reason for it. I certainly believe people *can* change, but I don't know how often they do so without a little nudge. I wanted to know what had nudged her.

Somehow I couldn't see Jo just waking up one day and deciding to sort herself out. And I knew she could be a manipulative brat when she wanted to be; I'd feel happier if there was a reason to think this wasn't all just play-acting on her part.

I thought back over her behaviour in the last few weeks – before she headed off to London. I tried to recall my impressions. One moment in particular jumped out at me for some reason. I'd been working late one evening and I'd bumped into Jo in the meeting room. I hadn't thought much about it before, but now, for some reason I couldn't get it out of my mind. There was something about it…

She was such a sneaky little bitch; I bet she was up to something.

That thought sort of hit me out of nowhere. I was a little shocked at myself. I must be *really* tired – and maybe a bit cranky. David always fussed about his blood sugar, making sure to snack if he trained – claimed he was as brusque as a doctor's receptionist if he forgot to eat. Maybe I'd contracted his tendency to hypoglycaemia. I should get up and find some food.

I pulled the sweatband off my head, breaking the Connection.

It wasn't until that moment that I realised I'd even been holding a Connection all this time. I shook my head to clear my muddled thoughts. I knew my own mind and I didn't like this feeling of mushy, moody daydreaming – losing my train of thought, dozing, forgetting I was Connected – it made me feel uncomfortable. I clapped my hands loudly, once, and jumped up. *Enough*, I thought.

I wrapped a towel around my damp neck and packed everything away. Then I locked up the barn and trotted up the hill towards the dormitory block, my bag banging against my back. My sweat-drenched clothes felt unpleasantly clammy in the chilly night air and I hurried to get inside.

I was showering, letting my mind wander, when my thoughts drifted back to what I'd been thinking in the barn: about Jo and our encounter in the meeting room. That memory seemed brighter than the others; it glinted like a broken bottle on a sandy beach, and I wondered why it was bothering me so much.

Jo had been running a little errand, she'd said. That thought, that she was up to something, my sudden vehement distrust of her, it had seemed so out of character for me that I was inclined to follow it up, to see if my subconscious was trying to tell me something.

Once I'd changed, I went back out into the cold and walked over to the main building. I looked up at the windows as I punched in the door code: everything was in darkness. I had to turn on lights everywhere I went: the entrance, the back corridor, the office. The place was deserted. I walked through the Professor's office, down the steps and into the meeting room. Turning on the light, I looked around, momentarily not seeing the thing I was looking for.

I ducked down and there it was, behind the table. I leaned over the table, reaching my arm out and pulled the mains adaptor out of the wall socket, holding it up to the light. Straightaway I knew my suspicions were correct. This wasn't what it appeared to be: the weight was wrong, even the kind of plastic seemed wrong, and there was no maker's name.

I went back out, through the Professor's office, and into the hallway. There was a maintenance cupboard with a few tools in it just past the main entrance. I headed there now, unlocked the door and rummaged around until I'd found a small enough screwdriver. I undid the screws holding the adaptor together and pulled off the top.

It was full of circuitry. This thing was a bug and I'd seen Jo planting it.

I didn't bother to lock up; I headed straight for the Professor's room, the two halves of the bug in my cupped hands, to tell him what I'd discovered. I was fairly sure he had a key to Jo's sanctuary, where all the computer equipment was kept. I wondered what we'd find in there if we looked.

I thought about knocking on Daniel's door too, asking him to join us. He'd know more about bugs and radio waves than I would; he might know what else to look for... but he was also devoted to Jo. I'd involve him once I was sure what was going on. Theresa would be a better bet. I was certain I'd seen a couple of semesters of Physics classes on her college records; she might know how bugs worked. And she'd have no problem investigating Jo.

Theresa was on the phone when I knocked on her door, but she hung up and said she'd join me in the Professor's room in five minutes. I didn't explain why I needed to see her.

Then I knocked on the Professor's door and he answered a moment later, a book in one hand and a pair of spectacles in the other that I knew he still liked to hold while he read even though he didn't need them any more.

"Susan?" he enquired, puzzled but friendly.

"We have a problem," I said, "and I think Jo Hallett is behind it."

The three of us – the Professor, Theresa and me – stayed up pretty late that night. The Professor found his spare key to the server room and we filed over there. It only took Theresa a couple of minutes to point to a little black box, with an antenna sticking out of it, and identify it as a receiver. Its audio lead was connected to the computer it sat on, which was how Jo would record whatever the bug overheard, Theresa said.

We couldn't get past the computer's security, and we didn't spend a long time trying. We left everything where it was and trooped back again, to the Professor's room, and he made tea. Then the three of us tried to work out what was going on and what we should do about it.

The look of deep, banked anger on the Professor's face was one I had never seen before and for the first time since I'd met him, I found myself thinking that you wouldn't want to get on the wrong side of him. Whatever Jo was up to, it seemed like a safe bet that she'd come to regret it.

Chapter 25 – Told by Jo

This is how the loss of a loved one feels. You start to wake, rising up out of nothingness, feeling light, cleansed by sleep. The world comes closer and you start to smile waiting for your day to start. And then it drops on you, all the weight of your problems, your pain. You remember what happened and you feel sick. You'd hoped it was a dream but wishing it away was the dream and now that you're awake it's back.

With me it wasn't loss, but it came to me in the same way. One moment I was waking, untroubled, unafraid – the next moment it all fell back into place and I found myself locked at the centre of a life gone wrong.

And with awareness came the instant weariness of knowing that today would be another fight.

And yet, on the heels of the weariness was a sort of strength. I pushed away the tired thoughts, the feeling that it was all too much for me to cope with. And that determination felt familiar. I knew that as long as I lived, I would start every day like this: shutting down the bad thoughts and choosing to be strong. And right now, I thought I could probably handle that.

For a moment after waking, I didn't move. I took stock. I was still lying on the bed, still dressed in last night's clothes – only now it was light outside. That meant it was at least half seven in the morning, probably later. I'd been out for over nine hours.

At least I was still in the spot where I'd passed out. For a second I'd worried that once I was unconscious *he* would have taken control. I'd have got up from the bed like some zombie rising from its grave. My body would have been sent out on some errand, doing god knows what. But here I was. I didn't appear to have moved. Maybe he'd been asleep all this time too.

But surely he wasn't asleep any more. With a sense of climbing dread, I waited for something to happen – for my body to jerk, to start moving of its own accord, to stand up without me willing it to.

It didn't happen.

I tried to detect his presence, to get some sense of what he was thinking, whether he was still there. But there was nothing. No sign that he was still in my head.

Then a final thought from last night slotted back into place: the necklace. It came back to me now. When I first saw that thing around my neck, I hadn't recognised it. But gradually it had started to look familiar. After a little while I could recall seeing it before, remember hearing about how my mother loved to make things like that; I thought I'd even seen it around her neck once or twice. But now those memories no longer seemed like mine. When I tried to recall seeing the necklace around my mother's neck, her expression came out wrong. I realised now it was just a fragment of an old photograph; her features frozen in the camera's flash. The memory of her wearing the necklace was a fake, a composite designed to fool me.

He had created that recollection – and others – layered them up from fragments of other things. I'd only been fooled because he'd never let me dwell on the inconsistencies; he would cut me off, distract me, redirect my attention.

Whatever the necklace was, it was something from his world, not mine. I remembered my decision to wear it at all times and now that felt fake too. The necklace must be his trap-door into my head, his tunnel under my defences. Somehow he'd found a way to put this noose, this yoke around my neck.

So perhaps he *was* out there in the ether, subtly influencing other adepts, whispering softly to them – but he had managed to go far beyond that with me; he'd established a permanent presence in my brain. I was convinced that as long as I wore this necklace, he would be in a position to control me. Without it, he might diminish to just a nagging thought or a persistent daydream. He'd be the frail influence I'd read about.

If breaking the necklace would break his hold then in a few seconds it would be done, and I was confident I could fight him for that long. I reached up and under the neck of my shirt. I grasped the fine gold wire. It was delicate, eminently breakable. If I just pulled hard enough it would stretch and snap and I would be free.

I pulled. I felt the wire digging into my neck. I pulled harder. I could picture a purple groove forming in my flesh as capillaries under the skin burst. I pulled harder still, wincing at the pain.

Stop. I heard the voice in my head, ringing clear like struck metal. For a second I froze, releasing the pressure on the necklace. Fear flushed cold water into my veins. My hand trembled at the sense of violation, the shocking closeness of his voice. But I wrapped my fingers around the gold wire and started to pull again.

Stop or your friends will die.

I will prove it to you. Call them. Speak to them. Even now they are in danger. Call the Professor and you will see. Speak to him and then decide if you want to do this.

I stopped pulling. What should I do? Was this a trick? But

what would it achieve except to buy him a couple of minutes? Why would he bother with that?

Perhaps he had sent someone to intercept me and they just needed a few more seconds to reach me. Was he stalling?

Gird yourself and wait. Once you see that no one is coming, call your friend. Then you will know what I can do.

Gird myself? I supposed he meant I should Connect, ready myself to fight off an attack. Did that mean he'd read my thoughts? Could he hear everything I was thinking? And what about his suggestion; was that a trick too? If I Connected, would that give him some extra power, enable him to better control me?

Your thoughts are like worms writhing; you must learn to compose yourself. You believe you are making a decision but all you do is tally your fears. Well, sit and tally and writhe as long as you wish. But if you remove my sign your friends will be killed, and then you will be killed, and I will find someone else to share my power with.

Now he was telling me to do nothing; did that mean I should act? I could feel his disgust at my panic, my paralysis and second-guessing. I calmed myself as best I could.

Help me for a short time and I will make no further requests of you. You know what I am looking for. I want the Marker and nothing more.

You have already profited from my presence. I have taught you so well that no one can stand against you. Soon you will be free and you will be invincible. What I ask is quickly done and easily so. You have everything to gain by helping me.

But if you fight me than you will have nothing and be left with nothing and no one living will remember you.

Then, once again, he commanded me Call your Professor.

I was shaking so badly that I could hardly pick up my mobile, but I gripped it in both hands and scrolled through the numbers until I found the Professor's. I dialled and waited for him to answer...

"Hello?" It was him.

"Professor, it's me, Jo. I need to talk to you," I said.

"Oh, is that what you need?" he said, anger quivering in every word. "Well I also need to talk to you, so we are in agreement. I want you to get on the first train from London, get yourself down here, and do it now," he said and then I heard him slam down the receiver.

I was stunned. I'd never heard the Professor talk like that. What had my tormenter done to make him act like that?

After the Professor hung up on me I just stood there. I didn't move.

I was upset, thrown off balance by his rejection. And I also knew that my situation had altered, that something important had happened at the field-station in my absence. Maybe it should have been obvious, but I couldn't work out what it was or what it meant.

Do you understand?

That voice, it sounded so loud and deep, and yet it made no sound; it was only in my head. But my mental acoustics must have been impressive because his words rang like trumpets at a coronation. But I *didn't* understand yet.

Why was he like that? What did you do? I thought, and I realised my words were reaching him.

I visited your friends. I caused them to realise what you had done, how you had spied on them. I put the knowledge of your betrayal in their minds.

Oh.

Despite the fact that I could feel my confidence shrivelling, I dug deep for some reserves of bravado. *Well you'll have to do more than get me fired from the project to scare me. I've survived a lot worse than that,* I said weakly.

Ahhh. You still don't see. I have proved that I can pass information to your friends. If you refuse to help me, I will pass information to your **enemies**. I will tell the Army of Witnesses about your companions and where to find them.

You know what they are capable of? Imagine how it will be for your friends if the Army's wolves find them. Can you picture what their assassins would leave behind? Then you would be completely alone, waiting for the butchers to come for **you**.

He allowed me a moment to consider.

I want a few days' more of your cooperation. It costs you nothing. And then I will be gone. You will be free to waste your long and pointless life however you see fit. Your friends will still be alive. And you will be safe.

I am patient. If you disappoint me, I can find someone else and start again. You will not have the same opportunity. And we are so close to finishing. You can almost taste your freedom; why would you doom your friends and yourself now?

Think on it, he said. Unnecessarily. I couldn't do anything else *but* think on it.

I didn't know if *he* was providing it or my own imagination was conjuring it up, but I could almost see the twisted bodies strewn through the project buildings. I could picture myself returning to find them like that, all dead. Daniel cut down, the Professor ripped apart. He could make it happen.

And however I turned it, whatever angle I looked at it from, it seemed like my tormentor had found a way to beat me. I tried to find some hope that he was only lying to me or telling half truths. What if… yes, what if he hadn't influenced anyone? Maybe he'd only *witnessed* events at the field-station and was now claiming the credit for them. That was a straw I could clutch at: maybe the truth was he didn't have the power to influence anyone but me.

How do I know you didn't <u>discover</u> my friends were angry with me and pretend that you made it happen?

Ask them when they learned of your deceit. It happened while you slept, after you decided to defy me. After you decided to tell them about me. It happened while I kept you here, insensible. Or do you doubt it was me who made you sleep? Does it all seem like a coincidence?

If it *was* all a coincidence, it had arrived right on cue. No way I fell asleep all by myself last night. It was like being anaesthetised. So I would concede that my unconsciousness was his doing. And why knock me out unless he had an errand to run elsewhere?

Would he put me to sleep in order to spy on the PAC for a few hours? He couldn't be sure he'd see anything. A few hours, randomly chosen, weren't much good for spying; but they might be perfect if you had a specific task in mind, like passing on information. So if I accepted that he could put me to sleep, how much did I want to bet that he couldn't also reach into other people's minds if he wanted to? Would I bet my life and the Professor's on it? Daniel's? The rest of the team's? That final straw had been snatched from my grip.

Unable to maintain my doubt, I felt resignation setting in like nightfall. For a moment I'd felt strong and defiant. I thought that discovering my enemy's presence would allow me to fight him. I'd had hope. But now, that hope was dimming. It would be so easy for him to execute his threat; all he would need to do was hint to the Army, just give them a *glimpse* of our location, our identities, and they would find us. I was certain that they were already straining at the leash, sniffing for our scent.

So what else could I do? I couldn't run, just tear off the necklace and make a break for it, leaving my friends to die. You needed a level of professional ruthlessness that I didn't pretend to possess if you wanted to pull off a really colossal act of cowardice like that. You needed real discipline. Guilt of that magnitude would skewer someone like me, and if I fled, I'd spend every waking hour squirming on its hook.

Could I make him let me go? Fake my own death, make it seem like an accident? He was in my head so I didn't see how. I mean, he was probably listening in on this very thought, so how could I deceive him? Unless he actually *witnessed* my death, I couldn't see how he'd buy it. And even then, if he thought I'd planned it, spite might still motivate him to hurt my friends.

I had no more straws to clutch. There was only one choice left open to me and he knew it. Now he was waiting until *I* realised it too.

Of course if you still doubt me, we could try another approach. I'll lay your reservations to rest by bringing the Witnesses down upon your friends and then you can beg me to help you escape when the wolves come for *you*. If the **prospect** of your friends' deaths won't motivate you, perhaps the **memory** of those deaths will do a better job.

OK, OK, I thought, *I get it*.

But then I realised something. My tormentor couldn't follow *all* of my thoughts. I had admitted to myself that he had won and yet he had given me a final sales pitch to close the deal. *I* knew I was beaten, but he hadn't picked up on it. Was there some way that I could use that? Could I learn to control which thoughts he saw and which ones he missed?

Hope twitched a little on its death bed.

I would have to be *so* careful. I couldn't even begin to make a plan against him until I could be sure I could conceal it and I couldn't even imagine what that plan might involve considering he could look out through my eyes and hear with my ears. I mean how could I even *begin* a task like that?

In fact, until I gained some measure of control over my

privacy, I shouldn't even be thinking this thought (OK. So I had to distract myself.)

I should think about... about the fact that my situation seemed so overwhelming that it was making me nostalgic for my old problems. (Yes.) I remembered grumbling that the work at the field-station was boring and that some of the people were unfriendly. I latched onto that memory and soaked up the irony of it. I mean, boo hoo. How did my earlier situation even register as a problem? That recollection seemed as remote as playground name-calling now. (Good. Let go of any resistance. For the time being.)

I felt a new emotion now – neither happy nor sad. Maybe it was acceptance. It was time to acknowledge my defeat.

What do you want me to do?

Ahh. Those words will save your life.

Good. Your first task is easy. I find myself concerned for your health. I think you need to take some more of your medicine.

I knew what he meant; the image slid into my mind along with his words. He wanted me to apply the patches I had worn before – the anti-depressants and the oxymethylphenidate. They must make his task easier, I guessed. Somehow they must make me more compliant, or maybe easier to monitor.

I'd last applied the patches right before that disastrous night, the night I'd dreamed of the ice, the night when he must have come to me for the first time. Those patches would both have run out a week later, but somehow it hadn't occurred to me to take them off before then, even though I'd been feeling fantastic and would no longer have felt a need for them. More of his twisted cognitive therapy no doubt: interrupting any thoughts he didn't approve of. So effective was his distraction that I hadn't thought to peel off the old patches until I'd returned to London, by which time they would long since have been depleted. And of course

I hadn't applied any more; I mean, why would I? I was feeling unstoppable. Trying to influence me to reapply them at that point might have made me suspicious and it probably hadn't seemed worth the effort; I was being an obedient puppet.

I hesitated now, though. Howlingly ironic though it was, I really didn't like the idea of medicating myself at this moment. When it was just me in my head things were very different. The patches had seemed like a harmless piece of cheating, a way of cutting a few corners in my day – but now the rules had changed. The drugs didn't feel like my slippery little friends any more; they'd switched sides and were working for him – and that made me feel queasy and vulnerable. It was like the difference between ending a heavy night's drinking passed out on your own sofa or down at the bus station. One was immature, the other was Russian roulette. Applying the patches now might mean more than giving up the fight; it might mean giving up the *ability* to fight.

Maybe I could say I'd left the patches in Cornwall.

You keep some in your ditty bag; I've seen them. Go and get them now.

Was he responding to my delay in acquiescing or had he read my mind that time? And what the hell was a 'ditty bag'? Wherever it came from, he didn't get *that* bit of vocabulary from out of *my* head, though I knew what he meant. I kept a couple of transdermal patches in my wash bag.

My instinct was to stall, but from what I could see, there was no compelling reason for him to be patient with me. He could have the Army kill the people I cared about and still get what he wanted. To him it would just be a gesture, a useful lesson. It would put only the smallest crimp in his plans. He'd just have to send me into hiding as soon as he tipped the Army off, and then keep me below their radar until I'd grabbed the Marker for him. He might even have a hiding place in mind.

Weighing it up, it seemed like he had a nice, big stick he could use on me and very little reason to hold back. If I stalled or refused to obey, he could obliterate the PAC just to see if my attitude improved. And he'd still retain one king-sized threat to hold over me: the prospect of my own violent death. I reckoned I was going to have to do as I was told.

So without any further delay I went into my bathroom, slipped out of my top and applied a patch to each of my upper arms: a metered dose of SSRI anti-depressant and another of OMP.

The anti-depressants would take weeks before they affected my mood, but I had no idea how soon they might influence his control over me. The drugs would begin to hit my bloodstream in minutes and then I guess we'd see.

I stared into the bathroom mirror looking for any clue that someone else was looking out through my eyes. I wondered how he felt looking at my reflection in the bathroom mirror and seeing my freckly chest, my second-best bra.

I remembered my little lesbian moment of a few weeks back and suddenly it made sense to me. I had a male consciousness lurking in my head, colouring my thoughts and supplementing my memories. So I wasn't turning gay; I was simply being controlled by a male presence.

You'd have to be quite the homophobe to see that revelation as a cause for celebration.

Listen, what do I call you?

For some time now, I have been called the Sleeper.

And when I get the Marker, how am I going to hand it over to you?

When the time comes I will show you. No more questions. We have work to do.

He'll show me? Not tell me? Interesting choice of language. *You're the boss. What's my next task?*

There was a pause.

Tell me, what will happen if you do not return to your friends today, as instructed?

I guess they'll call. A lot. And then they'll send someone. (No point in trying to lie about this.) *And I suppose if I duck whoever they send, they'll get worried and make me a priority, maybe come here en masse.*

So you need to find a way to stop them pestering us. *You* may determine how best to achieve that.

And remember, *I* have my *own* way to stop them interfering... but it is permanent. Invent something just as effective if you want me to spare them.

I didn't like how this was shaping up. *Wait, wait; I'm doing what you want; I'm not fighting you. You threatened my friends' lives to get me to behave and I'm behaving. You can't say you'll kill them anyway unless I do some other thing. There have to be rules. If you don't give me any reason to believe you'll spare them, then I might as well not help you.*

I see you are confused. Perhaps I should clarify your position.

Your friends will be no trouble to me if they're dead. But *you* want me to keep them alive. So you must make sure I never have a pressing reason to eradicate them. If they interfere, I will kill them; if you need to be taught a lesson, I will kill them. Make sure I *don't* have a reason to kill them and I will let them live.

Is that clearer now?

So psychopaths like sarcasm too. *OK, but how should I persuade them to leave me alone?*

You know *my* way; I'm giving you an opportunity to come up with a less bloody alternative.

Well, at least tell me what you did, exactly. What did you tell them about me?

I let them know you placed a device in their meeting

room allowing you to make a record of their conversations. I would imagine they also suspect you of reading their correspondence, their secret papers.

Right. Great. So they knew I was spying on them; what would they make of that revelation? Would they think I was working for the enemy, planning to betray them? I hoped not. Surely they wouldn't jump to that conclusion without evidence to the fact – say, some clue that I was being blackmailed by the Army. And there was no such evidence. Plus if the Army knew about the field station, wouldn't they simply have sent their people in to torture the truth out of everyone? Why screw around with bugging them? The PAC would see that, wouldn't they? I *couldn't* be an Army agent.

So they must have thought I was spying on them for my own personal amusement, rummaging through their secrets for kicks – like some teenage hacker – and now I'd blundered upon a secret they'd already decided I couldn't be trusted with.

And you know, for a moment, I honestly couldn't recall if that was how this had all started. Had I been doing this just for kicks, in the days before the Sleeper had arrived? What had motivated me back then? It all seemed like such a long time ago. I couldn't remember being that person, thinking like that. I might be up to my neck in trouble now, but at least my behaviour made some sort of sense to me; these days it was the *world* that was insane.

With the stakes so high, it seemed that the lives of my friends now depended upon my ability to find an alternative explanation for why I'd spied on the PAC – a reason that said 'leave me alone' instead of 'come and get me' – something that would keep them out of the Sleeper's way and therefore safe.

I'm going to call Daniel. He'll be sympathetic enough to at least let me speak.

There was a pause.

Acceptable. But I will consider any slips of the tongue to

be deliberate, so select your words with exquisite caution.

With all my heart, I wanted my call to Daniel to be a coded cry for help. I wanted to use some odd phrase only he would catch, introduce some subtle tone into my voice that only he would recognise. But for that to work I needed to exploit the fact that Daniel knew me well and the Sleeper didn't. The problem? Daniel might know me well, but the Sleeper was inside my head, and he held Daniel's life in his hands. Anything Daniel might spot would come through loud and clear to the Sleeper. Without a way to hide my true thoughts, secret messages were out of the question.

And I had only the haziest idea of how to conceal my thoughts. My only clue was a growing suspicion that strong emotion played a role, making it easier for him to read me. And I'd be most keyed up when I had the most to hide, which would tend to give me away – which meant for now, no tricks.

I dialled Daniel's mobile and he answered without delay. I could hear music playing and I guessed he was still in his room.

"Hey Josephine, what's up? I saw you'd left me a message; I was just about to play it," he said. Obviously he didn't know yet what the others had found out. The PAC would probably tell him last.

"Hey Daniel," I said wearily, taking a moment to organise my thoughts. "Well, no surprise I suppose, but I have a problem. You'll hear about it soon enough."

He sounded concerned. "Oh? Well, why not tell me now?"

Time to put on a show.

I allowed a good helping of the (very genuine) panic I was feeling to show through in my voice. Then I took a deep breath and launched into it: "You want to know what the problem is? I'm a little bit *freaked out* Daniel. Oh, I knew something was going on with the PAC; I knew you all were hiding some nasty secret – and I wasn't happy about it. I wondered what you could be doing that was *so* bad, but no one would talk to me. I was a part of it and no one would tell me what *it* was. So I decided to find out anyway."

"Ahh," was all he said. Thinking this through as I spoke, I realised, if I was going to be angry I'd have to claim I'd only just discovered the truth. Otherwise exploding now would seem peculiar.

There was outrage in my voice: "I knew it was bad, but… but last night I played a recording of a PAC meeting I'd made. I'd wanted to know what the hell I'd been dragged into so I bugged the meeting room. Maybe I shouldn't have done it, but everyone was lying to me and I wanted the truth. And given what I heard, I'm hardly the criminal here. You were talking about people being *killed*, about the PAC hiding from the killers, spying on people, plotting against them. I didn't listen to all of it. I'd heard enough. I still don't know what to make of most of it." I pushed the emotion a few notches higher. "I mean, are you people *insane*? What on earth do you imagine you're doing? I thought I was joining an academic team, I thought you had some groundbreaking project I could be part of, and I discover you're… I don't know what, part of some sort of cult – a cult that seems involved in more than a few *murders*."

"Jo," he said, trying to reassure me, "we haven't *killed* anyone."

"Are you sure?" I shot back. "Didn't you have a pretty good go with someone called Jan?"

"*He* was trying to kill Susan and David," he explained.

"He wanted to kill *them*, they wanted to kill *him*. In the end someone else murdered him first. I mean *listen* to yourself."

Now I spoke slowly and firmly, "I don't want any part of this. I want out. Please tell the Professor from me that I want him and his team to leave me alone. If *any* member of the PAC comes *near* me, if anyone tries to get in *touch* with me, I'll call the police. I swear. You freaks need to stay *away* from me."

I was out of breath with emotion now.

"Jo, listen. Don't do anything hasty, alright?" Daniel said, "We're really *not* the villains here. I mean, for goodness sake, it's *me*; you know *me*." He took a breath, almost a gulp. I could picture him pushing his hair back. "Look, take a bit of time. This all seems very weird, but if you think about it I'm sure you'll realise I wouldn't be a part of something unless I thought it was the right thing to do. Just please promise me you won't do anything until you've given yourself some thinking time?"

"I don't know, Daniel," I said, calming down a little, softening, "I don't know what to make of this. Maybe I *do* need some time."

Then I abandoned the calm: "But so help me, if I see a familiar face, if I get the impression that you've sent someone to shut me up I really will go straight to the police, and anyone else who'll listen, and I'll tell them everything I know about what you're up to. You and the Professor can explain the whole thing to the cops."

"You won't have to do that," he assured me, "I'll make sure you're left in peace to think things through. Take a bit of time, let the shock of this settle down for a while and then give me a ring. We can talk about it. When it's all sunk in a bit more we'll talk the whole thing over. OK? That's fair, right?"

I said nothing for a moment. Then I let myself sound small and weak and said, "OK, Daniel. Alright."

"OK then," he said, with warmth in his voice.

Hesitantly he added, "I wanted to ask you about something else, but it can wait. Maybe next time. Until then, take care."

"Sure," I said glumly and hung up. I hadn't needed to make him hate me, thank god, but he wouldn't be galloping to my rescue any time soon either. It was a painful thing to do, but I thought it had probably worked.

The Sleeper had turned the PAC against me and now I'd finished the job. Daniel would convince the others that I wasn't spying on them for kicks. He'd paint a very different story: that I'd just wanted the truth and now I was freaked out and threatening to turn them all over to the police. They weren't going to like me any better as a snitch than as a sneak, but it should keep them away from me for a little while. Unless I was mistaken, I'd just done a damn good job of cutting myself off from my only source of help.

Masterful. I believe the boy will do as you asked. He sounded pleased.

And this can form the pattern for our future enterprise, if you wish. I will name the destination and you may plot our course and take the trick. If you can achieve my aims without inflicting great injury upon your own then so be it. I can be fair if fairness serves me. The choice is yours.

I found his turn of phrase a little hard to follow but I was guessing this was the carrot to go with the big stick he'd been waving. He was saying if I followed his orders, he'd let me organise the details myself. I supposed it was a good offer: easier for him if he simply watched me do all the work – but good for me too, just in case I needed a little wiggle room to put my brilliant plan for personal and general salvation into effect. If only I *had* a brilliant plan.

What do you say?

Depends on how much a person likes guilt, I suppose. I've got a feeling I might regret coming up with ways for you to get what you want.

Anyway, what's next?

Next we investigate the address mentioned in Jan's papers. Find out what you can in advance and then we'll pay a visit in person.

I was happy enough with that request, at least the first part.

I could trawl around the Internet looking for info, during which time I could a) surreptitiously think about other things and b) avoid placing myself or others in immediate jeopardy.

By now, I was so paranoid about the Army that when I Googled the address, I only put in the general location. I didn't really expect the Army could check Google's records to see who searched for what, but who knew how much data-traffic the intelligence agencies monitored as it made its way between private citizens and their favourite web-sites. And if the intelligence community knew something then maybe the Army knew it too. That didn't stop it being sheer paranoia, but I felt better for rationalising a little.

Even keeping things general, the mystery of this address quickly revealed itself. Was it a flat, a room in a commercial building or a plot of land? None of the above. It was a berth. And I assumed there was something anchored in that berth. Presumably Jan had a boat, either a barge or a house-boat I would imagine, and it was on the river a little ways east of the Millennium Dome.

I had no idea how many house-boats there were dotted around the Capital, but I knew it was easy to forget that London still had miles of canal running through it. You'd turn a corner and happen upon a section of ancient waterway threading between loft-converted warehouses. Jan's berth was in a dock which let out directly to the Thames itself, but I wasn't able to find out much about it. Most mentions of that stretch of water dated back more than a century. The land around it seemed to be given over to a cement works now – and that was about all I could learn.

So much for spinning out the research; the next step was to go there. Time to consult my demonic master.

Do we sneak in or break in? Or make up some excuse to be there?

Suggestions? Remember, time is precious.

Well, it's the middle of the day. If we want to go now, it'll have to be in plain sight, I reckon. So we'd better come up with a reason to look around.

Which would be?

I don't know, maybe an estate agent. I've got the name Jan used to rent it and a few other details. I can fake up a letter from him that says I'm allowed to inspect the property, maybe with a view to finding a purchaser. I can also make up a couple of business cards that identify me as a property agent. That would make it easy for me to take pictures and ask a lot of questions.

That sounds promising. Get to it.

Great, I thought, without enthusiasm. First, though, I needed to take a shower and have some breakfast. I insisted upon it.

With that out of the way, I forged a letter and a couple of business cards. Jan had used the name James Jenkins on correspondence relating to the berth and I didn't have a sample of his signature for that name. On the other hand, I thought it was a fairly good bet that neither would anyone else – at least not on site. And anyway, who checks signatures except a bank? I found a good fountain pen and signed the letter with a flourish *somewhat* inspired by the way Jan signed his other pseudonyms.

In my wardrobe, I found a navy blue suit in some manmade material and a pale lilac blouse with some kind of ruched thing happening at the front. It looked sort of estate-agenty to me. Then I remembered that Noola had a wig. Before she'd had extensions and turned them into dreadlocks she'd had a nuked-blonde-with-dark-red-roots look. Frankly it made her look as though her hair had been irradiated and now her follicles were bleeding, but she seemed happy with it. She'd also bought a neat, redheaded wig to wear to job interviews and for dealing with those of a more conservative disposition when it came to coiffure. I went downstairs and swiped it. It wasn't an impenetrable disguise, but it was better than nothing.

In this get-up, I'd be taking the tube, not the bike, and doing some walking, so I dug out a long coat. I also found a big purse that looked businessy and inside it I put all the bits and pieces I planned to take with me: digital camera, notepad, tape measure – which raised a question.

Do I wear tribute? I think I can get the headband under this wig without it looking like my head's bulging oddly.

There was a longish pause and I wondered if there was anyone there. I hadn't had any luck yet detecting the Sleeper's presence. Did he disappear on who-knows-what errand from time to time and I didn't notice?

Then he answered. You can maintain the Quell state without my help? Otherwise I will have to take control.

I guess he didn't want us to make our way to the Marker's secret hiding place while broadcasting our presence to every nearby adept.

It's easy enough. And I can slip out of the bracelets in a second if I have a problem.

Very well.

I hadn't found the Quell state difficult and it meant I wouldn't have to fumble around looking for tribute if something bad happened.

I had one more idea for what to take with me: a metal detector. It might reveal something the Surfaces didn't. I wasn't intending to lug one of those long-handled beachcombing things with me, but I might be able to pick up a stud detector. Ingeniously enough it was a device that had nothing to do with the male physique and everything to do with locating pipes and wires inside walls, and you could get one from most hardware stores.

The only question was, how much should I be helping? If the Sleeper simply wanted me to hand over the Marker, and then he'd keep his word and let me go, then anything I could do to speed this quest along was a grand idea. If he pretty much planned to wipe me and the PAC out, then all I was doing was digging my own grave. Unfortunately I didn't have a lot of evidence to help me decide which it was. It would help if I knew why he didn't fetch the Marker himself. Was he incapacitated and that's why he needed it? I pictured a body wrapped from head to foot in bandages, like the soldier in white in *Catch 22* – but in this case masterminding his own cure through some as-yet-unexplained exercise of magical mind-control.

I knew that most physical wounds could be cured with the Healing surface – in fact most would cure themselves sooner or later without you even concentrating; you just had to Connect. So far as I knew, only extreme old age required the Marker – as the Healing surface didn't offer immortality, only a healthy and very long life. So maybe he was some dusty fossil in a wheelchair somewhere, his dry hands clutching his cane as he concentrated on making me run round London looking for his holy grail.

Either way, I couldn't quite figure out why he didn't have minions. How was he even alive if he was helpless and had no one to obey him? It seemed strange to picture an adept with superb control of his powers who, for some reason, had no followers and no fortune. With his powers, he should certainly be rich. It made sense that he was old – very old – so what had he been doing with his life up until disaster struck and he needed to be rejuvenated by the Marker? I couldn't see how a powerful adept could end up a bed-ridden pauper immobilised by old age. With money, servants or even a little mobility he could be searching for the Marker without my help. And without those things, how was he keeping himself alive?

As I was thinking all this, I was looking up the address of a hardware store where I could buy a stud detector. I was doing my best to guard my thoughts – though it was pure guesswork whether I was doing it right – but even if he could read me, I figured the Sleeper couldn't begrudge me my curiosity. He could *command* me not to think about who he was and where he came from, but he couldn't expect me to obey; nobody could really control their own curiosity.

I found a suitable store and called up a map to show me where it was. Then I hit print. I got out of my chair to grab the print-out and a sudden surge of disorientation hit me. I grabbed the edge of my desk to steady myself. The feeling was familiar, though the overwhelming intensity of it wasn't: it was the patches kicking in – and it was something more. For a second I stood there, not daring to move, clutching the desk for support. I thought I was going to throw up.

I could feel my mind getting softer, mushier, my thoughts losing definition. I could almost picture the barriers around my mind getting more porous as the chemicals reached my brain. I imagined I could feel the Sleeper pushing forward, wriggling further into my mind, worming his tendrils into my thoughts. And with that feeling came another sensation, an awareness of something in motion. A dizzy, spinning shape rose into my mind. It twirled and turned in on itself, like some abstract, geometric animation.

What was this thing? Had it spilled across the connection between our minds? I didn't know, but somehow its shape reminded me of Connecting.

I'd never really thought about it, but the sensation of Connecting was really about configuring your thoughts in a certain way – into a pattern, in fact. When I Connected I was bringing this pattern to the forefront of my mind. In its shape, the Connection pattern resembled the drawing I'd first seen when I'd tried to use magic that time on the moors. Those mental exercises I'd performed involved staring at elaborate patterns of ink on paper – someone's attempts to capture in a line-drawing the rich, moving shapes an adept must hold in her head.

The Quell state used a pattern too, though it was a very

simple one. And this new writhing shape that was forming in my mind reminded me of both of those others. Was it related to them somehow? And yet it seemed incomplete. I had the feeling that it would be a powerful thing indeed if it was whole.

A moment or two later and the shape began to fade. My disorientation lessened.

I didn't know what this experience meant or what had just occurred, but it seemed to be over now. I couldn't be sure, but my suspicion was that the Sleeper had pushed a little too hard as he tried to take advantage of the drugs' growing effect on me – and in his haste he had caused us both a few moments of disorientation and nausea. But who knew for sure?

I snatched up the map, grabbed my bag and headed downstairs and out into the cold. I was grateful for the jolting chill of the icy air and the feel of my heels hitting the hard, frost-lichened pavement. Walking the winter streets was simple, physical and sharply real – a few moments of normality to distract me from the war being fought inside my skull.

Chapter 26

A whiff of stagnant-pond-smell told me I was getting close to a reservoir of sluggish water. Of course I knew the river was just the other side of the wall, but despite all the junk that was pumped into it, the river itself seemed to be odourless. It was the musty water of a wet-dock I could smell.

The path I'd been walking along reached a flight of concrete steps that would take me up and over the wall. On the other side was the broad enclosure of a private dock and beyond it the river.

There were half a dozen house-boats lined up along a wooden jetty, packed side-by-side like piglets on a sow as my Pappy might have said, had he been a redneck instead of a banker. The jetty was on the land-most side of the dock. The dock itself was a square basin, maybe fifty yards on a side, which jutted squarely off from the broad and sinuous main channel of the Thames. I could just make out another inlet on the far river-bank, five hundred yards away. From a high enough altitude I imagined this section of the river would resemble a python that had swallowed a roll of quarters, sideways on. Kind of.

Beyond the boats, a thick wall separated the dock from the river, except for a ten-yard gap in the middle that was sealed by two low lock-gates that looked a little like paddles from a giant pinball game. I could see the exposed and gleaming steel pistons which attached the gates to the opening mechanism hidden under the dockside. My guess was that the gates were more or less watertight because the level of the river on the other side looked to be a few feet lower than in the basin. You obviously had to pick your moment to activate the buried hydraulics and swing the lock-gates apart; opening them now would flush the dock like it was a cistern.

There were six boats tied up to the wooden jetty, plus two derelict-looking barges along the side walls. A couple of the house-boats must have been nudging sixty feet in length, but none were much more than six feet wide – something to do with the width of the canals they evolved in, I supposed.

The wooden jetty began a few feet out into the water and you reached it by walking down a short ramp from the stone dock-side. The only way onto the ramp, though, was through a gate, which was guarded by a little sentry box.

On either side of that gate, a high chain-link fence screened off the jetty from anyone who might fancy their chances at jumping across from dry land.

I strode up to the gate, ready to present my pseudo-credentials and found the little guard-hut empty. A sign on the hut's door stated that it was manned 24 hours a day by PerimeterForce as part of their Instant Response Guarantee. The gate was unlocked, not even latched (nice work, PerimeterForce) so I strolled through and clattered down the ramp on my daring inch-and-a-half heels.

Down on the jetty, the berth-numbering system looked to be a little arbitrary, but after a little to-ing and fro-ing I found 4-14J, the address I'd seen on Jan's papers. It was the farthest berth from the ramp, and the boat it contained was set apart from the others. It looked quiet – deserted even.

Only one of the other boats showed any activity at all, and it was at the opposite end of the jetty. Its engine covers were up and a man in baggy overalls was leaning into the housing, tools spread out on a purple towel to one side of him. If he noticed me, he gave no sign of it and seemed unconcerned by my presence.

I took a good look at the boat in 4-14J. It was a little shabbier than the average, but not the shabbiest. Tiny, scruffy curtains were drawn on the dusty windows and the deck needed sweeping. Sun-faded red paint was blistering near the prow. Or was the prow at the other end? Let's just say the front. The rudder was clearly at the far end, the end that stuck out into the basin and towards the river.

All the other boats were snug up against the jetty, noses touching dry land, but 4-14J was standing off by several feet. There was a stretch of dusty black-green water between the wooden platform I stood on and the deck of the boat. The gap wasn't an insurmountable obstacle, but it made this boat the least likely to receive casual visitors.

I could see that the back of every boat was roped to the next and on 4-14J that rope had been shortened. That was what kept it from drifting in to the jetty. It also kept it close to its neighbour, and right now the two were as close as stink on a weasel as my non-existent Uncle Billy-Bob would say.

I broke the background litany of the Quell state and Connected, immediately stretching out with my senses to touch the boat, alert for the sparkle of recognition that would occur if another adept was operating nearby. My best bet, if I did detect someone, was probably to turn around and run – to thunder up the ramp and just keep going. I didn't have a sword with me and I wasn't sure I could use one anyway, so running like hell would be the better part of valour.

I did not tell you to Connect. He sounded furious. Oops.

Sorry. Well, no harm done. There's no one here.

I knew from the Sleeper's own shared knowledge that the best way to avoid a trap is to Connect early, while you can still get away. So why was he snippy? Didn't he want me to stay safe? Maybe he just liked to be consulted.

Trying to look like I knew what I was doing, I jumped onto the boat one berth to the left of Jan's, which also had its curtains drawn. I ran along its running board for a few feet and leapt onto the foredeck of 4-14J (if 'foredeck' is nautical for 'front porch'). No one peeked out from the boat I'd used as a stepping stone. The boat I'd landed on likewise failed to disgorge Army assassins, river police or angry pirates (in descending order of likelihood).

I was at the front and the door to the boat's interior appeared to be at the far end, so I needed to get back there somehow. There was probably a trick to it, but moving along the boat from stem to stern (or anyways from snout to tail) was extremely difficult. There was a flat lip of black-painted wood, maybe six inches wide, that jutted out from the steep side of the boat a foot or so above the water line. If I leant forwards, and grabbed hold of the roof of the boat, I could shuffle sideways along the lip, balancing myself with my hands. My shiny leather gloves were particularly unsuited to marine gymnastics, but I kept them on anyway.

Perhaps the right way to do this was to clamber up and walk along the roof itself, but that somehow seemed too conspicuous, like dancing on the table when you're supposed to be keeping a low profile. I attempted a shuffling sideways-hop, while trying to tuck my bag under my arm, and I managed not to jump right off the boat and into the cloudy depths below. Fortunately my ugly, black shoes were sombre enough – and thus unused enough – to still have some tread left on their plastic soles. I crabbed my way to the back porch of the boat, managing not to trip on the anchor chain or the rope that stretched across to the boat next door. Then I climbed down into a foot-well kind of a space that contained the rudder handle, the seat the driver would occupy, a couple of items of nautical paraphernalia and a pair of locked wooden doors leading to the interior.

I ducked down out of sight and gathered my focus. With my Surface senses spread out, sweeping across and into the boat, I panned quickly through the vessel without encountering any sign of an enemy. So no one was *currently* Connecting in there.

I altered my focus to scan for other possible dangers which might await me in there. It was difficult to get a clear picture of the cluttered and complex interior in any detail, but I didn't detect anything moving or register the signature of body heat. I did the same for the boats nearest me, and a quick pass found no heat signatures there either.

I suppose someone could be hiding in the water, but I doubted it. You couldn't create a decent Shield in water and you couldn't penetrate it properly using the Surface senses. Most adepts found immersion in water undesirable to the point of phobia. If no one was in the boat, they weren't likely to be under it; it should be safe to venture inside.

I took one last look up at the dockside above me and the flood-wall beyond. This was an ideal place to ambush someone, unless they were part dolphin. Only one (dry) way out, high ground on three sides and a river at your victim's back. I hoped there was no one up there on the wall right now, thinking those exact thoughts.

I turned my attention back to the boat. The low doors sealing off the interior were held closed by a padlock which was hooked through a chunky iron hasp. I squatted down, sitting on the backs of my heels to take a closer look, steadying myself by placing a hand on the overhang of the roof. Putting my other hand on the padlock, I closed my eyes and felt inside the metal for the mechanism and the tumblers. One, two, three, four. Once they were all lined up, I rotated the barrel and the bolt popped open. I set the lock to one side and opened the doors.

A breath of nasty, fungal air puffed up at me and I held my breath, turning my head for a moment to give it a chance to dissipate. Then I stepped down into the gloom.

Naturally the dim light didn't bother me. I closed my eyes and allowed the shapes of the things around me to register through the Push surface. It felt a little like pulling plastic-wrap over a tray of sandwiches, the wrap taking up the shape of what was beneath it as you tucked it into place. I could sense that the inner spaces of the boat were intricate and multi-chambered and it was immediately clear it was going to take me a while to examine them all.

The interior of the boat was dry and dusty, inhabited by some secretive species of nook-loving mould. The table and shelves immediately in front of me were empty and a discarded running shoe lay on the far bunk. I walked over to the bunk and sat down next to the sneaker, placing my bag on the rucked-up blanket by my side. Sitting still would make it easier to sweep through the hidden spaces of the boat, to search its recesses for hiding places. It was a lot of volume to cover in detail, but I got straight to work, beginning with the floor beneath my feet and combing the space below the deck in strips, working backwards in the direction of the jetty. The muddy blank of the water outside was like the frame around a picture I was studying.

Many times I sensed something within the structure or fabric of the boat, and had to pause to identify it. The engine compartment particularly was a nightmare. And I spent several minutes checking whether there was anything besides gasoline inside a gas-can that sat on the tiny foredeck. In that particular case, it would have been quicker just to go up there and tip out the contents.

None of these curiosities turned out to be the Marker sitting snug in some hidey-hole. At times during the search I was aware of the Sleeper's presence pressing in on my consciousness, scrutinising – and perhaps assisting – and I filed away the sensation, hoping it would help me to spot those moments when he was *least* aware of my thoughts and actions.

When I'd finished exploring the cavities nearest the hull, I leaned back against the bulkhead and let my focus infuse the timbers above my head, scanning within the woodwork of the top half of the boat – until once again I had traversed the full length of the vessel.

No luck.

Time to try something else, I thought, and dug the stud detector out of my bag. Like a geriatric house-painter, I ran the tip of the instrument in painfully slow strokes up and down the panelled walls, pausing each time the machine registered something. Most of what it told me I already knew – though on one occasion it found a metal spar running behind the back of a cupboard which I hadn't noticed before. It did me no good, though: a careful mental probe of the space around the spar failed to find anything of interest, like, say, the release mechanism for a hidden compartment. There didn't seem to be anything to find, which I guessed the Sleeper wouldn't be happy about.

It was now coming up on two hours since I'd arrived and I had completed my third exhausting scan of the boat – two occult and one electronic-with-occult-follow-ups – with nothing to show for it.

What now?

We keep looking. He was emphatic and I could sense his displeasure. This time instead of looking for the Marker itself, we look for clues: papers, hiding places where the Marker might once have been kept, any personal effects.

Ohh-kaaay. I was starting to feel drained. This was like

trying to read fine print in bad light while balancing on one leg. It was enough to give you a migraine after a while.

On the other hand, it was better than being dead, so I set to work again, inching my way along the craft, no longer looking for the bright hardness of filigreed metal, instead alert to the presence of anything soft and out-of-place. For variety, I worked in a spiral this time, corkscrewing my way along the boat from muzzle to fetlock, imagining that I was peeling it like an apple skin.

Twenty minutes of that and I was really starting to flag. A headache was swelling behind my eyes and I was beginning to feel dizzy and a little nauseous. My concentration kept slipping and at one point I even broke the Connection for a second, without meaning to – which brought a wordless rebuke from the Sleeper that reverberated through my mind like a slap in the face.

But then something changed and after that I sensed that he was taking a lot more of the strain, directing my focus with less input from me, like a pilot taking over the controls from an exhausted co-pilot… which was a much more innocent analogy than the reality of our relationship.

Even with his help, the muzziness in my head grew as the minutes rolled by and I realised that the pattern I'd glimpsed earlier was once again rising from the floor of my mind, contorting and folding in on itself like before. A metronomic chant went with it. It began to sound in my head, faintly at first, but soon quite discernible. The pattern was even more distinct this time, but I knew it was still incomplete. I still had no idea what it meant.

I sensed that the Sleeper was nearly as weary as I was, which I'd guess was why this pattern was leaking across the link between our minds. As he kept us both focussed on the search, and as we both grew more and more drained, I found myself catching glimpses of foreign images from the overspill of his memories – random snippets that I could tell came from him – slopping over the link and into my brain.

None of it was very clear or easy to interpret, it was all edges and out-of-focus corners of things, but I filed every impression away as best I could. I desperately wanted to know more about my tormentor; any clue about his origin or his real intentions might reveal something I could use. Above all I needed to know whether he really planned to let me go – me and the PAC – once he was done with me.

With the pattern in my head continually devouring itself and the influx of foreign thoughts tumbling along behind, it was getting a little hard to think straight. The Sleeper was putting all his attention into maintaining the search and, consequently, everything else was starting to slip. I found myself wondering how long he could keep at this, and a split-second later I felt the echo of that thought coming back to me. The barrier between our minds had become so weakened as he poured his focus into the unrelenting examination of the boat, that I was hearing my own thoughts as they made contact with his consciousness. I was experiencing them from his perspective as well as my own, creating a kind of mental echo. If I tried, I was fairly sure I could see through the barriers around his mind.

I tried not to allow my exhilaration to register for fear it would attract his attention. I disowned the feeling, refusing to react emotionally despite what this could mean. Gently, subliminally almost, I attempted to draw more of his thoughts towards me. It was the most peculiar sensation I can ever recall feeling. The dominant impression was of cold, but behind that was structure: rank upon rank of memory – just out of reach.

Afraid to disturb those dense-packed strata of memory, I turned my attention to the inward-folding pattern, attempting to bring it into better focus, to summon a little more detail from his side of our mental link. I hardly dared put any force or urgency behind my attempt; I didn't know what little thing might alert him to what I was up to. I tried to think calming thoughts and gently *drew* the images to me.

As I watched, my perspective on the swirling pattern tilted and I realised that it was one of a series of patterns, lined up in his mind like rifles on an armoury wall. It was difficult to count them, but I thought there were seven. Maybe more. Each was different and yet they were all related somehow. At the far end, I recognised the basic shape I had copied and taken out to the moors with me. It was the pattern for teaching novices to Connect. In fact (the knowledge crystallised within me all by itself) it was *called* 'Connect'. And next to it, was the simple, ghost-like inversion of Quell. Their geometry was straightforward compared with the tendrilled, multi-layered complexity of the other patterns, but I sensed they were all aspects of a common purpose – like keys on a keyboard.

Given that I knew the name and function of those first two shapes, I couldn't help wonder: what was the significance of the others? I focussed on the shape that lately had begun to invade my mind... and all by itself, a word dropped into my mind: 'Home'. Behind it I glimpsed another shape and another word, almost like the legend beneath an illustration in a book. Part of it coalesced in my mind: 'Pattern...'.

Whatever 'Pattern...' meant, it seemed more familiar than the rest. I didn't see how that could be but it was definitely reminiscent of something. For a moment I couldn't think what. Then it came to me: it reminded me of the necklace I was wearing. And as I thought it, the full legend revealed itself to me: 'Pattern Link'.

And the knowledge flowed in with the name. This was how the Sleeper had constructed my necklace. That first time, while I was unconscious but still Connected, he had established a temporary link to my mind, but it was too weak to last for long or to let him accomplish much. So he had worked fast and done his best to seize control of my drugged and boozy brain. He had used this symbol, Pattern Link, forcing it into my mind and directing its focus onto the few scraps and oddments of gold remaining in my jewellery box. The symbol's power had fused the metal, compressing and extruding it into a two-dimensional likeness of itself. As it neared completion, the Sleeper had caused me to place it around my neck. The cold metal had somehow softened and flowed until it reformed into an unbroken tracery around my neck and the Sleeper at last had a subject he could properly control. From that point on, he had a path straight into my psyche. He'd been able to influence, coax and manipulate me without me realising it. And I'd taken credit for every change he'd made, never suspecting I was sharing my head with a stowaway.

It was such a relief to unravel even a corner of this mystery and for a moment I was heady with the revelation.

Immediately I tried to calm myself.

Once I was a little more composed, I gently focussed in on the shape called 'Home' and painstakingly attempted to tease out the memories that went with it. I knew, somehow, that this pattern was the key to the Sleeper's plans for me and I had to discover what it meant.

Slowly I gathered the threads of his memory to me and knowledge began to weave itself together in my consciousness. His recollections were siphoning in a thin stream across the link between our minds, slowly and quietly.

Then I felt the Sleeper's thoughts shifting and I willed him not to notice what I was up to. I was nearly there. I almost knew its purpose. The Home pattern was for...

Then I had it, just as the Sleeper took control once again, his attention no longer on the search but turned back to rest upon me.

Well?

For a moment I thought he knew what I'd been doing. But then I realised that some part of my brain had been keeping track of his search, and if I thought about it for a second, I knew that he'd stopped because he'd found something on the boat. He had located a pouch – through the Push Surface it felt like a thin plastic wallet – taped underneath one of the boards of the deck in the next compartment along. He wanted us to go and investigate.

I got up off the bunk, now, stretching my lower back and rotating my head to relieve the stiffness I felt from sitting so long immobile.

I opened the bulkhead-door to the next compartment and stepped through into the compact space beyond. I'd stood here before when I ran the stud detector over the walls – and I'd found nothing then. In front of me was another door six feet ahead and there were cupboards to both sides. I knew they were empty except for a few tins of food. On my second mental sweep of the boat, I'd even searched inside the cans, in case they contained something other than baked beans, sweet corn and chicken soup.

On the floor ahead of me stretched a piece of fraying dark-blue carpet. It covered the middle strip of the painted decking along the centre-line of the boat. I bent down and ripped up the carpet, tearing it free from its tacks. Now I could see the wood beneath.

I needed to lift out part of the middle plank – a section about two feet long. But the piece I needed to remove was dogged into place by a couple of wooden pegs on the plank's underside. The pegs pivoted on dowels and locked under the boards on each side. The problem was that the pegs were inaccessible from above, so you couldn't tuck them out of the way until you'd lifted the plank – but you couldn't lift the plank free until you'd folded the pegs out of the way. It was another lock that only an adept could open – unless one was prepared to rip the floor up – or maybe fiddle around on your hands and knees for half an hour, sliding a steel rule between deck joints. I was pleased I didn't have to take either of those approaches.

I reached in and Pushed the pegs round on their pivots until they were flush with the sides of the plank. Then I got my fingernails under the sides of the board and pried it out of the floor. Sure enough, on the underneath was a clear vinyl wallet, the A4 kind that stationers sell for keeping paperwork in, and it was fastened to the bottom of the plank by two long strips of duct tape.

The wallet closed with a sort of toothless zip like they have on resealable food bags. I pulled the zipper open and lifted out the papers, walking back to the bunk with them and putting them in my bag. Then I went back and resealed the wallet, put the plank back in its place, and Pushed the pegs round until the board was locked down again. When that was done, I laid the carpet back in place and trod it down with my shoes.

I inspected my handiwork to see whether there was any sign that I'd been here. As I tipped my head down to squint at the carpet in the dim light, I suddenly felt like my brains were sloshing forwards in my head. It was a horrible feeling, brought on by my extreme tiredness. In fact I was pretty much dead on my feet by now. Just looking down at my feet had made me sway with exhaustion. I figured it was time that my all-powerful master called it a day and I got out of there before I actually fell down.

If the Marker was here, I think we'd have found it. So can we go through the papers back at the flat? I'm completely exhausted. We can figure out what they mean once we're somewhere safe.

Yes. We can return home now.

That was a relief; he was in a sensible mood. Most likely

he was knackered[1] too. His mention of home made me wonder which Home the Sleeper's pattern referred to; I was fairly sure I managed to keep my interest to myself, though. Having felt the echo of my own thoughts in the Sleeper's mind I had the beginnings of an understanding for the way our link worked – just a beginning, mind you, but I had a sense for what carried: what he might overhear and what he might miss. It was like learning to whisper all over again: every adult could do it (if they chose to), but little kids sometimes struggled with the concept. You had to learn to speak and be quiet at the same time – and I thought I could see how it might be done.

Did that count as a victory? The possibility that I could think without being overheard? If it *was* a victory, it was a small one. My overall position was definitely not strong. He could see through my eyes and hear through my ears and I had no way to stop that.

And, although I knew I could fight him for short periods of time, the medication would make it so much harder. With the drugs now flowing through my veins I doubted I would be able to seize control of my actions for more than a few seconds. And even then, the Sleeper still had a couple of threats he could use to command my total obedience. So it wasn't a victory, but it was an opportunity.

I needed a plan.

Damping my thoughts to a stealthy murmur, I thought back on the collection of patterns I'd seen ranked in the Sleeper's head. Besides Connect (which seeped into every adept's brain until you were hardly aware it was there) I knew pretty much what Pattern Link did – it made a necklace that could link two minds together – and at the last second, I'd grabbed a general idea of what Home was for.

---

[1] A posh British word meaning enervated or greatly fatigued

I believed Home would take me somewhere – somewhere *central*. Central to what, I wasn't sure. But from the halo of meaning around it, I could tell what use the Sleeper had in mind for it. He would use it to bring me to him. But of course he would wait until I was holding the Marker before he activated it.

On its own, that was a frightening thought – the idea that he had a way to instantly abduct me – but what *really* troubled me was the knowledge that the Sleeper had at least three more patterns, maybe more. I knew with the certainty of stolen memory that each one commanded a power outside of what any sane person had ever achieved.

I should explain what I mean by that. As he infused my mind with his own skill at magic, I'd acquired lots of other information too. And besides what the Sleeper had shared with me, I'd also pored over the PAC's collection of old manuscripts, and the notes they'd written detailed their speculations. The overall picture I'd assembled told me that the patterns the Sleeper possessed were what was known as Greater Powers. These were powers beyond what you could achieve through the standard seven Surfaces. In the PAC's notes they were sometimes flippantly referred to as 'guru level' powers. Adepts had known about them forever, though they were exceedingly rare, and there was one thing everyone agreed upon: they were out of reach to normal people – normal adepts, that is.

Only a few unworldly elders had ever mastered a Greater Power and to do so they'd had to spend the majority of their long lives ridding themselves of ambition and every other material and physical desire.

It was believed that only the enlightened could even *discover the existence* of a Greater Power. It took decades, at least half a dozen of them, to reach a state of affectless and transcendent emptiness within which one of the deep secrets of magic might be revealed. Most who tried never met with success and no one

– not one person in the recorded history of the world – had ever mastered a power and then resuscitated enough of their ego to put it to worldly use.

If you came by a Greater Power it was because you had obliterated your desires, your ego even. You couldn't master that power and then use it to take over the world. At least no one ever had, even though it was every power-mad adept's dream. The PAC's papers included just a flavour of the eternal and avid interest in the subject and those papers all agreed: no exceptions had ever been found. Greater Powers would not come to the ambitious or the worldly.

And when you catalogued the few enlightened souls who had manifested some Greater Power there were perhaps half a dozen gurus in all – depending on who you believed – maybe a couple more and maybe fewer. And in each case they had mastered only a single Greater Power.

From what I'd seen inside the Sleeper's mind – that plus a little arithmetic – I knew that he had mastered at least five Powers. *Five.* I'd seen the common or garden patterns – Connect and its simple inversion Quell – and then at least five others. It was unprecedented; even the knowledge that had spilled over from the Sleeper's mind itself told me that. He had done something no else had been able to do. That no one *should* be able to do.

I also recalled from the PAC papers that described the Marker that its creation was credited to a Greater Power so rare that it had only manifested itself once, in ancient China, at least a century before Julius Caesar was a twinkle in his father's eye.

Given what I now knew, I could guess that there was a pattern for making Markers too, presumably called Pattern Marker – just as Pattern Link had made my necklace, my mental shackle – and I could tentatively assume that the Sleeper didn't possess it. If he could make Markers, I couldn't see why he'd have me crawling around on my hands and knees looking for one.

I knew his control of the Surfaces was formidable because that skill had flowed into me, had been deliberately pressed into my head. And with that skill had come sufficient knowledge to place his abilities in context, to know that these were the skills of a great master. But it now seemed that he was something even more fearsome, something unheard of – a master of *multiple* Greater Powers who had *not* shed his ego, and who had very definitely not renounced his claim on this world. Somehow he had accomplished what a hundred generations of adepts had declared impossible (however much they'd wished the opposite was true).

Not for the first time I began to wonder what the Sleeper would do once he had the Marker in his grasp and had used it to regenerate himself. I had struggled with the question before, but now I knew two new things. First: he might very probably be the most powerful adept who had ever lived. And second: the pattern he carried in his head, the one called Home, would take me to him, wherever he was. Somewhere he had a body in need of repair and when the writhing shape that increasingly haunted my mind was finally activated, I knew I would find myself standing next to that broken-down body. I wondered, with a sick nervousness, what would happen after that.

And I knew that I'd find out soon.

With all those insights and fears swirling around in my head as I left the boat, I experienced a moment of total desperation. At my feet was a boat hook and for a split second I thought about picking it up from the deck and just whacking myself over the head with it. In my many layers of clothing, I'd flop over the side and sink down into the ooze without leaving a trace. I was sure I could do it before he could stop me and then it would all be over.

Maybe it would be better for everyone if I did it – better than unleashing the Sleeper on the world. It might even be the best death I could hope for now.

But I didn't do it. Not only was I afraid – we shouldn't underestimate the importance of that – but it would leave the Sleeper furious and vengeful. I'd be giving Daniel, the Professor and the others maybe a fifty-fifty chance of waking in the night to find an Army assassin at the foot of their beds. Even if I gave no thought to my own wellbeing, bringing my life to a sudden, violent end would do nothing to help my friends.

And from my friends, my thoughts turned towards my mother. Here I was, contemplating taking my own life and I'd been led to this point by my revulsion for her suicide. What was the word for that?

For a moment, my mind drifted back to a college English class I'd taken years before. The Professor who took the class was so picky that she interviewed every applicant individually, putting them on the spot with her fierce questions. She had commanded me, "Define irony." I forget what I replied at the time, something about it being a kind of higher justice invisible to most of those it affected. I think she'd been favourably impressed. She'd let me on the course at any rate.

But I think if I was asked what irony was now, I'd give a different definition. I'd say it was the piercing pain you felt when you realised what fate had done to the shape of your life.

As I made my way back to my flat I struggled to find some way to untwist the knot my life had been tied in.

Chapter 27

Nuclear weapons. That was the closest analogy I could find in the non-magical world. I'd seen inside the Sleeper's mind and there, lined up in his mental armoury, were five suitcases, each containing an atomic bomb.

Or maybe that wasn't a good analogy, because I had no idea what those symbols in his head might do. They were in the same league as the symbol which created the Marker, but what did that tell me? What was comparable to immortality? 'Pattern Link' had allowed him to pull me on like a glove and effectively possess me for weeks before I became aware of his influence and began to oppose him. What was comparable to demonic possession? And 'Home' hinted at something even greater: the source of magic, maybe: its central point. What might await me once he triggered that symbol? Was there some master control room for magic which the Sleeper had chosen for his lair? Was his proximity to the endpoint of Home what had given him access to this incredible arsenal of powers?

I didn't know what those remaining powers might be, the ones I hadn't been able to see, but that didn't stop my imagination generating bizarre or terrifying possibilities on a minute-by-minute basis. Adepts couldn't use magic directly on each another when both parties were Connected, but I pictured the newly rejuvenated Sleeper reaching through an opponent's Shield and dropping him in his tracks. Then I imagined some awful battlefield weapon, seeing a dozen soldiers turned to drifting ashes by a single, vengeful thought. A moment later I imagined a super-Shield, vast and thick, protecting a building and capable of turning aside a missile or absorbing its destructive force.

They were all just comic-book daydreams, recycled pieces of B-movie nightmares: my imagination could churn them out all day long – but that didn't mean they were impossible, untrue. Even if the truth was more subtle and low-key, more insidious than the flashy superpowers I was dreaming up, surely one of the five symbols would cause a shift in the balance of power in the world. Even the symbol I knew best, Pattern Link, could do that.

Once he was out in the world again, fit and young, the Sleeper could dig his claws into many more brains. There was no reason to think my necklace was for adepts only; it worked whether I wanted it to or not, regardless of whether I concentrated or not. What might he achieve with a few dozen of his zombies in the world? I didn't like to ascribe too much self-awareness to myself, but it had been my own vanity that had stopped me recognising that he was the reason for my newfound success. And I wasn't the only person in the world who suffered from vanity.

Might he not find vain and powerful people whose self-importance would never allow them to suspect that he was the power behind their throne? When I thought of egos so great they took credit for everything around them, was I not describing the leaders of the world? They were ripe for the picking.

Six months ago, all I had to worry about was a flaky temperament and my own genius for self-pity. By this time a week ago I had the vicious assassins of the Army to avoid. By this morning I had every reason to fear for my life and the lives of my friends at the hands of an enemy who had invaded my thoughts. And now, as much as I wanted to ignore it, I found myself fretting over what the Sleeper might do to the rest of the world once he was able to bring his power to bear on it.

In any sensible, believable version of reality this would not be my problem. A responsibility like this should not and could not fall onto shoulders like mine. It was so wrong as to seem almost like a global joke at my expense; I was being mocked by the hidden engine of fate itself[1].

Even as I acknowledged how ridiculous that last thought was – that it was just my old, neurotic impulses contributing their two-cents-worth – I was forced to admit that therapy couldn't cure *this* problem. There's nothing like discovering the fate of the world is now your responsibility to make you re-examine your feelings of being put upon.

The Sleeper was a problem bigger than the PAC and bigger than me. In fact it was a problem so serious, so huge, that it was almost a relief that I could think of no way to derail his plans; it lifted the responsibility off of my shoulders and demoted me to the status of helpless victim. If I couldn't stop him then I wasn't to blame for what he did.

And although that realisation was crushing, at the same time it was a comfort; it let me off the hook and allowed me to reconcile myself to the inevitable.

And then, of all the accursed luck, the beginnings of a plan began to occur to me.

---

[1]   Isn't it weird how feeling insignificant and possessing minuscule self-esteem doesn't stop a person also developing a sense of victimisation the size of a city block or allowing their paranoia to grow beyond all limits?

* * *

It was raining as I walked back from the tube station – spiteful Winter-in-London rain – and my wig was starting to look like the pelt of a drowned fox. I glanced around me and, seeing no one about, I pulled the wig off and stuck it in my bag. I tucked the gold headband in after it. Now at least it was my own hair that would frizz up and glue itself to my face.

I put as much urgency into my stride as I could, hoping I'd get to my front door before the icy raindrops worked their way any further down the neck of my coat. But I was so weary from the search of the boat that I didn't have a lot of speed on tap.

I knew I could save myself several minutes of exposure to the elements if I cut through Junkies' Alley so I left the pavement and crossed onto the gravel of the path, turning in under the shoulder-height branch of a fading plane tree. Fat, frigid droplets were brushed loose from the tips of its boney twigs and they pattered all around me and onto my skin.

I suppose I should have been concerned about the human reptiles who lurked in the grimy shadows here, but really, they were so thoroughly outclassed by the other menaces in my life I couldn't muster much of a sense of threat. I wondered if I should put my headband back on my head just in case they wanted to challenge that assessment, but I didn't bother. Any sense of peril I had after the tiredness had taken its cut was fully employed worrying about the Sleeper. And my emergency reserves of panic I was saving for the Army. Sorry, nothing to spare for the junkies, maybe next time.

I passed the iron stairs under which I'd seen a pair of predatory eyes tracking me that first time through here, but this time when I peered in, no one looked back. I reached the twist in the path by the big transformer and found I could see the road on the far side just up ahead of me.

And then I heard something.

"'Scuse me, wait a minute," a voice behind me slurred. Someone had been standing in the tall, shadowed bushes next to the grey enclosure of the transformer and now he crashed out on to the path, holding up a trembling hand that looked a little like a dying crab. He wasn't the one I'd seen before, but he just had to be a junkie. His eyes were mounted too deep in the black wells of their sockets and his cheek bones had risen to pallid prominence through the thin flesh of his face; he didn't get that way just by skimping on the wheat-grass and cutting a few yoga classes.

"Hold on, wanna ask you a question," he breathed, stumbling after me, sounding just as tired as I was. It would be almost funny, in a gallows-humour sort of way, if he chased me: me too tired to run, him too messed-up to catch me.

For some reason I said 'Sorry' to him – maybe it was some latent piece of middle-class programming reflexively triggered by his begging tone – and then I scuttled out onto the pavement at the far end of the path.

There was still an hour or two of daylight left, so I doubted he would actually chase me. But I slid my hand into my bag and explored with my fingertips until they encountered the cold smooth edge of my headband. I wasn't planning to stop, but I decided that if I looked round and saw him following me, I'd go back and deal with him: break a couple of bones, maybe. It would probably be doing him a favour – get him some medical attention. Otherwise I just didn't have time to be threatened by amateurs. I nudged those thoughts in the direction of our link, knowing how the Sleeper felt about junkies; he'd approve.

For some reason, that particular thought flaked loose another layer of false memory and I remembered something.

I'd already learned that my earlier, visceral hatred of junkies had come from him and now I discovered something else – and it didn't seem like he'd planted it deliberately. It was an intact fragment of knowledge that had somehow slipped across the link and embedded itself in my head. I drank in the flavour and scent of it, priming myself to recognise his signature from this scrap, to be alert for a similar imprint in my thoughts. But beyond this memory told me of him, it also told me something useful about the world – something that I might be able to use.

I looked back over my shoulder and saw that my would-be attacker hadn't even made it out into the daylight. My fingers withdrew from my bag.

Five minutes later I was home, the locks were on the door and I was upstairs, in the top bathroom, underneath a hot shower. The wig had made my scalp itch and now my skin was getting a good scrub. And the shower was a pretty good place to wrestle with the inadequate scraps of my plan. My mental autopilot could handle the soap-and-water side of things while the rest of my brain struggled with the life-and-death stuff.

If I could have strung the shower out for a couple of hours I would have done. This plan I had – that I was *beginning* to have – was a little insane – insane and complicated and it didn't work. I kept finding gaps in it. It was like taking a handful of pieces from three different jigsaw puzzles and hoping they'd make a picture – in my current predicament I'd have even settled for something abstract and modernist – but the more I looked the more holes I found.

And I wasn't putting this together sitting at one of those General's tables, crowded with model battalions arranged in rows, using a croupier's squeegee to fine-tune their deployment. I was struggling to find the one right combination of choices that would trigger all the events I needed to happen and I was doing it while putting a third application of conditioner on my distressed hair under water that had gone cold.

And the whole thing might even be possible, I might even be able to work it out, if I wasn't so goddamned tired. This was the most important piece of decision-making I'd ever had to do (or, I supposed, ever would do) and I could hardly stay on my feet for the fatigue that pulled down on my arms and eyelids and ladled tar onto my mental cogs.

The solution eluded me, despite the fact that I now had one huge and luminous ace up my sleeve. Despite my inability to assemble a coherent plan, I believed I had resolved one of the biggest intangibles in my situation. I reckoned I might have actually figured out the hiding place of the Marker, but I was so dizzy from exertion that I couldn't clarify my own thinking enough to feel sure. I didn't even think I could keep the Sleeper out of my thoughts for much longer. Fears pressed in upon me and I found myself worrying: what if my defences come down? What if he catches a glimpse of what I'm up to *and drags the whole thing out of me? Then I've lost whatever advantage I might have had.*

What advantage will you have lost?

Damn, damn, damn. He can hear me.

Yes, I can hear you. I'm inside your head, you unbelievable fool. What are you attempting to keep from me? It's something relating to the Marker isn't it? I can sense that much.

I got out of the shower, busying myself for a second or two by fussing with the towel. I struggled to blank my mind, to think only of nothingness. But it was impossible. It would have been impossible even if I were pin-sharp instead of dead on my feet. You just can't *not* think of something.

I am not inclined to give another lecture. I will simply prise that knowledge out of your head and that is not something you will enjoy. Once that is taken care of we can consider how you might benefit from an illustration of the price of disobedience; I am thinking particularly of the demonstration we discussed earlier, the scheme involving the abundant loss of life.

He was certainly getting a taste for the snarky speeches. I wasn't sure whether he *could* actually tear the knowledge out of my mind, but even if I'd been tempted to find out what *that* felt like, I had to be careful. I didn't want him rampaging through my brain, bursting through every barrier. I reckoned I could give up the location of the Marker without giving *everything* else away. And moreover, the jolt of adrenaline that came with being discovered had given me a temporary burst of strength which I was able to put to good use: I reckoned I now had a working idea of how to screen the bulk of my thoughts from his gaze – for as long as my concentration held. And I was becoming sensitive enough to his presence now that I was sure he wasn't overhearing this particular soliloquy.

But I could feel myself beginning to fade again almost immediately. I decided to tell him what he wanted to know before my mental defences collapsed completely. There was a time for resistance and this wasn't it. Wrapped in a bath-robe, I left the bathroom and flopped down on my bed, resigned to what was coming.

OK, here it is.

You were a nautical man once, right?

For a second, I could actually feel the shock radiating from his side of our link and into my mind. I'd caught him by surprise. And he was plenty tired too; he wasn't guarding his thoughts any better than I was. He hadn't expected my question, despite the many clues he'd allowed to slip through his fingers.

It's not a trick question. I just wanted to ask you something: that long-handled boat-hook thing we found on the house-boat; what do you think it's for?

There was a slight delay before he responded.

It is not a boat hook, as you call it. It is… unusual. Not a design I am familiar with. But then I do not consider a floating dog kennel to be a legitimate vessel. I have no knowledge of those waterborne dormitories. The owners might use such a pole for anything.

OK, next question. Why would a house-boat need an anchor chain?

And I'd done it again. I'd stopped him dead in his mental tracks.

He was thinking it through, trying to get ahead of me, I could sense it. The delay before he replied was even longer this time.

Perhaps… these 'craft' must stand off from shore from time to time. His words came slowly. He was unsure of himself. I could tell he didn't much like that feeling.

So why would the anchor be down when the boat is tied up in dock?

Yes. Yes, I see. Something has been attached to the anchor. You have impressed me. We will return to that place at once and raise the anchor.

Wait a minute. Just hold on.

Across the link, I could feel him bristling at being told what to do.

You refuse?

Not exactly. But first, don't you want me to tell you what the boat-hook thing is for?

He was fairly squirming with impatience now. He hadn't been able to contain his excitement when he realised where the Marker must be, and now he wanted to charge out there with all guns blazing. And yet he didn't want to miss something important. He was struggling to solve the puzzle that he knew *I* had already solved and he couldn't do it.

Tell me. **Now**.

Inwardly I sighed, and I realised that he wasn't the only one feeling a little irritation. I was running out of patience too.

You know, to be honest I've had more or less enough of you

ordering me around. If you're so smart, work it out for yourself.
And if you're so powerful, then you can _make_ me tell you.

It was a reckless thing to do, but the microscopic fragments that were all that remained of my god-given self-esteem could still prickle me like splinters. I felt, before I was done, I really had to take at least one stand against him. There would be plenty of opportunities for me to get myself killed before this was all played out and it just didn't seem right to allow that to happen without looking him straight in the metaphorical eye at least once and defying him. I'd been right a moment ago. There *was* a time for resistance and *this* was it.

For a second I couldn't tell how he was going to respond. And then a mass of ill-will struck the edge of my mind like an iceberg, peeling back the thin steel of my defences and bursting in towards the core of me. Its brutal bulk seemed ready to crumple me flat me like a Coke can.

I screwed up what little determination I had left and resisted him. It was like trying to lift a car off your chest. The weight just kept piling down on me. I could feel his strength, how much of it there was, and I could gauge it against my own. With a flicker of surprise I realised how powerful I actually was, but at the same time, I could see that it wasn't enough. He was going to win.

I struggled and fought for what seemed like an age, and gradually, inevitably, the weight descended on me. I must have looked like I was having a fit as I lay on the bedcovers twitching and straining at nothing. If I had been tired before, I was beyond that now, dropping down into a whole new realm of surreal weariness. If I kept this up much longer I really thought I would pass out. I held on until we were both woozy with fatigue and then, with a final, defiant thrust, I shoved him back momentarily and called a halt, acknowledging my defeat.

OK. Stop, stop, stop. You win. You win. I'll tell you.

He was masking it, but I knew he was just as drained as me.

He'd just had a little more practice at pushing himself than I had – centuries of hard discipline will do that for you. He was also boiling mad at my defiance; our earlier exchange had really rubbed his nose in my smartness. Funny how that never seemed to bring out the best in people, going back as far as I could remember.

The pressure on me dissipated and I awaited his response.

Now. Was all he said and it was deafening, like the blast of a fog horn experienced from close range. He didn't need to explain further.

Let me show you. I'll explain it all; I'll lay it out so you can see everything.

My arms and legs felt boneless with fatigue, but I rolled into an upright position and stood up. Then I went to my desk and fetched the papers we'd retrieved from the secret compartment in Jan's old desk. I selected one of the papers and laid it on the bed. It was a print-out of scheduled flight times between London and Rome and it was a couple of years out of date. Nothing very exciting there, it being information available to anyone with an Internet connection, but scribbled in the margins were a number of complex doodles.

I left them there and went to hunt through my bag, at last pulling out the papers we'd collected today from beneath the decking of the house-boat. I selected a single piece of paper, this time a receipt from a pharmacy, and placed it face down on the bed next to the list of flight times. On the back of the receipt was another of Jan's doodles, something long and thin, with a boxy outline at one end, lying next to a big shape like the side of a whale.

Then I fished out my laptop, fired it up and opened Illustrator – a drawing program. I'd had a lot of practice with it and was kind of a whiz at putting together complex diagrams – in fact I could draw faster with it than anyone I knew – and now I took Jan's doodles and re-drew them on the computer so that they became clear and neat. I could have roughed something out quickly enough, but instead I laid it on thick. I refined and added details until I could feel the Sleeper's patience fraying. I hit print and fetched the following hard copy:

You get it?
What is that? Explain it.
Look, just let me draw the second part. It'll make sense then.

I began a second drawing, working rapidly but still putting in more detail than strictly necessary. I knew it would annoy the Sleeper but I reckoned I could live with that, all in all. Maybe he'd get so angry with me he'd have a stroke and I could go back to my regular life – whatever form *that* might take.

Even though I'm normally wicked fast and accurate, exhaustion was relentlessly joggling my elbow as I drew. A couple of times I had to close my eyes and pause because I was actually finding it difficult to focus. I felt like I'd been up for days, maybe a week, but I pressed on. At last I hit print and fetched this:

It even had a little through-the-magnifying-glass section for extra detail.

Let me take you through it. On the first picture, you can see that there's a spike that sticks up from the side of the boat, under the waterline, right? You slide the hollow end of the boat-hook onto the prong and that lets you drop things down and thread them onto the spike, OK?

I tapped the first of Jan's doodles. If you squinted at it right you could see it as a muddled drawing of just that. The detail was much clearer in my version.

First you take a link of the anchor chain and drop it over the boat-hook and down onto the prong. Then you put the thing you want to hide in a bag and attach a cord to it. Put a loop in the end of the cord. Now you pass the loop over the pole and drop the bag over the side. The bag dangles from the spike and its cord sits on top of a link of the anchor chain. Now you can remove the stick. And that's the first picture.

I pointed to the second of Jan's doodles and then switched to my version of it.

If anyone hauls up the anchor chain without putting the stick in place, the rising chain lifts the loop of the bag free of the spike and the bag just drops into the sludge on the bottom. If you bring up the anchor like that you find nothing. But if put the boat-hook back in place first, you can haul the bag up. It's fiendish; I'm not surprised you took so long to get it.

Ouch. Maybe that last comment was a little too much. I could feel rage radiating across the link like desert sun through a windowpane.

Get up. We're going there now.

It's too late in the day. Get real. I can hardly stand.

Almost before I knew what had hit me, he had seized control of my motor functions. I was on my feet and hauling dry clothes out of the wardrobe with absolutely no conscious involvement on my behalf. Maybe I could have fought him but I hardly had the strength.

I'm sorry, I said, and tried to mean it. I didn't like being a puppet. Sure, being a willing accomplice was morally painful and guilt-inducing, but watching him pull my strings and march me round the room like his toy was hideous. It reduced me to an instrument of his will, which made me feel less than human. I resolved that I would at least retain control of my own limbs even if I had to relinquish everything else.

I'll do it. I won't fight you. I'll get ready and we'll go. You've won.

Cautiously I took back control and he didn't oppose me. I pulled on my clothes. Moving at all was an effort, but I didn't feel like baiting the Sleeper any more. It had already been an exhausting day and now we'd both used up what little energy had remained. If we clashed again, I didn't think there'd be enough left of my will-power to stop him reading my thoughts with as much as ease as leafing through a confiscated diary.

This time I didn't bother with a disguise. I chose jeans, solid boots and a heavy sweater for warmth. The only embellishment was a dark wool cap that I found on the floor of my wardrobe; I used it to cover the headband. The cap itched like crazy, which come to think of it was probably why it was on the floor, and I immediately regretted not picking out something different. But I didn't want to stretch the Sleeper's tolerance any further by dithering over my choice of outfits.

I was about to set off when I caught sight of all the papers lying on my bed. *Should probably tuck these away* I thought and gathered them up. I grabbed a folder from the bookcase and slid the papers in amongst some college paperwork, then I returned the folder to its shelf.

I pulled on a coat and clumped down the stairs. When I stepped out of the front door I found that the drizzle had let up. I judged that there was maybe an hour more daylight, although the street was already quiet. I'd only gone a few steps when I had to scratch my head furiously through the cap. I didn't stop, but a moment later I had to pull the cap off completely so I could get my fingernails into my itchy scalp.

Relax, I'll put it back on if we see anyone.

I neared the entrance to the cut-through, the Junkie's hang-out, and my feet slowed.

Why do you hesitate?

Um, don't you think we should go around? There might be someone in there and I'm asleep on my feet. It just seems safer to go round.

With both of us so tired, he wasn't having much more luck hiding his thoughts from me than I was from him. His weary anger was a constant presence. I think he was finding living in my head was a bit like sharing a dorm room with me; he'd had enough of my whining long since.

When he didn't respond, but just simmered to himself, I added: *Sorry, but just to be on the safe side.* There was a noticeable whimper to my mental tone and I could sense how irritating the Sleeper found it.

I do not cower from those parasites and I am getting tired of reminding you to obey me. The next time I even suspect you are defying me I will punish you. If I sense you are delaying me, I will kill your friends and then perhaps you will learn how to take orders instead of kicking at every instruction like a child in need of correction.

Wow. Someone was getting pretty pouty. But I didn't have the necessary grit to argue with him. I turned obediently into the alley and made my way once more through the dank semi-darkness.

In theory, I had nothing to worry about: the most powerful adept in the world was ready to assist me if I had to fight off a couple of over-medicated, ninety-pound purse-snatchers. Though, maybe in hindsight it would have made more sense to cover the enticing gleam of gold at my temples.

Even when I took a false step on the wet ground and in my numbed exhaustion nearly tumbled onto my ass it didn't seem like a big deal.

I'll admit that when I felt a clammy arm snake around my throat a cold draft of fear blew through me, but even then

I didn't doubt myself. Even though I was feeling a little high on exhaustion, I knew that in a second I'd lash out and there'd be shrieks and moans and unpleasant snapping sounds and a couple of addicts would finally have a good reason to dose up on morphine. All I had to do was focus...

And yet I couldn't. A second junkie kicked my legs out from under me and I went down, my collision with the ground knocking some of the wind out of me. The hard edge of a forearm (so skinny it felt like greasy cloth over naked bone) was still pressing hard into my windpipe and the acid stink of unwashed flesh was in my nostrils. I tried again to Connect and if my brain had been a gun, instead of a bang there would just have been a dry click. I was so weary that Connection wouldn't come. That's the moment when panic finally reared up, bellowing, and began to stampede through my brain. This was not good.

And then I felt the headband being torn from my temples and at that point it occurred to me that I might be in truly serious trouble. Despite the pain, despite the panic, my first fear was for how the Sleeper might react, what awful revenge he might take for allowing this to happen. Since he'd revealed himself, I'd been desperate to remove the necklace, but I knew that as soon as I did, I would be dooming my friends. In my mind it had become their lifeline, something I had to keep safe whatever else might happen – and even now I could feel grimy hands reaching for it.

I started to kick and scream (though no sound made it past the choke-hold on my throat). I struggled furiously even as I felt someone dropping their weight onto my legs. The pressure on my throat was making it difficult to keep breathing and I couldn't tell if the black clouds swarming across my vision were from lack of oxygen or some retribution the Sleeper had unleashed.

Just before my head hit the gravel, I felt hard fingers plucking at the clothing around my neck. Someone, somewhere said, "She's got a necklace on." And then I felt a new sort of pain as the gold wire at the back of my neck dug deep into my flesh. "Gimme the pliers," the other voice said and somewhere around that point I slid down into a nightmare where angry zombies with icy hands used a selection of tools to pull out my fingernails one by one and all I could think about was what would happen to my friends now that the link to the Sleeper had been severed.

Chapter 28

I knew an old guy once who told me about how, when he was younger, his worn-out Ford had been stolen. He was kind of surprised when the police called him, saying it had turned up, still drivable, some miles away. The police reckoned a couple of hippies stole it to get to a festival. This guy, who was kind of a hippy himself, got the bus to the police impound yard. "They ran off, but they left behind your things," the policemen said, handing over the car keys. *Hmm*, thought my friend, who always kept the car empty of belongings because the door locks didn't work properly. So he drove around the corner, pulled in, and performed a little inventory. The thieves had bolted, leaving behind a long afghan coat in his size, a handful of really cool bootleg cassettes, a full tank of gas and – when he popped off the plastic cover in the middle of the steering wheel – a brimming bag of grass, right where he always kept his own stash. What a nice story. I thought of it as I was coming round.

When I was about 90% conscious I realised that my face hurt, just on one side – the side resting on the gravel. I lifted my head and a boom of pain detonated in my head. Being choked unconscious had left me with a headache so large it seemed to cram my skull to bursting point. Broken bones, blood, severed limbs? I sat up, aware that I was lying in a puddle of oily rainwater and I began patting myself, figuring it was the easiest way to find out what was attached and what was broken.

I could hardly believe it when I failed to find any injuries. Well, any major injuries. I touched a tender spot on my scalp and my fingers came away bloody. The flesh of my scalp was already puffing up around the cut, but even in my most hypochondriacal moment I couldn't convince myself it was much of a wound.

Even though I was sitting up, I was aware that I wasn't thinking clearly yet.

Above me stretched the dark coral of bare plane tree limbs outlined against a dimming cloud-locked sky; around me was the alleyway. As I took stock, I pictured a miniature maintenance crew reconnecting downed circuits in my nervous system. The gravel on my cheek, the water-melon-sized headache, the cut on my scalp – each one made its presence felt in turn as the lights came back on in my brain. Next to arrive was a bone-deep ache in the muscles of my back and legs. I couldn't tell if I'd been kicked, fallen down, or just laid awkwardly in my stupor. Whatever the reason, I was stiff as a lacquered board.

Once the circuitry to my nerve endings was restored, my body's repair crew evidently set to work hooking up my higher mental functions. With a jolt of nausea reminiscent of sudden deceleration I remembered my situation. The feeling was like sleepily glancing at the bedside clock and having it occur to you that right now you're supposed to be in an exam. It was like that, except in a world where they kill your friends if your grades drop.

How long had I been disconnected from the sleeper? Phone gone, watch gone, no way to tell. OK, well… it was still light. In fact it didn't seem any closer to sunset than when I left the house. So I hadn't been unconscious very long. There'd only been an hour of daylight left when I closed my front door, so I couldn't possibly have been out for more than 45 minutes. My best guess, based on nothing more than intuition, was that I'd hardly missed any time at all – maybe five minutes. But even if I was right, that five minutes might seem like five hours to the Sleeper, who was suddenly disconnected from the world, unable to oversee his slave, and doubtless fretting that all his plans were going south. Cut off like that, his mind might be bubbling away, brewing up venomous schemes for reprisal. What might he have done already? And what if I was wrong and I'd been out for a lot longer than five minutes?

Losing consciousness had never been part of my admittedly sketchy plan. Everything else, though – believe it or not – was going better than expected.

You see, I'd figured out a way forward during a moment of surpassing despair. Hitting that low had made me realise something – something that finally allowed me to gather up the unruly strands of my planning and plait them neatly together. The secret had been to remove a single disruptive thread from the bundle. With that one gone, everything else came together tidily.

My mistake, it turned out, had been to expect too much, and that had prevented me from making any progress. Like those aspiring gurus I'd been thinking about, I'd been holding on to too many of my earthly needs; I could only achieve more by striving for less. Poetic sounding, isn't it? The practicalities, though, were grim.

My moment of clarity had struck when I tried to imagine the Sleeper releasing me. He would have his Marker, I would no longer be of use to him, and he'd simply send me away with a pat on the back and a heart-felt thank you. "Stay in touch," he'd call after me, waving.

Look a little closer and you'll see that there's something wrong with that picture. It just wasn't going to happen. He was never going to let me go. It was obvious.

So where did that leave me? I already knew that I couldn't run from him.

Put those two facts together and you arrived at this conclusion: it was no longer about me – simple as that. The Sleeper was going to kill me. And that realisation freed me to see things as they really were. If I withdrew just one requirement of my plan – the need for me to survive it – then everything else gelled. I could see a way to save my friends, even to hand them the Marker. And I could thwart the Sleeper for the foreseeable future – or until he could find another slave. And that could be a very long time if you factored in the memory that had surfaced as I was walking home. Just before I'd let the Sleeper overhear my thoughts about the Marker, it had come to me: there were no new adepts.

The old guard, virtually immortal as they were, took every opportunity to eliminate the up-and-coming competition. It was spelled out in the PAC manuscripts if you knew how to interpret them: a stranger was just a mortal enemy you hadn't met yet. There were no tender, impressionable young adepts for the Sleeper to prey upon, because if any arose, they'd be swiftly despatched by those currently in power. The PAC lived in camouflaged obscurity in a damp field in the middle of Cornwall mainly for that reason, and the four of us – the Professor, David, Susan and me – might well be the only candidates for mind control that the Sleeper had seen for a century – at least in this part of the world. The Sleeper had been very lucky to find someone as vulnerable as me.

But like I say, this wasn't about me. With that liberating thought in my mind, I realised that if I was able to remove myself from the picture in just the right way I could keep the Sleeper bottled up indefinitely. All I had to do was make my death look like an accident. Before, when I'd decided against trying to fool the Sleeper, it was because I couldn't see him buying any scheme I might have for *faking* my own death – but what if it wasn't faked? What if it was for real and the only fake part was making it seem accidental?

But how to pull that off? Step out in front of a bus? Total the bike at high speed? Sneeze while cleaning my service revolver? I'd keep those as my back-up options. Right away I figured the junkies would be my best hope. See, I didn't actually need them to kill me outright, just to mug me and steal the necklace. That would give me a little time out from under the Sleeper's gaze in which to set up the finale.

Of course, I couldn't be certain they'd jump me, but I could certainly push my luck. And I'd hit the Street Crime Jackpot on my first attempt.

By way of preparation, I'd completed what the Sleeper had started: the process of utterly exhausting the both of us. The junkies could only overpower me if I was defenceless, so I needed the Sleeper to believe that I was too tired to Connect. Not much play-acting required there. I'd sparred with him and struggled against his efforts to control me until both of us were weary almost to the point of collapse.

Then I'd goaded him until I could be sure he'd react angrily when I meekly suggested avoiding the alleyway and playing it safe. It was important that he remembered the decision had been his and not mine. And I thought I could rely on his expansive ego to dismiss any suspicions that I'd cleverly manipulated him.

It also hadn't required much acting skill to panic just before I blacked out. I really was frightened for the lives of my friends and the thought of what I had to do next had leant a real quality of desperation to the performance. With the exception of me passing out, things had pretty much gone according to plan. But what I couldn't predict in advance was whether I would survive the mugging.

If I didn't, then the drawings showing the location of the Marker, together with the papers giving the boat's location, were right there, in amongst my college paperwork, for the PAC to find. Earlier, I'd put my college ID in a different pocket from my wallet so that it wouldn't be stolen when the muggers swiped my cash and credit cards. So when the authorities found my body, they would pretty quickly link me to the Professor. My college employment records and my passport both listed the Professor as my next of kin, so there'd be a good chance that he would be the first to go through my things. I'd set things up so that the PAC could pick up the trail of the Marker.

But that was just a backup. I thought it was pretty unlikely that the junkies would kill me.

I was expecting to have to do that myself.

If I woke up after the mugging, my plan was to run a couple of quick errands and then retrieve the necklace. Just before I put it back on I'd have a simple task to perform – one brutal act before I could rest. I'd need to find something sharp and slice open an artery. Then I could restore the link to the Sleeper just in time for him to catch the final act. If I died while he was inside my head, monitoring my every move and sensation, there'd be no doubt in his mind.

I'd make it clear to him that in reclaiming the necklace from the muggers I'd been severely wounded. He'd have to take that part on faith, but he'd have seen through my own eyes the most important parts: the mugging itself, and then, a little later, me gasping my authentic last. It would be like he'd ducked out of the room to grab a soda during the last few minutes of my televised life story: when he left the heroine was being attacked, when he got back she was dying. He could fill in the missing part for himself.

What I wasn't sure of – what I wouldn't know until the

moment came – was whether I could do it. Kill myself, I mean. My plan was to inflict a good, deep wound in the thigh – make sure I found that femoral artery. I could bleed out from that in just a couple of minutes and in the meantime it would incapacitate me, preventing me from reaching help.

It wasn't instantaneous, though; I should have long enough to settle the necklace back in place and bring the Sleeper up to speed before I lost consciousness.

I was praying that I wouldn't lose my nerve when the time came, but there was a sick feeling in my guts like my internal organs had been scooped out and replaced with a couple of bags of iced water. I'd found myself hoping that the junkies would finish the job for me, so I didn't have to.

But, wouldn't you just know it, here I was still alive, sitting in a puddle of filthy rainwater and struggling not to throw up at the thought of what I had to do next. *Screw it*, I thought, and twisting onto my side, heaved the contents of my stomach into the weeds.

With that out of the way, it was time to get busy. According to my plan, if I was still alive after the mugging, I'd need to Connect in order to overpower my attackers and retrieve the necklace. For that I'd need tribute, and I'd already noticed some suitable jewellery in Noola's room when I'd moved her things. Of course I'd ditch the tribute before I put the necklace back on, so there was no danger of the Sleeper Healing my injuries. But first I had to get back to the house.

I staggered to my feet and tried to run. I took three wobbly steps and nearly lurched straight into a wall. I corrected my direction and set off, in a limping jog. I'd have laughed if I thought I'd be able to stop again: my agonising trot reminded me of a wounded pantomime horse.

I was desperate to get out of that alley and back to my house before any more time passed. I tottered along as quickly as I could and was soon outside my front-door. My house-keys were gone, but there was a spare set hidden beneath the straggly branches of the front garden's lone shrub. God knows what sort of spectacle I presented, but I managed to retrieve the key and get inside the house before any passers-by could spot me and shriek at the sight of a filthy, blood-spattered crazy-woman wrestling with a buddleia davidii.

If I was quick, I would have time to make one phone call before I had to return to the alleyway and conclude this awful, grim business. I'd gone over it a dozen times and in my plan, it was always the Professor I was going to call: the man in charge and the one who I most wanted a final chance to explain myself to. But as I ran up the stairs, slipping and stumbling, heading for the top room, it just came to me that I would call Daniel instead. It was like a parting gift to myself: the idea of hearing his voice brought a flicker of warmth to the nuclear winter that had taken hold inside my head.

I would call Daniel.

It's strange how the mountainous, unstoppable weight of destiny can turn on such delicate moments.

I searched out his number. My mobile was gone, so I called him on the house phone. It rang and rang, and for a moment I thought I wasn't going to reach him. While I waited, in agony for him to answer, I checked the time. Now I could see that it hadn't been more than ten minutes since the necklace had been cut from around my throat. Even so, ten minutes…

Daniel answered. "Hello?" he said, uncertainly. Maybe he had this number in his phone's memory and knew it was me. He wouldn't know what to expect; he was wary. But it was still mighty good to hear his voice.

"Daniel, it's Jo," I said, emotion threatening to catch in my throat. The old me would have cried at a moment like this. The new me came pretty close too.

He used that slow-paced, kind of hushed, talking-to-a-lunatic voice as he said, "Jo. How's it going? You feeling OK?"

Even that tone couldn't annoy me. I saw it for what it was: a sign that he was trying to reach out to me as carefully as he could. I let myself bask for a moment in the concern I could hear in his voice. I *knew* that calling him had been the right to do. I'd needed to hear how much he cared, before I... well, you know.

I said, "Daniel, I have some things to tell you. Now don't interrupt. You just have to listen and please, please trust me. Can you do that?"

Was that a lot to ask? "But Jo," he said, "wait a minute, there's something I need to tell you." He was suddenly all full of pep about whatever-it-was. Now that he'd realised I wasn't going to spaz out on him he was bursting to speak.

"Sorry Daniel, but that's interrupting," I said firmly. "Unless what you've got to say involves all of us getting killed very soon, then my speech takes precedence. Fair enough?"

"Killed?" he said, momentarily shut down. But only momentarily: "Well, OK. But believe me, you'll want to want to hear this."

By the way, that story earlier – the one about the hippy and his car – there was a point to it. The Sleeper was gone from my head right now, but he'd spent the last few weeks fixing up the place the way he liked it. He wanted his quest to succeed and all he'd had to work with was a whiney white girl with bad muscle tone. So he'd rammed as much of his guile and his gift for manipulation across the link as he could. Even though I'd pretty much learned to tell the difference between what was his and what was my own, that didn't mean I couldn't make use of what he'd left in my head.

With several big chunks of the Sleeper's Machiavellian play-book grafted into my head, I knew I could wrap Daniel around my little finger if I wanted to. I could push his buttons, get him to listen attentively, make him hear what I had to say.

It would be so easy, but something stopped me. I knew I could reel off some script the Sleeper had left me and have Daniel snapping to attention. But this was my last chance to talk to him and I wanted it to be *me*, and not some clone of the Sleeper, who spoke the words. I grew up not knowing how to control people – not having the confidence or the skill – and now I had both. It raised the question: in the past, was it only lack of opportunity that had stopped me from treating those around me as playthings or servants? Well, I had the opportunity now and I decided that for my last human act, I'd show a little restraint. I would let Daniel talk.

I said, "Daniel, I *beg* you, make every second count. You've got one minute to tell me whatever it is."

Bless him, he said nothing for a moment, realising I really meant what I said and figuring he needed to get his words out right. Then he launched into it: "OK. Remember when I helped you carry a load of your mum's things down to the bins? Well afterwards, I came back again and retrieved it all. You can shout at me later, but I was sure that one day you'd regret chucking that stuff out. I was planning to keep it until you were a bit less upset about it all. But I didn't want to make things worse, so I went through it all, in case there was anything bad in there – anything you didn't need to see. Shout at me later for that too. Anyway, I found something."

He continued, "It was a big Fedex envelope addressed to your mum and it was still sealed up. There was a receipt with the envelope. It was signed by Maria Revilla." He said the name slowly, unsure of the pronunciation.

Without thinking, I said, "My dad's housekeeper. Since I was little."

"OK," said Daniel, "well the date on it started me thinking. The receipt told me where Mrs. Revilla collected your mum's package from, so I Googled a newspaper story about your mother's death and compared addresses." Now he sounded each word out carefully, so there'd be no misunderstanding: "Your mum died outside that same Fedex office."

"What?" I said, finally beginning to understand. "Are you saying she was collecting a package when... when she died?" His minute was now up, but I was no longer watching the clock.

He said, "Your mum never got there so the company probably called again. Your housekeeper had to collect the envelope and for some reason she didn't put two and two together and link the address with your mum's death."

No surprise there. Mrs Revilla wouldn't have driven herself; she'd have just called a cab and probably handed the while-you-were-out card straight to the driver. Plus... the memories were coming back now. "When I was little, Mrs Revilla, she had kind of a drink problem for a while, I think. As a kid I'd figured she was just sad about my mom's death, but..." I was putting this together as I was talking, re-evaluating the judgements I'd made as a little girl: "but I when I think back, her loyalty was always to my dad. I don't think she even liked Mom, so... maybe she was drinking all along. Might explain why no one opened the door to the Fedex guy first time around, and how come the package needed collecting. No surprise she didn't recognise the address."

"Right, right" Daniel said, barely able to contain himself. "So your mum drove all the way across the city because that's where the parcel office was. And why would anyone kill themselves on the way to collect a package?" he said. "Jo, it *must* have been an accident."

I felt tears coming now. The Sleeper's instincts, still in place even without their owner present, rose up to push the emotion aside and I let them, was grateful for them. They allowed me to clamp down on the surging swell of roiled-up feelings.

Even so, I was pretty choked as I said, "Daniel?" It really wasn't much more than a throaty whisper. "I don't know what I'd do without you. I don't deserve you, but I do appreciate you. You know that, don't you?"

I felt a sudden urge to tell him everything and to apologise for every wrong thing I'd ever done. But again, those ruthless Sleeper reflexes blocked the impulse – and again I let them. There were other priorities than my guilty conscience here.

"Well, I…" he said and tapered off. Finally, something had taken the wind out of his sails. And thinking about wind and sails made me think of the Sleeper, the ice dream, the house-boat. I glanced at the clock, seeing that we were a whole minute over Daniel's allotted sixty seconds.

"But you… you should hear what else," Daniel was saying, his voice picking up speed again. "You'll never guess what was inside the envelope. Oh and you can shout at me later for opening it."

Two minutes fifteen since I'd said 'go'. Even having this conversation with Daniel was risking his life. I had to snap out of this and get moving.

"This is plenty for now, Daniel. Maybe, um, maybe another time," I said, choking up, knowing there wouldn't be any more times. Then I gathered up the emotion and put it away, getting it good and locked down this time. I cleared my throat and tried again. "There's no time right now, Daniel."

I needed to bring Daniel up to speed, maybe mumble a slightly coded goodbye, and then get going, before sentimentality wrecked everything. Except that I couldn't speak. Something was happening inside me. That makes it sound ominous, but it wasn't. It wasn't magical either. I think it was just the effect of Daniel's words, the meaning of them propagating through me. It was something to do with him and something to do with my mother and maybe something to do with me too: a ripple of hope fluttering through my chilly heart, simple and human. Maybe it was my mother's last gift to me. And I couldn't move while it unfolded inside me.

"Jo?" Daniel said, puzzled at my silence. "Jo?"

"I…" was all I said. What if? What if? It was all I could think for a moment.

And then I was suddenly free again. The change was completed. What if I didn't die? What if I fought to live? I could even see a kind of way that it might happen.

It would be risky – much riskier than going obediently to my death – I'd be gambling with everyone else's lives – but I wanted to fight – I needed to fight. If there was a chance of defeating the Sleeper then I should seize it. And with a rush of brilliant energy that burst through me like Summer returning to the frozen world, I knew that it was the right thing to do.

In a flash my plan rewrote itself and I realised that I would need an insurance policy, some way to protect my friends if my first attempt failed. And no sooner had I thought it than I realised Daniel could help me make it happen.

As if on cue, he said, "You wanted to tell me something?"

The words rushed out of me: "Daniel, something big is happening and we're all in a lot of trouble. You need to forget everything I told you last time we spoke. I was being forced to say those things. The truth is that I know everything the PAC has been doing, I know all about the Army Who Witnessed Creation, and I know about the Marker. I think I even know where the Marker is. And if you don't want it to end up in the hands of someone far worse than Jan then you'll do something for me." I debated telling him all about the Sleeper but that would just slow everything down at a moment when speed was vital. Possession took a bit of explaining.

Daniel didn't speak, just gave a surprised little sigh when he heard my words. So I started to tell him exactly what he needed to do.

340

And all the time I was speaking I was also thinking about what *he'd* told *me*. I mean, in a way it didn't make any difference. Without even meaning to, I'd made a sort of peace with my mother and this didn't change it. For a little while now, instead of looking up to her as a parent, our roles had somehow become reversed, and I'd been able to think about her almost as though *she* had been *my* daughter. Maybe it was something to do with having a centuries-old adept living in my head. And when I thought of her like that, I no longer saw her failings as grievances for me to resent; they were simply the burdens she'd had to carry and they were heavy indeed. They made her seem frail, in need of looking after, and all I felt for her now was pity.

And now Daniel had told me that she *hadn't* given up. Maybe her demons would have beaten her in the end, but somehow, knowing that she'd had more strength in her than I'd realised, that she'd still been fighting to live on the day when she died, well it made a difference. It made me wonder if there wasn't more strength in me too.

And as Daniel listened carefully, I told him, "I need you to come to London tonight and to bring something with you. This will sound strange, but you need to trust me about it." And I gave him the details. He wasn't crazy about fetching what I wanted – never mind that the details of where I wanted it brought were positively bizarre – but reluctantly he agreed.

I couldn't ask any more of Daniel, put him in any more danger, but the thought of reinforcements did cross my mind. "I don't suppose Susan Milton has come down off the ceiling yet. I imagine she's still pretty annoyed with me."

Daniel said, "I don't know. She took off suddenly. I think she's picking David up from the airport." I could almost hear him shrug. "I won't pretend she was a supporter of yours. She was the one who found out what you'd been up to. The last time we talked about you, she went off in a huff, but I think she's coming back tomorrow if you want to try talking to her."

Tomorrow? That wouldn't do me any good, and David Braun wasn't even in the country right now. For a moment I thought of trying to reach Susan on her mobile and explaining it all to her. Both she and David were pretty useful adepts – for novices – and with their help my plan might run a lot smoother, but I was down to my last couple of minutes here. Persuading Susan to cut me a break because I was possessed, well that was not a conversation you could rush. I would have to go it alone – as I'd always known I would.

"No problem," I said, trying to mean it. "So you'll do what I asked?"

"Yes," he said, quietly. "And you really won't tell me what this is all about?"

I hated keeping him in the dark, but I couldn't see any alternative. "I'm sorry Daniel. I would tell you if I could." I just couldn't have him jumping in to save me and getting himself needlessly killed.

It was time for me to go – past time really – so if I wanted to say some sort of goodbye, just in case, it had to be now. What to say?

I swallowed. "I just want you to know that I'm doing my best, Daniel. I'm doing what I think is right."

I think he really sensed, then, that this was serious. He'd heard the finality hiding behind my words, my need to sum things up.

"If it helps you with any of this," he said, with considerable pain in his voice, "I love you."

"Thanks," I sniffed, tearful despite the self-control I'd inherited from the Sleeper, "That helps a lot. Take care, Daniel," I added, and then I hung up.

I was sitting on the edge of the bed, the dead phone in my hands, and I felt like I could have stayed there without moving forever. But time was slipping dangerously fast through my fingers – time that would burn us all if I wasn't careful. I was beyond tired and the glimpse I'd caught of my reflection in the mirror made me look like I'd been hit by a garbage truck, but I had work to do. And there were still a couple of things to take care of before I left the house. I dashed into the bathroom, upended the little trash-can in there, and hunted around for what I needed. At the same time, I twisted one arm out of my sweater and wrestled with my t-shirt.

When I was done, I scooped the trash back into the bin and pulled my clothes straight again.

Then from my desk I fetched the spare key to Noola's room. I rushed downstairs, let myself in and rummaged through her things until I found her hidden jewellery box. I'd noticed a suitable replacement headband when I'd gone through her stuff, but now I needed bracelets too. She had a couple, but they were trashy looking things, and one of them seemed suspiciously like gold-plated crap. I had no idea how economical you could be with the gold and still be able to Connect. I hoped that Noola's cheap taste in jewellery wouldn't be the hairline fracture that caused everything else to fall apart.

With the gold in place, I summoned the Connect pattern and immediately felt the blossoming of my senses, as invisible membranes rose around me and displayed the essence of the world. I felt relief loosening the tension in my chest. I was tired, but not *too* tired. The Sleeper had believed my display of weakness earlier, in the alleyway, but the truth was, I still had a little left in reserve.

But I couldn't appear too chipper. Howling with the sting of it, I dug my fingernails into my scalp wound and dragged blood across my forehead: the worse I looked, the less suspicious the Sleeper would be. Then I deliberately collapsed the Healing field so that it wouldn't repair the damage I'd sustained. Now I just needed something to cover my head before I went out where people could see me.

The cap I'd worn before, the one I'd chosen because I knew it made my head itch, well that was wherever my bag was: gone. Instead I grabbed a baseball cap, jammed it down over my headband (ignoring the pain from my head-cut), and pulled the peak down to cover the blood streaked across my forehead. Then I rushed down the stairs, exactly like my life depended on it.

Out the front door, down the road and into the alleyway. By my reckoning it was now twenty minutes since they'd choked me unconscious on this spot; where were my muggers now? They must have some place where they holed up while their latest victim was recovering and staggering away, and I didn't think they were home-owners. I extended my awareness via the Surfaces, looking for body warmth and peering in through the walls and high windows on either side of the alleyway, probing into the corners and the crawl-spaces.

I sensed movement.

Then, sliding out from under the iron stairs came the junkie with the killer's eyes. He recognised me, I could see that. Languorously, he looked past my shoulder, checking for signs that I'd brought the cavalry with me. And then he glanced the other way, alert for someone approaching from behind him. Seeing no one around, he advanced on me.

I must have looked like I'd fallen out of a tree and into a dumpster. I was smeared with blood, and moss from the ground; I was dirty and bruised, and I still wore the same stained and filthy clothes I'd woken up in when I'd last stood here. I must have looked like an easy target.

As he stepped forwards, he dipped, picking up a length of wood with the bright edge of a broken hinge glinting from one end of it. Then he straightened, continuing to advance on me.

"I need my things back," I said, resting my hands on my thighs for support as a squall of tiredness blew through me and rocked me onto my heels. *Hmmm, mustn't fall down yet*, I thought to myself.

Seeing that I could hardly stand, he ignored my question and stepped close enough to swing at me. With surprising speed for someone with a medicated nervous system he whipped the lump of wood at me, aiming to catch me across the head. Instead, the weapon struck a barrier: a layer of air with the consistency of tank armour that prevented his blow from reaching me.

Then I Shattered the wooden club to splinters, leaving him suddenly speckled with cuts and clamping his stung hand between his legs as though I'd laid his palm open with a whip. I stepped forwards quickly and kicked him in the kneecap. Not hard enough to destroy it, but enough to send him pitching backwards. The brick wall behind him broke his fall.

Then I rearranged my Shield, and drew it inwards to clamp him around the throat, trapping him against the wall, unable to fall down. He writhed, his heels digging chunks from a section of scabbed asphalt, but his neck stayed trapped.

"Where are my things?" I asked, squeezing the Shield a little tighter and making his eyes stand out as though his brains were inflating.

He didn't speak but his gaze flicked over to the bulk of the heavy transformer. I left him hanging and explored in that direction with my extended senses. On the other side of the fenced-off electricity sub-station, through a narrow gap crowded with climbing weeds, there was a square of cement and a door, not visible from the alleyway. Behind the door was body heat.

I turned towards that heat, before remembering something. And then, pivoting back, I drove the second joint of my right thumb, backed by a tight fist, into his left temple. It was my first time hitting someone and I had only a fragment of the Sleeper's memory to guide me. I caught him square in the temple and released the Shield, allowing him to collapse on the ground, where he remained. But I damn near broke my thumb doing it. If the Sleeper had a real, physical body somewhere, he obviously had hands like elk hooves.

Leaving the downed junkie behind me I stepped over to the transformer. I laid the bushes flat ahead of me and scrambled through the gap between the enclosure's metal fence-posts and the wall, narrowly avoiding an abandoned syringe that would have driven itself up through the sole of my boot.

The muggers had found a way into some sort of utility building: a one-room brick structure with a few water company meters and pipes inside. I could feel movement and warmth on the far side of the door, beneath the pipework.

The door in front of me was closed. Reaching out with my hands I grabbed the door handle and pulled. It moved a little but wouldn't open. I felt behind the wood and detected a bar, dropped into place to hold the door shut. Something prevented me from moving it.

Well, no time for finesse. I flattened myself along the building's wall, to one side of the entrance, rotated a Shield into place, and then blew the door off its hinges and into the weeds. A spike of ejected doorframe whined towards me like a bullet and clipped my Shield, spinning off into the bushes like a severed airplane propeller.

I rolled my Shield around and stepped in through the doorway.

Inside I could detect two pairs of legs that disappeared beneath some dripping steel plumbing. And in the snug space behind the pipes I could feel a candle flame fluttering like a leaf against the Heat Surface. I Froze out the flame, leaving the two figures cowering back there in the little light that reached them from the doorway. They scrambled to their feet and edged to one side, beginning to emerge from behind the pipework. I heard a metallic snap that I took to be the catch of a knife opening.

346

A body rushed at me, just a shadow in front of my eyes, but clear as a Mondrian sunrise through the Heat Surface. He lunged head-first into my Shield, losing his footing in the impact. I felt rather than saw him stick himself with his own knife as he slipped. I wrapped the Shield tighter around me and reached out across the floor, probing for my belongings.

On cue, the other junkie, the one I hadn't seen before, rushed me. I caught him as he slammed his head on my Shield and I morphed the barrier as quickly as I could to catch him and enfold him. Then, as mindful as I could be of my injured thumb, I hit him in the nose with the heel of my hand. He moaned loudly, making a noise that reminded me of an angry seal, and I released him and let him topple into the corner.

By now the other one was back on his feet, one hand clamped across his self-inflicted wound and the other one once again holding the knife. He didn't charge, just stood warily, holding the weapon between us. Did that make it my move?

I began to Heat the knife. It took a few seconds for him to notice and he shifted it in his grasp, unsure of what was happening. A moment later, he gasped and dropped it on the dusty floor. He back-pedalled and I stepped forwards, wrapped my hand in the loose sleeve of my sweater and picked up the knife by its handle.

I applied a little Freeze to the grip to stop it burning through my sleeve and then I roared out at the blade with Heat until it began to ripple with a crimson glow. The metal clicked and pinged from the heat. I gathered the cowering junkie into a wraparound Shield and advanced on him as he struggled, finding himself suddenly unable to move.

I held the glowing knife level with his eyes and asked, "Where is my necklace, the rest of my things?"

"Do I know you?" he stuttered helplessly, staring not at me but at the knife's glowing point.

I growled irritably and he flinched. "You don't remember me? You choked me unconscious about fifteen minutes ago if that helps," I explained.

"Sorry, sorry," he pleaded, as though an apology might be all I was after. And then he added: "It's over there." He nodded his head to towards the pipework and the space beyond. "Few things in a bag on the roof. Maybe yours too."

I ignored him for a moment and felt across the floor once more. I could sense a cardboard box and within it, bracelets and what I took to be my phone. Transferring my attention to the roof above me, I was able to sense a pressed-metal housing with slatted sides – something to do with the machinery here, maybe – and within the housing, a bag (canvas perhaps) full of hard shapes and something worked into filigree. That had to be the necklace. Focussing hard, I flipped the loose metal side off of the housing and gave the bag a good jolt with Push. It slid across the roof and dropped into the bushes just outside the door.

I can't imagine which member of the gang was steady enough on his feet to climb up there and conceal things, but it would have taken me a while to find that hiding place without help. Aware that I was still standing, holding a blisteringly hot blade close to his face, my captive asked tentatively, "Ahh, what are you going to do with that knife?"

I smiled at him.

"Stab someone," I said, shutting off the Heat and beginning to Freeze the whole blade. "It's important to put on a good show."

He was staring at me horrified, and I explained: "God knows what diseases a person might get from a knife like this, but it should be safe now." And, gritting my teeth, I rammed the blade deep into the flesh of my shoulder.

Even though the metal was cool, it felt like it was still at a thousand degrees. The knife went in about an inch and a half and stayed there when I removed my hand. For a moment, I was hopelessly dizzy with the pain.

I tried to steady myself and I wondered whether it had been easier to bury a knife in my shoulder knowing that my original plan had called for the wound to be a death sentence. Horrible though this had been, it was still easier than the sacrifice I'd been preparing myself for. Now that I'd decided to live, this wound only had to demonstrate how desperately hard I'd fought to regain my link to the Sleeper.

Again, a tumble of dizziness spun my brain, and then hysteria threatened to take me for a second as I giggled, thinking what would happen if I passed out now, what these two would do to me, and how events would unravel for the PAC without my help. Thankfully, a moment later, the dizziness faded.

"Sorry about this," I said, my teeth gritted against the pain. I squeezed the Shield around the trapped junkie's throat until he couldn't breathe. I'd recognised his sleeve from when that skeletal arm had slipped itself around my neck, and I knew he was the one who'd half throttled me. It made this easier to do.

Less than a minute later his expression had gone from desperate to peaceful and I let him drop. His chest still rose and fell and I turned away from him. I gave the box in the far corner a Push and it slid out from under the pipework. I tipped it up with the toe of my boot and turned out the contents. Then I grabbed anything that looked familiar. Gathering those things up, I went outside and dropped it all on the ground next to where the bag had landed. Then I emptied out the bag onto the ground.

There, on top of the pile, lay the mangled lattice of my necklace. It was stretched and distorted and the sight of it devastated me. I hadn't expected it to be ruined and I didn't see how I was going to mend it. I'd pictured repairing a broken link or two with a few dabs of Heat, but I could see the filigree was pulled completely out of shape. Dozens of the hair-fine strands had elongated or snapped completely.

Still, I wrapped it around my throat, holding it in place using the arm that didn't have a knife stuck in it.

And felt nothing: no sense of the Sleeper's presence.

Hello?

I knew my thoughts weren't reaching beyond the confines of my own skull. Some subtle psychic ambience was missing, the micro-echoes I'd learned to associate with a functioning mental link. When you knew what to listen for, it was the difference between speaking from a stage and talking into a pillow.

With no way to contact the Sleeper, my plan was starting to disintegrate. A curl of panic, like a rising wave sweeping towards shore, was rearing up inside of me. I pushed it down, refusing to lose control now. I *had* to re-establish the link to the Sleeper, there *had* to be a way – and I *had* to find it now.

I was always telling people how smart I was; it was time to prove it. I had to think: to put the nausea and weariness and hurt to one side, and concentrate on working this problem through. There had to be something I could do.

And at last, a possibility occurred to me.

I remembered the glimpse I'd caught of the Sleeper's thoughts, the layered bulk of his memories and the neat array of Patterns, like live butterflies pinned in a row, their wings still beating in slow-motion, each shape cycling through its own sequence of convolutions. I could see those shapes clearly if I closed my eyes. I picked out the shape of Pattern Link and tried to bring its exact form into focus. And to my shock, as I concentrated, it flared and expanded in my mind, blossoming into fullness and suffusing me with its distinctive power.

Hardly knowing what I was doing – what *it* was doing – I felt the breaks in the necklace merging together and the tortured strands healing themselves, tightening back into their proper arrangement. The metal tensed and gathered like tendons pulled tight and the necklace settled itself over the torn skin of my neck from where it had recently been ripped.

Its work completed, the Pattern began to drain and collapse, its petals turning to ash, just as I felt the breaking storm of the Sleeper's presence rolling back in on me like my own personal typhoon. I snuffed out the remnants of the Pattern as swiftly as I could, hiding it from his awareness.

Then I could do what I'd been yearning to do for most of today: I could rest. I let my knees buckle, closed my eyes and collapsed like a human accordion. Only desperation had kept me from passing out before now and I no longer kept up that fight.

Let this all be *his* problem for a while.

Chapter 29

I stopped battling the exhaustion, the pain, the symptoms of growing blood-loss, and let myself drift away. My physical body still existed somewhere, off in the distance, but it was miles from where my disconnected mind tumbled gently through space, rolling over and over towards nothingness.

As though I was watching it happen through the foggy lens of a cheap telescope I could see my distant body crumpling, my limbs losing tension like noodles in hot water. I felt a sense of relief as the world receded. I guessed that I would catch a last glimpse of my body at about the moment my good shoulder hit the dirt. Finally, I could rest.

And then, with a jolt, the Sleeper snatched control. I'd dropped to my knees, but before I could topple sideways to lie in the soot-specked weeds, he reanimated my limbs, pulling tension back into my muscles and halting my collapse.

Let me sleep, I pleaded, a little deliriously. *I can't do any more.*

Far from being sympathetic, the Sleeper exuded prickly suspicion. Plainly, he couldn't tell whether he'd been conned and my stuporous wilting wasn't helping him discover the truth.

His mind bellowed at me: If you have deceived me here, you will **pay**. And he did that thing with his words where they rang like angry trumpets.

Well if that's your attitude, I thought, and once again dropped backwards into the waiting arms of fatigue, which carried me away, not just from my body but from the Sleeper as well. I left him in sole and unopposed control of my body. I allowed my mind to simply loll. Psychic dead weight.

Far away, I was vaguely aware of him orienting himself, looking out through my eyes, forcing my body to stand. He stuffed a few things into the bag that lay at my feet and hefted it in a way that would hide from casual observers the hilt of the knife protruding from my shoulder. Then he pushed his way through the bushes, squeezing past the buzzing grey bulk of the transformer.

Back on the gravel path, he stepped over the inert junkie I'd discarded there. Then he retraced my earlier route, along the alleyway, out onto the street and back towards the house.

How many did you kill? he asked as we left the alleyway behind us. His tone suggested he was almost impressed. The question drifted up to my untethered mind from far below. I answered like in a dream, words appearing without my involvement. *Don't think anyone's dead. Just settled them down a bit.*

My voice slurred in my head like I was drunk. I was really only half conscious, and thinking at all was an effort I couldn't be bothered to make.

I caught distant glimpses of what he was doing, but it was intercut with moments of delirium where I floated, blissfully lost among imagined fragments of June sky.

The Sleeper had got us home and all the way upstairs. I barely registered our progress – though I was absent-mindedly aware of taking a spill on the final set of stairs before my room. Diluted and vague, the pain of a banged elbow came through as though it had happened a long time ago. Everything had such a dreamy quality to it, as I continued to let my consciousness drift like an inflatable lounger in a forgotten Summer swimming pool, leaving it to the Sleeper to pick my body off of the carpet and get me up those last few stairs. Once in my room, he steered us towards the bathroom.

The change of scenery did nothing to revive me; all that white tile was the perfect blank canvas for my imagination, which projected swatches and snapshots of dream colour against the out-of-focus, bare ceramic.

But reality came whistling back into razor-edged focus when the Sleeper leant over the sink, grasped the handle of the knife, and pulled. The pain centres of my brain lit up like a lightning strike. He might as well have connected the hilt of the knife to the mains.

With the blade removed, he kept the heel of my hand pressed into the nova of the wound and drew down the Healing Surface so that it was folded and concentrated around the hole in my flesh. My other hand braced us against the edge of the sink as I felt my knees suddenly dip, unstrung by sudden light-headedness.

But gradually the crackles of high-voltage pain that raked my nerves began to dissipate and the blood that I could feel welling, and then running hotly down my side, slowed from a trickle to a drip, and then stopped completely.

He took me back into the bedroom, dropping me into a chair, and allowed the Healing focus to dilate, spreading it out like a blanket across my other injuries. The scratchy throb from my scalp-wound grew steadily duller and the hard straps of pain in the muscles across my back began to loosen their aching grip.

After thirty minutes wrapped in the Healing field, the only injury remaining was the clotted hole in my shoulder – within which I could feel new fibres of skin and muscle itching as they sought each other out, twitching like insect antenna, then brushing together and knitting tight. The process began to slow once the worst of the damage had been undone.

Bathe, put on clean clothes and then we will set off. I want to retrieve the Marker tonight.

I just laughed. Out loud. I didn't mean to; this wasn't like earlier when I *wanted* to bait him, but I just couldn't help it. I'd figured the best way to allay his suspicion that he'd been conned·was to share with him my total helplessness and physical disarray. Before the mugging I'd been running on fumes. Now I had the healthy skin tone and alert expression of an organ donor, post-donation. My clothes looked like I'd found them when I was unclogging a drain. And my brain was badly-made Jell-O.

The final touch, driving a knife into my shoulder, had been about buying me a little time. I wasn't sure it was necessary, but I didn't want the Sleeper thinking we were good for any more active duty today. I needed to give Daniel a chance to run that errand for me just in case I needed it. It hadn't occurred to me that the Sleeper would assess the perforated bag-lady he saw in the mirror and declare her ready for action.

For some reason, he seemed to think he could wring a bit more useful work out of me today before I dropped dead in my tracks like some Victorian pit-pony. Exhaustion had my heart thumping painfully in my chest as though something in its mechanism had been thrown out of alignment by the abuse I'd racked up recently. This was madness and I roused myself to tell him so. A few, final drops of adrenaline leant me some eloquence.

You're welcome to try, but personally, I haven't got it in me. If the Marker is there, then it's been there for a year. It will still be there in twelve hours. Can I remind you that I'd put in a pretty full day even before I got choked unconscious and stabbed. I know it must be frustrating having to tolerate my frailty, but I think it's pretty clear that I've reached my limit for today. Can't we interpret the fact that I got the snot beaten out of me by a couple of emaciated dopeheads as a clear sign that I've been overdoing it? In case we run into trouble when we go to fetch the Marker, I wouldn't mind being able to put up a bit of a fight. Right now I can neither see straight nor use both of my arms. I mean come on.

The shoulder will be healed by tomorrow. And in the morning we won't need to break into the dock; we can just walk in. There'll be less risk of trouble and we'll be in infinitely better shape to handle any problems.

I reckoned he was probably convinced, but I needed to give him a way to save face if he wanted to concede the point. I figured I'd give his ego a pat and let him blame this all on me. *I don't know how you're managing to keep going, but I just don't have anything like your stamina.*

No, you don't, he snapped. Understand that this is the last allowance I will make for your weakness. If you have to ask me to take pity on you again I will take that opportunity to put you permanently out of your misery.

I took that huffing and puffing to mean that he was reluctantly agreeing with me.

Understood. I tried to sound meek but sincere.

That really was a relief. Now I was free to get out of my filthy clothes. I didn't even want to think about the long-term health risks of rolling around in that alleyway. I suppose it was the least of my worries, but it made my skin crawl. I found a black garbage sack and put my sweater and jeans straight in there. They weren't worth saving. If I wanted something suitable for getting mugged in again, I'd just start fresh with a new outfit.

Then I stripped off the rest of my things – including Noola's jewellery – and took my third shower of the day. Thank god for hot water, is all I can say. It was no substitute for a couple of weeks drowsing in the sun on a quiet beach somewhere, but it was still bliss to my battered body. I tied a hand towel over my shoulder to keep the direct force of the shower from hitting the partly healed wound and that seemed to work OK. After I'd scrubbed and scoured for a few minutes I began to feel less contaminated, like I'd erased the filth from the alleyway.

Tempting though my soft bed was, I made a heroic stand and ignored its beguiling call for another half an hour while I returned Noola's jewellery to her room and made myself a huge sandwich, which I ate accompanied by an enormous glass of milk. I don't normally drink milk, but somehow it seemed like the thing to do, like I was giving the Healing field a few more nutrients to work with than if I'd just drunk water. Or maybe it just reminded me of being a kid.

Finally I crawled into bed. It must have been all of 8pm but I felt like I'd been anticipating this moment for weeks. The ridiculous excess of pain, adrenaline and exertion I'd experienced today had dramatically narrowed my sense of perspective. I couldn't think in terms of the big picture right now. I had food in my belly and clean cotton sheets beneath me. As far as I was concerned, tomorrow was another lifetime for a different me to handle.

I set my alarm for 6am and let the lapping waves of sleep work their way up my body. I felt them lift me free of the Earth and pull me down with them into that ancient, dark ocean where I lay drowned in dreamless black for a small eternity.

Sometime in the night I thought I heard something, but sleep had trapped me under its colossal weight, as though it owned me now, and I couldn't have stirred to investigate the sound if my life depended on it. Which, naturally, it did.

* * *

Eventually I awoke to the sound of my clock radio. Its buzzer sounded exactly like the collision warning of a passenger plane from a disaster movie I'd once seen, which might explain why my first thoughts on that morning were 'Pull up, pull up.'

I cut off the alarm with an unsteady swat of my palm, and then I just lay there for a moment, letting my waking mind re-integrate itself after the elemental disorder of sleep. Any residue of drowsiness was driven out of me by the cavalry charge of problems galloping back into position.

This was the day. Despite my resolve to fight, there was an excellent chance that this was the end of the line for me. Somehow I knew that at the bottom of that anchor chain there really was a watertight bag – I could picture it – and it really did contain the Marker. I believed Jan's scribbles proved it.

The Sleeper had been driving me towards this day ever since he had first chanced upon the marinaded wreck of my boozed-up, drug-dilated brain, lying prone and inviting, still Connected to the magical ether. It took me back to the moment when I'd seen that opium-sprawled junkie with the needle dangling from his arm. That was how I must have looked to the Sleeper. He was like a car-thief finding a drunk passed out at the wheel, the engine still running. Who knew how many decades he'd scrabbled uselessly at the iron-hard minds of resolute, disciplined adepts, unable to get any purchase. Even David and Susan, novices though they were, each had more willpower than any three other people I knew. While the Professor, despite his genial manner, had a core of granite.

If finding a slave hadn't been a big enough prize for the Sleeper, there, in my recent memory, were references to the Marker. It was like stealing the keys to the entire candy store from a baby.

And while I'd slept last night, another of his plans had reached culmination. Without needing to analyse it, I could sense that the Home Pattern was there in my mind – whole and ready now. Unless I stopped him, the Sleeper would activate it as soon as my fingers touched the Marker.

Somehow our link had deepened and expanded, and when I thought about it, I found I could even catch blinks of detail, shutter-quick glimpses through the Sleeper's own eyes: millisecond flashes looking down at his ruined body in its mineral prison.

I couldn't properly interpret those tightly compressed images, couldn't really say what I was looking at, but I knew approximately what they meant. Somewhere, the Sleeper lay crippled and physically powerless, unable to move – but possessed of an intact mind. That mind had curled like a lurking spider underneath the surface of the magical world, watchful, alert – ready to dart out and snatch up a suitable victim.

Then I had come along and he had ensnared me.

In a fair fight, I didn't kid myself that I could beat him. And now that he'd weakened my mental defences with the drug-patches, I knew I stood even less of a chance. But since that talk with Daniel, I'd realised that if I could just hold my nerve, I might be able to deal the Sleeper a blow that would leave him drowning in doubt and despair.

With that thought hidden in my mind, like a gun tucked into the back of my jeans, I readied myself to return to the boat. Another hour basking in the invisible warmth of the Healing Surface had reduced my shoulder wound to an ugly knot of reddened skin: an ache and an eyesore, but not a liability any longer.

I didn't bother with the idea of dressing up and impersonating an estate agent. Neither the Sleeper nor I had the stomach for charades. We both knew that this was the finale, what I think they call the endgame. If along the way I had to assert myself a little and deal with a security guard then so be it; as soon as my fingers touched the cold metal of the Marker, all mundane concerns would be behind me.

I trudged down the last flight of stairs and approached my front door. I hoped that the Sleeper would interpret my leaden reluctance as a sign of weakness or fear. I could hear winter rain intermittently pattering against the front-room windows and I paused for a moment to look at the heap of coats piled over the coat rack and to find something warm and dry to wear. The decision was made easy when I noticed that my favourite fleecy jacket had slipped off its peg and lay on the floor by the front door. I picked it up, dusted off a grubby sleeve and zipped it around me. With a hand that felt as heavy as regret itself, I opened the door and stepped out into the spit and squall of the raw and chilly morning.

Chapter 30

Out on the street, some of the inevitable grimness of my mood lifted and a little gallows humour started to work its way in. Probably just the early stages of hysteria, but I'd much rather laugh at something serious than face it with humourless maturity. Why multiply the unpleasantness of the situation by refusing to joke about it?

Under my Chicago Bears cap, I was wearing gold. My wrists too were gilded. In my mind, the quiet, refrigerator hum of the Quell state kept me from Connecting.

I was walking to the station. By unspoken agreement with the Sleeper I was leaving the bike where it was. If he had his way, then I'd have no need of a quick getaway. Or rather, I'd be performing one of the quickest getaways in history, courtesy of the Home pattern. That wasn't exactly how *I* intended for things to turn out, but I didn't want to make the Sleeper suspicious by advertising the fact. I don't know what I was *supposed* to think was going to happen once the Marker was in my possession, but I wasn't about to bring the subject up. So there was no discussion, I just headed for Stockwell tube.

Once I reached the station, I queued for a ticket. My mind was on other things, when a fit-looking, twenty-something white guy struggling with a heavy backpack lurched away from the machine in front of me and struck me with the trailing edge of his pack. The gnarled metal pull of a zipper caught me across the cheek, scoring the skin. I drew my breath in sharply at the unexpected pain, dabbing instinctively at my face. My finger came away with a smudge of red on it.

The man turned angrily to see who had obstructed him and snarled at me, "Why don't you watch where you're going?" Then he pushed his way towards the ticket barriers.

Hmmm, I thought to myself. I was waiting for the anger to come, but there wasn't any. I'd expected, now that I could mentally separate the Sleeper's feelings from my own, that I'd sense more of the old me – and the old me would never have been able to let something like this pass.

But it seemed like such a small thing compared with what else was going on; I just couldn't get very worked up.

Thinking about my calmness, I decided that it probably came down to how you see other people. When I used to feel like a failure, I kind of looked up to everyone else and that made the way they treated me seem like a judgement; rudeness like I'd just experienced would make me feel sorry for myself for ages.

On a good day, I might have managed to view other people as equals: being snarled at by a stranger would feel like a challenge; it'd make me punchy.

But now all I saw was some young idiot putting his own problems on public display. He was obviously late, he couldn't manoeuvre his bag without bumping into people and in his tiny reality that was a major deal; it had stretched his patience to breaking point. That wasn't annoying; it was just a bit embarrassing. If you couldn't handle outsized luggage without losing your self-control, how would you handle the big things?

How would you face your own death? I found myself hoping he lived a long enough life to get a little perspective.

Or he could maybe share mine; I seemed to have a little too much perspective right now.

The man with the rucksack had only taken a couple of steps when a short, black guy standing behind me sucked a little air through his teeth to make a tutting sound and muttered, "That's just rude." Then he called out, "*You* watch where *you're* going. You hit this lady, you know."

Out of the corner of my eye, I could see that the guy behind me was about half the size of the man with the rucksack. I smiled. He didn't know I could kill the man who bumped me without losing my place in the queue. He didn't know whether the guy with the rucksack would decide to make an issue out of this. He just knew he was standing up for me, and I liked that.

Sure enough, the rucksack guy turned, anger twisting his lip, and took a step towards the man who'd scolded him. His face had a look that suggested he viewed this as the final straw.

I supposed that now there'd be shouting and maybe a fight. I wasn't in the mood.

I stepped forwards and placed my palm on the rucksack guy's chest, halting him. "Remember how late you are," I said, looking into his eyes, "You don't have time for this." It wasn't some Jedi mind-trick; it was just the truth. He was only acting like a baby – a very tall, muscular baby – because he was under pressure.

The rucksack guy pulled the focus of his scowl away from the defiant man behind me and angrily met my gaze. Then he glanced at my cheek. I caught the microscopic drop in his self-esteem as he registered the cut, noticed the beads of fresh blood, realised he was to blame. Then he turned huffily away, nearly bumping into a truly enormous man who looked like he might break rocks for a living – perhaps with his hands.

The guy behind me gave a wheezy chuckle: "He'll be lucky

he don't have some sort of *accident* this morning."

He amused himself for a moment, laughing at that, then asked me quietly, "How's your face?"

I turned a little and smiled warmly at him. "I'm fine, thanks," I said, and in a strange way I realised it was true.

He appraised the damage. "That's a bad scratch," he said, pretending to look worried. Then he laughed and said, "Luckily, you still pretty." The way he said 'pretty', it didn't have any 't's in it. *Pri-eee.*

I giggled. Nerves, I suppose. I mean it wasn't really funny and I don't think I've ever made a sound that you could describe as a giggle before. I'd be flirting next.

It was a shame dear Daniel wasn't around to help me with that. He'd waited a long time for some flirting from me.

I bought my ticket and made my way down onto the platform. Jammed in with a few hundred hassled-looking commuters, I found myself smiling again. What a psychiatrist might make of that, what with the swirling currents of death and self-sacrifice all around, I didn't know, but it felt quite natural. Who knew why? Not me.

A few stations along, I changed trains, and this time I was heading against the crush. When I emerged into the wintry grey of the wind-bitten morning, the rain had stopped. That was an improvement, though feral gusts still snapped at my ears and the back of my neck. I tugged my collar a little higher and wondered why the Sleeper was so quiet. We'd had a brief discussion about tactics a few minutes back, but that was it.

You still there?

It was probably safe to tweak him a little now. He couldn't afford to disappear off and rat out the PAC's location to the Army; he had to keep a constant eye on me. His holy grail was due to make an appearance in a little while.

Attend to your surroundings, not me, he grumbled, clearly

not in the mood for banter.

His words seemed damped, muffled somehow. And I realised why, as soon as I thought about it. I'd been blocking him out of my head. Not completely, but I'd subconsciously narrowed our link to restrict his access to my thoughts. I hadn't even had to concentrate; the simple act of wanting to be alone with my own musings had restricted the flow of communication between us. It was moderately impressive. Another month or so and I'd really be able to give him a run for his money.

There, you see? Gallows humour.

On the last section of the walk to the dock, I took things pretty slowly, keeping an eye out for anyone nearby. When at last I reached the concrete steps that would take me over the wall and down into the basin of the dock, I stopped and had a proper look around. There was some activity far-off: the machinery of the cement works rumbled and boomed distantly like a spent thunderstorm, but there was nobody close by.

For some reason, I was much more keyed-up than the last time I was here. I had a sense of danger that wouldn't leave me.

I climbed the first few steps slowly, glancing over the crest of the wall and then pulling back. Beyond lay the guard-hut, the high fence and the wooden walkway that led down onto the pontoon decking where the boats were tied up. The tethered vessels looked just as they had before, with Jan's set off to one side and back from the others. Having seen nothing to alarm me, I raised my head again and took another, longer look.

I worked my gaze across the dock like it was a painting I was restoring: careful to bring out every detail and not to miss a spot. I couldn't see any signs of life. The boat with the engine trouble was quiet now, no evidence of the mechanic or his tools. The guard-hut seemed deserted too. I'd anticipated needing to do something about the guard and now I wondered if he *ever* showed up.

Cautiously, I worked my way up the steps, over, and down onto the dockside beyond. It felt a little like walking through a minefield: the surroundings looked innocuous enough but there was a finite chance that if I put a foot wrong something would blow up in my face.

Ordinarily, I might Connect now. If there was a trap, I should trip it and run. But last time we'd been here, the Sleeper had been angry with me over that. And just now, on the train, he'd made his wishes clear. I wouldn't Connect without his permission.

It seemed that my survival wasn't the first priority; recovery of the Marker was. I just had to get it in my possession – whatever the cost – and then he would bring me Home. So despite the fact that I'd be a lamb to the slaughter if the Army were lying in wait, he didn't want me to run. No, my job was to get onto that boat and to reach the Marker first.

I walked cautiously past the guard hut.

No sign of anyone within, though a dark-blue uniform jacket hung from a peg in the tiny interior. Did that mean the guard was nearby? If he was patrolling, he'd be pretty cold without that heavy wool serge between him and the elements.

I moved slowly down the gangplank which led to the floating pontoon deck and the boats beyond. I wanted to be alert to anything out of the ordinary, but it was obvious that the buffeting wind would drown out anything less than a shout, and my gaze was blurry with tears as the winter chill stung my eyes.

I reached the wooden decking and walked to the far end: the closest point to Jan's boat. With a last scan of the surroundings, I jumped onto the boat adjacent to Jan's, ran down the full length of its running board and leapt across to 4-14J, to land with moderate grace next to the rudder, in the recessed well at the back of the vessel.

Nothing happened: no sirens or yelling.

I picked up the pole that lay by my feet. Its hollowed square end was just as I remembered it, obviously intended to attach to something. I lowered it over the side of the boat, wondering how one located the up-tilted spike that it fitted onto. It wasn't possible to see more than an inch through the mud and algae in the water.

Leaning out a little, I noticed a groove notched into the handrail. It was one of many dents and pocks along the outer edge of the boat, but it looked a little bit more deliberate than the rest.

I laid the shaft of the pole into that groove and, using it as a guide, slid it down into the water. After a little poking around, the tip of the pole encountered something near the hull. I rotated the pole, trying to settle it onto the metal spike there. After a little trial-and-error I got it, and the pole slipped down into place. If I'd wanted to I could have let go now and the pole would have stayed put.

Next I had to raise the anchor chain. It was a simple mechanism: a little drum-winch with a hand-crank at one end like the starting-handle for an old-timey car. With one hand steadying the pole (because I didn't relish diving in to retrieve it if it fell) I gave the handle a turn and the anchor chain began to rise.

And then it stuck.

For a moment I couldn't see why, but by leaning out and peering back at the winch, I discovered a padlock with an elongated loop that went through one of the links of the anchor chain and fastened to a metal eyelet bolted to the handrail. I tried to reach below the padlock and pull the chain up by hand.

Yeah. That wasn't going to happen. It weighed a ton, the angle was impossible and the chain was slippery. Problem.

Should I Connect? I need to break that lock.

There was a pause as the Sleeper considered his reply.

Yes. But remember to move quickly once you do.

I stilled the gentle, rhythmic oscillation of the Quell state that was looping in my mind. It ceased, and straightaway I felt the Surfaces rise and expand around me, filling like sails catching the breeze, and opening like the petals of an enormous, unseen flower. Without waiting for the sense of Connection to complete, I immediately reached out with the Shatter surface and cracked the mechanism of the padlock. I hooked my hand beneath the winch and pulled the fractured lock free.

It took only a second and even as my hands reached for the padlock, impressions began to flow in from the Surfaces. I grabbed the handle of the winch and began to wind up the chain at the same instant that fear solidified into reality.

One by one, three citrus-yellow stars flared: three clusters of gaseous light, like soft miniature suns, silently rising out of the featureless sea of the Presence Surface. Three adepts.

It was curious how the Presence Surface presented its threats so comfortingly: cool, graceful radiance to indicate the location of a killer. One was near me, on one of the other boats; the other two, no doubt ready to block my retreat, were beyond the dock wall, at the extreme limit of detection.

From the Sleeper's point of view, I only had to touch the Marker, to get it within my grasp, and the battle was over. I could feel him wordlessly pressuring me to work even faster as I frantically hauled on the handle of the winch. I obeyed as best I could, but I was desperately trying to think how this affected *my* plan – because *my* plan required me to destroy the Marker. And that was going to be suicidally difficult in the middle of a one-sided fight with a trio of assassins.

I know, my plan doesn't sound very impressive or sophisticated. And I suppose it wasn't, but I'd realised something. I'd realised that hate is over-hyped as a motivator; what keeps people going for the long haul is hope. The Marker was the object on which all the Sleeper's hopes rested and I planned to obliterate it in front of his eyes.

368

And if that wasn't enough to crush him, I had a final trick up my sleeve. I had a gift for him, something he had been after for a while now. Irony had finally taught me a useful lesson, and the lesson was that sometimes giving people what they want is the best way to hurt them.

And all I would have needed to put my plan into effect was about a minute or so of peace and quiet. Which wasn't going to happen.

Even as I struggled to invent a way out of this situation, at the same time as I was furiously working the winch handle, I saw a man step out onto the roof of a boat several vessels down from me. He was young, slim and dark-haired and he appeared to be wearing a suit, beautifully tailored from some silky charcoal-and-green cloth. He was the man who had chased me when I'd visited Jan's house in Notting Hill.

He yelled something melodious but insistent that I couldn't understand. Panicked, I yanked the winch handle even harder, figuring that I still had a couple of seconds before he crossed the intervening distance and reached me. I wanted to put a Shield in his way, but I was draped half over the side of the boat, dragging on the winch lever with one hand and steadying the pole with the other: there was no way to raise a Shield without getting in my own way.

Now the man stepped lightly from one boat to the next, and then the next, covering the six or seven foot gap with no more exertion than if he was stepping off a kerb. As he closed the distance, the dreary sunlight glinted from the gold stripe across his temples.

Glancing down, I saw that one skewered link of the anchor-chain was now working its way up the pole. And resting on top of the threaded link was a loop of braided steel cable. I reached down and grabbed the cable, pulling on it and hauling against the suction of the water.

I heard the man's heels thump down on the next boat along just as a tan-coloured sack on the end of the wire broke the surface, pouring water from its folds, and rising into the air. I straightened up and reeled in the wire, simultaneously placing a slab of Shield between the boats so that the young man's approach was blocked.

What I'd do next I didn't know. I could feel the Sleeper focussing on the Home pattern, bringing it to the forefront of our joined minds, ready to activate it. I was careful not to grab the bag itself – only the wire – so that he wouldn't be tempted to activate the pattern yet. Besides which, he'd be a fool not to have me check the contents first.

Pick up the bag, he commanded me, but I ignored him. I had only moments to act. Could I destroy the Marker before the man in the suit reached me? Perhaps I should relinquish it to the Army in exchange for letting my friends and I live. Then the Sleeper's revenge would mean nothing. But I couldn't trust them any more than I could trust him.

A clatter of thumping wood gave me a split-second's warning that something else was going on, but not enough time to react. Then it all happened at once. The Sleeper poured his will across the link, trying to activate the Home pattern in my mind. I blocked him, amazed he would take even the smallest risk that the Marker wasn't in the bag.

Simultaneously, the young man pressed forwards, frowning as he found his path blocked by my invisible Shield.

And a new sun rose, blindingly close, bursting through the Presence Surface right behind me.

And as all these things were taking place, the woman who'd crashed out of the cabin doors behind me stepped forwards and cracked me firmly across the back of the skull with the cold iron pommel of a drawn sword.

The ringing blow whited out my senses for a second and shot

numbness through my nerves, slackening my grip, so that the bag slithered free of my fingers and plopped back over the side of the boat like an escaping octopus.

Momentarily unable to balance, I staggered and fell backwards, banging my head on the way down, to lie blinking and dazed at the feet of a tall, fair-haired woman who held a sword, now turned point downwards, just above my sternum. In a single, quick motion she flipped the circle of gold from around my head with a twitch of her sword tip. The move incidentally sliced an inch-long cut into my scalp and shut down my Connection to the Surfaces with the finality of an axe-blow through a power cable.

I was still dazed from the impact, but despite the excruciating sensation that my skull had just been rung like a bell, I recognised her. She looked exactly like a sketch Susan had made of the assassin Karst. Well not *exactly* like: her perfect, pale features were distorted by a partly-healed scar which ran down one cheek and tugged the corner of her beautiful mouth into a lopsided smirk.

That had to hurt, I thought.

"Danik. The bag," she called, in unaccented, but somehow foreign English. As she spoke, she kept her eyes on me. She was staring intently at me, but not quite into my eyes. It was as though she was trying to see through my flesh.

"You're *young*," she said incredulously. "You have never been old, have you? Who has sent a child here?"

She moved, placing the point of her sword just below my ribcage and leaned forwards a little. I gasped for breath as the blade exerted painful pressure and threatened to rip through my clothing.

"You can tell me," she said, confidentially, "Who sent you?"

Meanwhile, the man Danik took a final light step across the five foot expanse of water and came to rest, apparently quite steadily, on the narrow handrail of the boat, the soles of his immaculate leather shoes somehow gripping the wood. The gusting wind fluttered the hem of his jacket but had no apparent effect on his balance.

He bent his knees, placed a gloved hand on the winch and dipped his other hand down to scoop up the metal loop where it lay, threaded over the pole, resting on the anchor chain. Straightening, he began to reel in the wire, careful not to splash any water onto his clothes.

"We've been here so long," he observed, his voice higher and softer than I'd expected. "that I was beginning to doubt you." His words were directed to Karst.

Karst ignored him and whispered once more to me, "Who sent you?"

From where I lay, I could see the stitching on his shoes, the ox-blood leather so dark it was almost black. I stared at his feet while Karst waited for me to answer her. I wondered what kind of person dressed like that.

"I really think she's no more than thirty," Karst said to Danik. "A strange choice. Perhaps she's a decoy, so be alert."

"We could torture her a little," Danik said, his quiet voice sounding playful and a little shy.

Karst shook her head. "I'm not in the mood. If it's in the bag then we're finished here. And so is she." She glanced over the side of the boat into the opaque midnight-teal of the water. "Maybe put her down there when we're done," she gestured with a nod over the side and shivered slightly as if to say rather-her-than-me. It seemed like it was the water itself and not the dying that made her shudder.

Danik flipped the bag up over the rail and down onto the seat by my head. "Do the honours," he said, and Karst lifted her sword off my sternum and pushed its point through the bag and into the wood of the deck-planks beneath. Then Danik grabbed a corner of the bag and pulled, the material parting around the blade as though it were a scalpel cutting through… through something innocuous and unrelated to my current situation.

Inside the bag was a sealed plastic envelope, like the one we'd found beneath the floor of the cabin inside, but this one contained a complex, intertwining filigree in some pearlescent silver metal.

Grab it. The thought boomed into my mind.

Karst had removed my headband, but not the necklace. The Sleeper could still retrieve me if he chose to. But even if I was tempted to obey him, I'd seen how fast that sword could move and I had no illusions about beating Karst's reflexes. Still, I thought, it was splendid to see that even in this predicament, the Sleeper could still find a way to dramatically shorten my life, even when I was down to my last couple of minutes.

I wondered if making a grab for my headband would be any easier. I might as well try, I thought. It couldn't make matters any worse. Careful not to betray my intention by tensing up, I prepared to make my move, at the same time attempting to ready myself for the bite of Karst's sword.

Chapter 31 – Told by Susan Milton

The Professor was even angrier than *I* was when he heard – and saw – what Jo had been up to. I think a big part of that was probably disappointment. I blamed Jo for what she'd done, but I think the Professor blamed himself as well. None of us like that particular sensation.

Even so, Jo's... well you had to call it betrayal, didn't you? It seemed like a pretty solid reason to get worked up. Theresa showed us how the technical side of it worked. Apparently Jo could just log in from elsewhere and pick up recordings of our meetings. It just seemed so *organised*. It took Jo's maverick streak to a new level, beyond what you could blame on petulance, and made it seem positively calculating.

The morning after it all came out, Jo had called the Professor. He came and found me afterwards; told me what had happened. He was embarrassed about how he'd acted. He'd let her have both barrels and then he'd hung up.

I gently suggested that she deserved it, but that didn't really mollify him.

He explained, "It's about what's *best*. She might have deserved another dressing down but that's an excuse, not a reason. If my behaviour makes things worse instead of better, then it was the wrong thing to do – provocation notwithstanding."

He added, "And when I scold others for their lack of self-control, it sits better with me if I'm not red in the face and bellowing at the time. Hypocrisy rather undercuts my point, don't you think?"

We were having this chat at my desk and at about that point, Daniel showed up. I motioned subtly for him to give us a minute. But I suppose Daniel was a little preoccupied because he didn't notice my gesture and instead came right over.

"Hey Daniel. This isn't the best time. Can you give us five minutes?" I asked.

He seemed pretty dejected and ignored my question. "I just spoke to Jo," he said.

That was the first of two calls she would make to Daniel that day. Later on, she would phone a second time and retract everything – but of course I didn't know that then. At the time I just wanted to know what she'd said. I changed my mind about making Daniel wait. The Professor would want to hear this too.

I said, "I'm guessing it wasn't good news." It sounded a little more flippant than I'd intended but no one seemed to notice.

Daniel relayed the conversation he and Jo had had, about how she wanted to be left alone. When he'd finished, the Professor and I were silent for a moment, considering.

"Where does that leave us?" I asked, wanting to hear what the others thought.

We kicked that question around for a little while. The Professor and I also filled in some blanks for Daniel. He knew the highlights of what Jo had been up to and we added a few of the specifics. We'd been planning to tell him later in the day anyway.

Daniel didn't try to defend her. I suspected he was doing a

little of what the Professor had been doing: blaming himself. All he said was, "I think she knew she was being shut out of something and she didn't like it. Mind you, this wasn't how I expected her to act. She must have been…" He didn't finish that thought. He was obviously going over old conversations the two of them had had; you could almost see his lips moving.

Knowing that both of them were supporters of Jo in their own ways, I decided that it fell to me to kind of state the case for the prosecution – or at least push the conversation in that direction. I said, "Jo doesn't make it easy to be on her side, does she?"

No one touched that remark. The Professor asked Daniel, "Do you think she's serious? Would she go to the authorities?"

"I don't know," Daniel admitted with a gloomy sigh. "I wouldn't have thought so, but she seemed really worked up over what she'd discovered. She was almost frantic about us keeping out of her way. I think we have to do what she wanted: give her a few days to calm down."

"You don't think," the Professor asked gravely, "that's she's somehow being coerced?" He looked like he hadn't wanted to ask that question.

Daniel ran his fingers through his hair and looked even more frustrated. "I don't know what to think. I'm sure she's not betraying us, but there must be something going on. What I can't work out, though, is why she wouldn't want help if she'd got herself into some sort of trouble. She knows she can trust me. And she knows I wouldn't have made her beg; she could have just dropped a hint or two. But there was nothing."

I said, "So she didn't ask you to do her some favour… and not tell us? She just called to say we should all stay away?"

What I didn't know when I asked that question was that I was a little early. The call asking Daniel to do her a very unusual favour was still some hours away.

I scrutinised Daniel pretty closely as he replied. He was self-conscious but earnest: "She didn't ask me to do *anything* for her, except convey the message. And you know I'd only help her if I believed it was the right thing to do for all of us."

He obviously knew what I was hinting at. "Sure, sure," I said, "I just felt I had to ask. I'm not criticising your loyalty to Jo, I was just asking whether it was a factor here." I summed up, "So we just leave her alone for a while? You agree with that, Professor?"

"I am *far* from happy over this," he said, and there was that angry edge in his voice again, the one that hadn't existed when I'd first met him – the edge I knew belonged to his youth, until the Healing Surface had brought it back to life.

I could see that Daniel noticed it too, was maybe a little taken aback. The Professor concluded, "There will be words to be said, but this is not the right time. For now, I think we allow Jo time to reflect, and to accustom herself to the alarming world she has insisted upon entering."

"OK. Well I guess that's settled then," I said and there were nods all round.

The Professor took his leave and Daniel looked about ready to head off too, but I stopped him. "Have you got time for a tea break, Daniel? I want to ask you something," I said.

He looked mildly intrigued and perked up a little. He said, "Always a pleasure, never a chore. Will there be Kit-Kats?"

I smiled, reflecting on Jo and him, and thinking that he probably deserved someone better. Why couldn't he take an interest in someone a bit more stable, like Theresa for instance?

"There may be," I said, noncommittally. I logged off from my computer, got up, and grabbed my purse.

We walked downstairs together, heading for the refectory. As we walked, I said, "I just wanted to know a bit more about what's been going on with Jo. I've never really got to know her. In fact, I think I've missed out that part and gone straight to thinking she's kind of a pest." Then I added, "Sorry," because it wasn't my intention to offend him.

He shrugged, looking unhappy again – like he wanted to argue with me but was having a few doubts himself.

I said, "I mean, honestly, she *is* kind of a pest, but for all I know she might have her reasons. I remember that she got a sudden new lease of life – really started making an effort. I was even beginning to think I'd been wrong about her. Then all this happened. I realised I have no idea what goes on in her head."

"Yeah, well I'm not as much of an expert on that as I thought I was," he said. "You know, the day Jo turned over her new leaf was the day after she had some bad news about her mother."

Delicately I asked, "I thought her mother had died when she was little?"

He said, "When Jo was five. The thing is that she doesn't remember anything from then so it's all a bit of a minefield. Almost anything she finds out is likely to be a shock." He paused. "Anyway, I don't want to talk too much about her private business."

He was obviously debating with himself about how much more to say. "The day before, Jo and the Professor had a few words. I think the Professor said more than he'd meant to about Jo's mother, and Jo took it badly. I mean it was very depressing stuff. Then the next day she was a changed person. Totally over it, apparently."

I suggested: "Sometimes bad news is like that. It can make you consider where your life is going – maybe push you to make some changes."

"I'm sure there was some of that," Daniel said. "She definitely didn't want to follow in her mother's footsteps, but it still seemed very sudden and very… *complete*."

"How do you mean?" I asked.

"I don't know," he shrugged. "There was no transition, I

suppose. She was just different." He paused a moment, snorted, and then said, "I thought maybe she'd finally realised what a fabulous person I was." Then he rolled his eyes a little to make it clear that no one could *really* be so foolish.

"So you and she…" I didn't say more. I wasn't even quite sure what I was asking. I was just looking for more information. I suppose I wanted to understand exactly what had tipped me off to Jo's deception. Something about it bothered me. I was half expecting Daniel to reveal something that would solve the mystery for me and then I could say: "Yes, that was it. I *knew* I'd noticed something peculiar." But it didn't happen.

He said, "We had a really nice evening in the pub. Jo got completely plastered. But in a good way. Not depressed drinking. It was actually the happiest I'd seen her for a long time. I made sure she got back to her room without falling down a well. I, er… I thought maybe we'd reached some sort of understanding. Like maybe we were a bit closer now." He was obviously finding this embarrassing to talk about. "But when I saw her the next day it was like a month had gone by. No hangover and she was a new person."

"And so far as you know," I said, "nothing happened between her getting home and you seeing her the next day?"

"I think she threw up," he said. "And she had a trippy sounding dream about being frozen."

"Frozen?" I asked.

"Stuck in the middle of a load of ice. She said it made her see that she'd been stuck solid in the middle of her life and it was time to thaw things out – or something like that. But what got her to the point that she was dreaming about making this big change, I don't know. Maybe they're putting Prozac in Southern Comfort now. Not that Prozac was what she needed."

I'd gone quiet for a moment, not paying attention to the last couple of sentences. I was fixated on what he'd said about her dream. "She dreamed about being surrounded by ice? So, exactly how did the dream go?"

"I don't know. If Jo said any more about it I can't remember it. You think it's important?" he asked.

I said, "I'm starting to wonder if Jo's mixed up in something a lot worse than we thought."

I didn't like this, not at all. How many people dream about being stuck in ice? I never had – at least not before the previous evening.

Maybe it was a favourite if you lived in Alaska or something, but not in Southern England in the fall. And yet Jo and I both dreamed of being trapped in ice – her, right before she changed, and me, just before I became suspicious of her.

I *knew* I'd read something about shared dreams, but I couldn't remember what. It was in one of the manuscripts we'd acquired earlier in the year, I was sure of it – one of the manuscripts we kept hidden away and didn't talk about outside the group, because the authors had been adepts.

Daniel, meanwhile, seemed to think I was accusing Jo of something, some conspiracy. He said, "Come on. She's done something stupid but she's still our friend. She hasn't risked anyone's life, for goodness sake."

"I wouldn't be so sure about that," I said. There was tension in my voice now. I didn't have the answer to this puzzle, but I knew where to look for it – and I knew I wasn't going to like what I found. "I'll talk to you later, Daniel. I've got something to do."

"If it's about Jo, then so do I," he said, and there was a certain amount of defiance in his voice. But I was already miles away, trying to remember which document in the PAC library dealt with dreams.

In retrospect, it might have been better to share what I was thinking with Daniel. I certainly would have done if I'd known he was going to get a second call from Jo later that day. But as it was, when she called, all he could tell her was that she had no allies any more among the PAC.

If I'd still been around I might have been able to set him straight on that point, but I was miles away by then, working on a plan of my own.

Chapter 32 – Told by Jo

I knew this was going to hurt.

I couldn't see a way to avoid Karst's sword completely, but maybe I could still reach my headband in spite of whatever she did to me. I'd psyched myself up to the point where I didn't think I was going to hesitate when my opportunity came, and now I was just waiting for the right moment – ideally when Karst was in the middle of saying something.

Determined to act soon, I gave myself a mental countdown from ten. But I'd only reached seven when Karst and the one she called Danik both reacted – to what, I couldn't tell, but it was like a subtle shiver had passed through both of them.

Karst's sword was still hovering near my sternum, but her eyes flicked up to scan the barrier wall that ran around the outside of the dock.

"Ideas?" she said. *How about not killing me?* I thought, but it seemed she was addressing Danik.

"Our Asian friends getting greedy? One Marker not enough for them?" he suggested. Then his eyes closed for a moment and he said, "I see two of them, moving."

"Yes," she agreed, "heading for the steps." I gathered from this that they'd only now become aware of the adepts beyond the wall. When I'd detected them earlier, I'd assumed that everyone but me was part of the same team – but obviously I was wrong.

The two behind the dock wall must have withdrawn after I became aware of them, because they obviously hadn't registered with Danik or Karst until this moment.

If they weren't working with my current aggressors, I had to wonder who they were. Regardless, they might be a useful distraction. Maybe I had a little longer to live after all. Possibly several minutes. I decided to hold off on making my suicidal grab for either the headband or the bag until I saw what happened next.

"If we have to fight, let's not stay on this *jävel* boat, eh?" Danik said. He sounded annoyed, but not worried.

I couldn't tell if either of them was genuinely concerned about the two newcomers. Their manner was as blasé and unruffled as before, but I thought I could still discern a slight shift in their postures, a tightness around their eyes. There was obviously some ethic of stratospheric cool they were both determined to adhere to, but it didn't extend to *total* nonchalance in the face of an advancing enemy.

Danik made as if to step across to the next vessel along with one of his dainty leaps, but the crunch of breaking wood and a distant cracking noise a split-second later stopped him. Someone had shot a piece of the handrail to splinters. With a bullet.

For a second, both of them blinked. Ordinary humans would have flinched; experienced soldiers might have ducked for cover; but these two – with a century or more of conditioning under their belts – their instincts were to wrap themselves in Shields. Eyesight was a distraction.

Which was my cue. For a moment, Karst was pouring her focus into folding the Shield Surface around her – it was automatic, reflexive. I doubted she had left a gap through which to stab at me if she noticed I'd begun to move.

By the time her eyes opened a half-second later, I was no longer directly under her blade. She saw me, but just too late to skewer me. Instead the tip of her sword plunged into the deck about an inch from my receding shoulder. And her Shield prevented her from trying again. It would take a moment for her to shift that invisible barrier and in that time I was able to grab my headband and set it back on my head.

Once again the universe blossomed, its hidden dimensions opening like gargantuan petals, and I was Connected. Karst's sword could still cut me if I let it, but at least she wouldn't be able to crack my skull like an Easter egg with just a sharp thought and a twitch of her nose.

I pulled in my Shield Surface, wrapping myself in its protective cloak, putting some solid air between my skin and the tip of Karst's rapier.

It was getting a little crowded here, to say the least. But for our Shields, Karst could probably have reached out and touched me if she'd stretched her arm a little.

I glanced up at the concrete steps and saw something that surprised me. A tall order you might think, given all that was taking place at the moment, but nevertheless it was true. Susan Milton was running towards me, a long canvas bag clutched in her hand. She had reached the bottom of the concrete steps and was now moving towards the guard hut. Behind her, I could see the black stick of a rifle muzzle protruding over the top of the wall. I couldn't see whose shoulder the weapon was clamped to, but I had my suspicions.

Danik chose that moment to test his luck. He was in an absurd position, still balancing on the handrail, a foot and a half away from the fist-sized hole the bullet had made. He undoubtedly had a Shield in place between him and the sniper, but he couldn't stay put. And I suspected that in him an adept's dislike of water was particularly strong. He sprang from his perch, his motion no longer dainty, but powerful and rapid like some sort of hunting animal. There was no preamble, he was simply in the air. And then a second later he was on the deck of the adjacent boat just in time to stop a bullet – or at least to slow it down a little.

The impact punched an exit-hole from the sleeve of his suit, instantly outlining it with red, in the general area where his left elbow would have been. Squeamishly I snatched my eyes away before they could lock onto the rent in his sleeve and focus on the excavated flesh beneath.

Danik had jumped out past the limit of his Shield, as he'd had to in order to reach the other boat, and evidently the sniper had been expecting that. The rifle had been aimed at the spot where Danik would land. All the sniper had needed to do was squeeze the trigger.

Danik handled having a chunk of his arm torn out through a hole in his sleeve a little better than I would have – which is to say he remained conscious. Nevertheless, screeching like a broken steam pipe, he toppled backwards into the water and into silence.

Karst swore. In German. One of the few words I knew in that language. But she still didn't register genuine distress. If I'd had to decode her expression I would say it read: 'Great! Another crappy day at work'.

Susan had passed the guard-hut now and was at the start of the gangplank that led down to the floating jetty. The sniper, meantime, had apparently decided that the time for gunfire was past because he'd leapt up from his rifle and was now on the concrete steps heading our way, his gun abandoned. As I'd suspected, the figure was David Braun.

Karst, muttering something under her breath, leaned over the side of the boat, allowing herself to fall outwards so that I thought she was about to belly-flop into the water. At the last moment she grabbed the handle of the winch to stop her fall, and steadied herself. Then, with the point of her sword held up towards the sky, she reached down and snagged Danik's collar. With extraordinary strength, she pulled herself upright and at the same time wrenched Danik's body half out of the water, flopping him onto the handrail on his stomach, where he remained. A hard line across the arch of his back was brought into definition now and I recognised it as the outline of a sheathed blade concealed beneath his jacket.

Then Karst twisted round and stroked the edge of her sword along the rope that joined the rear of this boat to the next. The motion was like a bow on a violin string and the strands separated at once.

While she'd been doing this, I'd tried to reach the Marker, but it was on her side of our back-to-back Shields.

I was getting nowhere with that, so I began searching my environment using the Surfaces, looking for some feature of our surroundings that I could use to my advantage.

I found two.

Meanwhile Karst flipped herself back onto the boat at about the same time that Susan reached the bottom of the ramp. Karst snatched the plastic wallet holding the Marker off the deck, where it lay just out of my reach, and slid it into the cross-over wrap of her stylish jacket. Then she ran towards the front of the boat, as though she and Susan had agreed to meet there and she didn't want to be late.

I took the opportunity to kick Danik in the head, but despite looking like a drowned rat, he still had a partial Shield in place. My boot was deflected away from his temple, but it still slammed into his shoulder, so it wasn't a complete loss.

He grunted and raised his head, staring venomously at me. I suspected all I'd done was rouse him from his daze. A second kick from me struck a much expanded Shield and did no damage at all. I desisted.

Susan was now standing on the deck in front of the boat. As I watched she finished pulling a sword from the bag she carried. She rolled her wrist a couple of times, causing the tip of the blade to tear through the air with a sound like a bedsheet ripping. Her face was blank but set. I felt a surge of pride and respect and gratitude, all mingled together, seeing her standing there ready to take on my tormentors. I also felt a heave of fear, knowing how formidable Karst would be, how unequal this fight would be.

Karst, for her part, had grabbed the rope that ran from the boat's nose to the deck and was pulling on it, one-handed. Infinitesimally at first, the boat gradually moved towards the jetty.

Karst had transferred her sword to her left hand while she held the rope, and it seemed equally at home there. Perhaps after a century or two of practice, everyone is ambidextrous. It was not a comforting thought.

The boat slid in towards the deck and in a moment Karst and Susan would be in range of each other's swords. But David wasn't far behind Susan. He was carrying a black nylon bag similar to the one Susan had just discarded.

With a moment to spare before the bladework commenced, Susan darted her eyes towards me and called out: "How are you doing? Is the Sleeper still in there with you?"

So she'd worked it out somehow. I suspected she'd dug out the document I hadn't been allowed to read, the one the Sleeper had forced me to delete my copy of – the one that undoubtedly mentioned a vivid dream common among novice adepts, a tendency towards strange moods, and the nickname given to the force responsible: the Sleeper.

And it was a good question: was the Sleeper still in here with me? He was awfully quiet.

What is there to say? he ventured.

"I think he's waiting to see how this all turns out," I said. I felt I should offer some words of explanation: "When I found out he was in my head and I tried to get rid of him, he threatened to tell Karst about all of us unless I obeyed him."

That got Karst's attention. "You let *the Sleeper* control you?" she interjected, her tone mocking. "He's a ghost; he's nothing. And you've been doing his bidding." She tutted and announced to no one in particular: "This is the result when children play with magic. This should never have happened."

She sounded disgusted. Then, without warning, Karst was in motion, lunging towards Susan and unloading a staccato sequence of overlapping cuts at her head and torso.

Susan parried furiously, but Karst moved so rapidly it was difficult to even *see* the path of her sword, never mind defend against it.

Thankfully none of the attacks reached their target but the final reverse clipped a two inch section from the end of Susan's heavy blade; it bounced away across the jetty, ringing each time it struck the decking.

Susan gasped, clearly startled by the machine-like speed of the assault. She stepped back a little just as David arrived. For his part, he didn't stop, but turned a little to his left and leapt onto the next boat over, running along its roof – which quickly brought him level with Danik, who was hauling himself to his feet. The two boats were very close now and the two men were separated by just a couple of feet of water.

Time for me to make a contribution.

"Su… uh, Serena" I said calmly, realising at the last moment that I probably didn't want to use her real first name, "can you practice your tank training for a moment? You be 'it'."

I used the name that she and David had used when I'd spied on them in the barn. I now understood the term referred to wrapping yourself in a Shield, like a tank in a war movie; you trundled along slowly and relied on your impenetrable armour to protect you from close-quarters attack.

Susan glanced towards me, unsure. "Now," I said urgently. Karst looked over at me, unable to decode my message or discern the threat. She shifted her blade a little, unsure of which direction an attack might come from.

I gave Susan a second to comply and then pushed as hard as I could through the Heat Surface.

The first time I'd been here, I'd found a gas-can tucked into a corner in the nose of the boat. I'd searched it as a possible hiding place for the Marker. When my senses encountered it this time around, I already knew what it was. I'd been driving heat into for thirty seconds now and, when I judged that Susan was ready, I focussed hard and heaved the temperature of the petrol up towards its flash point.

A moment later, the can ruptured.

A lot of times when a bomb goes off on TV, they don't use dynamite or plastic explosive, or whatever the script claims is in the bomb; they use what I was using: gasoline and air. So when the gas-can exploded, there was a moment of unreality, of familiarity, like I was just watching this on television, like it was staged. But the thunder of sound was shockingly real, as was the bucking of the deck and the blaze of heat that spilled over the top of my Shield and stung the skin of my face.

For Karst, who was standing two feet from the centre of the explosion, it must have seemed like the whole world had turned to flame. Her Shield caught some of the blast, but there were plenty of gaps: she'd wanted to give herself freedom of movement to use her sword and it had cost her dearly.

The explosion spun her into her own Shield and splashed fire up along her side and across her face. The force of the blast itself was modest, definitely subsonic, but the heat was ferocious.

In a moment her jacket was ablaze and her hair burned along with it. I expected her to jump over the side, into the water, but instead she curled into a ball. The flames around her compressed, tightened… and then went out.

The boat itself was still burning and rocking, fire was running across the deck, spilling out onto the water. A black umbrella of smoke was roiling above us and climbing into the sky. Beneath the spreading black cloud Karst herself was sealed in a spherical Shield, cut off from any oxygen. I suspected someone with her extraordinary strength and athleticism wouldn't need to breathe for a minute or two if she didn't want to. Incredibly, throughout it all, she'd maintained her grip on her sword.

Susan's Shield protected her completely, though she looked plenty surprised. Danik too sustained no fresh injuries. David had a burning sleeve to contend with, but he simply stepped away from Danik and calmly lowered his arm into the water. No fuss or panic.

Karst, on the other hand, finally registered some emotion. She uncoiled from her foetal ball and yelled something. I assume it was some German swear word, but it was way beyond my limited grasp of Teutonic vulgarity.

Danik was on his feet now, trying to draw his sword from its sheath across his back, but he was struggling. It was slung in such a way that it was easiest to reach with his left hand, but too much of his left arm had been removed when the bullet had struck him to make that practical, so he was clawing beneath the collar of his jacket with his right.

As he fumbled he spoke. "Plan?" he enquired of Karst, and his tone sounded strained but far from hysterical. But despite his composure, blood was running freely from the cuff of his sleeve, splashing onto the boards and pooling on the deck by his feet. It was spreading in my direction and I tried not to stand in it.

Karst didn't answer immediately. She was pawing at the

fused and charred remains of her jacket, trying to find the Marker amid the layers of charred cloth. Her skin had bubbled red on her hands and face but the muscles and tendons beneath seemed to still be working.

She pulled a strip of burnt cloth free and the Marker tumbled to the deck, dropping into a patch of burning gasoline. She bent slightly, obviously about to reach into the flames and seize it, when Susan jumped forwards and jabbed with the jagged tip of her blade towards the Marker. Karst snatched her hand back just in time. She straightened and gave Susan her attention.

Over her shoulder she called, "Danik. Get the Marker. If you get a chance, kill those two," she tipped her head towards David and me. "I'll clear us a path." So saying, she took a step towards Susan.

A wrinkle formed between Karst's pale blue eyes and she said, "I know you, don't I?" And a moment later: "You burned *Jan* like this, didn't you?"

Susan didn't answer. She clearly sensed that Karst was about to attack again and she was doing her best to be ready. Flames were burning in pools and puddles all around her, the fire on the boat was really starting to take hold, but Susan appeared undistracted; her focus remained on Karst.

I was looking around me, trying to size up the situation. I had no sword and no skill with one, so I couldn't fight. David was about to engage Danik – who had finally managed to draw his blade – and I was hoping the latter's horrible wound would hamper him, or at least throw him off mentally, otherwise things would go badly for David, I felt was sure. And Susan was about to face a second attack from a scorched and shaken-up Karst. But Karst – despite the awful transformation the fire had brought to her skin, her hair and her clothing – seemed undaunted. I wasn't sure Susan could survive for more than a few seconds against her.

Whether they'd meant to or not, David and Susan had cornered two superior opponents, neither of whom would want to swim for it. In the water, the two assassins wouldn't be able to create Shields and they risked being skewered as they tried to get back on dry land. Worse still, with a rifle added to the equation, they weren't even safe if they stayed in the water. And remaining on board a burning boat wasn't likely to appeal to them either, so their only hope would be to go *through* Susan and make it back to the dock.

As far as I was concerned, I needed to destroy the Marker and I needed either to neutralise the two assassins or at least get David and Susan out of their path. With seconds leaking away and my mind racing, I could see no way to make it happen. No way, except through sacrifice. My sacrifice. The 'Plan B' I'd been hoping to avoid.

I slipped my hands into my pockets and my fingers encountered the familiar shapes within. Daniel hadn't let me down. He had fetched my favourite fleece from my room in the project's dormitory, all the way up to London. He had pushed it through my letterbox to lie at the foot of the coat rack. And before he had done so, he had put the drug-patches in my pockets.

"Hey!" I yelled, loud enough to get everyone's attention. "Before the killing starts I have a favour to ask." As I spoke, my mind was pushing, prodding, feeling its way, wriggling under damp stone looking for a particular spot.

For a second I appeared to have everyone's attention. "Erm, Serena?" I said. "Give everyone my apologies and say something nice to, erm, that guy I like, please."

She nodded, but with a questioning look. She was wondering what I was going to do. Last time I'd spoken cryptically there'd been an explosion; this time, everyone tensed.

Then there was a distant cracking sound, followed by a prolonged creak and a bass grinding noise. It was deep and low, like the sound of an avalanche beginning.

"Danik," Karst snapped, "*do* something about her."

Danik turned obediently and tried two or three times to get the tip of his sword through my Shield, but without any luck.

A second later, as the grinding sound continued, I caused one of the many spots of flame around us to flare. It was hardly noticeable with so much fire around us, just a six-inch stretch of rope burning a little more brightly as I Heated it. But it was a section of the rope that joined the front of the boat to the jetty.

The low groaning grew in volume and then, suddenly, the boat lurched and the water shivered. Several of the boats around us pitched; a couple knocked hulls. No one was fighting; everyone was trying to figure out what was happening.

"What is she doing?" Danik demanded, glancing at Karst. He had finally reached the limit of his sang-froid and sounded distinctly rattled. Karst had no reply for him.

Now a gurgling noise grew until it matched the grinding sound for volume. The barge on which we stood drifted back from the jetty, apparently under its own volition, and as the tether rope pulled tight, it severed with a pop at the point I'd been super-heating.

Now it became obvious what I'd done. I'd found the mechanism that opened the dock gates and I'd activated it. Water was rushing out of the dock into the river, where the level was currently about two feet lower. Boats were being pulled taut on their lines and ours – no longer tied to the jetty – was being swept towards the opening jaws of the gates.

Even though this was my idea, there was one thing I hadn't predicted. As water poured out of the dock and swirled around the boats, the dead security guard rose to the surface and I got my first look at him. He was about sixty, dark-skinned and a little paunchy around the middle. His features, though slack now, were gentle looking – though I suppose looks prove nothing.

Nevertheless, it hurt me to see his discarded body floating there. I felt my reticence over what I planned to do to the two assassins melting away.

I hopped up onto the roof of the boat and walked towards Karst, who eyed me warily and tracked my approach with her sword-tip.

"Stop the gates opening," Danik called to her. I glanced back to see him looking around most unhappily now. His eyes shifted from the gates, to the water, to the receding dock, and back again.

"I can't find the controls. I'm not an engineer," she snarled.

"Well, break it then," he yelled.

"You've got worse problems than that," I said. "Check out the fuel tank. It's right beneath your feet – over this way a little." This last was addressed to Karst, who involuntarily glanced downwards, though there was nothing to see.

She would be reaching out with her mind, encountering the fluid volume of the brim-full tank, sensing the bubbling focus of Heat at its centre. Even as she was learning about the threat from beneath her, the stern of the barge was gaining speed as it slid towards the opening gates.

"Cool it down," she shouted. But at that moment I Shattered the top of the fuel tank, letting in air to mix with the hot vapour. It was only a matter of time, now, before the expanding fumes encountered the dozen or so fires scattered across the surface of the boat.

Karst was struggling to cool the overheated fuel below, but my control was better. And as she fought to undo what I'd done she stared at me, real concern in her eyes. I said, "It's worth it to take you two with me." And then I smiled and stepped a little closer.

Now I was directly above the tank and part of it lay in the zone of protection around me, the personal space which another adept couldn't attack with magic. Now there was nothing she could do to stop me bringing a large fraction of the petroleum to a raging boil, Heating it until the volatile vapour poured out of the ruptured tank like steam from a kettle, expanding until it encountered a naked flame.

"Five." I said slowly and deliberately. And a moment later: "Four."

I locked eyes with Karst. "Three."

A muscle twitched in her blistered face as the boat slid out into the river.

"Two."

"The Marker?" called Danik.

"It'll survive a fire," said Karst.

"One," I said.

"Zero."

As I said it, Karst snatched at the Marker – coming away empty-handed because my Shield was in the way – and then, without stopping, she kicked off and dived into the water.

Danik stood, staring at the water, a horrified look on his face. And then he tucked himself into a ball in the stern.

Swiftly I grabbed the Marker, stepped down into the prow and curled up small, following Danik's example at the other end of the boat.

This time the explosion was much more forceful because half the interior of the boat had filled with gasoline vapour – the evaporated fuel mixing with the air and needing only a spark to unleash it. My Shield was slammed so hard by the expanding fireball that it cracked the planks I was anchoring it to. The centre of the boat was ripped open and flame swarmed around me, the heat held at bay by my Shield, but the irresistible brilliance of the fire almost blinding me. The deck beneath me pitched up as the vessel came apart and I was just able to catch a last glimpse of the dockside before fire blotted out everything. For a moment,

I had seen David, back on the lip of the dock wall, the rifle once again in his hand, settling the weapon on its stand and putting his eye to the scope.

At least they would get Karst. Danik I suspected was in no better shape than me: surrounded by fire and about to be tangled in wreckage at the bottom of river.

And then I heard the Sleeper's voice. Got you, he said, as the Home pattern bloomed into life and a wall of black iron seemed to spring up between me and the flame, sealing it off and plunging me in an instant into total, icy darkness.

I felt my body cease to exist and with it went my consciousness.

Chapter 33

I was inside my dream – the dream of ice – and once again I felt the piercing sting of irony. It was fast becoming my most hated sensation and yet again it had caught me by surprise. Maybe that's in the nature of irony, but I hadn't expected to be humiliated so close to the end of everything.

I mean you know how it is: enlightened people look beyond the little things, they try to see the bigger picture, the hidden themes in their lives. And thanks to Freud, every little thing means something, or can tell you something about who you really are, what you secretly want. With the years of therapy I've had, when I dream, of course I analyse it and try to find the meaning beneath the surface – especially when it's the first dream I've had in years. It goes without saying that I know better than to take it at face value.

And yet here I was, standing inside that dream. It wasn't symbolic of anything; it was real and just as I'd pictured it – and I felt stupid for ever thinking it was anything else.

When the Sleeper had first come to me, my mind had been filled with images of ice – a thousand miles of it on every side, shot through with old, slow, clear-blue light. I had seen myself trapped, twisted and calcified by my old life and in front of me lay two possible destinies: the cracked and settled husk of a dead future, if I followed in my mother's footsteps, or the glowing, glorious opalescence of the alternative: the possibility of true freedom.

And I stood now, within that plane of ice, looking at the calcified figure of the present, the dead husk of a failed future, the liberating glow of a better alternative – the three symbols from my dream – and I saw that they were real.

The walls around me truly were solid ice, cracked and fissured and ancient. At my feet was the rag-bound skeleton I'd believed symbolised my mother's fate. Whatever process of decay it had undergone was long since completed.

To one side of me was that soft compression of illuminated air that I'd mistaken for my salvation. What it really was I could only imagine. Gentle light, like down feathers, welled up within it and floated away into the space around me.

And finally, on the far side of the frozen bubble in which I stood, was the Sleeper, the living, mineralised corpse I'd imagined was a kind of ghost of Christmas Present.

I'd dreamed it all, and then, just as I'd done all my life, I'd made it about *me*. Always afraid that I was irrelevant, that I didn't matter, I'd twisted everything until I was somehow at the centre of things, the reason it was all happening. And when I'd finished rearranging and reinventing the world so that it revolved around me alone, I'd found that I couldn't bear it. The weight of it was crushing me.

In my version of reality, every random setback was personal, and every personal misfortune was malicious. If everything happened for a reason, then failure was a judgement, a verdict on me, and I couldn't stand it. Life with no meaning might be unbearable, but so was the opposite.

And then the Sleeper had saved me. He had pushed me aside and run my life at a reckless gallop searching for his own immortality. I was superfluous, irrelevant, subsumed. Not only was I not at the centre of the world, I wasn't even at the centre of my own life. And being connected to him was like being electrocuted, clamped to the current which burned through him like a torrent of lightning. It had paralysed me, then convulsed me and finally incinerated me, leaving nothing but a fine ash of my former self. My old view of the world was gone.

And now I faced the Sleeper at last. His sunken corpse was partly fused with the icy wall at his back and yet it pulsed with mineral life. The fat of his flesh had flowed with time and reduced, and the skin had hardened into milky glass which revealed the dark, glittering blood beneath, shot like verdigris threads through a marble mortuary slab.

His face was simply a wrapped skull, the skin pulled as tight as stretched paper by starvation. The glinting band of gold across his brow was now mortared to his cranium by accretions of lime and silted ice, built up steadily by years of dripping moisture. The remains of his moss-furred clothes hid the wreck of limbs beneath and whatever time had done to his torso.

He plainly had not moved for a century or more, and yet he wasn't dead. His eyes were sealed – the delicate, dried leather of their lids pulled drum-tight across the sockets which must themselves have dried up decades back – and yet I had the sense of being watched by him. He had lain where he fell and the wall had begun to grow up around him, the ice to swallow him, and yet he hadn't died.

Was I witnessing a stalemate between the action of the Healing surface and the forces of starvation and thirst? Or maybe here, at the source of magic, the rules were different.

I looked away from him and down at the bundled corpse by my feet and noticed for the first time the handle of a knife jutting from the rags, the blade caught in the crevice between two gristly vertebrae. Looking beyond, I saw of one of the long bones from its arm lying on the far-side of the corpse, separate from his body. The shaft of the bone was pitted and nicked as though it had been gnawed.

And what was this light that fell like blossoms carried on a summer breeze through a gap between the worlds? It could be only one thing. It must be Home – the point at which magic entered the world.

I began to see what had happened here.

The Sleeper had wanted power – more power than any adept had ever possessed. He wanted control of a Greater Power and at the same time he wanted to hold on to his ruthless ambition – then he could turn that Power upon the world like a weapon. And he had a plan for how to make it happen.

He had searched the world until he found himself a guru, some solitary, half-mad devotee so bereft of human greed and drive that he might actually penetrate the veil and embrace one of the great secrets. And the Sleeper would have looked for a particular kind of holy man – someone obsessed with the source of magic. Then, the Sleeper would have sheltered him, protected him and watched over him. And when the wise man had finally received his answers, the Sleeper would have been there too.

And I now knew the form that answer would have taken. The guru's mind would have received a pattern, the key to a Greater Power, and that pattern would have been Home.

However he had done it, the Sleeper had persuaded his holy man to activate the pattern he had received and to bring it to life. He had found someone capable of travelling to the source of magic and he had somehow hitched a ride.

Plainly his first act once the journey was complete was to run his victim through. The Sleeper would not want to share the seat of power; he would want to keep the throne for himself. But

I wonder if this is what he'd been expecting. Wouldn't he have imagined halls of gold, a palace in the clouds, the imagery of whatever romantic tales he'd grown up listening to?

The reality was a bubble in the bleak vastness of an ice sheet, which contained a glowing ball of energy – no way out and only a fresh corpse for company.

There was nothing to live on and yet he had not died. He had been trapped here, his body failing even as the Healing Surface kept his mind alive, maintaining the vestiges of a metabolism, moving a trickle of thickened blood through his arteries. With nothing to do, not even the capacity to move, he had turned inward. Whereas his holy-man had voluntarily cut himself off from the concerns of the world and the clamouring of the flesh, the Sleeper had it forced upon him: he was walled away from the world he'd known and his body was turning to ice. He had nothing to occupy him but the pursuit of Greater Powers and the search for a way out of his prison.

Nothing would have happened for the longest time, until the Sleeper thought he was going mad. But then, eventually, the Sleeper had begun to learn things. As the silent decades stacked up, he had unearthed first one, then another pattern and still he didn't find what he needed. Perhaps, eventually he would have discovered the one he needed: Pattern Marker. But would he have been able to construct his own Marker to resurrect his derelict flesh? He couldn't move any more. And the one I held in my hand now was made of platinum. I doubted whether there was any more of that particular metal hidden in this bubble. No, he was trapped here until he could summon another to help him. And in the meantime, he dreamed he was back on his ship, far out to sea, and he waited.

All these thoughts had run through me in a few seconds. Much of it was the Sleeper's own memory that had seeped into mine and I was remembering it as I gazed down on him. Across the link I sensed his mind stirring.

Place it upon me.

Now I was staring at the body from which that detached voice emanated. I was standing in the same prison that had confined him until thirst began to kill him and hunger drove him to gnaw the flesh of his dead companion.

I am going to suffer the same fate. I shared the thought with him.

No. We have a little water here and before the hunger becomes unbearable I will be reborn. Then, while you sleep, I will end your suffering and you will feel no pain. Your burden will be lifted – it is your deepest and most secret wish, to feel no pain, and I can grant it for you.

So were we both getting what we wanted? He would have a new life and I would be rid of mine.

You know there's a difference between calling something a burden and wanting to be rid of it. Burdens are often things we're so attached to that we won't let them go no matter how heavy they become.

I sensed a ripple of irritation in him. He had waited a long time for this moment. There will be time enough for poetic thoughts. You have something that I need. It is of no value to you. Please be good enough to hand it over.

It's true, I suppose, that you have the power to give me the most important gift I could wish for – but it isn't death. In fact you've already given it to me. You let me catch a glimpse of the world through your eyes.

It's also true that my life has been wasted on me and I can see why you might think the solution was to take it away from me completely, but I think all I needed was for you to try.

You've shown me death and I realise I don't like it. You've shown me what happens when people don't find a way to take some pleasure in what they have and I don't like that either. And you've shown me the suffering of others and I definitely don't care for that either.

Which brings me to you...

What are you talking about?

I'm talking about a question that's been bothering me. From your point of you, you've won. You've got everything you wanted: a means to build yourself a new body and a slave to fetch it to you. It's right here – right where you want it. So tell me, what happens next?

You want to know my plans for the future?

No. I want to know how you intend to put them into practice. This place killed you once. With a new body, all you've bought yourself is another painful death. I want to know how you plan to escape.

Give me the Marker and I will show you. If you have truly had a change of heart then you do not have to die; I can take you with me.

Then you do have a way out?

I have a plan, if that's what you are asking, but first I need to be whole again. Neither of us can leave until I am reborn.

Right, right. Of course. Because only you can get us out of here and there's not much point in you leaving until you have some meat on those bones.

Exactly. I am prepared to reward you for your assistance. You need never work a day in your life or want for anything again.

And all I have to do is bring you this? I brandished the Marker.

Indeed. His impatience was palpable now. So bring it here.

You've promised me death, then you've pardoned my life, now you're offering me a future of luxury and idleness. And all you want is the Marker.

I'd better not keep you waiting.

I stepped over the corpse at my feet and approached the Sleeper's slumped form. His head was turned and I was so close now that I could see the pulpy flesh at the back of his neck, see the trembling of the skin as a livid blood-vessel throbbed beneath. The Healing Surface had preserved the tissue around his spine so well here that it could still pulse and flex, in contrast with what I could see of the rigid mineral carapace of his lifeless chest – only the flesh needed for brain function seemed to have been sustained.

I took a chilly hand from my pocket and made ready to lay the Marker across his partly covered rib-cage. My own heart was pounding in my chest with the tension of the moment. After this, there'd be no turning back.

Then I reached over, spread the patches on the skin of his neck and squeezed them firmly into place. Unlike the patches on my own arms, these were fresh and full of drugs, and there was a whole string of them. Mine, on the other hand, were spent. When my link to the Sleeper had been broken and I'd rushed back to the house, I'd hauled these discarded patches out of the trash and swapped them for the live ones the Sleeper had made me wear. The drugs in my system had dissipated by now – which was probably why the Sleeper had said so little since we'd left the house this morning: I'd been shutting him out. Only when I addressed a remark directly to him had he been able to speak with me. And I hoped that meant I had enough strength for what came next.

With a row of patches in place on the Sleeper's neck I jumped back so that I wouldn't be entangled as he brought a Shield to bear. Then I tucked the Marker into my fleece and zipped it closed.

The Sleeper howled wordlessly at me and the pressure of

his fury began to pile down on my mind like the weight of time itself. He threw against me the lonely centuries of madness, the burning resolve that had kept him alive. He raged and threatened me, he insulted and maligned me, and then he simply beat against my defences with the strength of a hundred thousand days of determination and need.

I staggered backwards, dropping to sit on the ice, alongside the last victim he had claimed.

He was stronger than me. Despite the gifts he'd given me, the wiles he'd shared with me, the portion of his own strength he'd leant me – he was stronger.

And I was weaker. Much weaker. Horribly, corrosively weak.

There was no way to resist him, no way to defend against his onslaught.

So I gave him the gift he had wanted since he had found me: the freedom to completely enter my mind.

I pulled aside my defences and opened up the shameful, piteous recesses of my worst doubts and bleakest fears to him. I let him into my sulking bitterness, my sullen rages, my self-loathing fits of spite and the uncounted endless nights where I lay sleepless and inconsolable, feeling sorry for every bad thing that had ever happened to me and every good thing that never would.

He had never known such weakness, never let it touch him, and now it was inside of him and he was choking on it.

I pulled down the walls that kept my demons at bay and let his driving, battering presence flood in and wash over the lot. He could have it. I was sick of it. Like him I wanted to live. But unlike him I had a life to return to. Everything he'd known and every friend and enemy he'd ever made were no more, gone down to dust and long passed out of memory.

He had anger and desire and ambition – enough to overcome

me – but I had a home and a world I wanted to return to. I had friends I needed to make up with, relationships to build, real, honest sights and tastes and colours to experience. He had the black-and-white of willpower, but he had no anchor, no connection to the vivid, living warp and weft of the world and that fact was killing him.

The truth was that I could do for him what he had wanted to do for me. I could lift his burden.

It was the least I could do for him.

So as we struggled and fought, twisted and heaved, I reached out to him and I took from his mind the secret he had piled his hopes upon.

The Home symbol had a mirror-image, a reverse, and it was his way out. I grabbed that whole chunk of his mind and pulled it away – visualising as I did all the things I wanted to live for and releasing to him all the bad history I needed to leave behind.

I spread out my hands – one to touch the Sleeper and the other to reach his victim, so that his body too could be back in the real world and not rotting away to nothing here.

Then I made it happen: the Inverse Home pattern flared and opened, and the black iron walls dropped down as they had before, and I knew I was on my way back.

And with his last ounce of spite, before the long delayed moment of his death finally caught up with him, the Sleeper gave me another of his patterns – turned one loose upon me that I hadn't seen before. Its name was Revoke and it was the worst curse he could think to hurl at me. So, even as I struck the water of the dock, returning to the spot from where I'd been snatched, I felt the Surfaces fold in on me and the sense of Connection come undone and seal itself off from me with a finality it was impossible to doubt.

The water closed over my head in a world shrunk down to

what my five original senses could detect – and the metal band around my head was now nothing more than jewellery.

Chapter 34 – Told by Daniel Maclay

I looked after Jo until whatever had been in that river water was finally killed by the antibiotics.

I won't lie to you; I enjoyed it. Not so much her helplessness – though there was a little bit of guilty pleasure from knowing she couldn't answer back – but really because I'd wanted to help her for so long, to make her struggle easier and finally here was something I could do.

And I got back a very different Jo. It was still her, but it was as though we'd known each other as teenagers and then she'd gone away to war or spent years exploring the Amazon and now she was back, older, wiser and stronger. I felt like we were meeting up again after many years apart and the fact that it had really only been a few weeks didn't make the changes seem any less real.

The ordeal she'd been through sounded so traumatic that I couldn't see how she'd survived it, but somehow it had forced her to overcome the problems that had troubled her for years.

It was a painful story to listen to, as she spared us no detail, no matter how ashamed it made her – and the telling of it took several hours, with David, Susan, the Professor and me gathered around her bed.

She cried a lot in the beginning. I couldn't tell if it was relief or the memory of what she'd been through, but it seemed natural, cathartic. It wasn't the strangled weeping that had sometimes gripped her in the past: when the sobs seemed like they were tearing something inside her and I couldn't bear to see it and know I couldn't help.

Now she cried as though it was helping her to heal. The first time was when she told the Professor how it had all started out. And then again when she apologised to everyone for what she'd put them through. Susan cried too, which is something I didn't expect to ever see – especially as she'd been no big fan of Jo in the weeks gone by. I also saw a tear in the Professor's eyes at one point, but he was smiling at the time, so I wasn't sure how to read it.

And she cried a third time when she talked about injuring the women whose home she'd broken into – and then she swore to do something to help her.

When she'd finished telling her side of things, she was desperate to know what had happened after she had disappeared, whether David had been able to eliminate Karst and Danik once and for all.

So Susan told her about how Danik apparently went down with his ship – which Jo had apparently been expecting, but she was on tenterhooks to know what had happened to Karst. Had she escaped or had a shot from David's rifle finished her off? She sounded as though both possibilities terrified her equally.

David told her it was neither. Karst was found floating near the boat. In the explosion, some piece of flying debris had cracked her skull. And unconscious, she had drowned. David had screwed up his determination, ready to pull the trigger – and his relief at not having to do it was nothing short of jubilant.

He'd watched Karst's and Danik's bodies floating out beyond the dock-gates – face down in the water – until he'd been sure they weren't about to move. And then he'd tucked his rifle back into its bag, and he and Susan had concealed their swords and moved away from the dock.

Susan had been on the point of diving in and swimming to the wreck, determined to see what had become of Jo and whether she could be helped... until David had told her what he'd seen through the scope of his rifle. He had to tell her twice, assuring her it was true. He had seen Jo vanish just before the flames hid her from view. The bubble of her Shield was empty for a split-second before it collapsed, drawing the fire in with it. Jo was gone.

So the two of them had withdrawn, wondering what to do, puzzling over what Jo's disappearance might mean. The emergency services were arriving and they'd had to hide for a while. David had found a vantage point – an old, abandoned crane – which he climbed, carrying the scope from the rifle so he could spy on the clean-up operation. The security guard's body was recovered first, and then the lifeless remains of the two Army assassins were retrieved some distance downstream. Soon afterwards, a fire-boat arrived to extinguish the last remaining chunks of burning debris.

Then, just as he was about to climb down, David heard the faint echo of a cry, and saw two policemen hauling a struggling figure from the water. Maybe an hour after she had disappeared, Jo was back and she was alive.

The two stashed their weapons and approached, telling the police that their friend had insisted on going to investigate the first explosion while they themselves had searched for a phone box without success.

Apparently, the second explosion had destroyed any evidence of gunfire and seemed to provide an explanation for the three floating bodies. Jo was credited with trying to rescue the others and she didn't dispute the suggestion – in fact she was too exhausted and waterlogged to say much of anything.

David and Susan brought her back and I took over the job of looking after her once it became apparent that she was sick, as well as battered and utterly exhausted.

On the third day of her convalescence, she was sitting up in bed and I was stroking her hair. I had done it once while she slept, because she seemed to be having a particularly unpleasant dream. She'd woken with a start and I apologised, was worried she'd think it was creepy rather than reassuring.

"Keep doing it. It's nice," she'd said and I'd kind of got into the habit if I was sitting close by, talking to her.

On this occasion, though, I had brought her something. It was the book I'd found inside the package her mother had been going to collect when she had been killed. It was a book on home-schooling. Jo was leafing through it, a tear rolling down her cheek, and every now and then she'd smile.

She said, "I can picture her reading to me, you know? When I was little. I could never do that before. She had a lovely voice. I think she would have made a good teacher."

I said, "She'd be proud of how much you've learned without her, I think."

"I hope so," was all she said and we left it at that. I'd wanted to tell her about the book when we'd talked before, but it had turned out better this way.

She put the book down and looked at me. "You got me through this," she said.

I shook my head. "I was hardly involved at all," I said.

"You were a friend when I didn't have any friends," she said. "You found out the truth about my mother when I needed a reason to be hopeful. You trusted me even when I asked you to bring me the drugs, even though you despised them. And you gave me something to come back to when I was fighting for my life."

I butted in, "And I wrote a song about you, but since we don't have a singer right now, you'll have to wait to hear it."

"A song," she said, as though she wasn't sure she believed it. "What happened to Tammy?"

"She's travelling. I persuaded her to go," I said.

"And did she take a lot of persuading?" she said, teasingly.

"Not really. Asking her to sing the song I'd written about you seemed to do the trick. Anyway, it's better for both of us this way."

"I won't argue with that," she said, moving across so that she could rest her head on my arm.

We didn't speak for a few minutes and I wondered if she was asleep. Then she stirred a little and spoke drowsily: "I hope *you* get sick soon. Then I could look after you." She turned over and snuggled down into the pillow. So quietly it was almost a whisper she said, "I'd like that." And then she slept.

Copyright © 2006 Robert Finn

The Author asserts the moral right to be identified as the author of this work.
All rights reserved.

First published in 2006

1

Proudly published by

Snowbooks Ltd.

120 Pentonville Road

London

N1 9JN

Tel: 0207 837 6482

Fax: 0207 837 6348

email: info@snowbooks.com

www.snowbooks.com

British Library Cataloguing in Publication Data
A catalogue record for this book is available from the British Library.

ISBN 1-905005-067
ISBN13: 978-1905005-062

Printed and bound in Great Britain
Set in 9.5/13 Times, and Arial
using Adobe InDesign CS2
Typesetting errors? Email corrections@snowbooks.com